Victor Hugo's

Les Misérables

The Classic Story
of the Triumph of Grace
and Redemption

Adapted for Today's Readers by Jim Reimann

INTERIOR ILLUSTRATIONS BY SERGIO MARTINEZ

DISCARD

WORD PUBLISHING
NASHVILLE
A Thomas Nelson Company

Victor Hugo's Les Misérables

Copyright © 2001 Jim Reimann

Published by Word Publishing, P. O. Box 141000, Nashville, Tennessee, 37214, in association with the literary agency of Alive Communications, Inc., 7680 Goddard Street, Suite 200, Colorado Springs, Colorado, 80920.

ISBN 0-8499-1687-9

Printed in the United States of America
0 1 2 3 4 LBM 9 8 7 6 5 4 3 2 1

To Pam,
who has extended
a great deal of grace to me over our
twenty-nine years of marriage

All my love,
Jim

INTRODUCTION

———————————— ❧ ————————————

first published in 1862, Victor Hugo's *Les Misérables* has become a well-known classic. However, primarily due to its great length and to language that has become increasingly difficult to understand over time, few people of our current generation have endeavored to read it. Unfortunately, most people who *are* familiar with *Les Misérables* only know it from their exposure to the Broadway play or to various Hollywood movies.

Until a few years ago, I was one of those people. Then a friend of mine encouraged me to read the book. What I discovered was a masterpiece and a writing style virtually unmatched by today's writers. And to my dismay I discovered that much of the beauty and several meaningful episodes of the story were not included in any movie version or the play. I came to realize that even after seeing the play and each of the various movies several times, I still had not known the full story of *Les Misérables*.

Although the book is a beautiful work, much of the main storyline gets lost among its many tedious portions. Many of the classical writers of Hugo's day were paid by the word, which often made them more verbose than they might otherwise have been. According to Victor Francois, who in 1922 published a book of French lessons based on *Les Misérables:*

> *Les Misérables* is one of the longest novels in any language. It comprises five parts, which are divided into forty-eight books which in their turn are subdivided into three hundred and sixty-five chapters with as many different titles. The first edition . . . had no less than 2,550 pages.

Only one-third of the whole book deals with the real story; the other two-thirds are nothing but fastidious digressions on the most varied subjects, such as the making of cheese at Pontarlier, the battle of Waterloo, French slang, convents, old Paris, Paris sewers, etc.

Accordingly, I have attempted to tell "the real story." It is the story of Jean Valjean and the power of grace to redeem a life and to totally transform it. I have also attempted to maintain the beautiful pictures that Victor Hugo so masterfully painted with the words of his day—but in a way that today's readers can better understand.

Much of the work of condensing the original book was done through the careful scrutiny of my friend in Atlanta, Dick Parker. Dick, thanks for your diligent work and for the many phone calls as we discussed various aspects of the story. Credit should also be extended to two translators long since deceased: Isabel Florence Hapgood, whose 1887 English translation of *Les Misérables* was used as the basis for this book, and Charles Edwin Wilbour, whose 1862 translation was used for minor portions as well. I also owe a debt of gratitude to my friend Winston Maddox in Tucson, who first encouraged me to read *Les Misérables*. What a blessing I would have missed!

May you now discover the real story of Jean Valjean, and be as stirred by its message of grace as I have been.

—JIM REIMANN
May 2001

LES MISÉRABLES

CHAPTER ONE

---　✧　---

Early in October 1815, about an hour before sunset, a man traveling by foot entered the little town of Digne. Only a few of the town's inhabitants saw him from their windows or doorways, but those who did stared at him with a sense of uneasiness. It would have been difficult to imagine a vagabond more miserable in appearance.

He was average in height, somewhat stout and sturdy, and despite his unkempt look, he was in the prime of life—forty-six to forty-eight years of age. His cap had a drooping leather visor that partially concealed a face darkly tanned by sun and wind and dripping with perspiration. He wore a yellow shirt of thick linen that was loosely fastened by a silver clasp and a thin necktie that had been twisted like a rope, yet partially revealed a hairy chest. His blue trousers were threadbare, with one knee worn white and the other ripped. He also wore an old gray, tattered jacket, patched on one of the elbows with green cloth sewn on with string. On his back he carried a knapsack similar to those of a soldier. It was obviously new, and although very full, it was securely buckled. He held a large, knotty walking stick, while his sockless feet wore iron-toed shoes. Beneath his cap was his formerly shaved head—now covered with nothing but short, coarse bristles. They stood in stark contrast to his long, matted beard. The heat and sweat, not to mention his dusty journey by foot, added a complete air of filthiness to his totally miserable condition.

No one knew who he was, and those who saw him assumed him to be an aimless drifter. But from where had he come? Perhaps he had come from the south or from the seashore, for he had entered Digne on the same street

Emperor Napoléon had used seven months earlier on his way from Cannes to Paris. He must have been walking all day because he appeared very tired. Some of the women in the old market at the edge of town had earlier seen him pause under the trees on the Boulevard Gassendi to drink at the fountain by the promenade. He must have been quite thirsty, for some children who had been following him also saw him stop just a couple of hundred steps farther on for another drink at the fountain in the market itself.

Once he reached the corner of the Rue Poichevert, he turned left and headed toward the town hall. He entered the building, where he remained for a quarter of an hour. Upon exiting he removed his cap and humbly saluted the military policeman seated on the stone bench near the doorway. The policeman did not return the salute, but watched him intently as he walked away, and then entered the town hall himself.

At the time in Digne there was a wonderful inn at the sign of the Cross of Colbas. The innkeeper was a highly esteemed man by the name of Jacquin Labarre. Upon hearing the door open, yet without raising his eyes from his stove, Jacquin asked the traveler, "What may I do for you, sir?"

"I need food and lodging, please."

"That's an easy request to fill," replied the innkeeper. But as he turned his head to glance at the man, he noticed his meager appearance, and added, "Do you intend to pay for it?"

The man then took a large leather pouch from the pocket of his jacket, and answered, "I have money."

"In that case, we are at your service," said the innkeeper.

The man returned his money pouch to his pocket, removed his knapsack from his back, and set it on the floor near the door. Continuing to hold the stick in his hand, he then seated himself on a short stool near the fire. October evenings are cold in Digne, since it is located in the mountains, and having now stopped walking for the day, he had become somewhat chilled. Yet as he sat on the stool, the innkeeper continued to pace back and forth, scrutinizing him.

"Will dinner be ready soon?" asked the man.

"Immediately," replied the innkeeper.

While the drifter continued warming himself by the fire with his back turned to the innkeeper, Jacquin Labarre pulled a pencil from his pocket. Then tearing off a corner of an old newspaper that was lying on a small table near the window, he wrote a couple of quick lines in the blank margin. Simply folding it, he then entrusted the scrap of paper to a child. The innkeeper whispered something to the lad, who apparently served as his kitchen helper and errand boy, and then the child ran in the direction of the town hall.

All of this went unnoticed by the traveler, who again inquired, "Will dinner be ready soon?"

"Immediately," repeated the innkeeper.

The errand boy quickly returned and handed the scrap of paper to Jacquin. Eagerly unfolding it, as though he were expecting a reply, the innkeeper read the note carefully. Then tilting his head to the side, he appeared to be pondering the message for a few moments. He then walked toward the stranger, who seemed to be immersed in some disturbing thoughts of his own.

"You cannot stay here, sir," he said.

Beginning to stand, the traveler exclaimed, "What! Are you afraid I won't pay you? I'll pay in advance. I have money, I tell you!"

"That's not the problem."

"What is it then?"

"You have money . . . " said the innkeeper.

Yet before he finished his thought, the stranger interrupted with, "Yes, I do."

"And I," continued the innkeeper, "have no rooms available."

The weary traveler, regaining some sense of tranquillity, responded, "Then put me in your stable."

"I can't."

"Why not?"

"Because all of the stalls are filled with horses."

"Very well, then," countered the stranger. "Just give me a small corner of the loft with a little bed of straw. We can see to it after dinner."

"Sir, I can't give you any dinner either."

This declaration, spoken in a subdued but firm manner, struck the traveler as a personal threat. Standing fully upright, he shouted, "But I am dying of hunger and have been walking since sunrise. I have traveled more than thirty-five miles today, I have money, and I want to eat!"

"I have no food," responded the innkeeper.

Upon hearing these words, the stranger burst into laughter, pointed to the fireplace with their stoves, and retorted, "Nothing? With all that!"

"All that food is spoken for already."

"By whom?"

"By a large group of travelers staying here."

"How many are there of them?"

"Twelve."

"But there is enough food here for at least twenty!"

"Sir, it belongs to others. And they have paid for all of it in advance."

At this, the traveler seated himself again, and without raising his voice, said, "I'm at your inn, I'm hungry, and I'm going to stay."

The unwilling host then leaned close to the stranger's ear, and in a very harsh tone which made the man jump involuntarily, declared, "Go away!"

Bending forward, the traveler jabbed at some hot coals in the fireplace with the ironclad tip of his stick. He then spun around, and just as he began to open his mouth in sharp reply, the innkeeper glared at him and added in a very strong, yet subdued, tone, "Stop! I've had enough of your talk! Do you want me to tell you who you are? I know your name. You are Jean Valjean. As soon as I saw you walk in here, I suspected you were up to no good. So I sent a message to the town hall, and this is the reply I received. Can you read?" The innkeeper then handed the fully unfolded note to the stranger. The weary man glanced at the paper that had now traveled from the inn to the town hall and back. After a brief pause, the reluctant host continued,

"I'm in the habit of being polite to everyone. But to you I say, 'Go away!'"

The traveler, looking dejectedly toward the floor, walked toward the door, picked up his knapsack, and made his slow departure. This supposedly fine inn was closed to him, so he began to seek out some humble public place of shelter, however lowly it might be.

As he walked in the now cold twilight, he saw a glimmer of light at the end of the street. A pine branch swayed in the wind before an iron sign. He walked toward the sign, which was outlined in the fading light of dusk, and finally saw it designated a public house of shelter. This humble inn, located at the corner of the Rue de Chaffaut, had two doors by which to enter. One opened onto the street, while the other opened onto a small yard covered with manure. He did not dare to enter by the street door, but slipped into the yard, hesitated, and then timidly raised the latch to open the door.

"Who goes there?" asked the manager of the inn.

"Someone who wants supper and a bed for the night."

"Good! That's exactly what we furnish here." The host continued, "There's the fire, and supper is cooking in the pot. Come and warm yourself, friend."

Things appeared to be improving for the weary and hungry traveler, until one of the men at the table recognized him. The man was a fish salesman who had earlier been at the Cross of Colbas Inn run by Jacquin Labarre. Just thirty minutes before, he had witnessed the conflict between Labarre and the stranger. From his chair he motioned to the manager of this public inn, who walked over to him. They quietly exchanged a few words, as the traveler once again became deeply absorbed in his own thoughts.

Quickly returning to the fireplace, the innkeeper abruptly laid his hand on the stranger's shoulder, and then demanded, "I want you to get out of here!"

The traveler turned around and gently replied, "You know who I am?"

"Yes, I do."

"Please let me stay. I have already been turned away from the other inn."

"And you are being turned away from this one as well."

"But where would you have me to go?"

"Anywhere but here!"

So the tired man picked up his stick and his knapsack and stepped into the cold once again. As he walked, some children who had followed him from the Cross of Colbas Inn, and who seemed to have been lying in wait for him, began throwing stones at him. Lurching toward them in anger and wildly waving his walking stick, he dispersed the children like a flock of birds.

Soon he came to the local prison. Next to the door hung an iron chain that was attached to a bell. Almost as soon as he rang the bell, a small window covered by a grate in the door was opened by one of the guards. "Sir," the traveler said, as he politely removed his cap, "would you kindly let me in so I may have lodging for the night?"

The voice behind the grate replied, "This is a prison—not an inn! Get yourself arrested and I'll let you enter." Then the guard abruptly slammed the door of the grate in the stranger's face.

The beleaguered traveler then found himself on a little street bordered on both sides by many gardens. Some of the gardens were edged by beautiful hedges, which brought an aspect of cheerfulness to the street. In one of the gardens he caught sight of a small, one-story house, with one window brightly lit. Peering through that windowpane, he saw a large white room with an inviting bed that was covered with a printed, soft cotton bedspread. A cradle sat in one corner of the room, while a double-barreled gun hung from the wall. A table with chairs surrounding it sat in the center of the room, and was set for dinner. A copper oil lamp illuminated a thick white linen tablecloth. A pewter jug filled with wine shone like silver in the light, and a brown tureen of steaming soup sat on the tempting table as well.

Sitting at the table was a man of about forty years of age. He had a happy and inviting countenance and bounced a small child on his knee. Nearby sat a very young woman, nursing a baby. The father laughed, the young child giggled with glee, and the mother simply smiled with joy.

With his hunger growing by the moment, the traveler weakly tapped on the windowpane. The family did not hear him, so he tapped once again. He then heard the woman ask her husband, "Did I just hear someone knocking?"

"No," replied the husband.

The stranger tapped a third time. This time the husband stood, grabbed the lamp, and opened the door of the small house.

"Excuse me, sir," began the traveler. "Would you consider selling me a bowl of soup and allowing me a corner of the shed in your garden as a place to sleep? Would you please? For money?"

"Who are you?" demanded the man of the house.

The stranger replied, "I have just traveled from Puy-Moisson and have walked all day long. I have walked more than thirty-five miles. May I please stay—if I pay?"

"I would never refuse to lodge any respectable person who would pay me," answered the man. "But why don't you go to the inn instead?"

"They have no room."

"That's impossible!" exclaimed the husband. "This is not a market day, nor is there a fair going on in town. Have you been to Labarre's inn?"

"Yes, I have."

"Well, then?"

The traveler replied with obvious embarrassment, "I don't know. He just wouldn't allow me to stay."

"Have you tried 'what's his name,' on the Rue de Chaffaut?"

With increasing embarrassment, the stranger stammered, "He wouldn't allow me to stay either."

At this point the townsman's countenance abruptly changed to a look of distrust. He eyed the newcomer from head to toe, and suddenly exclaimed, with a bit of trembling in his voice, "Are you the man . . . ?" Upon taking another look at the stranger, the man then took a few steps backwards, returned the lamp to the table, and reached for his gun on the wall.

The man's wife instinctively pulled her children into her arms and took refuge behind her husband. With her nursing breast now uncovered, and with a look of fright in her eyes, she whispered, "This is the bandit of the French Alps!"

Then the husband, after having scrutinized the man for several more moments—as someone would eye a poisonous snake—returned to the door and shouted, "Clear out!"

"For pity's sake . . . please, a glass of water?" asked the traveler.

"A shot from my gun!" retorted the townsman. He then slammed the door, and the stranger immediately heard two large bolts slide firmly into place. A moment later the window shutter closed, and the sound of an iron bar being placed against it could be heard from outside.

By now the darkness of night was nearly at hand, and a cold Alpine wind was beginning to blow. Yet in the dim twilight that remained, the traveler noticed a small grass hut located in another garden bordering the same street. Determined to find shelter, he climbed the wooden fence and jumped into the garden. Approaching the hut, he saw its door to be quite low and narrow, and assumed it to be one of the small buildings a road worker would construct for himself as temporary shelter on cold days. He himself was now suffering from hunger and exposure to the elements, and saw the hut—at least at a minimum—as shelter from the cold. This sort of hut was not typically occupied at night, so after crouching low to the ground, he crawled through its door. Inside he found some warmth and a somewhat comfortable bed of straw. Exhausted, he lay there for a moment, fully stretched out on his newfound bed. Feeling unable to move another muscle, he nevertheless reached to unbuckle one of the straps of his knapsack in order to remove it from his back and use it as a pillow. At that very moment he heard a ferocious growl. Quickly raising his eyes, he saw the head of an enormous dog faintly outlined at the entrance to the hut.

The poor traveler realized he had unwittingly invaded the dog's house. Although he was a strong and somewhat large man, he armed himself with his stick and used his knapsack as a shield. He then made his way as best he could through the small door, which caused the rips in his ragged clothing to become even larger.

With some difficulty, he climbed back across the fence and found himself once again alone in the street. Without a place of refuge, without any shelter, without a roof over his head, and now having been chased from a miserable dog's house, he dropped his weary body onto a large, cold stone. As he was lying there, too tired to even sit, someone passing by heard him exclaim, "I'm not even as good as a dog!"

After some time, he pulled himself up again, only to resume his long walk. He headed out of the town, hoping to find some tree or even a haystack in the fields that would provide some small amount of shelter. He walked for quite a while with his head now drooping. Once he felt he was far from any possibility of human habitation, he lifted his eyes and intently searched the landscape around him. He found himself in a field, and just ahead of him was a low hill resembling a shaved head. Its grain had recently been harvested, and only the stubble remained. Except for that stubble nothing stood on the hill but a deformed tree, now writhing and shivering in the cold wind just a few paces ahead.

With his surroundings showing little hope of shelter, the traveler decided to retrace his steps. Returning to Digne, he found the gates of the town now closed. Digne had sustained a number of sieges during the religious wars of ancient times, and in 1815 was still surrounded by the old walls and the square towers that flanked them. He discovered an ancient breach in the wall and entered the town again.

By now it was eight o'clock in the evening. As before, being unacquainted with the town, he walked the streets at random. He passed the building of the local magistrate and then continued past the town's seminary. As he passed through Cathedral Square, he shook his fist at the church.

On another corner of Cathedral Square was a printing office. The proclamations of the Emperor and the Imperial Guard to the army, brought from the island of Elba and dictated by Napoléon himself, were printed in that very establishment. Completely fatigued, and now totally without hope of food or shelter, the traveler lay down on a stone bench in the doorway of the printing office.

Just at that moment an old woman walked out from the church. She saw the poor man stretched out on the bench shrouded in shadows. "What are you doing here, my friend?" she asked.

He answered harshly and with anger, "As you can see, my good woman, I'm sleeping." The kind woman, not worthy of such treatment, was Madame la Marquise de R.

"On this cold bench?" she asked.

"I have had a mattress of wood for the past nineteen years," replied the stranger, "and today I have one of stone."

"Have you been a soldier?"

"Yes, my good woman, a soldier."

"Why don't you go to the inn?"

"Because I have no money."

"So! All I have myself is four sous in my purse," said Madame de R.

"Give it to me anyway," demanded the stranger.

The woman handed over the four sous, but added, "I know you can't find lodging at an inn for such a small sum of money, but have you tried? You certainly can't spend the night like this. No doubt you are quite cold and hungry. Surely someone would give you lodging simply out of charity."

"I have knocked on every door."

"And?"

"And . . . I have been turned away everywhere."

The kind woman lightly touched the man's arm, and then pointed to a small house on the other side of the street, next to the seminary. "You have knocked on every door?"

"Yes."

"But have you knocked on that one?"

"No."

"Then knock there."

CHAPTER TWO

That same evening, Monseigneur Bienvenu, the Bishop of Digne, shortly after his daily stroll through town, was hard at work in his room. In his position, one with great responsibilities, his duties were never ending. The eight o'clock hour found him still at work, writing with a certain amount of difficulty on little squares of paper placed upon a large book lying open across his knees.

Madame Magloire entered his room, as she was accustomed to doing, to get some silverware from the cupboard near his bed. A moment later the bishop, sensing that the dinner table must be set and that his sister was probably waiting for him, shut his book, rose from his table, and entered the dining room. He entered just as Madame Magloire was putting the finishing touches on the dinner table. An oil lamp sat on the table next to the fireplace, which was already lit with a wood-burning fire.

Madame Magloire was in a heated discussion with Mademoiselle Baptistine, haranguing her on a topic very familiar to her and the bishop: the importance of having strong locks on the door of the house. It seems that while Madame Magloire had been buying some provisions at the market, she had learned of an evil-looking prowler who was in town and looked very suspicious. She fearfully ranted, "Even now he must be roaming about town, and people who return to their homes late tonight may be in for a very unpleasant surprise. And because the police are very badly organized, and there is no love lost between the chief of police and the mayor, people need to protect themselves by using some common sense, barring their windows, and locking their doors quite well."

Madame Magloire strongly emphasized these last few words, primarily for the benefit of the bishop. Yet having just come from his rather cold room, the bishop quickly sat in front of the fire and began warming himself, with his mind on other topics. Since the bishop had totally disregarded the remark meant especially for his ears, Madame Magloire repeated it. Then Mademoiselle Baptistine, wanting to satisfy Madame Magloire without displeasing her brother, timidly said, "Did you hear what Madame Magloire said, Brother?"

"Vaguely," replied the bishop. Turning in his chair, he placed his hands on his knees and raised his kind face toward the elderly servant woman, Madame Magloire. With his countenance joyful and illuminated by the bright fire below, he asked, "Come now, what's the matter? Are we really in any great danger?"

Madame Magloire responded by sharing her entire story again, but this time with even more exaggeration. Although she was unsure of the facts herself, she related, "It seems that a barefooted beggar—a dangerous wanderer—is at this very moment in our town. He tried to find lodging at Jacquin Labarre's inn, but was turned away. He walked into town via the Boulevard Gassendi and was roaming the streets around dusk tonight. He is a criminal and has a very scary face."

"Really!" the bishop responded.

His apparent eagerness to continue the conversation, spurred Madame Magloire to proceed triumphantly, unwittingly believing she had brought the bishop to the point of being alarmed. "Yes, Monseigneur, this is all true! Everyone says there is going to be some kind of catastrophe in this town tonight. Here we are, with such poor police protection, living in a mountainous region, and even without streetlights! The streets at night are black as ovens, indeed! And, Monseigneur, Mademoiselle Baptistine agrees with me that . . ."

"I have said nothing!" interrupted the bishop's sister.

Yet Madame Magloire continued as though Mademoiselle Baptistine had not protested at all, "We believe this house is totally unsafe! And if you, Monseigneur, will permit, I will ask the locksmith to come and replace the ancient locks on our doors. Nothing could be more terrible than the kind of latches we have, which can even be opened from the outside by anyone passing in the night. We need bolts on these doors! Please, Monseigneur, if only for tonight. I know you are in the habit of saying, 'Come in,' even in the middle of the night, to anyone who knocks on our door. Actually, they don't even need to ask permission, for they could open it themselves!"

At that very moment there was a very loud knock on the door. True to form, the bishop answered it by shouting, "Come in!"

The door swung open rapidly, as though someone had given it a determined push. In walked the stranger who was still searching for shelter. With his stick in his hand and his knapsack still on his back, he stopped just inside, leaving the door open behind him. His eyes shone with a look of roughness and fearlessness, yet they seemed weary at the same time. The light from the fire made him appear sinister and terrifyingly ghostly.

Madame Magloire, unable to find the strength to scream, stood trembling, with her mouth wide open. Mademoiselle Baptistine, turning toward the door, saw the man, and then nearly jumped in terror. But upon turning again toward the fireplace to see her brother's reaction, she became much more calm once again.

The bishop fixed his eyes on the stranger with a sense of peacefulness. As he opened his mouth, undoubtedly to ask the visitor what he needed, the man rested both hands on his walking stick and directed his gaze at the old man and the two women. Yet before the bishop could utter one word, the stranger began to speak in a loud voice.

"Listen. My name is Jean Valjean, and I am a convict. I have served nineteen years in prison and was liberated just four days ago from the chain gang. My destination is Pontarlier. I have been walking for four full days since leaving Toulon, and have traveled more than thirty-five miles today alone. When I arrived in Digne this evening, I went to an inn and was turned away because of my yellow passport, which I had previously been required to present to the officials at the town hall. At that point, I went to another inn, only to be turned away again. Both places demanded that I leave, refusing me food and lodging. I then went to the prison, but the jailer would not admit me. I even attempted to find shelter in a doghouse, only to be bitten by the dog, and chased off as though he were a man himself. You would have thought that dog knew who I was.

"Next I walked into the fields outside of town, intending to sleep in the open air. I decided I would sleep under the stars, only there were none. I thought it was going to rain, so I walked back to town, simply to seek shelter under a covered doorway. Across the square from here, as I was lying on a stone bench, a kind woman pointed to your house, and told me, 'Knock there.'

"So I have only done as I was told. What is this place? Are you running an inn here? I have some savings from my nineteen years of labor in prison—one hundred and nine francs, and fifteen sous. I can pay you. I have money, and at this point paying you means nothing to me. I am extremely weary and hungry, having walked such a long distance today. I just need to know, are you willing for me to stay?"

"Madame Magloire," the bishop said, "please set another place at the table."

Valjean took several steps inside the room, moving closer to the lamp sitting on the table. As though he had not quite understood the bishop, he continued to speak. "Stop," he resumed. "Didn't you hear what I said? I am a convict just released from prison." Reaching into his pocket, he pulled out a large sheet of yellow paper and unfolded it. "Here is my passport—yellow, as you can see. This is why I am turned away wherever I go. I can read it to you, for I learned to read in prison in a school they had for those who choose to learn. This is what my passport says, 'Jean Valjean, discharged convict, has been nineteen years in prison: five years for breaking into a house and burglary, and fourteen years for having attempted to escape on four occasions. He is a dangerous man.' There you have it! Everyone else has turned me away. Are you willing to have me? Is this an inn? Will you allow me something to eat and a bed on which to sleep? Or even a place in the stable?"

"Madame Magloire," the bishop said, "please put clean sheets on the bed in the alcove." She obediently began to follow the bishop's instructions to her.

Then he turned to Valjean and said, "Please have a seat, sir, and warm yourself. We will be having dinner in a few minutes, and your bed will be prepared while you eat."

At this point Valjean seemed to comprehend what he was hearing. The expression on his face, which had been somber and even harsh, now reflected a mixture of astonishment, doubt, and joy. He then began to stammer like a madman, "Really? You are going to allow me to stay, and not turn me away! I'm a convict! You called me sir! You haven't said, 'Get out of here, you dog!' which is what people always say to me. I was so sure you would turn me away that I decided to tell you who I was immediately. Oh, how kind that woman was who directed me here! I'm actually going to eat! And have a bed with a mattress and sheets, like the rest of the world! You are good people. Excuse me, Monsieur Innkeeper, but what is your name? I will pay whatever you ask. You are a fine man. You are an innkeeper, are you not?"

The bishop replied quite simply, by saying, "I am a priest who lives here."

"A priest!" exclaimed Valjean. "What a fine priest you are! Are you not going to ask any money of me? You are the priest of this parish? Of this big church? And I am a fool, for not having noticed your skullcap."

As he spoke, Valjean set his knapsack and stick in the corner of the room, returned his passport to his pocket, and then seated himself. Mademoiselle Baptistine looked pleasantly at him, as he continued, "You are humane, sir, for you have not shunned me or treated me with contempt. A good priest is a very good thing. Will you ask me to pay?"

"No," answered the bishop, "keep your money. How much did you say you have—one hundred and nine francs?"

"And fifteen sous," added Valjean.

"One hundred and nine francs, and fifteen sous. And how long did you say it took you to earn that?"

"Nineteen years."

"Nineteen years!" exclaimed the bishop, then he sighed deeply.

At this point, Madame Magloire returned to the room with a silver fork and spoon and placed them on the table. Turning to the woman, the bishop said, "Please place those as close to the fireplace as possible." And turning to his guest, he said, "The night wind is quite harsh in the Alps. You must be very cold, sir."

Each time the bishop used the word *sir*, his voice seemed so kind and gentle that Valjean's face lit up. For a convict to be called sir felt to Valjean like a glass of water might have felt to one of the shipwrecked sailors of the Medusa. Having been discredited and dishonored for so long caused him to thirst for this kind of consideration.

"This lamp sheds only a very dim light," the bishop said. Understanding his true intent, Madame Magloire went to the Monseigneur's bedroom, got two silver candlesticks from his cabinet, returned to place them on the table, and lit them.

"Priest," Valjean said, "you are a good man. You do not despise me, and have received me into your house. You have even lit extra candles for me. And you have done all this, in spite of the fact that I did not conceal from you my past, my true identity, or my unfortunate situation."

The bishop, who was sitting close to him, gently touched his hand. Then in the truest sense of love and caring, he said, "You did not need to tell me who you were. This is not my house—it is the house of Jesus Christ. And His door never demands to know the name of those who enter, but only requires that they have a need. You are suffering and are hungry and thirsty, so you are welcome here. And please do not thank me or say that I have received you into my house. No one is truly at home here, except those who need a place of refuge. In fact, as a passerby, you are much more at home here than I am myself. Everything here is yours. I have no need to even know your name. Besides, I already knew it before you told me."

Valjean's eyes opened wide in astonishment. He exclaimed, "Really! You knew what I was called?"

"Yes," replied the bishop, "you are called my brother."

"Stop, dear priest," Valjean protested. "I came here with great hunger, but you have been too good. I don't understand what has happened to me."

The bishop looked at him, and kindly asked, "You have suffered a great deal?"

"I was forced to wear prison clothes and had a ball and chain attached to my ankle. I slept on a plank of wood in the heat and the cold. I was beaten and shackled with a second chain for nothing at all. I was sent to solitary for saying only one word. And even when sick or asleep I would be chained. Dogs are treated better! Nineteen years! Now I am forty-six years old and must travel with a yellow passport. That is my life."

"You come from very difficult circumstances, indeed," responded the bishop. "Yet there will be more joy in heaven over the tear-stained face of one repentant sinner than over the white robes of a hundred just men. If you emerge from your sad past with thoughts of hatred and of wrath against mankind, you are deserving of our pity. If, however, you emerge with thoughts of goodwill and peace, you are more worthy than any one of us."

In the meantime, Madame Magloire had served supper: soup, made with water, oil, bread, and salt; a little bacon, a small piece of mutton, figs, cheese, and a large loaf of rye bread. Of her own accord, she had also added to the bishop's ordinary menu a bottle of fine old Mauves wine.

Then the bishop's face was immediately illuminated with an expression of merriment common only among hospitable people. "To the table!" he shouted excitedly. As was his custom, he asked his guest to be seated on his right, while Mademoiselle Baptistine, who remained perfectly calm, took her seat to his left.

The bishop asked God's blessing upon the food, and began to ladle the soup for the others at the table. Valjean began to eat with the enthusiasm of a half-starved man. Then the bishop abruptly declared, "It seems that there is something missing on the table."

In fact, Madame Magloire had only set the table with the bare necessities of silverware—one fork and spoon for each person. Yet whenever the bishop had a guest for supper, it was his desire that the full place setting of six pieces per person be placed on the tablecloth. He saw this simple luxury as innocently pretentious, but something that added charm to an otherwise austere home, and would lend some dignity to the poor.

Without saying a word, but fully understanding the bishop's remark, Madame Magloire left the room. A moment later three full place settings of silver glittered on the tablecloth, symmetrically arranged in front of each person seated at the table.

Once they had completed their dinner, the bishop wished his sister a good night. He then took one of the two silver candlesticks from the table, handed the other to his guest, and said to Valjean, "Monsieur, I will show you to your room." The weary traveler followed the bishop.

The small house was arranged so that in order to walk to the chapel, where the traveler's alcove and bed were situated, it was necessary to pass through the bishop's bedroom. As they passed through that room, Madame Magloire was busily returning the silverware to the cupboard near the head of the bed. This was always one of her final duties before retiring for the night.

The bishop showed his guest to the alcove, where a bed with fresh linens had been made. Valjean then placed his candle on the small table. "Good night, my brother," said the bishop. "May you sleep peacefully tonight. Tomorrow morning, before you leave, we will be happy to share a glass of warm milk with you from our cows."

"Thank you, dear priest," Valjean replied. Yet hardly had he spoken these kind, peaceful words before his expression changed so much that if the women had seen it, they would have been terrified. It is difficult to understand what may have prompted him at that moment. Perhaps he was attempting to convey some sort of warning, or obeying some instinctive impulse that even he did not understand. Nevertheless, he turned abruptly toward the old bishop, folded his arms, looked at him with a piercing gaze, and exclaimed in a rough tone, "You really are going to put me here in your house! And this close to yourself!"

Then just as abruptly he stopped, and finally added with somewhat of a sinister laugh, "Have you really thought this through, sir? How do you know that I am not a murderer?"

The bishop replied, "That is the concern of our good and gracious God." Then in a solemn way, the bishop raised two fingers of his right hand, and while moving his lips as a person who is praying, he bestowed a blessing on Valjean. The guest did not bow, and without turning around or looking behind him, the bishop left the alcove.

When the alcove was in use, a large woolen curtain, which was drawn from wall to wall across the chapel, concealed the altar. As the bishop passed by the curtain, he knelt and said a brief prayer. A moment later he walked through the garden, thinking and meditating, with his entire heart and soul wholly absorbed in the grand and mysterious things that God reveals at night to those whose eyes remain open.

As for Valjean, he was so fatigued that he could not fully appreciate the clean, white sheets. After blowing out his candle, he dropped fully dressed onto the bed, where he immediately fell into a deep sleep.

The bishop returned from his garden just as the clock struck midnight. A few minutes later all the inhabitants of the small house were sound asleep.

CHAPTER THREE

———————— ⚜ ————————

J ean Valjean had been born into a poor peasant family in Brie, a small village not far from Paris. He did not learn to read as a child, and once he became an adult, he took a job pruning trees in Faverolles. His father's name was also Jean Valjean, while his mother's maiden name was Jeanne Mathieu.

As a child Jean Valjean had a somber and quiet disposition, which is somewhat typical of children with an affectionate nature. On the whole, however, there was nothing striking about his appearance. He had lost his father and mother at a very young age, losing his mother to what was known at the time as milk fever—not to mention a lack of medical care for her sickness. His father was also a laborer who pruned trees and had fallen to his death from one of those trees.

After his parents' deaths, the only remaining family member Jean Valjean had was an older sister, who raised him. She had provided food and lodging for her younger brother as long as her husband was alive. Yet his sister was widowed when Valjean was twenty-five years old, and when her seven children were from one to eight years of age, Valjean then stepped in, and with the tables now turned, supported his sister who had raised him. He saw this responsibility as his duty, something not uncommon among the peasants of his day.

Valjean spent his younger years in meager, manual labor—always toiling for little pay. And because of the long hours he worked, in order to provide for his sister and her children, he had never had the opportunity to find a woman and to fall in love.

During pruning season he earned only eighteen sous a day. Once that season ended he would then hire himself out as a reaper, a teamster, or as a common laborer. He took any job he could find, as did his sister, although there was little she could do while caring for seven little children. They were a sad lot, living in misery, and facing nothing but their slow demise. And when it seemed nothing could get worse, they encountered a very difficult winter in 1795. Valjean had no work, and the family had no bread. No bread—and seven small children!

One Sunday evening, during this bitter winter, Maubert Isabeau, the baker at the Church Square at Faverolles, was preparing for bed when he heard the sound of glass breaking. The noise seemed to be coming from the front of his shop, and he arrived there just in time to see an arm reaching through the hole in the glass, which had apparently been made by a fist. He saw a hand quickly grab a loaf of bread that was then pulled outside through the window.

Isabeau quickly ran outside, as the thief attempted to get away as fast as he could run. Yet the baker continued to pursue him and finally overtook him and made him stop. In the meantime, the thief had thrown the loaf of bread away. However, the evidence of his bleeding arm betrayed him. The thief was Jean Valjean.

Valjean was taken before the court and charged with breaking and entering an inhabited house at night, and with theft. The fact that he owned a gun, was well known as an excellent marksman, and had previously been charged with poaching, did not help his case. Therefore, Valjean was found to be guilty by the court, and with the legal codes being very explicit, was condemned to spend the next five years in hard labor in prison.

Many times while imprisoned, Valjean could be seen weeping. His heavy sobbing would often impede his speech, but he could be heard to mumble, "I was only a pruner of trees in Faverolles." Still sobbing, he would raise his right hand and gradually lower it seven times, as though he were patting the seven heads of his dear nieces and nephews. Seeing his apparent love for them, it was easily discerned that his crime had been done for the sake of those poor, hungry children.

Whenever he would be sent by the prison to another place of backbreaking work, he was forced to sit on an open cart with a heavy chain around his neck. In fact, all the things that had once constituted his life were now erased, including his name. He was no longer Jean Valjean, but was prisoner number 24601.

Toward the end of his fourth year in prison, with only one year remaining to serve, Valjean's first opportunity came to escape. His fellow prisoners assisted him, which was common in such a sad place. He got away, but was captured on the evening of the second day. At this point he had neither eaten nor slept for thirty-six hours. Upon being taken before the court once again, he was condemned for this new crime to serve an additional three years in prison—now a total of eight years.

During his sixth year in prison, Valjean had his next opportunity to escape. Although he took advantage of the opportunity, he could not fully run away. When he was missing at roll call, the guards fired their cannon as a warning, and a night patrol found him hiding under the keel of a boat under construction nearby. He resisted the guards who seized him, which added rebellion to the charge of escape. The new case against him was punished by an additional five years, two of which were to be served in double chains. Now his sentence amounted to thirteen years in all.

In the tenth year of Valjean's sentence, another escape opportunity presented itself. Once again he tried to escape, but succeeded no better. Three more years were added, now making his sentence sixteen years. Then during his thirteenth year, he made his last escape attempt, succeeding only in being recaptured within four hours. The cost for those four hours was three more years, for his sentence was extended again—now to a full nineteen years.

Finally, in October 1815, he was released. He had entered prison in 1796—serving nineteen years for having broken a pane of glass and for stealing a loaf of bread! Jean Valjean had entered prison weeping, sobbing, and in full despair. He emerged from the prison still totally dejected, but as a man without any show of emotion and with an expressionless face.

When Jean Valjean heard the strange words, "You are free," the moment seemed amazingly impossible to him. It was as though a strong ray of light from the living suddenly penetrated his entire being. He was overcome by the idea of freedom and liberty, but the bright light within him quickly faded. He had hoped for a wonderful new life, yet was soon to discover the only kind of life his yellow passport would provide.

The very day after being freed from prison, Valjean saw some men working in the town of Grasse. They were unloading some bales in front of an orange-flower perfume distillery when he offered his services. Needing more help, the foreman accepted his offer, so he immediately set to work. He was intelligent, strong, and good with his hands, and the foreman seemed pleased with him. While he was at work, a policeman passed by, observed him briefly, and then demanded to see his papers. Valjean produced his yellow passport, which the policeman quickly reviewed and handed back to him. With this done, Valjean resumed his work.

While he labored, he questioned one of the other workmen, and was told that the daily pay for this work was thirty sous. Yet when evening arrived, and he presented himself to the owner of the distillery to be paid, the man handed him only fifteen sous, without uttering one word. Valjean protested, but was told, "That is enough for you!" And when he persisted in his protest, the owner looked him straight in the eyes and said, "You must beware of the prison."

Once again Valjean felt that he had been robbed. The state and society had taken everything from him while in prison, including most of the meager savings he had been able to accumulate. Now it was happening to him as a man who was supposedly free.

Valjean's freedom from prison was not true deliverance. He had been set free from his chains, but not from his sentence.

CHAPTER FOUR

s the cathedral's clock struck two in the morning, Jean Valjean awoke. What had actually awakened him, however, was that his bed was too good. It had been nearly twenty years since he had slept in a bed, and although he was still wearing all of his clothes, the feeling was so new to him that his sleep was disturbed.

He had slept more than four hours, and his weariness had subsided. He was not accustomed to many hours of sleep, so he opened his eyes and stared into the darkness surrounding him. Then he closed them again, intending to sleep some more. Yet he was unable to sleep again, for his mind was filled with various thoughts. One of those thoughts that kept coming to him, and which drove all of the others away, had to do with the six sets of silverware and the silver ladle placed on the dinner table by Madame Magloire.

His mind struggled with his thoughts for a full hour. When three o'clock struck, Valjean opened his eyes again, abruptly sat upright, and stretched out his arm to reach his knapsack, which he had thrown into a corner of the alcove. Almost without realizing it, he then swung his legs over the side of the bed, placed his feet on the floor, and found himself sitting on the edge of the mattress.

Just as abruptly, he stooped down, removed his shoes, and set them quietly on the mat beside the bed. Then he resumed the struggle with his thoughts, as he became motionless once more. He remained in this position, and perhaps would have stayed like this until daybreak, except that the clock suddenly struck again, indicating the half hour. That stroke of the clock seemed to be saying to him, "Come on!"

Valjean rose to his feet, hesitated another moment, and listened intently. All was quiet in the small house, so he walked straight ahead with short steps toward the window. Looking out, he noticed the night was not very dark. A full moon was only occasionally covered by thick clouds being driven by the wind. This created sufficient light indoors, enough to enable him to see his way through the house, except when the clouds briefly covered the moon.

He began to examine the window and found that it was not covered with any grating. It opened onto the garden and was only fastened to the house with a small pin. He swung it open, but as he did so, a rush of piercingly cold air abruptly penetrated the room. He then closed it immediately and began to thoroughly scrutinize the garden. A low, white wall that would be quite easy to climb enclosed it. Some distance away, at the far end of the garden, he could see only the tops of trees that were spaced at regular intervals, indicating that the wall separated the garden from a street planted with trees.

Having finished his survey, Valjean threw his knapsack over his shoulder, put his shoes in his pockets, and put his cap on his head, making sure to pull its visor down near his eyes. He felt for his walking stick and placed it next to the window. Then holding his breath and walking as softly as possible, he headed toward the door of the bishop's bedroom. Once there, he found it ajar, for the bishop had not closed it.

Valjean listened intently but did not hear a sound. He pushed the door gently with the tip of his finger, moving with the sly and uneasy gentleness of a cat. The door yielded to the pressure, opening ever so slightly and silently. He waited for a moment, and then gave the door a second and bolder push. It continued to yield in total silence. The opening was now large enough to allow him to enter, but near the door stood a little table at an angle to it, blocking his entrance. Recognizing the difficulty, he knew it was necessary to make the opening a bit larger, whatever the cost.

Having decided his course of action, he gave the door a third push, with more force than his previous efforts. This time a hinge, in need of oil, suddenly broke the silence with a hoarse and prolonged squeak. Valjean shuddered, as

though the hinge rang in his ears with the piercing and awe-inspiring sound
of the trumpet of the Lord on Judgment Day.

He stood still, petrified like a statue of salt, not daring to make any
movements. Several minutes elapsed while he remained motionless. The door
was now wide open, so he cautiously peered into the bishop's room. As he
waited and listened, Valjean realized the squeaking hinge had not awakened
anyone in the small house.

Taking a step, he entered the room. He could hear the measured, peaceful
breathing of the sleeping bishop across the room. He came to a sudden halt,
having arrived at the side of the bed in the small room sooner than he would
have thought. In spite of Valjean's terrifying gaze above him, the bishop
continued sleeping in profound peace.

A ray of dim light from the moon seemed to render a confusing view of
the crucifix hanging over the fireplace. Jesus appeared to be extending His
arms to both of them—as a blessing for one, and as a pardon for the other.

Suddenly Jean Valjean walked rapidly past the bed, without glancing again
at the bishop, and headed straight to the cabinet near the head of the bed. The
key was sitting there, so he took it and quickly opened the cabinet, which
plainly revealed a basket full of silverware. He grabbed it and walked back
across the bedroom with long strides, without taking any precautions at this
point to keep his noise to a minimum. Reentering the chapel, he opened the
window, grabbed his stick, and climbed over the windowsill. Now that he was
outside, he put the silver in his knapsack, threw the basket aside, hurried
across the garden, jumped the wall as easily as a tiger, and fled by foot.

The next morning at sunrise the bishop was strolling in his garden when
Madame Magloire ran to him in utter panic. "Monseigneur, Monseigneur!" she
exclaimed. "Do you know where the basket of silver is?"

"Yes," replied the bishop.

"Jesus the Lord be praised!" she said, "for I could not find it."

As she spoke, the bishop picked up the basket that Valjean had thrown
into the flower bed. He handed it to Madame Magloire, and said, "Here it is."

"But it's empty," she said. "Where is the silver?"

"Oh!" the bishop exclaimed. "It's the silver that troubles you? Not the basket? Well, I don't know where the silver is."

"Good God! It has been stolen! That man who was here last night has taken it," Madame Magloire declared. Then, in an instant, the elderly woman rushed into the chapel with a liveliness and alertness that betrayed her years. She entered the alcove, but quickly returned to the bishop. He was bending over a plant in his garden that had been broken by the basket as it had been tossed aside. The bishop calmly sighed as he examined the plant, but stood up straight upon hearing Madame Magloire shout, "Monseigneur, the man is gone! The silver has been stolen!"

As she uttered this exclamation, her eyes fell upon a part of the wall in the corner of the garden. It was marked with obvious signs of having been recently scaled. "Look at that! That's the way he went—down the Rue Cochefilet. How disgusting! He has stolen our silver!"

The bishop remained silent for a moment, then raised his dark eyes, and gently said to Madame Magloire, "In the first place, was that silver ours?"

"Was that silver ours?" The woman was dumbfounded, only able to repeat the question.

Another moment of silence ensued, before the bishop continued, "Madame Magloire, for too long I have kept that silver wrongfully. It belonged to the poor. And what was that man, if not poor?"

"Oh, dear Jesus!" retorted the woman, "I'm not concerned for my sake, nor for Mademoiselle Baptistine's. It makes no difference to us. It's for your sake, Monseigneur. What will you eat with now?"

The bishop simply stared at her with a look of amazement. "Oh, come now. Aren't there such things as pewter forks and spoons?"

Madame Magloire only shrugged, saying, "Pewter has an odor."

"Iron forks and spoons, then."

At this the woman made an expressive grimace, and offered, "Iron has a taste."

"Very well, then," said the bishop, "We'll use wooden ones."

A few moments later he was having breakfast at the same table where Jean Valjean had sat the previous evening. As he ate, the bishop cheerfully remarked to his sister that no one really needs a fork or spoon, even made of wood, to dip a small piece of bread in a cup of milk. His sister did not say one word in response, while Madame Magloire grumbled under her breath.

"What a nice idea," Madame Magloire muttered to herself, as she served the meal, "to take in a man like that! And to let him sleep so nearby! How fortunate that he did nothing but steal! Oh, my Lord! It makes me shudder even to think about it!"

Just as the bishop and his sister were finishing breakfast, there was a knock on the door. "Come in!" the bishop called.

The door swung open, revealing a disturbing sight on the small porch. Three men stood there holding a fourth man by his collar. The three were policemen, while the fourth was Jean Valjean.

One officer, who appeared to be in charge of the other policemen, stepped through the doorway. Upon entering the house he approached the bishop and saluted him. "Monseigneur. . . ." he said.

Hearing the word *Monseigneur,* Jean Valjean, who seemed completely downcast and dejected, raised his head with a look of astonishment. "Monseigneur?" he questioned. "I thought he was just the parish priest."

"Silence!" demanded the officer. "He is Monseigneur the bishop."

In the meantime, Monseigneur Bienvenu stepped forward as quickly as his advanced age would allow, and spoke before the officer could continue. "Oh! Here you are!" he exclaimed, looking at Jean Valjean. "I'm so glad to see you. I can't believe you forgot the candlesticks! They are made of pure silver as well. Surely you could sell them for more than two hundred francs. Please take them with the forks and spoons I gave you."

With his eyes now wide open, Valjean stared at the honorable bishop with an expression of astonishment that no human tongue could possibly describe.

"Monseigneur," said the officer, "then what this man said is true? But when we encountered him, he appeared to be a man who was running away. And once we detained him to look into the matter, we found this silver, and . . ."

"And he told you," interrupted the bishop with a smile, "that it had been given to him by a kind old priest who had given him lodging for the night? I see how this looks and understand why you have brought him back here, but it is a mistake."

"In that case," asked the officer, "we can let him go?"

"Of course," answered the bishop.

As the policemen released their grip on him, Valjean instinctively shrank back a step or two. "Is it true? I am released?" he questioned, in an almost inaudible voice, as though he were talking in his sleep.

"Yes, you are free to go. Do you not understand?" said one of the policemen.

"Yet before you go, my friend," added the bishop, "here are your candlesticks. Please don't forget them again." Then stepping to the fireplace, he took the two silver candlesticks from the mantel, and took them to Valjean. To the women's credit, they looked on without uttering a word or making any gesture that would betray the actions or words of the bishop.

By now, Jean Valjean's entire body was trembling. He mechanically reached for the two candlesticks, but with a look of bewilderment on his face.

"Now," said the bishop, "go in peace. By the way, when you return, my friend, it is not necessary for you to come and go through the garden. You may always use our front door. Remember, it is never shut with anything but a latch—day or night."

Then, turning to the policemen, the bishop continued, "You may take your leave, gentlemen." At this, they immediately departed.

By this point Valjean looked like a man ready to faint. The bishop leaned closely toward him and said in a quiet voice, "Do not forget. Never forget that you have promised to use this silver to become an honest man."

Valjean, who had no recollection of ever having promised anything, remained silent. Yet the bishop had stressed each and every word as he had uttered them. He then resumed in a very somber tone, "Jean Valjean, my brother, you no longer belong to evil, but to good. I have bought your soul from you. I take it back from evil thoughts and deeds and the Spirit of Hell, and I give it to God."

CHAPTER FIVE

———————— ⚘ ————————

J ean Valjean left the town as though he were again fleeing it. He set out so hastily through the fields that he took whatever road or path he came upon, and did not realize he was actually running in circles. He wandered around like this the entire morning, without having eaten anything, yet without feeling hungry.

He was at the mercy of a number of new sensations and thoughts. He was aware of a sense of rage, but he did not know against whom it was directed. And in light of the words spoken by the bishop, he did not know whether to feel touched or humiliated. At times a new strange emotion overcame him— one that struck at the hardness he had acquired over the last twenty years of his life. This state of mind wearied him.

As the long day finally came to an end, with the sun casting long shadows across the landscape, Valjean found himself on a large plain that was absolutely deserted. He saw nothing on the horizon except the Alps—not even a church spire from a distant village. He had walked some nine or ten miles from Digne, and was now seated near a path that cut across the open plain.

While still in the midst of his distressing thoughts, he suddenly heard a joyful sound that was barely audible. Turning his head, he saw a young lad of ten or twelve years, obviously from Savoy in southeastern France, walking down the path singing. He had a hurdy-gurdy crank organ hanging from his hip, while a small box on his back held a tiny monkey. The boy was one of those happy and gentle children who traveled from place to place with their knees showing through the holes in their trousers.

As he walked, from time to time he would playfully toss a few coins into the air. These coins probably represented his entire fortune, and among them was a forty-sous piece. The child stopped next to a bush near Jean Valjean, yet without seeing him. He tossed his coins once more, but although he had been catching all of them quite skillfully, he now dropped the forty-sous piece. It rolled across the ground straight toward Valjean, who stamped his foot upon it.

The young lad, following the path of his coin, walked straight over to the man. "Sir," said the child, innocently and with childish confidence, "that's my money."

"What's your name?" asked Valjean.

"Little Gervais, sir."

"Go away," retorted Valjean.

"Sir," resumed the child, "give me back my money." Valjean simply dropped his head, making no reply. The child began again, "My money, sir." Yet Valjean's eyes remained fixed on the ground. "Give me my money!" cried the child. "Give me my piece of silver!"

It seemed as though Valjean did not hear him, so the child grabbed him by the collar of his jacket and shook him. Then he tried unsuccessfully to move Valjean's big iron-toed shoe from atop his treasure. Once again he yelled, "I want my silver! My forty-sous piece!"

The child began to weep. Valjean then looked up, but remained seated. He had a perplexed look on his face, and simply stared at the child. Then grabbing his walking stick, he yelled in a strange voice, "Who's there?"

"I, sir, am Little Gervais!" replied the child. "Please give me back my forty sous! Take your foot away, sir!"

Valjean responded, still seemingly confused, "Oh, it's you! You're still here?" He then abruptly stood to his feet with his shoe remaining over the piece of silver and shouted at the child, "Go away!"

The child, now trembling in fear, stared at him for a moment, but suddenly turned and ran away as fast as his short legs would carry him. He did not even dare to look back. Yet with all that he was carrying, the child was forced to stop to catch his breath just a short distance away. Valjean heard the lad sobbing, in spite of being absorbed in his own thoughts.

Some time later the child had disappeared and the sun had completely set. Darkness now surrounded Valjean. He had eaten nothing all day, and he had a bit of a fever. He had stood in place, not moving a muscle, ever since the lad had run away. His breathing was heavy, and suddenly he shivered, as he began to feel the chill of the evening air. He then firmly pulled his cap over his forehead, somewhat mechanically pulled his jacket closed and began to button it, and stooped to grab his walking stick once again.

At that moment he caught sight of the forty-sous piece that his foot had ground halfway into the dirt, but which was now shining among the pebbles. A look of total shock flashed across his face, as he muttered between his teeth, "What is this?" Valjean stepped back several steps, unable to detach his gaze from the coin, as though it were an eye intently staring back at him. He darted toward the coin, seized it, and stood erect again, while shivering convulsively and casting his eyes toward the horizon like a wild animal seeking a place of refuge.

All at once he began running in the same direction that the child had traveled. After about thirty paces he stopped, looked around, but saw nothing. Then he shouted with all his might, "Little Gervais! Little Gervais!" He paused for a moment, yet there was no reply. Valjean began to run again, and from time to time would stop to shout into the solitude, "Little Gervais! Little Gervais!"

In this same manner he covered a very long distance, searching and shouting, but he saw no one. Finally, as the moon was rising, he stopped where three paths intersected. He gazed into the distance and shouted for the last time, "Little Gervais! Little Gervais! Little Gervais!" His shouts died away in the mist, without even awakening an echo. Valjean muttered yet again, "Little Gervais!" but in a feeble and nearly inaudible voice.

This was his final effort. His legs suddenly gave away beneath him, as though an invisible power had abruptly overwhelmed him with the weight of his evil deeds. He fell onto a large stone, now totally exhausted, with his fists clenched in his hair and his face on his knees. In grief, he cried out, "I am a miserable, despicable person!"

As his heart seemed to burst, he began to weep uncontrollably. It was the first time he had wept in nineteen years. While his tears continued to flow, it seemed a bright and glorious light penetrated deep into his soul. It was extraordinarily bright, and was delightful and fearsome at the same time. His past life—everything from his first sin, his inward hardness, his nineteen years in prison, his plans of taking vengeance into his own hands, his theft at the bishop's, and even to his latest sin of stealing forty sous from a mere child—flashed across his mind. This latest sin seemed all the more monstrous and cowardly since it had come immediately after receiving the bishop's pardon. Valjean had never witnessed anything so penetrating, nor had he ever been confronted with the magnitude of his sins so clearly.

As he continued to examine his life, it seemed horrible to him while the darkness of his soul frightened him as well. Yet in the meantime a gentle but bright light rested over his life and his soul. To Valjean, it was as though he beheld the light of heaven shining into the heart of a man who had been filled with the deeds of Satan himself.

No one knows how long Jean Valjean wept like this or what he did afterward. And no one knows where he went next. No one ever knew. The only thing known for sure is that on that very same night a messenger, who arrived in Digne about three o'clock in the morning, saw a man kneeling, as if in prayer, on the shadowed pavement outside the door of the bishop's residence.

CHAPTER SIX

--- ⚜ ---

uring the early 1800s, in the town of Montfermeil near Paris, there was an inn called The Sergeant of Waterloo, which was so named in honor of its owner. His name was Thénardier, and he and his wife ran the inn. And if the owner were to be believed, he had been a sergeant throughout the campaign of 1815, and had even conducted himself with valor. The sign over the inn was evidence of one of his "feats of arms," for he had painted it himself. Indeed, he did know how to do a little of everything—but badly.

If the truth of the battle of Waterloo were to be told, however, Thénardier was nothing but a nocturnal prowler who walked through the blood of the battlefield at night stripping the dead of their valuables. At this particular battle, he had moved the body of an officer to higher ground in order to better see what he might steal, and in doing so had inadvertently saved the man's life. The wounded officer, just returning to consciousness, had raised a feeble arm to briefly detain Thénardier, and said to him, "You saved my life. Who are you?"

The thief answered quietly, not wanting to be detected, "Like you, I belong to the French Army. If the enemy catches me here, I will be shot. I have saved your life, but now you are on your own."

"What is your rank, sir?" the wounded man asked.

"Sergeant."

"And what is your name?"

"Thénardier," was the thief's response.

"I will not forget your name," the officer said. "And please remember mine. It is Pontmercy."

One evening three years later, during the spring of 1818, the Thénardiers' two little girls were playing in the yard at the front of the inn. The older of the two, who was about two-and-a-half years old, held her eighteen-month-old sister in her arms. The children, who were happily playing with each other, were both dressed in somewhat elegant clothing. Their eyes were bright, and their clean cheeks were filled with laughter. Their mother, whose looks did not offer a very favorable first impression, stood nearby watching them carefully.

Another woman, who was approaching the inn on foot, held a child in her arms. She struggled somewhat, for she also carried a large bag made of carpet, which seemed to be quite heavy. The woman's child was one of the most divine creations possible to imagine. The beautiful child was a little girl, appearing to be two or three years old. The child's clothing was equally as elegant as that of the two other children playing nearby. She wore a bonnet of fine linen and lace, as well as a lovely dress tied about the waist with colorful ribbons. She appeared healthy, as evidenced by her rosy cheeks. Yet all that could be said of her eyes is that they were very large with magnificent lashes, for she was sound asleep.

The child's mother, however, appeared quite needy and poverty-stricken. She was dressed as a working woman, but one who was on the edge of becoming a peasant once again. Her name was Fantine.

She spoke to Madame Thénardier, saying, "You have two beautiful children, madam." The children were indeed lovely, but Fantine knew that bestowing compliments on their young could disarm even the most ferocious creatures.

Madame Thénardier nodded and thanked Fantine, and asked the traveler to have a seat on the bench next to her by the door. The two women then began to chat. "My name is Madame Thénardier," said the mother of the two little girls. "My husband and I run this inn." The woman had a rough complexion and was somewhat thin, but masculine, in her build. And there was a certain oddness that seemed to envelop her, and showed itself in her smirk of a smile.

As they talked, Fantine began to tell her story. She related that she was a working woman and that her husband was dead. It seems that her work in Paris had ended, and she was on her way to seek employment elsewhere, perhaps in her own native area. She had left Paris that morning and had walked most of the way. And because her child was so young, she had carried her nearly the entire time. As Fantine had done so, her little jewel had fallen asleep in her arms. Having said this, she tenderly gave her daughter a sweet kiss, which caused her to open her eyes. Those beautiful eyes were big and blue—like her mother's. Just then the child began to laugh.

Madame Thénardier then said to all three children, "Run along and play." Small children take to each other so easily that within a minute or so the two Thénardier children were happily playing with their visitor, digging small holes in the dirt. Then the two women continued their discussion, when Madame Thénardier asked, "What is your little one's name?"

"Cosette," Fantine responded.

"How old is she?"

"Nearly three years."

"Oh, then she's the age of my older child," Madame Thénardier stated.

In the meantime, the two sisters continued playing with their new playmate as though they had known her for some time. They were playfully digging in the dirt with their heads touching one another as they laughed and giggled in glee.

"How easily and quickly young children get acquainted!" exclaimed Madame Thénardier. "One would think that the three of them were sisters!"

This last remark was exactly what Fantine had been hoping to hear. She immediately seized on the statement, reached for Madame Thénardier's hand, looked intently into her eyes, and asked, "Will you keep my child for me?"

Madame Thénardier made a quick movement in a gesture of surprise, but one that indicated neither her assent nor her refusal. Fantine continued, "You see, I cannot take Cosette to the countryside, for my work will not allow it. In fact, it is nearly impossible to find work when you have a child—people are ridiculous in the country. It was nothing but the goodness of God that caused me to pass by your inn. And once I caught sight of your lovely little children— so pretty and so clean—I was overwhelmed. I said to myself, 'Here is a good mother. This is the perfect situation, for these three girls will be like sisters!' Madam, it will not be long before I return. Will you keep my child for me?"

"I must see about that," replied Madame Thénardier.

"I will pay you six francs a month, madam."

At this, a man's voice from inside the inn could be heard to say, "Seven francs a month, with six months paid in advance!"

"Yes," added Madame Thénardier. "Six times seven would be forty-two."

"I will pay that," agreed Fantine.

The man's voice chimed in again, "And fifteen more francs in advance for initial expenses."

"That makes fifty-seven francs in total," figured Madame Thénardier. She then hummed softly, as though satisfied with the numbers.

"I can pay that," agreed Fantine once again. "I have a total of eighty francs. That will leave me enough to get to the countryside, if I travel by foot. And once I earn more money there and can set some aside, I will return for my sweet daughter."

Again, the man spoke: "Your little child has an outfit?"

At this Madame Thénardier finally offered, "That is my husband speaking."

Fantine responded to his question, "Of course she has an outfit," and then directed a quiet comment to Madame Thénardier, saying, "Yes, I understood him to be your husband." Continuing, she added, "Cosette is my treasure. She has more than one outfit, too! Even one that some may say is extravagantly beautiful. She has some things by the dozen, and silk gowns, like a little lady. It's all here, in my bag."

"You must hand it all over to us," the man said in a matter-of-fact way.

"Of course I will leave them with you," Fantine responded, "It would be quite strange for me to take her clothes, and leave Cosette naked."

The man replied, "That's good," as he finally leaned outside the door, revealing his face for the first time.

With the bargain now concluded, Fantine spent the night at the inn. The following morning she handed over the money and Cosette's clothes, and then packed her carpetbag that was now much lighter as a result. She then set out on her journey, with the intention of returning very soon.

People often arrange such things quite calmly, but this type of situation can create a tremendous sense of despair. In fact, a neighbor of the Thénardiers, who saw Fantine shortly after she had left Cosette, related to them, "I just saw that young woman crying so hard as she was leaving that it almost broke my heart!"

Yet after Fantine had departed, Monsieur Thénardier said to his wife, "This money will enable me to pay the note I have coming due tomorrow for one hundred and ten francs. I was short fifty francs, and without this the bailiff would have come for me. My dear, you played the mousetrap quite nicely with our little ones."

"And without even knowing it!" said the woman, with a sly smile.

Fantine, the poor mouse who had been caught in that trap, was a pitiful specimen. Yet a cat rejoices even over a lean mouse. By any human standard, the Thénardiers were dwarfs in their character in matters of truthfulness, and given the right opportunity, could be extremely cruel. When it came to other ethical traits, Madame Thénardier could have been considered to be lower than an animal, and her husband was nothing better than a corrupt scoundrel. And as they advanced through life, they were only more prone to lean in the direction of evil.

The Thénardiers' wickedness, however, did not lead to prosperity, for their inn was in financial difficulties. Thanks to Fantine's fifty-seven francs, Monsieur Thénardier had been able to avoid being arrested by the bailiff by paying his note on time, yet the very next month he was in need of money again. Therefore, he and his wife took little Cosette's entire wardrobe to Paris and pawned it for sixty francs.

As soon as that money was gone, the Thénardiers began to see the little girl merely as a child they were caring for solely out of their "sense of charity," and began to treat her accordingly—not as the equal to their own daughters. Since Cosette no longer had any clothes of her own, they dressed her simply in worn-out petticoats that were meant to be undergarments. And even these were cast-offs from their daughters and were nothing but tattered rags by the time she wore them.

They fed Cosette with whatever was left, after their family had eaten. She ate somewhat better than a dog, but certainly worse than a cat. In fact, the family's dog and cat were her eating companions, for she was forced to eat with them under the table from a wooden bowl that was similar to theirs.

Soon Fantine had found work and somewhat established herself at Montreuil in the north of France. She wrote, or actually had someone write for her, a letter every month to the Thénardiers to inquire about Cosette. Invariably, they would simply reply, "Cosette is doing wonderfully well."

At the end of the first six months, Fantine sent another seven francs for that month, and then continued to pay on a very regular basis for several more months as well. But before the first year was quite over, Monsieur Thénardier told his wife, "This woman is doing us no favor! What does she expect us to do with her measly seven francs?" So he wrote Fantine to demand twelve francs per month, and since she had been convinced by them that her child was "so happy and doing so well," she agreed to the increase.

It seems that some people cannot love their own without hating someone else. This is exactly how Madame Thénardier was, for she loved her two daughters passionately, which caused her to hate Cosette. So this poor, sweet child, who knew nothing of the world, or even of God, was constantly punished, scolded, and beaten; yet all the while seeing two other creatures like herself living in the brightness and happiness of dawn.

Madame Thénardier was incredibly vicious and wicked in dealing with Cosette. Therefore, her daughters, Éponine and Azelma, observed their mother and became equally as brutal in their treatment of her. They were smaller and younger than their mother, but were nonetheless exact copies of her.

A year passed—then another. All the while, the people in the village said to each other, "Those Thénardiers are good people. They are not rich themselves, but look how they are raising that poor child who was abandoned by her mother!" In their ignorance they believed that Cosette's mother had forgotten her.

Over time Monsieur Thénardier learned by some obscure means that Cosette was most likely an illegitimate child, and used that information against Fantine to exact an increase to fifteen francs a month. He also told the girl's mother that "her little creature" was "growing and eating more" and then threatened to send her away unless he had more money each month. He would rant and rave to his wife, "I'll send the little brat into the streets. I must have an increase!" Fantine paid the fifteen francs.

From year to year the child grew, but so did her wretched condition. For the first two years she was primarily the scapegoat of the other girls' pranks, but shortly before she turned five years old she became the servant of the household. It was heartbreaking to see this poor little child, dressed in nothing but her old linen rags that were full of holes, shivering in the bitter cold of winter. There she would be, sweeping the street before daylight, with an enormous broom in her tiny red hands, while tears stained her large, beautiful eyes.

The people of the neighborhood would often see Cosette, and dubbed her "the Lark." The villagers, who were fond of bestowing nicknames on people, saw this trembling, frightened, and shivering little creature, as no bigger than a bird. And like a lark, she was up before daybreak—before anyone else in the house or the village was awake—and would be at work in the street or the fields.

Only this little lark never sang.

CHAPTER SEVEN

wo years before Fantine had left her little Cosette with the Thénardiers in 1818, the town where she found work had seen an important event. The town was Montreuil in the north of France, and the event had to do with the local industry. What had taken place there had greatly added to the prosperity of the little town, not to mention the surrounding area.

As long as anyone could remember, Montreuil had been known for the making of a special kind of black glass trinkets and jewelry. This industry had never prospered, however, because the cost of the raw materials was always so high. It seems that near the end of 1815 a stranger had established himself as a resident in town and had been inspired with an idea to change the manufacturing process of those trinkets. By simply substituting a different resin for another, and by bending the clasps rather than soldering them together, he set off a revolution.

In less than three years the inventor of these changes had become rich, which was good. But what was even better was that nearly everyone around him had become rich as well. The man had been a stranger to the industry and to the town when he arrived there. Nothing was known of his background, and it was rumored that he had come to town with very little money—only a few hundred francs at the most. It was with this meager amount of financial capital, along with an ingenious idea, that he had made his fortune, and the fortune of the entire surrounding countryside. Yet when he had arrived in Montreuil, this man had the appearance, the clothing, and the language of a common laborer.

He had made his humble entry into the little town just at nightfall on a December evening with a knapsack on his back and a walking stick in his hand. On that very evening a large fire had broken out in the town hall, and the stranger had rushed into the flames, risking his own life. He saved the lives of two children, both of whom belonged to the chief of police, explaining why the officials had totally forgotten to ask him for his passport. Then, because of his reputation as a local hero, they were embarrassed to ask for his passport, but had simply asked him his name. He was called Monsieur Madeleine.

He appeared to be about fifty years of age and typically seemed somewhat preoccupied. In spite of that, he was a good-natured man and offered employment to nearly everyone in the area. His only condition for employment was, in his words, "Be an honest man" or "Be an honest woman."

Although Monsieur Madeleine was a prosperous businessman, and was the impetus behind the dramatic turnaround of the industry in which he had made his fortune, it seemed his primary concern was not the business itself. His chief concern was for people, for he was constantly thinking of others, not himself. Within five years of his arrival in town, he was known to have some six hundred and thirty thousand francs in his account at the Bank of Laffitte in Paris, yet during this same time period he had spent more than one million francs of his own money to benefit the town and its poor. He was considered to be a religious person, something that was looked upon quite favorably during that time, and he attended mass every Sunday.

In 1820 Monsieur Madeleine and his service to the community had become so renowned that the king of France appointed him mayor of the town. Madeleine declined the appointment, but after being beseeched by other notable people, the citizens he encountered in the streets, and with additional pressure from the king himself, he relented and accepted the position. But the final nudge that swayed his decision was what an old woman angrily shouted from her doorway: "A good mayor can be a useful thing! Why are you running from all the good you could do?"

From his first day as mayor, he remained a simple man. His hair was gray, his eyes were penetrating, and his skin had the suntanned complexion of a laborer, yet his countenance was that of a thoughtful philosopher. He always wore a hat with a wide brim and a coat of heavy cloth, which he kept buttoned to the chin. He fulfilled his duties as mayor, but other than that one exception, he kept to himself, seldom speaking to others. His primary pleasure consisted of taking daily walks through the open fields.

Madeleine always ate his meals alone while reading a book. He loved books, which he saw as cold, but safe, friends. As a result of his avid reading, and his desire to cultivate his mind, each passing year saw his somewhat unrefined language grow to be more gentle and polished.

Although he was no longer young, he was known to be a man of amazing physical strength. He would always offer his assistance to anyone who needed him, whether the task was to lift a horse, push a wagon from the mud, or stop a runaway bull by the horns. And whenever he went out his pockets were full of money, but empty upon his return. He performed a multitude of good deeds, concealing his involvement, just as others would try to conceal their evil deeds.

People perceived Monsieur Madeleine as one who was happy and sad at the same time. They would often say of him, "Here is a rich man who is humble. Yet he possesses a certain happiness without contentment."

His room was furnished very simply. There was nothing there even worth mentioning, except that on his fireplace mantel stood two antique candlesticks, which appeared to be made of silver.

Before Madeleine was appointed mayor, near the beginning of 1820, the local newspaper of Montreuil printed an announcement of the death of Monseigneur Bienvenu, Bishop of Digne, who had died at the advanced age of eighty-two. The following day, Madeleine was seen dressed totally in black—even with black crepe on his hat to further signify his grief.

His mourning prompted a great deal of speculation in town, especially regarding his past. Of course, it was assumed that some relationship must have existed between him and the venerable bishop. Yet the great deal of conversation swirling around him actually served to raise his esteem even more in the eyes of the townspeople, especially among the wealthy. One evening an elderly woman, who was considered to be the "leader" in this petty world of gossip and who was no longer able to constrain herself, ventured to ask him, "Sir, you are no doubt a cousin of the late Bishop of Digne?"

"No, madam," Madeleine responded, simply.

"But," resumed the elderly woman, "you are in mourning for him."

He replied, "It is because I was a servant in his family in my youth."

Another topic that prompted additional speculation in the community was Madeleine's treatment of the young lads from Savoy, who traveled the country as chimney sweeps. Each time he would see one of these boys, he would stop the lad, inquire as to his name, and then give him some money. The youths told each other about this, and a great many of them began passing through Montreuil as a result.

Over the course of time all the speculation regarding Madeleine's past subsided. His level of respect among the people continued to grow until he was as highly regarded as the Bishop of Digne had been during his life. People traveled from more than thirty miles around to consult with Madeleine. He settled differences, prevented lawsuits, and helped to reconcile enemies. The people came to regard him as their judge, and with good reason, for an understanding of the law seemed to be written on his soul.

In spite of his growing esteem, however, there was one man in town who escaped the contagion. He was an employee of the French government, and opposed everything Madeleine did, as though some imperceivable, yet unstoppable, instinct kept him uneasy and alert.

Frequently, as Madeleine walked along the street receiving affectionate greetings from the people, this French official of lofty stature, wearing a heavy gray coat and hat and armed with a thick cane, would abruptly begin to follow him with his eyes. He would stand there slowly shaking his head with his arms folded, while a sneer would cover his face, as though he were saying, "Who and what is this man? I'm certain I have seen him somewhere. Whatever the case, I will not be fooled by him!"

This man, whose stern features were almost menacing, was named Javert, and he worked for the police. Madeleine had made his fortune and had already become highly esteemed before Javert had been assigned as a police inspector in Montreuil, so he had seen nothing of Madeleine's beginnings in the town.

Javert was regarded by the townspeople, especially those who were vagrants, with sheer dread. Even the mention of his name would often cause a person to tremble in fear, and encountering his face unexpectedly would shake someone to the foundation of his soul.

He became like an eye, full of suspicion and conjecture, which stared unblinkingly at Madeleine. Madeleine had certainly noticed the scrutiny, but it appeared to be of no importance to him. He never questioned Javert about it, and he never sought him out, but neither did he seek to avoid him. He endured that embarrassing and nearly oppressive gaze without even appearing to notice it. In fact, he treated Javert with grace and courtesy, just as he did the rest of the community. Madeleine's sense of tranquillity and confidence, in spite of this relentless scrutiny, caused Javert some obvious disconcertedness.

Nevertheless, there was soon to be an occasion that would produce a crack in the otherwise firm façade portrayed by Madeleine. One morning, as he was walking along an unpaved alley of Montreuil, he heard a noise and then saw a group of people beginning to gather. He approached and saw an accident. A man by the name of Monsieur Fauchelevent was lying beneath his cart after his horse had lost its footing and fallen.

It seems this man was also one of the few enemies Madeleine had at the time. When Madeleine had arrived in the town, Fauchelevent had been a lawyer whose firm was failing. Therefore, he was forced to watch Madeleine, a simple workman, grow rich, while he himself faced ruin. This had filled him with jealousy, and at every opportunity he had done whatever he could to cause harm to Madeleine and his business. Upon becoming bankrupt, he was left with nothing more than this very cart and horse. He then earned his living using his only remaining possessions as a vehicle for hire.

Fauchelevent's horse had two broken legs and could not stand, and the old man was trapped under the wheels of his cart. To make matters worse, the cart was heavily loaded, and its entire weight was resting on the man's chest. The men gathering around him had tried unsuccessfully to drag him free, and now one wrong move might kill him. It quickly became evident that his only hope was to have the vehicle lifted from him.

Javert had witnessed the accident and had already sent for a jackscrew to lift the cart. When Madeleine arrived, the people respectfully stood aside. Just then, Fauchelevent cried out in pain, asking for help.

Madeleine turned to those around him, and pleaded, "Is there a jackscrew available?"

"We have already sent for one," answered one of the townspeople.

"But how long will it take to get it?" Madeleine continued.

"We have sent word to the nearest blacksmith, but it will still take a good quarter of an hour," was the answer.

"A quarter of an hour!" exclaimed Madeleine.

As they waited, the cart continued to sink more deeply into the mud. It had rained the previous evening, and the ground was completely soaked. It became evident that waiting even five more minutes might result in the old man's chest being crushed.

"It's impossible to wait a quarter of an hour! It will be too late! Can't you see that the cart is sinking?" Madeleine exclaimed to those around him.

"We have no other option, but to wait," one man responded.

But Madeleine continued, "There is still room under the cart for one man to crawl beneath it and to raise it with his back. A minute more and this poor man will be gone. Who here has a strong back and legs? I offer five louis to the man who will do it!"

Yet not a man in the group stirred. "Ten louis, then!" shouted Madeleine.

At this, all the men present dropped their eyes to the ground, until one of them muttered, "A man would need to be devilish strong. And even then he runs the risk of getting crushed himself!"

"Come now!" Madeleine insisted, "Twenty louis!" Yet the same silence remained.

One of the men finally spoke: "It's not our will that is lacking."

Javert, whom Madeleine had not previously noticed in the crowd, added, "What is lacking is strength. One would have to be a hulk of a man to lift a cart like this on his back." Then, with his eyes fixed upon Madeleine and while emphasizing every word he uttered, he said, "Monsieur Madeleine, I have never known but one man capable of doing what you ask."

Madeleine shuddered. Javert then added, with an air of indifference, but without removing his eyes from him, "He was a convict."

"Is that right?" asked Madeleine.

"Yes, in the prison at Toulon," Javert stated. At these words, Madeleine turned pale.

Meanwhile the cart slowly continued to sink. Monsieur Fauchelevent screamed, "I can't breathe! My ribs are breaking! Do something!"

Madeleine glanced about once more, before asking, "Is there no one here who wishes to earn twenty louis and save this poor man's life?" Again, no one stirred.

Javert reiterated, "Like I said, I've only known one man who could take the place of a jackscrew, and he was that convict." Madeleine raised his head, met Javert's steely gaze, and smiled sadly. Then, without another word, he fell to his knees and crawled under the cart.

The others held their breath as they watched Madeleine, who was now almost flat on his stomach. He made two vain attempts to lift the vehicle from the mud. They pleaded with him to come out, after which the injured old man himself said, "Go away, Madeleine! Can't you see I'm fated to die? You are going to be crushed as well!" Madeleine did not reply.

At this point, it was nearly impossible for Madeleine to make his way from underneath the cart. Yet suddenly the enormous weight above him seemed to shake, and the wheels began to emerge from their ruts of mud. The men suddenly rushed forward, helped to further lift the cart, and finally pulled the old man to safety. It seems the commitment and bravery of one man had suddenly given strength and courage to them all.

Fauchelevent was extremely fortunate, for although he was badly bruised and sore, his worst injury was a dislocated knee and a broken kneecap. Madeleine instructed the injured man be taken to an infirmary he had established for his workers in his own factory building, and which was staffed by two Sisters of Charity. When the poor man awoke the following morning, he found a thousand-franc bank note on his night stand along with a note in Madeleine's handwriting that said, "I am purchasing your horse and your cart." Of course, the horse was dead and the cart was broken beyond repair.

Fauchelevent recovered fully, except that his knee remained somewhat stiff. Madeleine, on the recommendation of the Sisters of Charity and their priest, found the man a job as a gardener in a convent for nuns on the Rue Saint Antoine in Paris.

It was shortly afterward that the king had appointed Madeleine mayor of the town. The first time Javert saw Madeleine in his new role as the town's mayor, he shuddered in the manner a watchdog might experience upon smelling the scent of a wolf on his master's clothing. From that time forward Javert avoided the mayor as much as possible. Yet when his duties as a policeman demanded it, and he was then required to see Madeleine, he addressed him with profound respect—at least outwardly.

CHAPTER EIGHT

———————— ⚘ ————————

When Fantine finally made her way to her native area and hometown of Montreuil, no one remembered her. Yet the door of Monsieur Madeleine's factory was like the face of a friend to her, for she was offered work almost as quickly as she walked through it. The type of work was entirely foreign to Fantine, so she was not very skilled at it. Therefore, she earned very little each day, but at least enough for her to earn a living. Her problem was solved.

The fact that Fantine was now earning a living brought her great joy. She saw the opportunity to make an honest living through her own labor as a blessing from heaven. Her entire attitude about life changed and became more hopeful. She began to take pride in her appearance once again, and found some pleasure surveying herself in a new mirror she purchased. She was still very young and had beautiful hair and lovely white teeth, which gave her an engaging smile.

Fantine was able to forget many of her recent difficulties—yet she thought constantly of Cosette. As she did so, however, she was almost happy, for she saw the possibility of their being together again soon as being bright. She leased a small room and was able to furnish it on credit based on the fact that she was gainfully employed. Buying on credit, however, showed a lingering trace of her tendency to plan poorly for the future.

Since she was not married, she was very careful to never mention her little girl. Yet she continued to write the Thénardiers in order to inquire about Cosette, being forced to rely on a public letter writer since she only knew how to write her own name. The fact that she sent letters so often did not go unnoticed by the other women in Fantine's work area. This and other factors caused rumors to be spread about her and oftentimes a coworker could be heard to say, "She has some unusual ways about her."

Because of this, and due to the other women's insatiable hunger for gossip, Fantine was watched. In addition, many of them were obviously jealous of her golden hair and her beautiful teeth. Many times the women would notice her wiping away a tear, caused by Fantine's thoughts of her dear Cosette.

Her public writer was a good old man, but one who could not fill his stomach with red wine without emptying his mouth of secrets. As a result, it was discovered that Fantine had a child and that her letters were addressed to a Monsieur Thénardier—an innkeeper in Montfermeil. This led people to whisper to each other, "She must be that sort of a woman."

One of the gossip mongers even made a trip to Montfermeil, talked with the Thénardiers, and said upon returning, "For just thirty-five francs I have learned all about it. And I have seen Fantine's child."

At this point Fantine had been at the factory for more than a year. One morning the foreman of her workroom, who had heard the gossip, handed her fifty francs from Mayor Madeleine. He told her that she was no longer employed there, and that the mayor also wanted her to leave the neighborhood.

The timing could not have been worse for Fantine, for this happened to be the very month that the Thénardiers had once again raised the monthly fee for caring for Cosette to fifteen francs. Fantine was overwhelmed. She could not leave the neighborhood, because she owed for her rent and her furniture, and fifty francs was insufficient to cover those debts.

In response to being fired, Fantine could only stammer out a few words, begging the foreman to reconsider. However, he retorted by ordering her to leave the shop immediately, and added that she was only a moderately good worker anyway. Filled with shame, but even more overcome with despair, she left the factory and returned to her humble room.

Some people advised Fantine to see Mayor Madeleine about her situation, but she was afraid to confront him. Besides, she knew him to be a just and good man, and saw the fifty francs as evidence of that. She decided to submit to his decision.

She began searching for work as a servant in the neighborhood, literally going from house to house. Yet no one would hire her, and she could not leave town because the second-hand furniture dealer she still owed threatened her by saying, "If you leave, I will have you arrested as a thief." And her landlord, demanding his back rent, said to her, "You are young and pretty. You can pay!"

Fantine then divided her fifty francs between her landlord and the furniture dealer. She also returned three-quarters of the furniture, keeping only her bed. She now found herself without work, with nothing but a bed, and still fifty francs in debt.

Finally, she found work making shirts for soldiers at the nearby garrison. She earned only twelve sous per day, while her daughter cost her ten of that. It was at this point Fantine began paying the Thénardiers on an irregular basis.

Worse than learning to live on little is learning to live on nothing, which is equal to living in misery. This seemed to be Fantine's fate. She learned how to live the entire winter without a fire for heat, and learned to use her petticoat for a blanket, and her blanket for a petticoat. By eating her meals by moving from one window to the other, she also learned to use her candle sparingly. She acquired quite a talent for squeezing as much as possible out of a sou, and thereby regained a little courage and hope.

A saintly old spinster named Marguerite, who lived in her building, taught her many of the lessons of how to best live a life of poverty. Marguerite had a strong belief in God, living a life of true devotion to Him, and was charitable to all people—whether they were poor or rich. Among the poor of that day were many such virtuous people. No doubt many of them will find a place in the world above, for God will bestow another sunrise on them.

Excessive work fatigued Fantine, and she developed a dry cough, which became worse over time. Oftentimes she would say to her new friend, Marguerite, "Just feel how hot my hands are!"

Yet in spite of her excessive work, Fantine earned too little and her debts continued to increase. The Thénardiers, who were not being paid promptly, constantly sent her postage-due letters, whose contents drove her to further despair. One letter reported that Cosette was entirely naked in the cold winter weather and that she needed a woolen dress. They demanded she send at least ten francs to pay for one. Fantine carried the letter around all day, reading it over and over, and worrying about her sweet Cosette.

That evening she walked to the barbershop at the corner of the street. Upon seeing her, the barber exclaimed, "What beautiful hair!"

"How much will you give me for it?" she asked.

"Ten francs."

"Then cut it off," Fantine said, reluctantly. Her lovely golden hair fell to the floor. She immediately purchased a wool-knitted dress and sent it to the Thénardiers, which made them furious. Of course, it was only the money they wanted, so they gave the dress to their daughter, Éponine. The poor Lark continued to shiver.

"My child is no longer cold. I have clothed her with my hair," Fantine thought. She began wearing a small round cap to conceal her shorn head, but remained a lovely young woman. As her plight became darker and darker, the more radiant was the little angel in the depths of her heart. She would say, "When I get rich, I will have my Cosette with me again," and she would laugh. This would often aggravate her cough, which was becoming worse, and she was beginning to experience night sweats as well.

Fantine had long shared in the universal admiration of Mayor Madeleine, but she had now come to hate him. She had convinced herself that it was he who had turned her away and was the cause of her misfortunes. She sank lower and lower, even taking a lover, who beat her and then left her as quickly as he had shared her bed. Fantine had a sense of rage in her heart, and had actually taken to the man in a fit of disgust.

One day she received a letter from the Thénardiers that said, "Cosette has a sickness that has been making its rounds in our area, and she needs some expensive medicine. This is ruining us and we can no longer pay for it. If you don't send us forty francs before the end of this week, your little one will be dead."

Fantine burst into a scornful laughter and said to Marguerite, "Oh, they're good! These stupid peasants! Where do they expect me to get forty francs? That's equal to two Napoléons!"

Later, as she walked across the town square, she saw a crowd gathering around a man standing atop his carriage. He was a quack dentist, who was offering full sets of teeth, opiates, and elixirs for sale. Fantine mingled with the group and began to laugh with the others at the somewhat humorous presentation. The quack "tooth-puller" suddenly noticed her and exclaimed, "You have beautiful teeth, young lady. I'll give you a gold Napoléon for each of your two front teeth!"

"How horrible!" Fantine retorted.

"Two Napoléons!" grumbled a toothless old woman. "She's a lucky girl, indeed!"

At this, Fantine fled, covering her ears as she ran. Yet the salesman continued to shout at her, "Think about it, my beauty! Two Napoléons! If you change your mind, you can find me at the Inn of the Tillac d'Argent."

The next morning Marguerite entered Fantine's room before dawn, for they worked together in order to use one candle instead of two. She found Fantine seated on her bed, pale and frozen. She had been sitting there all night and had allowed her candle to burn completely down. Marguerite was upset over this tremendous wastefulness, and scolded, "You've let the candle burn out! Has something happened?"

She looked at Fantine and her closely cropped hair, and it seemed to Marguerite that Fantine had aged ten years since the previous day. She then asked, "Fantine, what's the matter with you?"

"Nothing," replied Fantine, calmly. "In fact, quite the contrary. Now my dear child will not die of that awful illness. I am content." She then pointed to two gold Napoléons glittering on the table.

"Oh, Lord!" cried Marguerite. "That's a fortune! Where did you get them?"

Fantine simply smiled, as the fading candle illuminated her face. Her smile was sickening, for the corners of her mouth were stained with blood. Dark holes were now where her beautiful teeth had once been. That very day she sent forty francs to Montfermeil. Yet it had all been a ruse perpetrated by the Thénardiers to extort more money from her, for Cosette was not sick.

Fantine's downward spiral continued in earnest. What she was paid for sewing shirts was reduced to nine sous per day—seventeen hours of work each day for only nine sous! And her creditors became more pitiless than ever, especially the Thénardiers. They wrote her that they had been much too patient and generous, and immediately demanded one hundred francs, or they would put Cosette out of their house and into the cold streets.

"How can I raise that kind of money?" Fantine thought. Unable to see any way out of her hopeless demise, she reasoned, "I will sell what is left." So this unfortunate creature became a woman of the night.

Fantine's history was that of society purchasing a slave—purchased from hunger, cold, loneliness, and destitution. It was a deplorable and heart-wrenching bargain. Misery makes it offer—society accepts.

People of that day claimed that the sacred law of Jesus Christ governed their civilization, but it certainly did not permeate it. And they claimed that slavery had disappeared from European society altogether, but this was untrue. It still existed—its name was prostitution.

There was now nothing left of what was formerly known as Fantine. She had turned to stone, having lost everything. She had resigned herself to whatever her fate may be, and became indifferent—as death resembles sleep. Her thoughts became, "Let the clouds fall on me, and the oceans sweep across me. What difference does it make?"

Fantine had reached the depths of despair, but in error believed she was beyond all hope, for no one is beyond the reach of the One Who can see beyond the darkest shadow. His name is God.

CHAPTER NINE

---❧---

One snowy evening eight or ten months later, in January 1823, Fantine was walking back and forth on the street by a military officers' café. In spite of the cold, she wore a revealing dress, which left her neck, shoulders, and back completely bare. A man inside began hurling insults at her, such as, "How ugly you are!" and "You have lost your teeth!"

She did not answer him, nor did she dare to even look at him, but continued walking in silence. Her walking back and forth, however, brought her under his sarcastic scrutiny with dismal regularity. Being ignored, the man chose to escalate his unruly behavior. He sneaked up behind her, scooped up a handful of snow, and threw it at her. It struck her on the bare skin of her back, which caused her to roar with rage. Fantine pounced on him like a panther, burying her fingernails into his face.

Her screaming attracted a crowd who made a circle around them, and who then began laughing, jeering, and applauding as the two struggled. Suddenly Javert emerged from among them, grabbed her by her satin belt, and demanded, "Follow me!" Recognizing him, Fantine immediately became quiet, turned pale, and began to shake in terror. Yet during all the commotion, her attacker slipped through the crowd and ran away.

Javert dragged her behind him to the police station. She submitted mechanically and was afraid to utter a word. Once inside, she fell down in a corner of the station, motionless and crouching like a terrified dog. A sergeant brought Javert a lighted candle, while Javert seated himself, took an official-looking form from his pocket, and began to write. When he had finished, he signed the paper and handed it to the sergeant. As he did so, he said, "Take three men and escort this creature to jail." Then, turning to Fantine, he said, "You are to serve six months."

"Six months! Six months in prison!" she screamed. "But what will become of Cosette? My daughter! My poor daughter! I still owe the Thénardiers more than one hundred francs. Do you realize that, Monsieur Inspector?" She crawled on her knees before him with her hands clasped, and begged, "Monsieur Javert, I plead for mercy. If you had seen the beginning you would know I am not in the wrong. I swear to you before God—I am not to blame! Have pity on me, Monsieur Javert!"

"Are you quite finished?" Javert responded. "I have let you have your say, and you will get six months. Now march! The Eternal God in person would have done no more for you."

At these words, Fantine realized her fate was sealed. She sank down, mumbling to herself, "Have mercy, O God!"

Moments earlier, without anyone realizing it, a man had entered the station, had stood there quietly, and had heard Fantine's desperate appeals to Javert. As her guards turned to lift her from the floor and take her to her cell, the man emerged from the shadows of the room, and said, "Just a moment, please."

Javert swung around and saw it was Mayor Madeleine. Javert removed his hat, and spoke somewhat begrudgingly, by saying, "Excuse me, Monsieur le Mayor?"

Yet before Madeleine could respond, Fantine sprang to her feet, and with one bound pushed the policemen aside and stood face-to-face with the mayor. Before anyone could stop her, she glared at him, laughed mockingly, and then spit in his face.

Madeleine wiped his face, and continued, "Inspector Javert, set this woman free." At this, Javert couldn't believe his ears and suffered the most violent upheaval of emotions he had ever felt in his life. These words also had no less effect on Fantine, who now clung to the damper of the room's stove, reeling from the impact of the mayor's demand.

Inspector Javert, now pale and cold, and with a look of despair on his face, finally responded in a firm tone, "Monsieur le Mayor, that cannot be done."

"Inspector Javert," replied the mayor, in a calm and conciliatory tone, "You are an honest man, and I feel no hesitation in explaining matters to you. Here is the truth of this case: I was passing through the area, just as you were leading this woman away. There were still groups of people standing around, so I made a number of inquiries and learned the whole story. It was the man who initiated the assault and was in the wrong. He was the one who should have been arrested by the police."

Javert retorted, "But this vile, despicable creature has just insulted you, Monsieur le Mayor!"

"That's my concern," replied the mayor. "My own insult belongs to me, and I can do as I please about it."

"I beg the mayor's pardon, sir, but the insult is also to the law," Javert insisted.

"Inspector Javert, conscience is a higher law. I have heard this woman, and I know what I am doing. Heed this well—she will not serve a single day."

"But . . ." Javert stammered.

"Leave the room, sir," demanded the mayor. Javert submitted, bowed low before the mayor, and finally left the room.

Fantine moved away from the door and stared in amazement as the inspector walked away. Nevertheless, she was in a state of strange confusion. She saw these two men as giants—one a demon and the other an angel. She was dumbfounded that the very man she had abhorred for so long, and whom she felt was to blame for all of her woes, had become her liberator—the angel who had defeated the demon. Another thing that amazed her was that at the very moment she had insulted him in such a hideous way, he had saved her. Had she, then, been mistaken about this man? As she pondered this possibility, she felt the icy chains of hatred beginning to melt and crumble within her. A bright light of unspeakable joy, confidence, and love was already dawning in her heart.

Once Javert was gone, Mayor Madeleine turned to Fantine with great emotion in his voice, as one who is close to weeping and finding it difficult to speak. Yet he spoke in a deliberate tone, and said, "I knew nothing about your plight, but I believe what you have said. And until tonight I was even unaware that you had left my factory. Why didn't you appeal to me? Nevertheless, that is history at this point."

He continued, "Now—I will pay your debts, and will send for your child, or you can go to her. Also, you may live here, in Paris, or wherever you please, for I will take care of you and your child. You will not be forced to work, unless you would like, for I will provide the money you need to live. I want you to be happy and honest again. And what's more—I believe that if everything is as you say, and I am not doubting you, you have never ceased to be virtuous and holy in the sight of God."

All this was overwhelming to Fantine. To have Cosette again! To leave such an infamous lifestyle! To be free and happy! She was only able to blindly gaze at the mayor as he spoke to her, for she was seeing the beautiful realities of paradise suddenly beginning to blossom from the very midst of her misery and despair. Fantine was unable to speak, and began to sob. She knelt before the mayor, and before he could stop her, she grabbed his hand and pressed her lips to it. Then she fainted.

Monsieur Madeleine had Fantine moved to an infirmary that he had set up in his own house. He entrusted her care to the Sisters of Charity, who put her to bed. She had developed a burning fever and spent much of the night delirious and raving. At long last, however, she fell asleep.

Toward the middle of the following day, Fantine awoke. She heard someone breathing nearby and pulled the curtain back that separated her bed from the remainder of the room. She saw Madeleine standing there, looking at something on the wall above his head. His eyes seemed full of pity, anguish, and supplication. Looking to the wall where his eyes were fixed, she saw a crucifix that was nailed there.

At that point, Monsieur Madeleine seemed transformed in Fantine's eyes.

He seemed to be bathed in light, as he was absorbed in prayer. She gazed at him for a long time, not daring to interrupt him. Finally, she asked, timidly, "What are you doing?"

Madeleine had been there for at least an hour, waiting for Fantine to awake. He took her hand, felt her pulse, and asked, "How do you feel?"

"Very well, thank you," she replied. "I think I'm better. This is nothing."

Finally responding to her first question as though he had just heard it, he said, "I have been praying to the Martyr there on high." But then he finished the thought silently to himself, "For the martyr here below."

He had spent much of the night and the morning making inquiries regarding Fantine, and now knew her history in all its heart-rending details. He continued, "You have suffered a great deal, poor mother. But now you have a portion with the elect, for I believe God uses our difficulties to help transform us into His saints. I trust that taking this step from your hell of misery will be your first step toward heaven."

That very night Madeleine wrote to the Thénardiers. Fantine owed them one hundred and twenty francs, but he sent them three hundred instead, telling them to use the overage to immediately bring Cosette to Montreuil, where her sick mother needed her. The letter delighted Monsieur Thénardier, who said to his wife, "I think our little Lark is becoming a cash cow! We can't let her go now. I think some idiot has taken a fancy to her mother."

Monsieur Thénardier replied by sending a formal bill for a little more than five hundred francs. Over three hundred francs of the bill were for a doctor and for medicine—not for Cosette, for she had not been ill—but for his daughters, Éponine and Azelma. It seems both of them had prolonged illnesses. Of course, he did not note this deception on the bill. Madeleine immediately sent another three hundred francs, and wrote, "Bring Cosette here quickly."

Yet Thénardier told his wife, "We should not give up the child just yet."

In the meantime, Fantine did not recover, but remained in the infirmary. She was very kind to the Sisters of Charity, who took care of her. One day the nuns heard her talking during a high fever. She said, "I have been a sinner, but having my child beside me will be a sign that God has pardoned me. It was for her sake that I was evil, and that's why God will pardon me. Once Cosette is here, I will feel the blessings of our gracious God. It will do me good to see that innocent creature. She is an angel, for at her young age the wings have not fallen off."

Madeleine took time to see her twice a day, and each time she would ask him, "Will I see my Cosette soon?"

He would answer, "Tomorrow, perhaps. She may arrive at any moment. I'm expecting her soon."

At this, her pale countenance would grow radiant, and she would declare, "Oh, how happy I'm going to be!"

Not only did Fantine not recover, but also from week to week her condition worsened. Some time later, the doctor listened to her chest, shook his head, and told Monsieur Madeleine that her condition was very grave. The doctor asked, "Doesn't she have a daughter she desires to see?"

"Yes," Madeleine answered.

"Then you should hurry and get her here!" the doctor urged. Madeleine shuddered at these words.

Just then, Fantine asked, "What did the doctor say?"

Madeleine forced a smile, and replied, "He said your child should be brought to you quickly. That will restore your health."

"He's right!" she agreed. "What can the Thénardiers be doing—keeping my Cosette from me? Ah, but now she is coming. Finally I will see happiness close beside me!"

Madeleine assured her, "I will send someone to get Cosette. If necessary, I will go myself."

Fantine dictated a message to Thénardier, which Madeleine wrote for her and had her sign. The message was this: "Monsieur Thénardier, You will deliver Cosette to the bearer of this note. He will pay you for everything still owed. Respectfully, Fantine."

In the meantime a serious matter intervened. It seems that as much as we may chisel the block of stone that comprises our lives, the dark vein of destiny seems to constantly reappear.

CHAPTER TEN

*O*ne morning Mayor Madeleine was in his study, handling some pressing matters related to his work as mayor. He was working quickly, in case he needed to make the trip to retrieve Cosette himself, when he was told that Police Inspector Javert wished to speak with him. The mayor responded, "Show him in, please."

As Javert entered the mayor laid down his pen, turned around, and said, "What is the matter, Inspector Javert?"

"Monsieur le Mayor, a criminal offense has been committed."

"What offense?"

"A lowly agent of the authorities has failed to show proper respect to another official in a very important matter. I have come to bring this fact to your attention, as it is my duty to do," Javert replied.

"Who is the agent?" asked the mayor.

"It is I," answered Javert.

"You?" questioned the mayor, with an expression of surprise. He then added, "And who is the official who has a reason to complain about your actions?"

"You, Monsieur le Mayor," responded Javert. At this, the mayor sat upright in his armchair. Then in a somber tone and with his eyes downcast, Javert continued, "Monsieur le Mayor, I have come to request that you ask the proper authorities to have me dismissed."

Hearing this, the mayor opened his mouth in amazement, and started to speak. Javert interrupted him to say, "I know what you are going to say—that simply handing in my resignation will suffice. But resigning is an honorable thing, and I have failed to do my duty. I should be punished and should be dismissed, not just allowed to resign." After a pause he added, "Monsieur le Mayor, the other day you treated me severely—and unjustly. All I'm asking today is that you treat me severely again—but this time with justice, according to the law."

"Come now! Why?" exclaimed the mayor. "What is this nonsense? What have you done to me that makes you guilty of a criminal offense?"

"You will understand, Monsieur le Mayor." Javert sighed deeply and then resumed, still somberly and sadly, "A few weeks ago, shortly after the incident with that woman, I was so furious that I informed against you."

"Informed against me?" the mayor questioned.

"Yes, to the chief of police in Paris," Javert continued.

The mayor, who was not in the habit of laughing—anymore than Javert himself—burst into laughter, and said, sarcastically, "What did I do? As mayor, did I encroach on their police responsibilities?"

"Not as mayor, sir. As an ex-convict," Javert said, coldly. Hearing this, the mayor became livid. Javert, who had still not raised his eyes to the mayor, resumed, "For some time I have thought you to be someone else, and have made a number of inquiries concerning your background, but found little. Yet because of your appearance, your slight limp, your incredible strength— especially your being strong enough to free poor Fauchelevent, who was trapped underneath his cart—I had you confused with someone from my past. I know this sounds absurd! But, because of this, I took you for a man named Jean Valjean."

"Who? What did you say the name was?"

"Jean Valjean—a convict I knew some twenty years ago when I was a prison guard in Toulon. It appears that soon after being paroled from prison Valjean robbed a bishop's home, and shortly thereafter even robbed a lad from Savoy on the road, using a weapon. Then he seemed to disappear, and the authorities have searched for him for the last eight years. I thought you were Valjean, and my anger toward you drove me to denounce you before the chief of police."

The mayor picked up a file of papers from his desk, and with an air of indifference, asked, "And what did the chief of police have to say?"

"He said that I must be crazy," Javert answered, "and he was right."

"I guess it is fortunate for me that you think so," the mayor said, smiling.

Yet Javert added, "I am forced to do so, since the real Jean Valjean has been found."

Mayor Madeleine dropped the file from his hand, fixed his eyes on Javert, and said in a strange but questioning tone, "Oh?"

Javert continued, "It seems, Monsieur le Mayor, there was an old fellow by the name of Monsieur Champmathieu in the area near Ailly. He was a very poor man and last autumn was arrested for stealing some apples. Because the jail was in bad condition, an examining official had him transferred to the prison in Arras to await trial. It was there that a prisoner by the name of Brevet, who was also an ex-convict, saw Champmathieu and exclaimed, 'I know this man! He is not Champmathieu—he is Jean Valjean!' Of course, Champmathieu denied it, but there were two other convicts in the prison, both of whom were serving life sentences and had served with Valjean. They were the only two convicts remaining in prison who would have known Valjean, and when the authorities showed Champmathieu to them, they did not hesitate, but immediately agreed with Brevet. Besides, the thief is the right age—fifty-four—and the right height. Rest assured, he is Jean Valjean.

"It was at this very time that I had sent my concerns regarding you to the chief of police in Paris. He told me I had lost my mind, for the authorities already had Valjean in their custody. Since I thought you were Jean Valjean, you can imagine my surprise. He even invited me to go to Paris to see for myself."

"And?" interrupted the mayor.

"And," Javert replied, with his face as stern and somber as ever, "it is true. There is no doubt in my mind. That man is Jean Valjean."

Madeleine turned toward his desk, picked up the file again, flipped through the pages, and began writing, as though he were very busy. Turning to Javert, he said, "That will be all, Inspector Javert. Actually, I have little interest in your news. This is a waste of our time, and I'm sure we both have work to do." He then dismissed Javert with a wave of his hand.

Javert did not leave, but said, "Excuse me, Monsieur le Mayor. . . ."

"What is it now?" demanded Madeleine.

"I still must remind you of one thing," Javert insisted.

"What is it?"

"That I must be relieved of my position."

The mayor replied, "Inspector Javert, you are a man of honor, and I respect you. But you have exaggerated your fault. Besides, it is an offense against me. I think you deserve a promotion, not a demotion, and I want you to retain your position."

"I am not looking for you to treat me with kindness," Javert argued. "In fact, your kindness to others has only served to increase my anger toward you. I want no part of it for myself. Your brand of kindness puts a lady of the night above a lawful citizen. Your kindness would put a worthless man above those who are superior. Your kindness is what I see as false kindness—the kind that disrupts society. Good God! It is easy to be kind—the difficult thing is to be just! Come now, if the tables were turned, I would not be kind to you. Monsieur le Mayor, I must treat myself as I would treat any other man. I must follow the law."

"We'll see," said the mayor, as he offered his hand.

Javert drew back, and said in an angry voice, "This must not be. A mayor should not offer his hand to a police spy—for from the moment I abused my power, I have been no better than a spy." Then Javert bowed deeply, and walked toward the door. Before leaving, however, he wheeled around, and with his eyes still downcast, added, "I will continue to serve until I am relieved from my position."

Mayor Madeleine stood there thinking, as he listened to Javert's determined footsteps fade away on the pavement outside.

Mayor Madeleine was, of course, none other than Jean Valjean. Yet from the moment of his remorseful prayer, immediately after his encounter with Little Gervais, he was a totally different man. What the bishop had wished to make of him, he had become. And it was more than a simple transformation—he had miraculously become a completely new creation.

Once he had left Digne, he had succeeded in disappearing and soon sold the bishop's silver—except the candlesticks. He kept them as a reminder of what the bishop had done for him—and as a reminder of his admonition: "Do not forget. Never forget that you have promised to use this silver to become an honest man. You no longer belong to evil, but to good. I have bought your soul from you . . . and I give it to God."

Valjean sneaked from town to town, covering France, but finally settled in Montreuil. It was here he became so successful and prosperous. He had come to feel safe from the possibility of being recaptured by the authorities, and lived in peace. Valjean truly regretted his past life, but was hopeful as he looked to the future. He had only two remaining objectives in life: to conceal his name and to sanctify his life—or, as he saw it, to escape men and to return to God.

These two objectives of Valjean's life were so closely intertwined in his mind they had nearly become one. Yet whenever they conflicted, the man others knew as Mayor Madeleine would never hesitate to sacrifice the first to the second—his security to his virtue.

This explains why—in spite of what may have been more prudent and sensible—he kept the bishop's candlesticks, openly mourned for the bishop, gave money to the little lads from Savoy who passed his way, and saved Fauchelevent's life, despite the disturbing insinuations of Javert. It seems Valjean sought to follow the example of the truly wise, holy, and just—living as though his first responsibility was to others, not himself.

Yet nothing of the magnitude of this current situation, as presented by Javert to him, had ever presented itself in the past. Never before had he faced so serious a struggle. His immediate instinct was to expose his true identity and take the place of Champmathieu in prison at once—a painfully difficult decision. The thought passed, however, and Valjean said to himself, "We will see. We will see." He thereby suppressed his first generous instinct, and retreated from heroism.

It would have been beautiful, especially after the bishop's holy words to him, if Valjean had not hesitated for an instant. After so many years of exhibiting true repentance, he should have walked resolutely toward the gaping precipice before him, at the bottom of which lay heaven. It would have been beautiful, but it was not to be. Instead, he was carried away, at least at first, by his instinct of self-preservation.

At times he would barricade himself mentally against future possibilities. He would even rise from his chair and bolt his door as if locking them out. And he would often extinguish his light as though he might be seen. Yet what he desired to close his door upon had already entered, and what he tried to keep blind was already staring him in the face. It was Valjean's conscience—or more precisely—it was God Himself.

Nevertheless, he deluded himself at first, for he had a feeling of security and solitude. Once the door was locked, Valjean felt invincible, and once the candle was extinguished, he felt invisible. Finally he tried to take a personal mental inventory. He set his elbows on the table, leaned his head on his hands, and began to meditate in the dark.

Valjean thought, "Where do I stand? Is this a dream? Is what Javert said really true? Who can that Champmathieu be? Is it really possible that he resembles me? How could life have been so peaceful yesterday, and change so quickly? I did not expect anything like this. How will this end? What should I do?"

Nothing but anguish resulted from this mental turmoil. It overwhelmed his will and his reason, from which he desperately sought some help and resolution. Valjean's head was burning, yet gradually vague outlines began to take form in his thinking. He began to catch a glimpse, not of his entire dilemma, but of some of the details. He also began to recognize the fact that he was actually in control of his situation. His thinking grew more and more clear as he came to understand his predicament.

Valjean realized he was becoming a thief once more, and the most repugnant kind of all, for he was robbing another person of his life, his peace, his place in the sunshine, and his very existence. He was becoming an assassin—he was murdering, at least morally, this poor man. He was inflicting on him a terrifying living death—a death called prison.

Ironically, to surrender to save the man, to assume his real name, to become the convict Jean Valjean once again—out of duty—was in actual fact the only thing that would achieve his resurrection, and close forever the hell from which he had finally emerged. Appearing outwardly to return to it was the only way to escape it in reality. It must be done!

In spite of the unfortunate mistake of misidentification leading to this dilemma, doing nothing would nullify his entire life, making it worthless. His repentance from past sins would also mean nothing and would be wasted. Valjean felt as though the bishop was present once again, with his eyes fixed upon him. He knew the bishop now saw Mayor Madeleine, with all his virtues, as an abomination; and saw the convict Jean Valjean as pure and honorable. Men saw his mask, but the bishop saw his face. Men saw his life, but the bishop beheld his conscience.

He knew what he must do—go to Arras and reveal the false Jean Valjean and denounce the real one. This would be the greatest of sacrifices, while ironically being the most profound victory at the same time. It was the last step for him to take, but it must be done. In this one sad step he would enter into sanctity in the eyes of God alone, and return to infamy in the eyes of men.

Without realizing he was speaking aloud, he said, "I will do my duty. I will save this man." He then took his financial account books and put them in order, and threw a file of loan papers into the fire, releasing many poor debtors from what they owed him. And then he thought of Fantine.

"Wait a moment!" Valjean exclaimed to himself. "What about that poor woman?" At this point a new crisis presented itself.

Fantine, abruptly appearing in his troubled thoughts, produced an unexpected ray of light. Suddenly everything seemed to be undergoing a change of perspective. He exclaimed, "Until now I have considered no one but myself, and whether I should hold my tongue and conceal my true identity, or denounce myself and save my soul. I only considered whether to be a respected, but despicable, mayor—or an infamous, but honorable, convict.

"What about this woman, who has already suffered so much, and who possesses so many praiseworthy qualities in spite of her downfall? And to think I have unwittingly been the cause of her great misery! And what about her child? I promised her mother—do I not owe something to her for the evil I have done? What will happen if I suddenly disappear? The child will be destitute and hopeless once her mother dies."

Then, reversing his previous decision, he argued, "If I do not denounce myself, I will remain Madeleine. Too bad for the man who is Jean Valjean! I am no longer he, and I no longer even know Valjean." Looking at his face in the mirror above the fireplace, he continued, "I am not Valjean—I am someone totally different now.

"I must not cower before the consequences of this new decision. In fact, there are objects in this very room that could tie me to that old Jean Valjean. Those threads must be broken, for they could betray me." Taking a small key from his pocket, he unlocked a hiding place built into the wall. Inside this hidden cabinet were a blue linen jacket, an old pair of trousers, an old knapsack, and an iron-tipped walking stick. He had kept all these things, including the candlesticks, in order to remind himself of his starting point. Yet he only allowed the candlesticks to be in plain view.

Valjean cast a cautious glance toward the door, as though he were afraid someone would open it despite the bolt that locked it. He then threw everything but the candlesticks into the fire. As the knapsack was consumed in the flames, it suddenly revealed something that sparkled amid the ashes. He bent over and recognized it as a coin—the forty-sous piece stolen from the little lad from Savoy.

As the fire roared, his eyes abruptly fell on the two silver candlesticks sitting on the mantel. Seizing them, he thought, "The entire being of Jean Valjean is still in them. They must be destroyed as well!" He stirred the hot coals with one of the candlesticks.

In a moment more, they would have both been in the fire. But he suddenly heard a voice within him shouting, "Jean Valjean! Jean Valjean!" The hair on the back of his neck stood up, as he listened to what seemed to be a strong voice arising from within his soul.

The voice continued, "That's right, Valjean! Destroy these candlesticks! Forget the bishop! Forget everything! Destroy this man, Champmathieu, too! That's right. Applaud yourself. Here is an old man—an innocent man—whose whole misfortune lies in your name. Your name weighs like a crime upon him, and because of it he is condemned to finish his life in abject horror. That's good! Be an honest man—remain Monsieur le Mayor. Remain honored and esteemed, enrich the town with your factory, feed the poor, and raise the orphans. Live your life of happiness. Just remember—while you are here in the midst of your joy and light, there is a man wearing your prison clothes, who bears your name in disgrace, and who drags your chain across a cold prison floor. Yes, these are great plans, you wretched creature!"

Perspiration streamed from his brow as he fixed his wearied eyes on the candlesticks. Yet the voice within had not finished, and added, "Jean Valjean, all the voices around you will bless you. But there will be one voice, which no one will hear, cursing you in the dark. All those blessings from others will fall back before reaching heaven, and only your curse will rise and be visible before the eyes of God."

The voice had come from the most obscure depths of his conscience, but had been quite startling and strong. In fact, he had heard the last words so distinctly that he glanced around the room in terror. "Is someone there?" he demanded aloud. Then after laughing a somewhat maniacal laugh, he said,

"How stupid I am! There's no one here!"

Yet there was One Who was there, but He was not of those the human eye can see.

Valjean returned the candlesticks to the mantel. He now recoiled in equal terror before both opposing decisions he had made—one after the other. Either seemed equally fatal. And try as he may, he kept returning to the heart-rending dilemma that lay at the foundation of his tumultuous thinking: Should he remain in paradise and become a demon? Or should he return to hell and become an angel?

Thus was the severe struggle of this unhappy soul in his astounding anguish. Yet this unfortunate man stood in the shadow of another Man, a mysterious Being, Who eighteen hundred years before had taken upon Himself—amid all of His sacredness—all the sufferings of humanity. While the olive trees of Gethsemane shivered in the fierce breath of the Infinite, He drank of the terrible cup before Him—a cup dripping with darkness and overflowing with shadows in the depths of a world that had obscured even the flickering light of the stars.

CHAPTER ELEVEN

━━━━━━━━━━━━━━ ⚜ ━━━━━━━━━━━━━━

A lthough he did not realize it, Mayor Madeleine of Montreuil was somewhat of a celebrity. For seven years his reputation for virtue had filled the town, the surrounding villages, and even reached outside the entire district. And beyond the prosperity he had brought to Montreuil, there was not one of the one hundred and forty nearby communities that was not indebted to him for some benefit he had provided.

The judge presiding over the current court session at Arras was certainly acquainted with his name—something he held in common with everyone, since the mayor was so profoundly and universally honored. Therefore, when the court clerk handed the judge a note with the name Madeleine on it, and which said, "This gentleman desires to attend the trial," the judge immediately wrote at the bottom of the paper, "Admit him." At this, the clerk quickly ushered the mayor into the courtroom where the trial had commenced some hours before.

The courtroom was quite large, but poorly lit. No one paid any attention to the mayor, for all eyes were directed toward a wooden bench to the judge's left. On this bench, illuminated by several candles, sat a man between two guards.

"So this is the man," Madeleine thought instinctively. Yet his eyes had not sought him out—they had gone there quite naturally, as though they had known him beforehand. As he scrutinized the poor man, he thought he was looking at himself, except that the man seemed older. His face was not quite the same, but his demeanor was exactly that of the old Valjean. He had the same short, bristly hair, and the same suspicious and untamed eyes that Valjean had the day he had entered the town of Digne. He seemed to be full of hatred and anger, which only served to hide his soul beneath a multitude of fears—fears probably collected through years of serving time in prison.

The mayor said to himself with a shudder, "My God! Is that what I am to become again?"

Only the judge and the district attorney prosecuting the case seemed to notice Mayor Madeleine, and both bowed slightly upon seeing him. Nearly terrified that others would now recognize him, he dropped into a chair immediately behind him, and attempted to conceal his face. He then looked around the courtroom for Javert, but did not see him.

Just as the mayor had entered the courtroom, the defendant's lawyer had rested his case. During the three hours of the trial thus far, the crowd had been observing this strange man, who was a miserable specimen of humanity. He had been questioned and appeared to be either profoundly ignorant or extremely cunning, yet, whichever was correct, he was gradually bending beneath the weight of his terrible likeness to Valjean. And several witnesses had already been heard who were unanimous in identifying the man.

Nearing the conclusion of his case, the district attorney said, "The man on trial here today is not only a plunderer and a thief who has stolen fruit, but is also an old offender who has violated his parole. Yes, he is an ex-convict of the most vicious and dangerous type, a criminal named Jean Valjean, whom justice has sought for many years. Eight years ago, after being paroled from the prison at Toulon, he committed a violent robbery, attacking a small lad from Savoy named Little Gervais and then stealing his money from him. This is a crime under article 383 of the penal code, and I reserve the right to try him for this crime later, after we have judicially established his true identity. His most recent theft of stealing a branch full of ripe apples is the one he stands accused of today. Later he will be judged for his old crime."

After the district attorney finished his statement, the debate between the prosecution and the defense had come to an end. The judge then asked the accused man to stand, and addressed him by saying, "Did you or did you not climb the wall around the Pierron orchard, break off a branch, and steal the apples—that is to say, did you commit the crimes of breaking in and theft? Also, are you the ex-convict, Jean Valjean—yes or no?"

The prisoner replied, "I have stolen nothing. I am a man who does not have something to eat every day, and as I was coming from Ailly, walking through the countryside after a rain shower, I found a broken branch on the ground with apples still on it. I picked up the branch without knowing it would get me into trouble. I have now been locked up for three months, have been beaten, and do not understand what is happening to me. At times, the guard next to me nudges my elbow and whispers, 'Answer now.' But I don't know how to answer. I'm not an educated man and I'm poor. You say I'm someone named Jean Valjean, but I don't know the man. My name is Champmathieu. I don't understand why everyone has pursued me so furiously."

The prosecuting attorney, who had remained standing, then addressed the judge, "Monsieur le Judge, I would like to recall the convicts Brevet, Cochepaille, and Chenildieu, as well as Police Inspector Javert. I would like to question them one last time as to the identity of the prisoner, in regards to the ex-convict Jean Valjean."

"I wish to remind you, sir," replied the judge, "that Police Inspector Javert was called away by some official duty as soon as he had given his testimony."

"Thank you, Monsieur le Judge," responded the district attorney. "In that case, I wish to remind the gentlemen of the jury of that testimony made here several hours ago."

He then read from Javert's statement, which said, "I have no need to see the court's evidence or hear the prosecution's persuasive arguments to know that the prisoner's denial is an absolute lie. I recognize this man perfectly, and he is not Champmathieu. He is an ex-convict named Jean Valjean, a man who is very dangerous and to be feared. It is extremely unfortunate that he was released at the expiration of his prison term. He served nineteen years of hard labor for theft, and made five or six attempts to escape. Besides the theft from Little Gervais, and his recent theft of apples, I also suspect him of a theft committed at the house of His Grace, the late Bishop of Digne. And there is no doubt in my mind that this man is Valjean, for I saw him very often when I was an officer of the prison guard in Toulon. I repeat—I recognize him perfectly."

Javert's precisely worded statement had a visually profound effect on the jury and the spectators in the courtroom. In spite of this convincing testimony, however—and in order to remove any possible doubt in the minds of the jury—the district attorney insisted on recalling the other three witnesses, Brevet, Chenildieu, and Cochepaille.

One after the other, the convicts once more positively identified the prisoner as Jean Valjean. One of the men testified to having been chained to Valjean for five years, while another, referring to the accused man's build, testified to his incredible strength. Each man appeared to be making his statement sincerely and in good conscience, and after each one finished a murmur seemed to rumble through the courtroom.

"Silence!" the judge demanded. And then, with all the evidence having been presented, he began his concluding remarks of instruction to the gentlemen of the jury.

At that very moment someone stood and cried out, "Brevet! Chenildieu! Cochepaille! Look at me!" The sound of the voice was intensely chilling, sad, and filled with a sense of dread, all at the same time. All eyes in the courtroom were instantly riveted on the man who had spoken, and who had risen from his seat and was now standing before the judge.

As though exclaiming in one voice, the judge, the district attorney, and some twenty people or more—all who recognized the man—spontaneously shouted, "Mayor Madeleine!"

The clerk's candle illuminated the mayor's face as he stood there with his hat in his hand. He was extremely pale and was trembling slightly. His hair, which previously had been gray, had turned completely white during the one hour he had been there, due to the tremendous emotional stress now weighing upon his life.

Before the judge or the district attorney could utter a word, and before the guards could stop him, the mayor—whom they knew as Madeleine—was standing in front of the witnesses, Brevet, Chenildieu, and Cochepaille. "Don't you recognize me?" he asked. All three remained silent, but each indicated with a shake of his head that he did not know him. But the mayor continued, "Gentlemen of the jury, this prisoner must be released! Monsieur le Judge, have me arrested. This man is not who you think him to be. I am Jean Valjean!"

No one breathed, for the initial murmur of astonishment was now followed by a profound silence like that of the grave. Every person in the courtroom experienced a feeling somewhat akin to that of religious awe, which overcomes people when something of grandeur has been done.

In the meantime, the judge's face was marked with a look of sympathy and sadness. He had quickly motioned to the district attorney, and they whispered a few words to one another. The judge then turned toward the public in the courtroom, and with everyone understanding his underlying suspicions, asked, "Is there a physician present?"

Without waiting for an answer, the district attorney explained to the jury, "Gentlemen, this strange incident is disturbing to each of us, I'm sure. We all know, at least by reputation, the honorable Mayor Madeleine of Montreuil. So if there is a physician in the courtroom, we agree with the judge in asking for you to attend to the fine mayor and to take him to his home."

The mayor, however, did not allow the district attorney to finish. He interrupted with apologies, but also with authority, and said, "Thank you, Monsieur le District Attorney, but I am not mad, and you are on the verge of committing a grave error. This man must be released! My conscience compels me to admit that I am the miserable criminal he is accused of being. I am the only one here who sees this matter clearly, and I am telling the truth. God is looking down from on high on what I am doing, and His approval will suffice for me. You may arrest me—here I am.

"Over the last few years I have done my best to conceal my true identity. I have lived under another name, become rich, been appointed mayor, and tried to reenter the ranks of the honest. It appears that is not to be. The court is right in saying that Jean Valjean was a miserable and dangerous man. It is true he robbed the dear bishop and that poor lad, Little Gervais. Perhaps it was not completely his fault. However, Monsieur le Judge, a man like Valjean, who has been so greatly humbled, cannot argue with the providence of God, nor can he offer any advice to society in general. Yet prison often makes a convict what he is, and the terrible infamy he experiences after parole causes great damage.

"Before being imprisoned I was a poor peasant, with very little intelligence. Yet prison changed me. I was stupid, but I became a very crafty criminal. I was a dumb, cold log, but I became a blazing fire of unrest. However, just as the harsh severity of prison ruined me, the forgiveness and kindness of one man saved me.

"I realize it is difficult for you to understand what I am saying. Yet if you will search among the ashes of my fireplace, you will find the forty-sous piece I stole from Little Gervais seven years ago. I know you must think I've gone mad, and the fact that you don't believe me is distressing. Nevertheless, whatever you may think—do not condemn this man! I can't believe these three men do not remember me. If Javert were here, he would recognize me. I have nothing further to add—except, arrest me!"

Then turning to the three convicts who had witnessed against the accused, the mayor said, "Brevet, I remember the knitted suspenders with a checkered pattern you wore in prison. Chenildieu, your right shoulder has a scar, caused by burning yourself with a hot coal, while attempting to remove a tattoo with the letters *TFP.* Yet they are still visible—isn't this true?"

"It is true," said Chenildieu, in amazement.

Speaking to Cochepaille, he said, "Isn't it true that on your left forearm are the letters marking the day the emperor landed at Cannes: the first of March 1815? Pull up your sleeve!"

With all eyes focused on him, Cochepaille turned up his sleeve. A guard held a candle near the convict's arm, and then nodded, indicating the date was indeed there. At this, the mayor turned to the judge and smiled in a way that was heart-rending. It was a smile of triumph, but also one of despair. The mayor then spoke sadly, "You can plainly see that I am Jean Valjean."

From this point forward it was as though each person forgot the role he was to play. The judge forgot he was there to preside over the trial, the district attorney forgot he was there to prosecute the case, and the counsel for the defense forgot he was there to defend the accused. Throughout the courtroom there were no longer any judges, accusers, guards, or spectators—there were only staring eyes and sympathetic hearts.

The mayor, now shown to be Jean Valjean, resumed, "I do not wish to disturb the court further, and will now depart from here, since you are not arresting me. I have many things to do. The district attorney knows where to find me, and can have me arrested whenever he likes."

Valjean turned and walked toward the door of the courtroom. Not one voice was raised in objection, nor one arm extended to deter him. There seemed to be something of a divine reverence about him, which caused everyone to stand aside. He walked slowly and deliberately, and upon reaching the door, turned to say, "Monsieur le District Attorney, I am at your disposal, and will await your command."

Then, turning to the audience, he added, "I know that all of you must consider me worthy of pity. But I should be envied, instead, for overcoming the temptation to remain silent. When I think what I was on the verge of doing. . . . Nevertheless, I would have preferred that none of this had happened at all."

The door opened and then was closed behind him by someone in the crowd. It was a small act of service in automatic response to a great godly deed. Less than an hour later, the jury's verdict set poor Champmathieu free. He left, however, in his somewhat normal state of confusion, not fully understanding what had just happened to him.

CHAPTER TWELVE

---

antine still had a fever and had experienced another sleepless night, although it was filled with happy visions. At daybreak she finally fell asleep, and Sister Simplice, one of the Sisters of Charity attending to her, took advantage of the opportunity to prepare Fantine's medications. As she worked in the makeshift laboratory in the next room, she looked up and was suddenly startled to see Mayor Madeleine, who had entered silently.

Letting out a faint cry of surprise, the nun exclaimed, "Is that you, Monsieur le Mayor?"

He replied in a quiet voice, "How is this poor woman?"

"Not so bad right now, but she has been very uneasy," Sister Simplice began. "She was very ill yesterday, but seems better today because she thought you had gone to Montfermeil to get her child for her." The nun did not ask the mayor if that were true, for it was plain to see he had not come from there.

The mayor responded, "You were right not to volunteer the truth to her."

"I know," the sister said, "but what will we say now? She will see you, Monsieur le Mayor, but will not see her child."

He reflected for a moment, and then answered, "God will inspire us with what to say. May I see Fantine?"

"She is asleep, but you may enter."

He entered Fantine's room, drew back the curtain, and approached her bed, while she continued to sleep. Her skin was extremely pale except for her cheeks, which were crimson. Her long golden eyelashes seemed to be the only remaining vestige of the days of her beautiful youth and innocence. They seemed to quiver slightly, although her eyes remained closed and drooping. In fact, it seemed her entire being was trembling, but it was as though some unseen wings were unfolding, ready to open wide and carry her away.

The mayor stood motionless beside the bed for some time, gazing on the sick woman and then in turn on the crucifix, just as he had done two months before—the first day he had come to see her in the infirmary. Fantine finally opened her eyes, saw him, and quietly said, with a smile, "And Cosette?"

Fantine made no movement of either surprise or joy—she was joy itself! That simple question, "And Cosette?" was asked with such profound faith, with such certainty, with such a sense of peace, and with such a complete absence of doubt, Madeleine could not find a word of reply. She then continued, "I knew you were there. I was asleep, but I saw you. I have seen you for a long, long time. I have been following you with my eyes all night long. You seemed to be in glory and were surrounded by all kinds of heavenly beings."

The mayor raised his eyes to the crucifix.

"But," she resumed, "tell me where Cosette is. Why didn't you place her on my bed as soon as I awoke?"

Fortunately for the mayor, the nun had notified the doctor, who now walked into the room. He came to the aid of Madeleine, and said, "Calm down, my child. Your daughter is here."

At this, Fantine's eyes beamed and her entire face seemed bathed in light. "Oh!" she exclaimed, "Then bring her to me!"

"Not just yet," cautioned the doctor. "You still have some fever, and must get well before seeing her. You don't want her to become ill, and besides, seeing her would unnecessarily excite you, harming you and making you weaker."

She vehemently argued, "But I am well! I tell you I am! I want to see my child!"

"You see how excited you are becoming," said the doctor calmly. "As long as you are like this, I must oppose your seeing your child."

Fantine insisted, "I don't have a fever any longer—I am well. I am perfectly aware that there is nothing wrong with me anymore. Nevertheless, I will calm down and not move, as though I were ill, in order to please you and the nuns. Once they see I am calm, they will agree, 'She must see her child.'"

She made a visible effort to be calm and still. Her sickness had made her very weak, and her efforts to remain calm were expressed in such a way that she became very childlike, "trying to be good" so she could see Cosette. While she made every effort to be quiet, she could not help but question Madeleine, "Did you have a pleasant trip, Monsieur le Mayor? How good you are to get Cosette for me! Tell me how she is. Did she handle the journey well?" Then with sadness Fantine added, "She will not recognize me."

He reached for her hand and said, "Cosette is beautiful and is well. You will see her soon enough, but now you must remain calm. You are getting so excited that you are pushing your blankets away, and all this talking and excitement will only worsen your cough."

In fact, nearly every other word of Fantine's was already being interrupted by terrible fits of coughing. After her coughing subsided somewhat, the doctor checked her breathing once more, and then excused himself, leaving the mayor and Sister Simplice alone with her.

It was evident that Madeleine, after his experience in court, had other things to tell Fantine. Yet now he hesitated. As he pondered what to say, Fantine suddenly exclaimed, "I hear her! I hear Cosette!" But she was hearing a neighbor's child playing outside the window. She excitedly resumed, "It is my Cosette! I recognize her voice."

The child's voice faded away. Fantine listened intently for a while longer, then her face turned sullen and she said, "How wicked that doctor is for not allowing me to see my daughter!" However, her thoughts quickly became happy once again as she thought of Cosette.

Madeleine held her hand and listened to her words as one listens to the sighing of a breeze. His eyes were downcast and his mind was absorbed in such deep reflection that it seemed to have no bottom. Fantine abruptly stopped speaking, which caused him to raise his eyes to her.

Suddenly she looked terrified. She seemed to stop breathing and sat straight up in the bed. Her face, which a moment before had been radiant, was now ghastly. Her eyes, wide with terror, were fixed on something at the other side of the room.

"What troubles you, Fantine?" the alarmed mayor questioned. But she made no reply. Her eyes remained fixed on what she seemed to see. Fantine slowly slid her hand from his and made a gesture, indicating he should look across the room.

Turning, the mayor saw Javert.

Fantine had not seen Javert since the day the mayor had rescued her from him. Her sickness caused her to comprehend little, but upon seeing Javert, there was one thing she was certain of—he had come to get her. She felt like her life was being drained from within her, and she could not bear to look at his fearsome face. She hid her face in her hands and shrieked in anguish, "Monsieur Madeleine, save me!"

The mayor had risen from his chair, and in the most calm and gentle voice possible, said, "Be at ease. It is not for you he has come." Then addressing Javert, he said, "I know why you are here."

Now aware the mayor's name was not Madeleine, Javert replied, "Valjean, be quick about it!"

Hearing Javert, Fantine had a terrified and confused look on her face. She thought, "If the mayor is here, what do I have to fear?" Then she saw something more incomprehensible than anything she had seen during her worst delirious bouts of fever. She saw Javert—the police spy—seize the mayor by his collar. When the mayor simply bowed his head, it seemed her world was coming to an end.

"Monsieur le Mayor!" Fantine shrieked.

Javert burst out laughing in a repulsive way that exposed all his gums, and exclaimed sarcastically, "There is no longer any Monsieur le Mayor here!"

Jean Valjean, making no attempt to free himself from Javert's grasp on his collar, said humbly, "Javert . . ."

But Javert interrupted, "Call me Monsieur Inspector."

Submitting, Valjean continued, "Monsieur Inspector, I would like a word with you in private."

"No! Say what you have to say openly!" Javert insisted.

Speaking openly but lowering his voice, Valjean began, "I have a request to make of you."

"Speak up!" Javert shouted.

"But you alone need hear what I have to say."

"What difference could that possibly make to me? I will not listen."

Jean Valjean turned toward Javert, and then continued very quietly but rapidly, "Grant me three days' grace! Just three days in which to find this poor woman's child. I will pay you whatever you ask, and you may accompany me if you like."

"You must think I'm crazy!" cried Javert. "Come now, Valjean, I have never thought you to be such a fool!"

"My child!" Fantine abruptly pleaded, having heard the mayor in spite of his attempt to keep his words from her. "Go find my child! I thought she was here. Please answer me, where is Cosette? I want my child, Monsieur Madeleine! Monsieur le Mayor!"

Javert stamped his foot in anger, and shouted, "And now the other criminal speaks! Hold your tongue, you hussy!" Then staring intently at Fantine, he added, "I told you there is no longer any Monsieur Madeleine and no Monsieur le Mayor. There is nothing here but a thief—a robber—an ex-convict named Jean Valjean! And I have captured him! That's what we have here!"

Fantine raised herself from her bed, propping her feverish body with her thin, weak arms. She gazed blankly at the mayor and Javert and opened her mouth as though to speak again. Yet a deep, deathly rattle resounded from the depths of her throat. Feeling cold, her teeth chattered, and she abruptly sat straight up, while her arms began to jerk convulsively. She thrashed about like a drowning person, and then suddenly fell back on her pillow.

As she fell, her head struck the headboard of the bed and fell forward toward her chest. Her gaping mouth uttered no sound, nor did her staring eyes appear to see. Fantine was dead.

Jean Valjean put his hand upon Javert's hand that held him, and while calmly pulling it away, said, "You have murdered this poor woman."

"Let's put an end to this!" shouted Javert, furiously. "I am not here to listen to your argument. A guard is outside, so march at once, or I'll have you tortured with thumbscrews!"

Valjean quickly reached toward the bed and twisted off an iron rod from the headboard. He held it like a weapon and glared at Javert, who had retreated toward the door. Then in a voice that was barely audible, he said, "I advise you to leave me alone!"

Javert was visibly trembling at the mayor's words. Valjean then turned and beheld Fantine's motionless body, with his face portraying a look of inexpressible pity. After a moment of meditation he bent over Fantine and spoke to her so softly his words could not be heard. He took her head in his hands and arranged it on the pillow, as a mother would do for her child. Finally, he smoothed her hair gently, and then lovingly closed her eyes.

At that very instant, Fantine's face seemed strangely illuminated. Perhaps it was the precise moment of death that signifies a soul's entrance into the great Heavenly Light.

Fantine's still warm hand hung over the side of her bed. Jean Valjean knelt down, gently lifted it, and kissed it. Then he stood, turned to Javert, and said, "Now, sir, I am at your disposal."

Inspector Javert locked Jean Valjean in the local prison, while the news of the arrest of the mayor of Montreuil created quite a stir in the town. Unfortunately for Valjean, nearly everyone deserted him at the news that he was a convict. In less than two hours' time, all the good he had done over the years had been forgotten. He was suddenly nothing but "a convict from prison."

That same evening, the mayor's housekeeper saw the front door open. From her vantage point she could only see the arm of the person who had entered—but she knew the sleeve of that coat and the hand that was reaching for a candle. It was the mayor!

Being terribly surprised at seeing him, it was several seconds before she could utter, "Monsieur le Mayor! I thought you were . . ." She hesitated to finish her sentence, out of respect for the man she still considered to be the mayor.

Valjean finished her thought for her, saying, "In prison? I was there, but I broke a bar of one of the windows, lowered myself to the ground, and escaped. I'm going to my bedroom. Please find Sister Simplice for me. No doubt she is still with that poor woman, Fantine."

The elderly woman quickly obeyed, while he climbed the stairs to his room. He glanced around the room at his table, his chair, and his bed that had not been slept in for three days. The housekeeper had cleaned the room and had found in the ashes of the fireplace two metal ends of a walking stick and a forty-sous piece, which she had placed on the table.

Valjean took a sheet of paper and wrote, "These are the two tips of my old walking stick and the forty-sous piece I stole from Little Gervais, which I mentioned in court in Arras." He then arranged his note, the iron pieces, and the coin on the table so they could be plainly seen upon entering the room. From his cabinet he pulled out an old shirt, which he tore in two. Then taking the linen pieces, he wrapped up the bishop's two silver candlesticks.

Hearing someone knock on his door, he said, "Come in!" It was Sister Simplice, whose eyes were especially red and whose face was unusually pale. She held a small candle in her hand, which was trembling slightly.

Jean Valjean had just finished writing another short note, which he handed to her and said, "Sister, please take this to the parish priest."

The note was not folded, so when he saw her glance at it, he said, "You may read it."

The note read as follows: "I beg you, sir, to take charge of all that I leave behind. Using the funds in my account, please be so good as to pay the expenses of my trial, and for the funeral of the poor woman who died here yesterday. The remainder is to be given to the poor."

Suddenly loud footsteps could be heard running up the stairs outside the room, while the elderly housekeeper shouted at the top of her lungs, "My good sir, I swear to you that not a soul has entered this house all day long. I have been by the door since morning."

A man's voice responded, "Then why is there a light on in the room upstairs?"

Valjean recognized the voice as that of Javert. He blew out the candle in his hand and quickly moved to the corner that would be hidden once the door was open. Sister Simplice fell to her knees by the table just as the door swung open.

Javert entered. The nun did not raise her eyes, for she was praying intently. The only candle still lit was the one on the mantel of the fireplace, but it shed very little light. Javert caught sight of the nun and stopped in total surprise. His first inclination was to leave immediately, but his duty propelled him in the opposite direction. He decided to ask at least one question.

Sister Simplice had never told a lie in her life, and Javert knew it. As a result, he held her in a certain place of honor and esteem. Then venturing to ask his question, he said, "Sister, are you alone in this room?"

The moment was incredibly tense, and the poor housekeeper felt as though she would faint. Just then the nun raised her eyes and said, "Yes."

"In that case," Javert resumed, "you will excuse me if I persist in my questioning. It is my duty. Have you seen a certain escapee this evening? He is Jean Valjean. Have you seen him?"

The sister replied, "No." She had now lied twice—one after the other. And she had lied without hesitation, as a person would do when sacrificing herself instead.

"Please pardon me then. I will now leave you alone," Javert said, as he bowed to the nun and promptly turned to depart.

An hour later, a man was walking rapidly through the trees and the night mist, departing Montreuil in the direction of Paris. The man was Jean Valjean.

CHAPTER THIRTEEN

S everal days after Jean Valjean fled from Montreuil, the police in Paris arrested him once again. He had taken advantage of his few days of liberty, however, to withdraw a considerable sum of money—some six to seven hundred thousand francs—from his bank account. He then hid the money in a place that only he knew.

When he was accused of theft, Valjean refused to defend himself. Not only was he pronounced guilty of robbing Little Gervais, but was also erroneously accused of being a member of a gang of robbers in the south of France. As a result, he was condemned and sentenced to death. Even though he refused to lodge an appeal, the king of France commuted his penalty to hard labor for life in prison.

Valjean was immediately transferred to the prison at Toulon, a place he knew all too well. But no longer was he prisoner 24601—he would now be known as prisoner 9430.

With their mayor now imprisoned, the people of Montreuil saw their prosperity vanish. His huge factory was shut down, his buildings fell into ruin, and his work force was scattered across the country. The small amount of trade that remained was now done strictly for money, instead of the general good, so there was nothing given to the poor any longer.

Some months later, near the end of October 1823, a ship by the name of *Orion* pulled into the port of Toulon for repairs. It was part of France's Mediterranean fleet and the year before had been in dry dock for repairs. Thick layers of barnacles, which slowed the vessel to half its normal speed, had been removed from its keel. This repair, however, had weakened the bolts on the keel, and it had now sprung a leak.

A warship the size of the *Orion*, now being repaired once again, always drew quite a crowd in the town of Toulon. One morning the people who had gathered to observe the ship witnessed an accident. A sailor high atop the main sail lost his balance while mending it. As he fell, he was able to grab hold of one of the footropes hanging from the bottom of the sail. He now swung violently back and forth at the very end of the rope high above the water and then above the crowd as they watched breathlessly below. The man's fall and the sudden jolt of grasping the rope had taken quite a toll on his strength. It was now all he could do to simply hang on to the end of it.

The poor man attempted to climb the rope to safety but was too weak to do so. And a rescue seemed so dangerous that no sailor volunteered to even attempt one. It was obvious something must be done quickly, for the man was so exhausted that he did not even dare to shout for help, fearing he would weaken himself further.

Suddenly a man was seen climbing the rigging with the agility of a tiger. The man was dressed in a red prison uniform and wore a green cap, indicating he was sentenced to life. As he climbed, a gust of wind blew his cap away, revealing his perfectly white hair and the fact that he was not a young man.

This convict, assigned by the prison to work in the shipyard, had immediately asked the officer in charge for permission to help as soon as he had seen the accident. While all the sailors trembled in fear and shrank from their responsibility, this man was willing to risk his life. The officer, instead of verbally responding to the man's request, had taken a hammer, and with one strong blow had broken the riveting that secured the prisoner's chain to his ankle.

In what seemed like centuries to those below, but was actually just seconds, the man climbed to the main sail. He then walked precariously along the bottom support of the sail as it swayed in the wind, tied another rope to it, and descended hand over hand to the unfortunate sailor below.

Now two men swung high above the water. The convict worked quickly to secure the sailor with his own rope, while he hung to the sailor's rope with his other hand. Once the man was securely tied, the convict climbed back to the bottom pole of the sail, pulled the man up, and then carefully carried him to the other sailors who had now climbed the mast.

At that moment the crowd broke into applause, convicts and sailors wept, and women embraced each other on the pier. And an impassioned cry could be heard from a number of people, who shouted, "A pardon for that man!"

In the meantime, the convict had begun to make his descent. With all eyes upon him, he suddenly ran along the pole of one of the lower sails, as though he would descend more quickly by dropping down one of its ropes. Yet as he did so, they saw him hesitate, stagger, and fall into the sea. The crowd, thinking the man's energy must be totally spent by now, shouted in horror for someone to help.

The poor convict had fallen between the *Orion* and another large vessel. Four men quickly launched a small boat, fearing the man would be pulled by the tide underneath one of the ships and drown. However, the man was nowhere to be found. He had not risen to the surface and seemed to have disappeared without a ripple. They continued to search until evening, yet their search was in vain, for they never found his body.

The next day the Toulon newspaper ran the following story: "17 November 1823. Yesterday, a convict assigned to the detachment of prisoners working on the *Orion* fell into the sea and was drowned. He had just saved a sailor from certain death, when he lost his footing and fell. The convict, whose body has not yet been found, was prisoner 9430, and his name was Jean Valjean."

The Christmas season of 1823 was particularly bright for the people of Montfermeil. The weather had been warm through the early part of the season, and they had not yet seen frost or snow. Many merchants from Paris had received permission from the mayor of the town to erect a marketplace in the church square. So many booths were erected that a number of them extended into the Lane du Boulanger, where the Thénardiers' inn was located.

On Christmas Eve, as a result of the busy marketplace, the Thénardiers' inn was filled with a number of traders and merchants who were eating, drinking, and smoking around the tables of their dining area. With just four or five candles burning, there was little light, but a great deal of noise. Madame Thénardier was cooking the supper, which was roasting over a roaring fire, while her husband was drinking with his customers and talking politics.

Little Cosette had become useful to the Thénardiers in two ways: She brought in the money her poor mother sent, and she was forced to serve them. Therefore, when the money ceased to flow from Fantine, due to her death, they kept Cosette anyway. In their thinking, she could at the very least continue to be a servant in their house.

Due to the high elevation of the plateau where Montfermeil was located, water was scarce. Therefore, it was necessary to carry water from a considerable distance to the inn. This difficult task had been assigned to Cosette. She was terrified at the idea of having to go to the spring in the dark of night, so the child attempted to make sure there was always plenty of water in the house before sunset.

This particular night, she was seated in her usual place—underneath the kitchen table near the chimney. She was dressed only in rags, while her sock-less feet wore only cold, wooden shoes. Her present task was knitting socks that were destined for the feet of the young Thénardier daughters—Éponine and Azelma—who could be heard playing and laughing in the adjoining room.

Every newcomer to the Thénardiers' inn and tavern would think of Madame Thénardier as the one in charge, since she always appeared to be busily working. This, however, was a mistake, for she was completely dominated by her evil husband. Yet she herself was quite a formidable person and not exactly kind. She loved no one except her own children, and feared no one except her husband. Actually, it would not be totally correct to say that she loved her own children, for often the cries of a very young child could be heard throughout the inn. It was a little boy who had been born to the Thénardiers during one of the previous winters, and who was now a little more than three years old. She loved to joke with her guests that the poor child was the result of "a very cold winter." Madame Thénardier had given birth to him and nursed him, but she did not love him. When he would cry, her husband would shout at her, "Would you please go see about the little brat?" Yet she did not want to be bothered and would allow the poor, neglected child to continue to scream in the dark. So her sense of motherhood certainly stopped with her daughters, while her husband seemed to have no parenting instincts at all. He had but one thought—how to enrich himself.

In spite of Monsieur Thénardier's craftiness and skill at deception, he was not even successful at his one and only goal. He blamed this on the fact that he had not yet found a "theater worthy of his great talent." In fact, he was near the point of financial ruin and was quite anxious because he owed more than fifteen hundred francs in various debts.

His theory of running an inn was to squeeze everything possible from the unsuspecting travelers who were unfortunate enough to come to Montfermeil near nightfall. He would continually seek to warp his wife's mind as well by demanding, "The duty of an innkeeper is to sell the traveler the following: stew, rest, candles, fire, dirty sheets, a servant, lice, and a smile. It is to stop the passers-by, empty the small purses, lighten the heavy ones, and shelter their family. It is to charge for an open window, a closed window, the chimney, the armchair, the ottoman, the stool, and the bed—whether it's a mattress of feathers or straw. We should charge for using our mirror every time they take a look—in short, to make the traveler pay for everything, even for the flies that his dog eats!" This man and woman were nothing less than craftiness and rage united—a hideous and terrible team.

As Cosette continued her knitting, four new travelers arrived at the inn. She knew these new customers would need water and suddenly remembered that the water tank was empty. The recent surge in business, a result of the nearby Christmas market, had greatly increased the inn's water consumption, and now she was fearful she would be forced to venture out in the dead of night. To make matters worse, she heard the customers saying, "It's black as an oven out there tonight," and "You would have to be a cat to go out there without a lantern!" Cosette trembled.

Suddenly, one of the peddlers staying at the inn said in a harsh tone, "My horse has not been watered."

"Sure it has," replied Madame Thénardier.

"I'm telling you it hasn't!" retorted the peddler.

At this, Madame Thénardier looked at Cosette and angrily said, "You little dog, go and water his horse."

"But, madam, there is no water," Cosette offered feebly.

Madame Thénardier then threw the door open, and shouted at the poor, frightened child, "Well, go and get some, then!"

Cosette dropped her head and walked to pick up the empty bucket near the chimney. The pail was bigger than she was, and would have easily held the child herself. She stood motionless before the open door with her bucket in hand, seemingly waiting for someone to come to her rescue.

"Get along!" screamed Madame Thénardier.

So the frightened little girl walked out into the cold dark chasm of the night, while the door closed behind her. She plunged into the darkness, making as much noise with her bucket as possible, as though the noise kept her company. The immensity of the night was confronting this tiny creature, so she did not look to the right or to the left, for fear of seeing something hiding in the bushes or the trees.

Finally Cosette reached the spring of water. She did not take time to breathe, but bent down toward the natural basin hollowed out by the water, and plunged her bucket into the dark water. Then, nearly filling the pail, she pulled it out and set it next to her on the grass. Realizing she was quite fatigued, she remained crouched on the ground for some time, then grabbed the bucket's handle with both hands, but could hardly lift it.

Straining with each step, she managed only about twelve paces before having to set the bucket down again. She continued in this way for some time, but was proceeding very slowly. Even by taking shorter and shorter breaks between efforts, she knew at this rate it would take more than an hour to return to the inn, and no matter what, Madame Thénardier would beat her. Upon coming to an old chestnut tree, she stopped for some time, hoping to get well rested. Then she summoned all her strength, picked up the bucket once more, and courageously resumed her march. Yet the poor, desperate little creature could not keep from crying out, "Oh, God! Help!"

At that very moment it suddenly seemed that her bucket weighed nothing at all. A hand, which appeared to her to be enormous, had just grabbed the handle and had easily lifted it. Looking up, she saw a large dark form, tall and straight, walking next to her in the darkness. This man had apparently walked up from behind her, but she had not heard him approaching. Without uttering a word, he had seized the handle of the bucket she was so valiantly attempting to carry.

Although her God-given instinct for this encounter might have been fear, she was not afraid. Abruptly, the man spoke to her, in a deep voice that seemed quite somber, "My child, this is very heavy for you."

"Yes, sir," Cosette replied, respectfully.

"Give it to me then," said the man. "I will carry it for you." Cosette let go of the handle as the man walked along beside her. "It really is quite heavy," he added, before saying, "How old are you, little one?"

"Eight, sir."

"And have you come from very far with this?" he questioned.

"From the spring in the forest," she answered.

"And how far are you going?"

"A good quarter of an hour's walk from here, sir."

The man said nothing for a moment, and then remarked abruptly, "Do you not have a mother?"

"I don't know," responded the child. And before the man had time to speak again, she added, "I don't think so. Other people have mothers, but I don't." Then after what seemed to be a moment of reflection, she continued, "I don't think I ever had one."

The man stopped, set the bucket on the ground, bent over the child and placed both hands on her shoulders, attempting to see her face in the dark. The faint light of the night sky vaguely outlined Cosette's emaciated face.

"What is your name?" asked the man.

"Cosette," was the seemingly unexpected answer. It was as though the man had received a massive shock. He looked at her again, removed his hands from her shoulders, and then quickly grabbed the bucket and began walking down the path once more.

After a moment he inquired, "Where do you live, little one?"

"In Montfermeil, sir, if you know where that is."

"Is that where we're headed?" he asked.

"Yes, sir."

He paused, then began again, "Who sent you out at such a late hour to get water in the forest?"

"It was Madame Thénardier."

The man resumed, attempting to sound indifferent, but with a tremor in his voice nonetheless, "And what does your Madame Thénardier do?"

"She and her husband keep the inn where I live," Cosette replied.

"The inn? Well, I will lodge there myself tonight. Will you show me the way?" asked the man.

"We are on the way there now," the child answered.

The man was walking quite fast, yet Cosette followed him without difficulty and no longer felt tired. From time to time she would look up at him with a sense of peace and indescribable confidence. No one had ever taught her to turn to Providence in prayer, nevertheless she felt the beginnings of joy and hope bubbling up within her, and she lifted her eyes toward heaven.

As they reached the village and approached the inn, Cosette timidly touched his arm and said, "Monsieur?"

"Yes, my child?"

"Will you let me take my bucket now?"

"But why?"

"If madam sees that someone has carried it for me, she will beat me," the poor child answered in a matter-of-fact way.

The man handed her the bucket as they came to the tavern door. Cosette knocked and the door swung open, revealing Madame Thénardier standing inside with a candle in her hand. Then with her voice filled with anger, she yelled at the child, "Oh, it's you! You wretched creature! Mercy, but you have taken your time! This little hussy has been amusing herself!"

"Madam," Cosette answered, while trembling all over, "here's a gentleman who needs lodging."

Madame Thénardier, with an obvious air of false sincerity, speedily replaced her gruffness with a forced smile. Then she eagerly focused her eyes on the man, and said, "And this is the gentleman?"

"Yes, madam," the man replied, as he slightly tipped his hat with his hand.

She knew that wealthy travelers were typically not so polite, so this gesture, and a quick inspection of his clothing and bag, caused her fake smile to vanish. Her gruff tone reappeared as she said, "Enter, my good man."

So the "good man" entered. As Madame Thénardier continued to scrutinize the traveler, she noticed his threadbare coat, and his worn and battered hat. Then with a grimace on her face, she walked across the room to consult with her husband, who was drinking with some carriage drivers.

It was obvious they believed the man to be a common beggar, because Monsieur Thénardier looked up and exclaimed, "See here, my good man! I am very sorry, but I have no room left."

"Then put me wherever you like," the man replied. "Put me in the attic or the stable. I will still pay as though you gave me a room."

"Forty sous," the innkeeper demanded.

"Forty sous it is," the man agreed.

Overhearing the conversation, one of the carriage drivers leaned to whisper to Madame Thénardier, "Isn't the rate only twenty sous?"

"In his case it's forty," the woman retorted. "I don't lodge beggars like him for less."

"That's true," added her husband. "We could ruin our spotless reputation lodging such people."

Their new guest never took his eyes off Cosette. She returned to what the Thénardiers called her kennel, while her sad but beautiful eyes took on an expression never seen in them before. The poor child kept them riveted on the traveler.

CHAPTER FOURTEEN

The following morning, at least two hours before sunrise, Monsieur Thénardier was in the tavern with pen in hand, working by candlelight. He was busily preparing a bill for the traveler who had arrived the previous evening. It was for charges over and above the forty sous the man had already paid, and included an additional charge for the man's room—since the innkeeper had "miraculously discovered at the last minute" that he did have a room available after all, and did not have to put the man in the stable. His wife watched carefully as he wrote, while a faint sound could be heard in the house—the sound of the fragile Lark sweeping the stairs.

At least a quarter of an hour—and several erasures—later, Thénardier produced the following masterpiece:

BILL FOR THE GENTLEMAN IN ROOM 1

Supper	3 francs
Room	10 francs
Candles	5 francs
Fire for heat	4 francs
Service	1 franc
Total	23 francs

"Twenty-three francs!" Madame Thénardier exclaimed upon seeing the total. Her voice was filled with glee, but also a touch of hesitation, for she continued, "He won't pay that."

Her husband only laughed, coldly, and said, "He will pay. And when he comes in here, I want you to hand the bill to him." He then left the room, just as the traveler entered by another door.

Thénardier instantly turned and stood motionless in the doorway, yet only visible to his wife. The traveler had his bag, a bundle, and his walking stick with him.

"Up so early?" questioned Madame Thénardier. "Is the gentleman leaving us already?"

"Yes, madam, I am going."

"You have no business here in Montfermeil, sir?"

"No, I'm only passing through. What do I owe you, madam?" he asked. At this, she handed him the bill her husband had written. The man unfolded the paper, glanced at it, but as though his thoughts were elsewhere, he resumed, "Madam, is business good here in Montfermeil?"

"Monsieur, times are very hard! And to make matters worse, we have so few rich in this village. All the people are poor, you see. If it were not for a few rich and generous travelers like you, monsieur, we would not get by. We have so many expenses. And that child is costing us a fortune."

"What child?" the traveler asked.

"You know—that little one—Cosette, or the Lark, as she is known around here."

"Oh!" the man responded. "What if someone were to rid you of her?"

"Rid me of Cosette?" Madame Thénardier asked eagerly, as though she couldn't believe her ears.

"Yes," the man said, calmly.

Suddenly her red, angry face seemed to brighten, but with a hideous smile. Then, with her voice dripping with sarcasm, she said, "Take her, my dear sir! Lead her away—keep her—give her food, sweets, and drink—do whatever you please with the blessings of the good holy Virgin and all of the saints of paradise upon you!"

"Good. I will take her then," the traveler agreed.

"Are you really serious? You really will take her away?" the woman questioned.

"Yes."

"Immediately?" the woman asked, still unable to believe what she was hearing.

"Yes, immediately. Call the child," the man instructed.

At this Madame Thénardier screamed, "Cosette!"

Returning to the matter of his bill, not having noticed the total at first glance, the man asked again, "How much do I owe you?" Then as his eyes suddenly saw the amount, he exclaimed in surprise, "Twenty-three francs!"

"Good gracious, yes, it's twenty-three francs," she responded, as though it were nothing.

Without arguing, the stranger calmly laid five five-franc coins on the table, while saying, "Go and get the child."

At that moment, Monsieur Thénardier, who had overheard their entire conversation from his position in the doorway, walked toward the traveler, and said, "As to the child—I need to discuss the matter with the gentleman. Leave us alone, wife."

Madame Thénardier was amazed by what she knew was coming—a brilliant display of her husband's best talent. She was aware that a great actor had just walked onto his very own stage. She did not utter one more word, but turned obediently and left the room.

As soon as they were alone, the innkeeper offered his guest a chair. Monsieur Thénardier remained standing, however, while his face took on an expression of caring and kindness. "Sir, what I wish to say to you is that I simply adore that child!"

The stranger glared at the innkeeper, and with a look of disbelief, asked, "What child?" But as he did so, he set a one hundred-sous coin on the table.

Yet Thénardier continued, as though he hadn't heard the man, "How strange it is that one grows so easily attached to a child. What's that money for? Pick up your hundred-sous piece. I adore the child."

Once again the stranger demanded, "What child?"

The innkeeper retorted, "Our little Cosette, of course! You're not intending to take her away from us, are you? Let me tell you frankly—I cannot consent to that. I will miss the child too much, for she became as one of ours when she was just a tiny thing. Now it is true that she costs us a lot of money, and that she has her faults. It is true that we are not rich, and that I have had to pay more than four hundred francs to buy medicine for just one of her illnesses. But I had to do something, for heaven's sake! The poor child doesn't have a mother or a father. I have raised her!"

The traveler kept his eyes fixed intently on Thénardier, as the innkeeper continued, "Pardon me, sir, but I cannot just give away my child to someone passing by. Wouldn't you agree? Nevertheless, although you don't appear to be rich, you do seem to be a very good man—and if your desire were for her happiness, perhaps I would consider letting her go. But I must find that out, for it would be at great sacrifice to me. Of course, if I were to let her go, I would like to know what becomes of her, and would like to visit her from time to time. I would need to know that her foster father is taking good care of her."

Then, finally coming to the end of his act, the innkeeper, said, "I guess I should at the very least ask to see your papers. Your passport, please?"

The stranger, with his eyes seemingly penetrating to the very depths of the innkeeper's conscience, replied in a somber and firm voice, "Monsieur Thénardier, no one needs a passport to travel less than fifteen miles from Paris. If I decide to take Cosette, I will take her, and that will be the end of the matter. But you will not know my name, my address, or where she is. It will be my intention for her to never lay eyes on you again as long as she lives. I am breaking the chain that binds her foot to you. Does that suit you? Yes or no?"

Realizing the traveler had not been taken in by his act, the innkeeper cut to the heart of his true concern and insisted, "It will cost you fifteen hundred francs!"

The stranger pulled his old leather pouch from his coat, counted out the money, and laid it on the table. Then, placing his fist on top of the bills, he demanded, "Go get Cosette."

Madame Thénardier, who had been listening to the conversation through the partially opened door, walked back into the room. Then she called, "Cosette, come immediately!"

An instant later Cosette appeared. The traveler took his bundle and untied it. Inside was a complete outfit—all in black—consisting of a coat, dress, apron, scarf, woolen socks, and shoes. It all seemed to be the perfect size for a girl her age.

Then the traveler said to Cosette, "My child, take these, and go and dress yourself quickly."

The first rays of dawn were appearing when some of the inhabitants of Montfermeil beheld a poorly clothed old man walking along the road to Paris. He was holding the hand of a little girl who appeared to be in mourning, for she was dressed all in black. The small child's eyes, however, gazed at the sky, and were open wide, as if in wonder. She felt as though she were walking beside the goodness of God Himself in human form.

Of course, these two were Jean Valjean and Cosette. They traveled many miles that day—the day he had rescued Cosette from the claws of the Thénardiers—some in carriages and some on foot, until they reached Paris. The day was filled with many new and strange emotions for the child, and although she was very tired, Cosette never complained. Jean Valjean realized her weariness as she began to drag more and more on his hand as they walked. Therefore, he put her on his back, after which she placed her head on his shoulder and promptly fell into a deep and peaceful sleep—the first she had known in years.

Along a deeply rutted dirt road near the outskirts of Paris sat a very humble looking building. At first glance it appeared to be nothing more than a thatched house, but in reality it had as much space as some cathedrals. It was quite hidden from the road by the surrounding trees, revealing only one door and window. To the postman it was known as Number 50-52, but the neighborhood knew it as the Gorbeau House.

Jean Valjean, still carrying the sleeping Cosette, stopped in front of the house. As though they were wild birds, he had chosen this deserted place to construct their nest. Fumbling through his pocket, he finally withdrew a key and unlocked the door. Then quickly entering, he climbed the staircase with the child.

At the top of the stairs he took another key from his pocket and opened another door. As the door swung open, it revealed a somewhat spacious attic room, furnished with a mattress on the floor, a table with several chairs, and a stove in the corner with a fire already burning. Since it was evening the room was dark, except for the dim light shining through the window from the street lantern outside. Across the room was a dressing area with a cot, where Valjean laid Cosette without waking her.

After lighting a candle, he sat at the table and gazed at the sweet child's face with a feeling of profound joy, kindness, and tenderness that was inexpressible. Cosette slept with a look of tranquil confidence that is characteristic of only those who are extremely strong or extremely weak. The little girl had fallen asleep without knowing who carried her or where she was going.

Valjean knelt by the child's bed and gently kissed her hand. It had been nine months since he had kissed the hand of the small girl's mother—who had also fallen "asleep." As he did so, mixed emotions of sadness and happiness filled his mind, while thoughts of heaven once again filled his heart.

Cosette continued to sleep as the sun was rising. A faint ray of light from the December sun penetrated the attic window, casting long threads of light onto the ceiling. Suddenly a heavily laden cart passing along the road shook the entire building like a clap of thunder. The shaking of Cosette's small bed startled her, and she abruptly cried out, "Yes, madam! Here I am!" She then sprang out of bed with her eyes still half shut, and reaching toward the wall, asked, "Where's my broom?"

Before Valjean could speak, however, she opened her eyes and beheld his smiling face. Then she uttered, with an air of joy and surprise, "It's true! This is not a dream! Good morning, monsieur." Then she added, as if from habit, "Must I sweep?"

He answered with only one word, "Play!" So Cosette spent her first day of freedom with this kind man, yet didn't bother attempting to understand what had happened to her. She simply played, and seemed inexpressibly happy.

At dawn the following day, Valjean sat motionless by Cosette's bed again, waiting for her to awaken. As he gazed at her, he felt as though something new had entered his soul. He had never loved anyone, and for twenty-five years he had been alone in the world. He had never been a father, a husband, or even a friend.

In prison Valjean had kept to himself, and his heart had been full of darkness and anger. His sister and her children had now become only faint memories. After being released from prison he had made every effort to find them, but having been unsuccessful, had nearly forgotten them altogether. All the tender emotions of his youth had long since fallen into an abyss, but when he looked at Cosette he felt his heart stir.

New emotions of love and affection awoke within his heart and rushed headlong toward that little child. Just watching her sleep, he trembled with pure joy. Here was a poor old man with a perfectly new heart filled with sweet love for Cosette.

Valjean was now fifty-five years old, and Cosette was eight. Yet it seemed that all the love that might have been possible through his many years was now focused into one indescribable light. It was only the second pure vision he had ever experienced. Just as the grace the bishop had shown him caused the dawn of virtue in his life, Cosette had caused the dawn of love.

Over her short life, Cosette had also become another person. She was so little when her mother had left her that she no longer remembered her. Like all children she had tried to love but had not succeeded, for her attempts had always been rejected. The Thénardiers and their children had spurned her love, and even the dog she loved had died. At eight years of age her heart was already cold, yet it was not her fault. She had the capacity for love but had never really had the opportunity for it. Now that it was presenting itself, she felt this new emotion just as Valjean did. Cosette loved this kind man from the very first day. And she did not see him as old or poor, but thought of him as handsome, just as she thought of their room as lovely.

The first story of their building was unoccupied, except for one room, which was inhabited by an old woman who did the housekeeping for Valjean. He had rented his room on Christmas Eve from this woman, and had represented himself as a gentleman who was coming there to live with his little daughter. He had paid her six months in advance.

For many weeks Valjean and Cosette lived a happy life in their modest room. She was filled with laughter, talking, and singing from dawn until dusk. He began teaching her to read and to spell. A thoughtful, angelic smile would cross his face as he taught her, for doing so dispelled his remembrance of why he had learned to read in prison—simply to accomplish more evil.

Teaching Cosette to read and allowing her to play became nearly all of Valjean's life. Yet sometimes he would tell her about her mother, and he taught her to pray. She called him, "Father," and did not know any other name for him.

He passed the hours watching her play with her doll and listening to her childish chatter. Life seemed good to him, and he no longer questioned the motives of people, but saw them as good and just. He saw no reason why he would not live to be a very old man, now that this child loved him. Valjean saw a complete future stretching out before him, illuminated by Cosette as a warm and precious light.

He protected her and she strengthened him. Thanks to him, she could walk through life—thanks to her, he could continue to walk in virtue.

CHAPTER FIFTEEN

Jean Valjean was careful not to go out during the day. At sunset each evening, however, he would walk for an hour or two—sometimes alone, but often with Cosette. He would seek out only the most deserted streets, and would often visit churches, the closest and his favorite being Saint Médard's. When Cosette did not go with him, she would stay with the housekeeper downstairs, but the child was always delighted when they would walk together. He would hold her hand as they walked, and speak sweetly to her.

They lived very modestly and kept only a small fire in their stove. On the street, Valjean was taken to be a poor man, for he wore his old worn coat and his battered hat. Occasionally, people he encountered on his walk would hand him a sou or two, which he would accept with a deep bow. Then making sure no one saw him, he would approach some poor beggar and give the coins away, while adding some money of his own. But this had its disadvantages, for in spite of attempting to do this anonymously, he became known as "the beggar who gives."

As a result, speculation began to grow over who this poor "rich" man could be. And to make matters worse, Valjean's old housekeeper and landlady, a quite cross-looking creature of a woman, was permeated with an inquisitive nature and a horrible sense of envy. She would continually watch him, scrutinizing his every move, yet without his suspecting it. She had even questioned Cosette, who had been unable to tell her anything, since the child knew nothing herself except that she had come from Montfermeil.

One morning this spy saw Valjean doing something that struck the old gossip as peculiar. He entered one of the uninhabited rooms on the first floor of the building while she observed him through the cracked door of the room across the hall. With his back turned toward her, she could see him fumbling in his pocket. He pulled out a pair of scissors and some thread, and then began to rip out the lining of his coat. Beneath the lining was a small piece of yellowish paper that she immediately recognized to be a thousand-franc bill.

The woman quickly returned to her room, wondering where such a man would get so much money. Just a moment later, he knocked on her door, handed her the bill, and asked her if she could get it broken down for him into smaller bills. He told her it was his quarterly government pension that he had received the day before. Yet she knew he had not left the building that day until six in the evening and that the government bank would have been closed at that hour. The old woman did as he asked, however, but not without mentioning her suspicions to a number of people. Therefore, that thousand-franc bill became the object of a great amount of speculation on the part of many a gossip up and down the street.

Near the well by Saint Médard's church, Valjean would often pass by a man who appeared to be a beggar about seventy-five years of age. The man was rumored to be some sort of policeman who at one time had worked in the parish, helping to maintain order in the church. Valjean never passed the man without giving him a few sous, as the man would sit there mumbling his prayers.

One evening when Valjean was out walking alone, he passed by the beggar who was in his usual place saying his prayers. Valjean placed a few coins in the man's hand, when the beggar suddenly fixed his eyes on Valjean, and then just as quickly dropped his head again.

Lightning seemed to flash through Valjean with a shudder. By the dim light of the street lantern, he had not seen the face of some unknown beggar, but that of a well-known and horrifying person from his past. He recoiled in terror, but continued to stand there, afraid to speak or even to breathe. He didn't know whether to stay or to run, but simply stared at the beggar, who no longer appeared to know he was there. Perhaps it was the instinct of self-preservation that kept Jean Valjean from uttering a word. Yet as he pondered the situation, he thought, "This man is no different than he's been any other night. I must be going mad! I must be dreaming! This is impossible!" Yet he hardly dared to confess, even to himself, that the face he thought he had seen was that of Javert.

A few days later, around eight in the evening, Valjean was in his room with Cosette, teaching her to spell. He heard the front door of the building open and close again—which struck him as odd for that time of night. He knew the old woman always went to bed at nightfall, in order to save her candles, but dismissed it, thinking perhaps she had taken ill and had gone out to get some medicine from the doctor. Yet, upon hearing someone climbing the stairs, he signaled for Cosette to be quiet as he listened.

After quite a long time of silence, he quietly looked through the keyhole of his door. He saw a light that seemed to form a sinister star in the blackness of the stairwell. Obviously, someone was there, holding a candle and listening. Several minutes later the light finally retreated, but he heard no footsteps, and realized that the person who had been listening had removed his shoes.

That night Valjean did not sleep at all and remained fully clothed as he lay on his bed. At daybreak, just as he was finally dozing off from fatigue, he was awakened by the creaking of a door at the other end of the attic hallway. Then he heard the same heavy footsteps he had heard climbing the stairs the preceding evening. As though shot from the bed, he sprang toward the door and once again peered through the keyhole. Whoever it was walked past his door this time without pausing. The corridor was too dark to see the person's face, but when the man reached the staircase a morning ray of light formed his silhouette, giving Valjean a complete view of his back. The man was of lofty stature, wore a long coat, and carried a large walking stick under his arm. The strong neck and shoulders were those of Javert.

When the old woman came to work in his room at seven in the morning, Valjean cast a penetrating stare at her, but did not ask any questions. She acted normally as she swept the floor, and then remarked to him, "Possibly you heard someone come in last night."

"Yes, I did," he replied, as nonchalantly, as possible. "Who was it?"

"It was a new tenant who has just rented a room here," she replied.

"What's his name?"

"I'm not exactly sure. It's Dumont or Daumont, or something."

"And who is this Monsieur Dumont?" Valjean questioned.

The old woman simply stared at him with her beady eyes, and answered, "A wealthy gentleman, like you." Perhaps she had no ulterior motive in saying this, but Valjean thought he detected one.

When darkness came, he descended the stairs and carefully scrutinized both sides of the street. It appeared to be absolutely deserted, although someone could have easily been hidden behind the trees. He quickly returned to his room and said to Cosette, "Come with me." Then, taking her by the hand, they departed.

Valjean deliberately took nothing but side streets and would often double back in order to make sure he was not being followed. There was a full moon, still near the horizon, casting quite a bit of light and long shadows onto the streets. Because of this, Valjean and Cosette were able to walk along the dark side of the street, while keeping an eye on the lighted side. By the time they came to the Rue Poliveau, he felt certain they were not being followed.

Cosette walked along without asking any questions—a passiveness that the suffering of the last six years had instilled into her nature. Of course, she had grown accustomed to feeling safe and secure when she was with Valjean, and instinctively trusted him to know where they were going. Yet he had no more idea where they were going than Cosette.

He trusted God—she trusted him. It seemed to Valjean as though he were clinging to the hand of Someone greater than himself—as though he felt the presence of Someone leading him—yet invisible. However, he had no settled plan or course to follow. He was not even absolutely sure that the man he had seen was Javert. And even if had been Javert, perhaps Javert did not recognize him as Jean Valjean.

Valjean stepped into the shadow of a doorway, thinking that if they were being followed, he could not fail to get a good look through the moonlight shining across the way. In fact, not three minutes had passed when four men appeared. All were tall, dressed in long, brown coats and hats, and held huge walking sticks in their hands. The man who appeared to be their leader turned and quickly pointed with his hand toward the direction Valjean had headed, while another seemed to indicate the opposite direction with considerable obstinacy. Just as the leader had turned, the moonlight fell upon his face, and Valjean was sure he was beholding the face of Javert.

Uncertainty had now ended for Valjean, but fortunately for him it still lingered with the four men. He took advantage of their hesitation—time lost for them was gained for him. He slipped from the doorway where he and Cosette had been hiding and into the shadows away from the men. He could tell she was becoming tired, so he lifted her into his arms and carried her.

No one was on the streets where Valjean walked and the street lanterns had not been lit because of the full moon. Now carrying the child, he doubled his pace and headed for the heart of Paris. Several minutes later he looked back, but still saw nothing but deserted streets. Seeing no one, he drew a long, deep breath.

While still fearing, however, that he was in imminent danger, Valjean saw a plain-looking building that appeared to be uninhabited. Rapidly surveying it with his eyes, he thought he could save himself if he could only get inside. He set Cosette against the wall of the old building, while instructing her to remain silent. The only door he saw was hidden in the shadows and was perhaps a promising entryway for them. As he examined it closely, however, he realized it was not a door at all. It had no hinges or a lock and through its rotting planks he could see nothing but slabs of solid stone. What appeared to be a door was simply a wooden decoration for the façade of the building. It would have been easy to rip away the rotting wood, but he would have found himself face-to-face with the wall once again.

He noticed a pipe running up the side of the building, and briefly thought of climbing up to the roof. However, it was three stories to the top, and how would he have carried Cosette with him? Besides, he now saw a man standing on the street corner, who would have certainly seen him climbing. Valjean quickly gave up this idea and crawled back along the wall around the grounds of the building to Cosette. When he reached her, he realized no one would be able to see them there, regardless of the direction they approached. Yet he reasoned they could not stay there long and that he must act soon.

At that moment Valjean heard heavy, deliberate footsteps some distance away. He risked leaning from the shadows to glance around the corner of the street. To his dismay he saw seven or eight soldiers in formation with their bayonets drawn. They were marching down the street toward him. There could be no mistake, he figured, that this was a patrol Javert had commandeered to assist him in his search. Indeed, he soon recognized two men with the patrol as those who had earlier been with Javert. At every alleyway the men would stop to search and then continue their march in his direction.

Valjean calculated that at the rate they were traveling he had about a quarter of an hour before they would reach him. He probed the recesses of his mind as to what to do next. Because of his past, he had two compartments in which to search—one held his saintly thoughts, while the other held the talents of a criminal. He had learned to use one or the other depending on his circumstances. Among these resources, thanks to his numerous escapes from the prison at Toulon, he also had the incredible ability to scale walls, often using nothing but his sheer muscular force.

Yet climbing any wall at this point would be a problem because of Cosette. Abandoning her was out of the question, and it would be impossible to carry her up the wall. The wall appeared to be about eighteen feet high, and to get the child over it he would need a rope. Then reaching into the criminal pocket of his mind, he noticed the lamppost across the street. In those days, the lamps were lit by a worker who would climb to the top using a rope, which was kept in a locked box at the base of the light. Valjean crossed the street in what seemed to be a single bound, broke the latch on the metal box with the tip of his knife, and quickly returned to Cosette. He now had a rope.

Then, without making one useless movement, he undid his necktie and tied it around Cosette underneath her arms. Taking the rope, he tied it to the necktie, and put the other end of the rope in his teeth. He quickly took his shoes and socks off, threw them over the wall, and began climbing. Putting his fingers into the mortar grooves between the blocks of stone, he found himself atop the wall within thirty seconds. Crouching on his knees, he looked at Cosette, who stared at him in amazement, but without uttering a word. In a quiet voice, he instructed the little girl, "Put your back against the wall." She immediately obeyed, as Valjean added, "Don't say a word, and don't be afraid."

Before Cosette knew it, she was also atop the wall. Then Valjean put her on his back and crawled on his stomach along the wall. Suddenly he heard the thundering voice of Javert yelling at the patrol to search the nearby alley. Valjean quickly slid onto an adjacent roof, lowered Cosette onto the grounds of the building, and then jumped down himself. Whether it was from sheer terror or from courage, Cosette had not breathed a sound through this entire ordeal, though her hands had been somewhat scraped by the stones of the wall.

Valjean found himself next to the building whose roof had served as his means of escape. He was now standing in some sort of a very large, unique garden. No one was there, which was not uncommon considering the late hour, yet it did not seem as though the garden was made to walk in, even in broad daylight. His first concern was to put his shoes and socks back on, and then he and Cosette stepped into a small shedlike structure to hide. Of course, a man who is running from someone never believes he is sufficiently hidden.

Cosette was now trembling and stood close to him, while they heard Javert's patrol searching the nearby alleys and streets. After about a quarter of an hour had passed, it seemed as though the sound of the men had finally become more distant. Valjean continued to hold his breath, however, as he held his hand gently over Cosette's mouth. The solitude of the garden in which they stood seemed strangely calm, as though the walls were made of the deaf stones mentioned in the Scriptures. The walls—and the garden inside them—

remained peaceful—not sensing a need to cry out, although all beyond them was in an uproar.

Suddenly, in the midst of this profound calm, a new sound arose. It was as divine and celestial as the noise of the patrol had been horrible. It was a hymn so beautiful and full of a sense of prayer and harmony that one would believe it to be a heavenly sound that only a newborn baby or a dying man would ever hear. The sound was the sound of women's voices and was towering above the garden, as it wafted its way from the gloomy building next to Valjean and Cosette. Just as the sound of demons seemed to be retreating, this choir of angels seemed to be breaking through the thick darkness of the night.

Valjean and Cosette fell to their knees. They did not know what they were hearing and they did not know where they were. Yet both of them—man and child—the penitent and the innocent—felt compelled to kneel. The voices they heard had a strange quality, for they did not appear to prevent the building from seeming deserted. To them the sound was the supernatural praise of an uninhabited house.

By now a cold night wind was blowing, which was typical of one to two o'clock in the morning this time of year. Yet the poor, weary, and trembling Cosette said nothing. She simply sat down next to Valjean and leaned her head against him without one complaint. At first he thought she fell asleep, but as he bent down to look at her he saw her eyes were wide open, and her thoughtful expression troubled him. He asked the child, "Aren't you sleepy?"

"I'm just very cold," she replied. The ground was damp, and with the shed open on all sides, the breeze seemed to grow stronger every second. Valjean lovingly removed his coat and wrapped it around little Cosette.

"Is that better?" he asked.

"Oh, yes, Father," was her sweet reply, as she laid her head on a stone and fell asleep.

Valjean sat down beside her and began to think. Now feeling somewhat safe, he began to regain his composure little by little. As he gazed at the beautiful child, he clearly recognized a truth that was to become the foundation of his life going forward. He knew that as long as she was near, he would need nothing else. And as long as they were together, he would never fear for his well-being, but only for hers. In fact, since giving her his coat, he was totally unaware that he was very cold himself.

In spite of his being lost in thought, he suddenly heard a peculiar noise. It sounded like the faint tinkling of a bell, yet it was quite distinct. Upon turning in the direction of the noise, he saw someone standing in the garden. A man was walking through the melon beds, and was stooping at regular intervals, as though he were spreading something onto the ground. The man also appeared to have a limp.

Valjean shuddered when he saw the man. Now sure that he was being pursued, he was suspicious of everyone and saw anyone as potentially hostile. He could not relax during the day because it might enable someone to recognize him, nor could he relax at night because it might allow the one searching for him the opportunity for surprise. Earlier he was afraid because the garden was deserted, but now he shuddered because someone was there.

Upon seeing the man, Valjean quickly took the sleeping Cosette into his arms and placed her on the ground behind a pile of old furniture being stored at the far end of the shed. Then he began to carefully scrutinize the man working among the melons. What seemed strange to him was that every time the man moved, the small bell sounded again. Valjean pondered, "Who is this man who has a bell attached to himself like a cow or an ox?"

As he wondered, he lightly touched Cosette's hands, and found they were icy cold. "Oh, my Lord!" he cried out, softly. Then he spoke quietly to the child, "Cosette." Yet she did not open her eyes. At this, he shook her quite vigorously, but she still did not awaken. He asked himself if she were dead and then sprang to his feet, now shaking from head to toe.

Cosette was pale and was now lying totally still. He knelt over her as she was spread out on the ground and listened to her breathing. She was still alive, but her respiration was so shallow and weak, Valjean feared she was at the point of death. He wondered how he could possibly warm her back to health? Without considering the possible consequences, he rushed from the shelter of the shed. He was certain he must find some way to put her beside a fire in a very few minutes, and then put her to bed.

Valjean walked straight up to the man he saw in the garden, as he pulled a hundred francs from the pocket of his coat. The man was bent over and did not see him approaching, when Valjean said, "One hundred francs!" Startled, the man quickly looked at Valjean, who continued, "One hundred francs, if you will give me shelter for the night." The moonlight fully illuminated Jean Valjean's terrified countenance.

With words of great surprise, the man exclaimed, "Monsieur Madeleine! Is it you?"

Hearing these unexpected words, especially at such a late hour and in an unfamiliar place, Valjean was greatly startled. The man, who obviously knew him as Mayor Madeleine, was a stooped old man who was partially lame. He was dressed like a peasant and wore a leather covering on his left knee, which had a small bell attached. His face was in the shadow of the moonlight and was therefore not recognizable to Valjean.

Trembling all over, the man removed his cap and excitedly continued, "Why are you here, Monsieur Madeleine? Where did you come from? Did you fall from heaven? That wouldn't surprise me in the least. And look how you're dressed, on such a cold night! You have no hat or coat."

"Who are you and what building is this?" demanded Valjean.

"Oh, pardon me, but this is too much!" exclaimed the old man. "I am the man you arranged this job for, and this is the house where you yourself had me taken. Don't you recognize me?"

"No," said Valjean, with a puzzled expression on his face. "And how is it that you know me?"

"You saved my life," the man answered.

The man turned slightly, and the moonlight outlined his profile. Suddenly Valjean recognized him as old Fauchelevent, the man he had once rescued from underneath his broken cart. Then he said, "Yes, of course, I remember you, Monsieur Fauchelevent. But what are you doing out so late tonight?"

"I'm covering the melons in the garden. With such a full moon, I figured it would be quite cold tonight, and I didn't want them to freeze." Then returning to the matter at hand, he added, "But tell me why you are here."

Valjean, realizing he was now known to this man—at least as Madeleine—still proceeded cautiously. Then, in spite of being the intruder, he reversed their roles and became the questioner by asking, "What is this bell you are wearing on your knee?"

"This," replied Fauchelevent, "is so I may be avoided."

"What do you mean? Avoided?"

Old Fauchelevent winked, and said with a slight smile, "Oh, yes! You see, there are only women in this house—many of them young girls. I am not to be seen by them, so the bell gives them a warning that I am coming. So when I come, they go."

"What kind of house is this?" Valjean questioned.

"Come now, surely you know."

"No, I really do not," replied Valjean, in a serious tone.

"But you got me the job here as the gardener?"

"Please refresh my memory, as though I knew nothing," Valjean insisted.

"This is the Convent of the Petit Picpus in the Saint Antoine Quarter," Fauchelevent reminded him. At these words, Valjean's memory seemed to be suddenly restored. As the memories came flooding back to him, he marveled how chance—or more correctly, Providence—had brought him to the very place he himself had recommended for Fauchelevent, after the old man had been crippled by the fall from his cart some two years before.

Valjean then mumbled softly, but with a sense of astonishment, "The Convent of the Petit Picpus."

"Exactly!" old Fauchelevent resounded. "But tell me Monsieur Madeleine, how in the world did you manage to get in here? For even if you are a saint, you are still a man, and no man is allowed in here."

"You're certainly here, aren't you?" retorted Valjean.

"Well, no one but me is allowed."

"Still," pleaded Valjean. "I must stay here." Then leaning toward the old man, he whispered in a somber voice, "After all, Monsieur Fauchelevent, I saved your life."

"Yes, I know. And I had to remind you of that," the old man responded.

"Well, you can now repay the favor, for what I did for you two years ago."

"It would be a blessing from God if I could do something for you! What do you want me to do?" Fauchelevent asked.

"I will explain everything," Valjean said, with a tone of assurance. "Do your have an extra room with a bed?"

"All I have is my small cabin over there, behind the ruins of the old convent. No one ever goes in there but me. It has three rooms in it."

"Great! It's settled then. Now, Monsieur Fauchelevent, I have two requests to make of you."

"Certainly, what do you need?" the man asked, kindly.

"First, that you not tell anyone what you know about me. And second, that you not attempt to learn anything more."

Fauchelevent responded with a reassuring look and said, "Monsieur Madeleine, I know that you can do nothing dishonorable, and that you have always been a man of God. Besides, it was you who got me this place to stay. It is yours, and I am your servant."

Then with a sense of urgency Valjean said, "Please come with me. We will go and get the child."

"There is a child!" the old man said in amazement. Then without saying another word, he followed Valjean obediently, as a faithful dog follows his master.

Less than half an hour later, Cosette's cheeks had become rosy once again by the heat of the fire, and she was sound asleep in the old gardener's bed. Once they had put little Cosette safely to bed, Valjean and Fauchelevent sipped on a glass of wine and ate a bite of cheese, sitting before the crackling fire. Then, with the only bed in the house being occupied by Cosette, the men lay their tired bodies onto beds of straw. Before he shut his eyes, Valjean mumbled quietly, yet loudly enough that Fauchelevent overheard, "I guess we will have to stay here forever."

This remark rang through Fauchelevent's ears all night long, causing him to wonder what had brought the dear Mayor Madeleine to him under such a cloud of mystery. And despite the fact that both men were very tired, neither of them slept at all that night.

So it was into this little house that Jean Valjean had "fallen from heaven," as Fauchelevent had expressed it. Valjean now knew for sure that Javert had found him out—that he had not been drowned when he fell from the ship in Toulon. Then knowing Javert was on his trail once again, he knew he would be doomed if he walked from the convent onto the streets of Paris. He felt like a whirlwind had picked him up and deposited him in this convent. Therefore, he had but one thought—to remain there.

For a man in this unfortunate position, the convent was both the safest and the most dangerous of all places. It was the most dangerous because men were not allowed to be there. If he were discovered, he would be charged with a flagrant offense, and there would be only one step between the convent and prison. It was the safest because, if he could manage to remain there, no one would ever think to look for him in such a place. The unlikelihood of a man being in this "impossible" place brought safety.

CHAPTER SIXTEEN

--- ⚜ ---

The next morning, Fauchelevent introduced Jean Valjean and Cosette to the reverend mother of the convent. The nun stood there with her rosary in hand and a veil covering her face, while another of the nuns stood nearby scrutinizing the strange man and the little girl.

The reverend mother then began her interrogation, by inquisitively saying, "I take it you are Monsieur Fauchelevent's brother."

"Yes, Reverend Mother," replied Fauchelevent, taking advantage of the nun's incorrect assumption.

"What's your name?" she continued.

"Ultimus Fauchelevent," the old gardener replied.

"Where are you from?"

The old man spoke for Valjean again, and said, "From Picquigny, near Amiens."

"How old are you?"

"Fifty," Fauchelevent answered.

"And what is your profession?"

"He's a gardener," Fauchelevent replied.

"Are you a good Christian?" the nun demanded.

"Everyone in our family is," retorted the old gardener.

"Is this your little girl?"

Continuing his ruse, Fauchelevent said, "He is her grandfather, Reverend Mother."

At this, the other nun whispered to the reverend mother, "He answers well." Of course, Valjean had not uttered one word. Then the two nuns consulted privately with one another for a moment or two in the corner of room.

Finally, the reverend mother turned toward the gardener and said, "Monsieur Fauchelevent, you must get another kneecap with a bell. Both of you must wear one."

Later that day two bells could be heard in the garden, and the other nuns of the convent could not resist the temptation to lift the corner of their veils for a better peek at the newcomer. At the far end of the garden the two men dug side-by-side, which was an amazing sight, especially considering their pasts. All day long the nuns' vow of silence was temporarily broken as they passed the word, "He's the assistant gardener—the brother of Monsieur Fauchelevent."

From that day forward, Jean Valjean was officially the assistant gardener of the convent, and his name was Ultimus Fauchelevent. However, he had been admitted to the convent primarily due to the reverend mother's concern for the child. She believed Cosette's future would be "quite ugly," as she put it, "without our help." The nun was immediately drawn to the unfortunate child and made a place for her in the convent's school as a charity case.

Cosette shared nothing of her past with the nuns and continued to think of herself as Jean Valjean's daughter. She knew so little about Valjean that his secrets were safe with her. Plus, she had suffered so much in the past few years that she was afraid of nearly everything—even to speak or to breathe at the wrong time. She was so conditioned to one wrong word bringing an avalanche down upon her that she kept quiet.

For Valjean, the convent became an island sanctuary surrounded on all sides by raging, dangerous waves. Therefore, its four walls became his world. He was able to see enough of the sky to maintain his sanity and sense of peace, and enough of Cosette to remain happy. It was the beginning of a very sweet life for him.

He was given a room in the old cabin with Fauchelevent and enjoyed working with him. Having once been employed pruning trees—in his years before prison—Valjean gladly returned to gardening and quickly became quite useful. He used his extensive knowledge of cultivation to graft the many trees of the convent's orchard, causing them to produce a much more abundant crop.

The nuns gave Cosette permission to spend an hour each day with Valjean. In comparison to the melancholy sisters, he was always happy and kind, so the child adored him. At the appointed hour she would run to the humble cabin and to Valjean, and whenever she entered, it became paradise. The more joy he tried to bring to Cosette, the more joy he received in return—which is the godly result of giving.

When all the schoolchildren would be given time to play outside, Valjean would stop his work and watch her running and playing from a distance, and he could always distinguish her laugh from the other students. Early in the morning or late in the evening, as he would be thinking of her, he would often gaze toward her classroom or dormitory window. In God's own way, the convent was contributing—as was Cosette—to the upholding and the perfecting of the late bishop's work in Jean Valjean.

The convent was the second place of captivity Jean Valjean had seen in his life. Prison had been a fearsome and terrible place, whose severe conditions had caused him to experience the sins of justice and the criminal abuse of the law. He had been a part of the prison, but was a spectator at the convent, and mentally contrasted the two places with feelings of anxiety.

Valjean thought of his former prison companions. How wretched were their lives! They toiled from dawn until dusk, and were permitted little sleep. And what little rest they were allowed was on their thin mattresses, only two inches thick, and in rooms only heated during the harshest days of winter. They were forced to wear the bright red clothing of prison, and were only given linen trousers in the very hottest weather and wool shirts on only the coldest of days. Even these meager concessions were treated by the guards as great favors extended to the poor prisoners. They were never given any wine and ate meat on extremely rare occasions. The convicts lived nameless lives and ultimately became their assigned number. They existed with nothing but their dejected eyes, quiet voices, and shaved heads—beneath the whips of the guards and in utter disgrace.

Then Valjean's mind turned to the sisters of the convent. They also had dejected eyes, quiet voices, and shaved heads. Yet these were not forced on them in disgrace, although they suffered the scoffs of the world around them. Their given names had been taken from them as well, and they were referred to only by common designations upon entering the convent. They never ate meat or drank wine and often waited until evening to eat anything at all. They wore a black woolen shroud, which was too heavy and hot for summer, and too thin and cold for winter. And their rules would not allow them to add or subtract anything to their attire, regardless of the season.

The sisters lived, not in warm rooms, but in austere cells where no fires were ever lit. And they never slept on mattresses even two inches thick, but on beds of straw. Finally, just as they were becoming weary each night after a long day of toil, they were required to kneel for prayer in an ice-cold, dark chapel with a stone floor.

The first captivity was that of men, while this was one of women. Yet through it all, these women seemed to have a heavenly air of innocence and holiness that is only brought to earth through godly virtue. The men often whispered to each other, bragging of their crimes, while the nuns spoke out loud only when confessing their faults.

These were two bastions of slavery. Yet in prison deliverance was possible, for the length of the legal term, no matter how long, was always in sight. And, of course, escape was a possibility as well. In the convent, however, the commitment was made in perpetuity. The only escape was at the far end of the distant future—the faint light of liberty that men call death. In the first, men were bound only with chains; while in the second, women were chained by faith.

What flowed from prison was a great curse, the gnashing of teeth, hatred, desperate viciousness, rage against society, and a reproachful view of heaven. Yet what flowed from the convent was nothing but blessings and love. In these two places, so similar but so different, were two kinds of beings who were quite dissimilar—yet attempting the same process in their lives: making amends for their faults.

Jean Valjean thoroughly understood the life of the prisoner and attempting to make amends for his crimes. But he did not understand the lives of these women, whom he saw as beings above reproach and without stain. He asked himself what their faults could possibly be. Yet a voice within his conscience replied, "One of the most divine gifts of mankind is the opportunity to give your life for the sake of others, and out of a thankful and forgiven heart to pray for someone else's forgiveness."

The first high wall he had seen held the tigers of prison, while the walls he now beheld surrounded lambs. This was a place of forgiveness, not of punishment, yet the latter was more austere and dark at times than the former. And the sisters of the convent appeared even more burdened with their task at times than any convict he had ever seen.

As Valjean meditated on these thoughts, his pride vanished. He scrutinized his own heart in every possible way, felt his own insignificance, and wept. All that had happened to him in the months since rescuing Cosette seemed to take him back to the bishop's holy admonitions. Cosette led him through love to the bishop's words, while the convent led him back to those words through humility.

Often in the twilight of evening when the garden was deserted, he could be seen on his knees on the walkway near the chapel. He would gaze through the very window he peered through on the moonlit night of his arrival, knowing the sisters were at prayer inside. He saw himself as kneeling before the nuns, as though he dared not kneel directly before God Himself.

His whole heart melted in gratitude to God, and his love for Him and others continued to grow. Many years passed in this way as Cosette grew into a beautiful young woman.

CHAPTER SEVENTEEN

I n 1831, in the area of Paris near the Rue Boucherat, Rue de Normandie, and Rue de Saintonge, lived an old man called Monsieur Gillenormand. He was a bit of a curiosity to his neighbors, primarily because he had lived to quite an advanced age. At one time he had been like everyone else, but had lived so long that he was no longer like anyone around him. He was a man of the previous century and had a haughty bourgeois air that he seemed to wear as a badge of honor. He was more than ninety years of age, yet stood erect, spoke loudly, drank hard, had all thirty-two of his teeth, and still needed to wear his glasses only to read.

Gillenormand would get a shave every day by a nearby barber, who was not only jealous of the old man but also detested him. The old man was proud of his self-declared discernment in all matters, and also boasted that he was extremely shrewd. He had very little belief in God, and would often stand with his hands in his pockets and declare, "The French Revolution is nothing but a bunch of lowlife scoundrels."

Gillenormand had a daughter of fifty years of age who was unmarried, but whom he treated as though she were eight years old. In a rage, he would often chastise her severely, and would have loved to see her horsewhipped. Because of her own prudishness, no one except her immediate family ever knew her first name. She always referred to herself simply as Mademoiselle Gillenormand.

Her father had once had another daughter as well. She was born ten years after his first one, and the two girls had little in common. Although sisters, their character and countenance were as different from each other as could possibly be. The younger of the two had a charming disposition and had married a heroic soldier at an early age. The older sister also had dreams of marriage, but her goals of finding the "perfect, wealthy man" were never realized. The younger had married the man of her dreams, but had died while still quite youthful.

Mademoiselle Gillenormand lived with her father and did his house-keeping. Besides this spinster and her elderly father, there was also a little boy who lived in their house. Monsieur Gillenormand always addressed the child in the sternest of tones, and would often wave his cane at the boy and yell, "Come here, you rascal!" or "Get in here, you good-for-nothing!" The child was the son of his deceased daughter and was, therefore, the man's grandson. Because of his harsh treatment, the boy would tremble whenever his grandfather was nearby.

At this same time, in the not too distant town of Vernon, anyone crossing the beautiful bridge over the Seine would often catch a glimpse of a man working his flower garden bordering the bridge. The man was about fifty years of age, although he appeared much older, and wore a leather cap and wooden shoes, while his trousers and coat were made of coarse gray cloth. Pinned to his coat was a faded yellow ribbon. His face, deeply tanned by the sun, had a large scar running across the forehead and down the right cheek. By comparison, his face was nearly black while his hair was nearly white. His body was now stooped, and he could often be seen with his hoe and sickle in hand tending or cutting his flowers.

At the far end of his small plot of land, away from the Seine, stood a small house. The man lived a quiet and humble life in the cabin without any family, but had a plain-looking woman who lived there as his servant and house-keeper. The tiny plot he called his garden was known all over Vernon for the beauty of the flowers the man cultivated there, and it was these flowers that provided his livelihood.

The man's name was Georges Pontmercy, and anyone who knew anything of French military history knew the name. When he was quite young, during the time of the Revolution, he had been a soldier in the Rhine Army. He had been equally adept as a soldier, handling a saber or a musket, or as an officer who could lead a squadron or a battalion of men. As a career soldier, he had later accompanied Napoléon to the Island of Elba, and at Waterloo was the leader of a squadron that captured the flag of the Lunenburg battalion. He had taken the flag to the emperor and had cast it at his feet, in spite of the fact that his face was bleeding profusely from a deep sword cut he had received during the battle. Napoléon, greatly pleased, declared to him, "You are now a colonel, a baron, and an officer of the Legion of Honor!"

Thinking he would not survive the war, Pontmercy humbly replied, "Sir, I thank you on behalf of my widow."

Despite the honors bestowed on him by the emperor, all that had taken place during the Hundred Days War was forgotten once King Louis the XVIII came to power. Pontmercy was no longer considered to be a colonel, a baron, or an officer of the Legion of Honor, and was sent to Vernon where he could be kept under surveillance. Yet he continued to sign his letters as Colonel Baron Pontmercy, and would always wear his yellow ribbon, which was the designation of an officer of the Legion of Honor. The Attorney for the Crown had warned him not to wear the decoration "illegally," as he put it, but Pontmercy retorted, "I don't know whether I no longer understand French, or whether you no longer speak it. All I know is that I don't understand what you're saying." He then defiantly wore the ribbon eight straight days, and because of the esteem he enjoyed among the people, the attorney did not dare prosecute him. Yet his pay was reduced to half the normal compensation for a retired soldier, which is what forced him to lease the smallest house he could find in Vernon.

Between the two wars, while Emperor Napoléon was in power, Pontmercy had found time to marry, and it was he who was the heroic soldier who had married the younger of Monsieur Gillenormand's daughters. The old bourgeois man had reluctantly given his daughter permission to marry, and had sighed at the time, "I guess even the greatest of families are forced into this." The new Madame Pontmercy became an admirable woman in every sense, and lived a life worthy of her famous soldier husband. Yet in 1815, she had died unexpectedly, leaving a small son, who became the joy of the colonel's life. However, Monsieur Gillenormand demanded possession of his grandson and declared he would disinherit the lad unless Pontmercy gave the child to him. The boy's father, believing he was doing what was best for the child, yielded to the grandfather, and then attempted to transfer his love to his flowers instead. After this, he tried to keep his lonely mind occupied with his trivial tasks or thoughts of his past glories.

Monsieur Gillenormand had no contact whatsoever with his son-in-law, but would occasionally refer to him mockingly as "His Baronship." He and Pontmercy had agreed that the colonel should never attempt to see his son or speak to him, under penalty of seeing the boy returned, yet disowned and disinherited. Gillenormand and his spinster daughter thought of Pontmercy as a man afflicted with the plague, and intended to raise the child in their own way. Pontmercy submitted to all of this, continuing to think it was in the boy's best interest, and that no one but the colonel himself was sacrificing anything.

Actually Gillenormand's estate did not amount to much, but the boy stood to inherit a considerable sum from Mademoiselle Gillenormand. She had inherited a large estate from her mother's side of the family, and her sister's son was her natural heir.

The boy's name was Marius, and he knew only that his father was living. No one volunteered any information to him, and he was discouraged from asking any questions. Yet due to his grandfather's whispers and innuendoes, he picked up the fact that his father was only to be thought of with a sense of painful shame.

While Marius was growing up in this way, Pontmercy would slip away from Vernon every two or three months, and like a criminal violating his parole would quietly sneak into Paris. He would conceal himself behind a pillar in the Saint Sulpice Church at the time the boy's aunt would take him to mass. Hardly daring to breathe, lest Mademoiselle Gillenormand should see him, he would stand there trembling as he gazed at his son.

The priest, from his vantage point near the altar, would often see a man standing quietly near a pillar of the church. He wondered about this man who stood there staring at a boy in the pew, while large tears streamed down the man's scarred face.

The priest's heart went out to him.

Marius Pontmercy pursued his studies well as a child, and upon finally being somewhat free from the hands of his aunt and his grandfather, the young man entered college and then law school. He did not love his grandfather, very much, for the old man's cynicism repelled him and wounded his spirit. And his feelings toward his father were nothing but a dark void. On the whole he had a stern personality, but was passionate to the point of fanaticism in his political leanings, declaring himself to be a Royalist. He was proud, yet generous, was a religious and enthusiastic young man, and was honorable and pure to a fault.

One evening in 1827, when Marius was seventeen, he returned home and saw his grandfather holding a letter. As soon as he walked in, his grandfather looked up and said, "Marius, tomorrow you must go to Vernon."

"Why?" Marius asked, with a puzzled look on his face, for he knew no one in that town.

"To see your father," his grandfather said dryly.

At this, Marius began to tremble. He had often thought about his father, but never dreamed he would be asked to actually see him. Nothing could have been more unexpected, or more unpleasant, in his thinking. What had been nearly a lifetime of estrangement was now being forced into reconciliation.

In addition to seeing his father in the wrong political camp, he was convinced that the "slasher"—as his grandfather called him on a good day— did not love him. To him, this was undeniable, since he had abandoned him into the care of others. Therefore, feeling he was not loved, he did not love in return. "Nothing could be more simple," he thought.

Marius was so taken back by his grandfather's words that he was speechless. His grandfather explained, "It appears your father is quite ill, and is requesting your presence." After a short pause, the old man added, "You must leave first thing tomorrow morning. There is a coach that leaves at six o'clock and arrives in the early evening. This message says for you to hurry."

Seeing his task as unpleasant, Marius nevertheless considered it his duty to obey. So the next evening at dusk, Marius found himself in Vernon. He asked the first person he saw for "Monsieur Pontmercy's house." He refused to say, "Colonel Pontmercy's house," for in his own mind he agreed with the restoration of the king, and, therefore, did not recognize his father's claim to either his title of colonel or baron.

The house was quickly pointed out to him. He rang the bell and a woman opened the door and stood before him with a lamp in her hand. Marius simply asked, "Monsieur Pontmercy?" The woman remained motionless.

Marius then demanded, "Is this his house?"

The woman nodded, at which Marius added, "Then may I speak with him?"

At these words, the woman shook her head.

"But I am his son!" insisted Marius. "He is expecting me."

"He is no longer expecting you," the woman said. Marius suddenly noticed that the woman was weeping, as she pointed to the door of one of the rooms.

Marius quickly entered the room, which was lit by only one candle sitting on the fireplace mantel. In the room were three men: one standing, one kneeling, and one lying on the floor. The one on the floor was the colonel, and the one kneeling was a priest who was obviously engaged in prayer. The one standing was the man's doctor.

Even in the dim light of the candle, a large tear could be seen on the pale cheek of the colonel, which had trickled from his now dark eye. The light of his eyes had been extinguished, yet the tear was not yet dry. Marius was just moments too late, and his father's tear was for his son's delay.

Marius gazed at his father, a man he had not seen for many years. He looked at his strong, manly face and his eyes that were still open, but which no longer could see him. He noticed his white hair and then his muscular arms, which bore the marks of many swords and bullet holes. Finally he contemplated the large scar across the man's face. The scar spoke of heroism, but something greater marked his entire countenance—the goodness of God.

As he reflected on the fact that this man was his father, and that he was now dead, a chill ran down his spine. Yet the sorrow he felt was no greater than he would have felt for any other dead man he would have happened to see.

The colonel had left no estate, and the sale of his furniture would barely cover his burial expenses. While Marius stood there motionless, the old woman handed him a scrap of paper. On the note, written in the colonel's own handwriting were these words:

> "For my son, Marius. Emperor Napoléon made me a baron on the
> battlefield of Waterloo. Since the Restoration disputes my right to the
> title, which was purchased with my own blood, I leave it to my son.
> He shall take it, and I am confident that over time he will be worthy
> of its use. Also, during that same battle, a sergeant by the name of
> Thénardier saved my life. I have heard that recently he has been
> running a little inn in Montfermeil, a village in the outskirts of Paris.
> If my son ever meets him, I want him to do all the good that he can
> for Thénardier."

Marius took the paper and kept it safe, not so much out of a sense of duty to his father, but out of a sense of vague respect for death that seems to be inherently demanded by the hearts of men. Nothing else remained of the poor colonel. Monsieur Gillenormand even had his son-in-law's sword and uniform sold to an old clothing dealer. And the dead man's neighbors devastated his beautiful garden and pillaged his rare flowers. Ultimately all the flowering plants were taken over by weeds and died as well.

After his father's burial, some forty-eight hours later, Marius returned to Paris and to his law studies. He wore a bit of black crepe on his hat, but had no more thoughts of his father than if the man had never lived at all.

In two days the colonel was buried, and in three—forgotten.

CHAPTER EIGHTEEN

⚜

Marius continued going to Mass on a regular basis, just as he had been taught in his childhood. One Sunday he attended church at Saint Sulpice, in the same chapel his aunt had taken him many times as a lad. This particular morning, feeling more contemplative than normal, he knelt down behind a pillar next to a velvet-covered chair. The service had hardly begun, when an old man who was one of the parish officers appeared, and said to Marius, "This is my chair, sir."

The young man promptly stepped aside, so the old man could be seated in his chair, but he stood throughout the service just a few steps away. Once the mass was concluded, the old man approached him and said, "I beg your pardon, sir, for having disturbed you earlier. You must have thought me rude, but please allow me to explain myself."

"There is no need of that, sir," Marius said.

"Yes, there is," continued the old man. "I don't want you to think badly of me. But, you see, I am quite attached to this place. I enjoy the Mass much better from here, for it is very special to me. It was in this very place that I often watched a poor, brave father come every two or three months for many years. I was able to find out that he had no other way to see his child, because he was prevented from doing so by family arrangements. The little boy never suspected that his father was there. Perhaps the poor child had never even been told that he had a father. The man stood behind this pillar so that he would not be seen—weeping all the while. That poor man adored the little fellow. I could see that plainly. Therefore, this spot has become holy in my eyes, and I have gotten into the habit of listening to the Mass from here.

"Once I even had the opportunity to learn something about the man. Some time ago I was visiting my brother in Vernon when I saw him. My brother was his priest and told me some of the poor man's history. It seems he had a father-in-law who threatened to disinherit the child if he, the boy's father, ever saw him. He sacrificed himself for his son's happiness and future inheritance. Apparently the man's father-in-law demanded this agreement because of the man's political persuasions. Some people just don't know where to stop! Just because a man fought at Waterloo doesn't make him a monster, and that is certainly no reason to separate a man from his child. He had a deep battle scar across his face, and his name was something like Pontmarie or Montpercy. He was one of Napoléon's colonels, and I believe he is now dead."

"His name was Pontmercy," Marius stated, but his face had turned ashen.

"Yes, that's it! Did you know him?"

"Sir," Marius offered, "he was my father."

The old man clasped his hands in delight, pulled them to his chest, and exclaimed, "Then you are the child! Yes, I guess he would be a man by now. Well, dear child, I can honestly say that you had a father who loved you dearly!"

Marius, feeling overwhelmed by what he had just learned, simply offered his arm to the elderly man and walked him to his house. The following day he said to his grandfather, "I have planned a hunting trip with several friends. May I have permission to be gone for three days?"

His grandfather replied, "Take four days if you like. Go and have a good time."

Marius had no intention of taking a hunting trip—except one to find out more about his father. Suddenly he had become obsessed with knowing all he could about this man who had loved him after all. He went straight to the library of his law school and searched all the files, newspapers, and histories of the Republic and the Empire for any mention of Colonel Georges Pontmercy. He devoured everything, and even went to visit one of the generals his father had served with during his military career. The general knew many details of his father's life in Vernon as well, and Marius was learning to see his father as the rarest of men—one who reflected all the best qualities of a lion and a lamb at the same time. In fact, the son was quickly traveling down the road of adoration when he thought of his father.

The young man's political ideas were also undergoing extraordinary transformation. Reading the history of his father and the history of those times startled and bewildered him. Up to that point the Republic and the Empire had only been monstrous words to him. Marius had always seen the Republic as a guillotine at dusk and the Empire as a sword in the night. Yet he was now beginning to realize that he had no more understood the politics of his country than he had intimately known his father. He felt he had not known either one and had willingly allowed a total darkness to cover his eyes. But now his eyes were wide opened.

Marius perused the many bulletins of his father's grand army. They were heroic stories penned on the very field of battle. He would always see the name of the emperor, and would often behold his own father's name. He felt as though the great Empire was presenting itself to him, and a flood seemed to be rising within him. At times it seemed his father was close enough to breathe on him and would whisper in his ear. Once, without fully realizing what was happening within him or what sudden impulse he was obeying, he sprang to his feet, stretched both arms out the window, and while staring into what appeared to him to be infinite darkness, he loudly exclaimed, "Long live the emperor!"

Like many converts to a new religion, Marius's political conversion intoxicated him. He threw himself headlong into it and went too far. Fanaticism for the sword took possession of him, for his political idolatry was divine on the one hand, but was becoming brutal on the other. He entirely shed his Royalist skin and donned the hide of a revolutionary. It was then that he went to an engraver and ordered his personal cards, which read: Le Baron Marius Pontmercy.

From time to time Marius would once again take one of his "hunting trips," and his aunt began to wonder where he was really going. On one of these trips, which were always brief, he went to Montfermeil. He went there in order to obey his father's instructions to find the old sergeant of Waterloo—the innkeeper named Thénardier. Yet the inn had failed financially, and no one knew what had happened to Thénardier.

This trip had taken Marius four days, and his grandfather said while he was gone, "This boy is becoming too wild."

The young man's grandfather and his aunt began to scrutinize his every move, and one day they thought they noticed something under his shirt, which was attached to a black ribbon and worn around his neck.

Marius's spinster aunt, Mademoiselle Gillenormand, had another relative she was quite fond of by the name of Lieutenant Théodule Gillenormand. He was her grandnephew, and the primary reason she was so fond of him was that she had so little contact with the young man. He was in the military and had all the qualities that made him a competent officer. He visited Paris so rarely that Marius had never seen him. Therefore, the two cousins knew each other in name only.

One morning while Marius was on another of his "hunting trips" away from home, his aunt's curiosity was overwhelming her. She was attempting to take her mind off of him by sewing, and had been working for several hours when someone knocked on her door. It was her grandnephew.

Uttering a cry of delight, the soldier's aunt exclaimed, "Théodule! It's so good to see you! What brings you to town?"

"I'm just passing through, and will be here only until evening. Our garrison is being transferred, and we had to come through Paris."

"Are you traveling by horseback with the rest of your regiment?" she asked.

"No, I asked for permission to visit you, and another soldier is taking my horse for me. I will catch up with my unit by coach. By the way, I wanted to ask you something."

"Yes, what is it?"

"Is my cousin Marius traveling today as well?" he asked.

"What makes you think that?" she questioned with surprise. Suddenly her curiosity regarding Marius was piqued even further.

"Well, when I got to Paris, I first went to book my seat on the coach for this evening," he began.

"And?" she said, attempting to pull the information from him more quickly.

"I happened to see the names of the other passengers, and Marius Pontmercy was one of them," he added.

"Oh! I wonder what he's up to. Where could he be going?" she wondered aloud.

"He's just traveling—like I am," he answered.

"Yes, but in your case it's your duty. In his case, I believe there's something strange happening."

Then an idea suddenly struck her, and she asked, "Would your cousin recognize you?"

"No, I have seen him from a distance, but I don't believe he has ever seen me," the young soldier answered.

"And where is the coach headed tonight?"

"Ultimately to Les Andelys, but I get off at Vernon, in order to catch another coach for Gaillon. I have no idea where Marius is headed," he explained.

"Listen, Théodule, I would like your help with something. Marius has been spending more and more time away from here, and I would love to know what is he is doing."

"Oh, he's probably just chasing some young woman's skirt," he said with a smile.

"You're probably right, but do me a favor. How about following Marius, if you can? Since he doesn't know you, it should be easy. And if you catch a glimpse of the young woman, then write to let me know all the details. I'm sure it will amuse Marius's grandfather, too."

Smiling again, slyly, he agreed by saying, "As you please, Aunt. I'd be happy to be my cousin's 'chaperone.'" Then, after receiving a hug from his aunt, the young lieutenant departed.

That evening Marius boarded the coach and promptly fell asleep, totally unaware he was being watched. Around sunrise the next morning the coach pulled into Vernon, and Marius stepped down and quickly began walking down the street. Since Théodule had several hours before his other coach was due to depart, he had time to follow his cousin.

A little peasant girl standing on the street corner, her arms loaded with bouquets of flowers, began shouting to Marius and the other travelers, "Don't forget to buy flowers for your lady!" Marius turned, walked to her, and purchased one of the finest selections in her nearby basket.

Lieutenant Théodule, watching from a distance, thought in amusement, "To deserve such a fine bouquet of flowers, this woman must really be something. I can hardly wait to see her." At this point he began following Marius out of his own sense of curiosity, not just because he had promised his aunt he would do so.

Marius did not notice he was being followed, and he walked past a number of attractive women, yet never so much as glanced at them. It seemed he saw nothing around him, which led Théodule to think, "He must be very much in love!"

Moments later the young soldier realized Marius was headed toward the church. "Great!" Théodule said to himself, "A rendezvous spiked with 'a bit of mass' is the best kind. There's nothing like trying to pull one over on God."

Yet once Marius got to the church, he continued right past it. Then he disappeared around the back of the building. "I guess he's meeting her outside. Perhaps I'll get an even better look at the lass," the lieutenant speculated.

Upon reaching the back of the church, however, Théodule stopped in amazement. He saw Marius kneeling over a grave. He had spread the flowers over the small plot and was covering his bowed head with his hands as he sobbed aloud. At the far end of the grave stood a plain cross, which was fashioned out of black wood. On the cross in white letters was written the name: Colonel Baron Pontmercy.

Marius' cousin suddenly realized that the "lass" was a grave.

It was to his father's grave that Marius had been going nearly every time his aunt and his grandfather had wondered were he was. Lieutenant Théodule was so taken back and deeply moved by his cousin's visit to a grave that he did not know what to write to his aunt—so he decided not to write at all.

Two days later Marius took the long coach trip back to Paris. Sweaty and tired by two full nights spent riding in a coach in just three days, he went straight to his room, and undressed to take a bath. He flung his coat and the black ribbon that he wore around his neck onto the bed.

Monsieur Gillenormand had heard his grandson return and slowly climbed the stairs to question him as to where he had been, yet once he reached Marius's room, the young man was already in the bath. As he looked around the room he suddenly spied the black ribbon that had piqued his curiosity for so long. Unable to resist the temptation, he grabbed it and the young man's coat and hurried downstairs.

Triumphantly swinging back and forth the locket that was attached to the ribbon, he strutted into the room where Mademoiselle Gillenormand was busy with her sewing. Then he declared, "Victory! We are about to expose the mystery!" He took the locket, gazed at it for several moments, and as though filled with a sense of pure rapture, pried it open with his wrinkled fingers.

Both the father and his daughter surmised they would find a portrait inside, yet to their surprise, when the locket was open, they found nothing but a carefully folded piece of paper. The old spinster, bursting out in laughter, said, "I know what that is! It's a love letter! Let's read it."

Then putting on her glasses, the woman unfolded the paper and began to read, "For my son, Marius. Emperor Napoléon made me a baron on the battlefield of Waterloo. Since the Restoration disputes my right to the title, which was purchased with my own blood, I leave it to my son. He shall take it, and I am confident that over time he will be worthy of its use."

It would be impossible to fully describe their feelings at this moment. It seemed as though the chill of death ran down their spines, and they did not say a word for a moment or two. Finally, Monsieur Gillenormand, rereading the note for himself, mumbled, "This is in the slasher's own handwriting."

Marius's aunt quickly returned the paper to the locket, as her father searched the pockets of the young man's coat. He pulled a blue paper packet from the coat, and taking it from him, the old woman began unwrapping it. Inside were the cards Marius had recently had printed, which read: Le Baron Marius Pontmercy.

Just as his grandfather was reading the card, Marius walked into the room. Then seeing his grandson, the elderly man said, with an air of sarcasm and superiority that seemed crushing, "Well, well, well. So you are a baron now. Congratulations!" Then he asked, "What is the meaning of this?"

Marius reddened slightly, and replied, "It means that I am the son of my father."

Monsieur Gillenormand laughed cynically, and said harshly, "I am your father."

"My father," retorted Marius, looking down, but with sternness in his voice, "was a humble and heroic man who served the Republic and France gloriously. He was one of the greatest men in our history and served his country for more than a quarter of a century. He lived through snow, rain, and mud, day and night, and was wounded twenty times or more for what he believed. He died abandoned, alone, and forgotten, and his only crime was to love two ingrates: his country and his son."

This was more than Marius's grandfather could bear to hear. At the word *Republic* he sprang to his feet. The old Royalist's face turned as bright red as a branding iron, while pure rage arose within him.

"Marius!" he screamed. "You are an abomination! I don't know what your father was, and I don't want to know! But I do know this: There were only scoundrels among those men. Anyone who served Napoléon or Robespierre was a thief and an assassin. They were all traitors who betrayed their king, and they were all cowards who fled before the Prussians and the English at Waterloo!"

At these words, Marius stood motionless for several moments. His mind was whirling. What was he to do? His father had just been trampled underfoot by his own grandfather! How could he possibly avenge the one without outraging the other? Finally, staggering as though intoxicated, he glared at his grandfather and thundered, "Down with that pig, Louis XVIII!"

Although Louis XVIII had been dead for four years, it was all the same to Marius, and his meaning was certainly understood. The old man's face, which moments earlier had been crimson, turned whiter than his hair. He responded, coldly, "A baron like you and a bourgeois like me cannot possibly live under the same roof." Then pointing a trembling finger toward the door, and with the lightning of anger flashing across his eyes, he shouted, "Get out!"

Marius left. The following day Monsieur Gillenormand said to his daughter, "Send sixty pistoles every six months to that bloodsucker, and never mention his name to me again."

The young revolutionary had left without saying—or even knowing—where he was going. All he had was thirty francs, his watch, and a few clothes in a bag. He hired a carriage and instructed the driver to take him to the Latin Quarter.

Only God knew what was to become of Marius.

CHAPTER NINETEEN

꧁

uring this period, despite appearances to the contrary, certain
revolutionary wind currents began to stir. They had begun as breaths
in 1789 and 1793 at the beginning of the Revolution, and were in the
air once again. In Paris at this time there were many new political groups,
including the Friends of the ABC, whose stated purpose was to foster the
education of children and the elevation of mankind.

They were known as Friends of the ABC, because in French, ABC is
pronounced ah-bay-say, exactly like the French word *abaissé*, which means
abased. Thus, they considered themselves to be "friends of the abased" or
"friends of the people." They were in the embryonic stage of forming their secret
society, and their numbers were few. The group had two meeting places in Paris,
one near the fish market in a wine shop called Corinthe, and another on the
Rue Saint Michel in a little café called Café Musain, whose back room soon
became their primary meeting location.

When they met they would smoke and drink, gamble and laugh, and
shout about a number of issues while whispering about certain ones. Nailed to
the wall was something nearly sure to draw the suspicion of any good
policeman—an old map of the French Republic during the Revolution and
before the restoration of the king.

The majority of the Friends of the ABC were students who were on quite
good terms with the working classes. The principal leaders were three young
men by the names of Enjolras, Bossuet, and Courfeyrac, who had formed such
a strong bond of friendship that they had become like family.

Enjolras was an only son, was rich, and was a charming young man, but was quite capable of being terrible. He was angelically handsome, but had a savage side as well, for depending on the circumstances he could be as pious as a priest or as defiant as a well-trained soldier fighting for his life. He was indeed a priest of the ideals he held, and had only one passion—to overthrow any obstacle that stood in his way.

Bossuet seemed to be a happy but quite unlucky fellow, for his specialty was not to succeed at anything. Yet to counter his unluckiness, he seemed to laugh at everything. At twenty-five years old, he was already bald, and had already run through the complete inheritance his deceased father had left him. The house and land he had inherited had been used as collateral for a risky venture, and now nothing remained.

Courfeyrac brought a sense of balance to his friends and tried to keep them from extremes. He was the center of the group in nearly every respect. His father was known as Monsieur de Courfeyrac, a designation of aristocracy, which led the young man to refer to himself simply as Courfeyrac.

Each of these young men was quite different, yet they all believed in only one religion: progress. They thought of themselves as sons of the French Revolution, and even when laughing and joking, they would suddenly become serious at the mention of the date 1789.

One afternoon, as Bossuet was leaning on a doorpost of Café Musain, a carriage passed slowly by, as though the driver was not sure where he was headed. Seated next to the driver was a young man who had a rather bulky leather bag at his feet. Sewn onto the bag was another piece of leather imprinted with the name Marius Pontmercy.

Seeing Marius, who looked out of place in the area, Bossuet called out, "Where do you live, my friend?"

"In this cab," Marius answered.

"You must be very rich," Bossuet said, with a smile, "because your rent on that 'house' must be nine thousand francs per year."

Courfeyrac emerged from the café just as Marius explained by saying,

"Actually I've only used this carriage for the last two hours. I need to get rid of it, but I don't know where to go."

"Then come to my place, sir," Courfeyrac said, as he climbed onto the carriage. Then without waiting for a response, he instructed the driver to go to the Hotel de la Porte Saint Jacques. That evening Marius found himself in a room of the hotel right next door to Courfeyrac, and within a very few days the two had become friends.

One morning Courfeyrac's increasing curiosity as to Marius's political persuasion led him to abruptly ask, "By the way, Marius, do you have any political opinions?"

Seemingly taken back by the question, Marius retorted, "How dare you ask that!"

Yet Courfeyrac persisted by saying, "What are you?"

Relenting, Marius mumbled, "I'm a Bonapartist Democrat."

Because of Marius's admission, the following day Courfeyrac introduced Marius to the Friends of the ABC gathered at Café Musain. Then leaning close to Marius, he whispered in his ear with a smile, "I have just introduced you to the Revolution."

Marius had now become part of a group that would immediately begin to challenge and stretch his thinking. Quiet by nature, he had fallen into a hornets' nest of ideas with young men who were used to making those ideas known as flamboyantly as possible. Initially uneasy with his new surroundings and friends, Marius was nevertheless up to the challenge and eager to learn more.

Life for Marius, now separated from his aunt and grandfather, became very difficult. He endured tremendous hardships and times of great misery, even being forced to "eat" his clothes and his watch, for he sold whatever he could to afford food. Marius also learned to "eat" of the many indignities of the poor. He suffered days without bread, nights without sleep or even the use of a candle, a hearth without fire, weeks without work, and finally a future without hope. His remaining coat had holes at the elbows, and his only hat evoked the laughter of even the street urchins. He would often find his door locked due to his rent being late, and would then be forced to endure the sneers of his neighbors. He was humiliated and saw his dignity being trampled, yet he was learning that often these are the only things a person has to devour.

Marius took whatever work he could find, and would take his meager earnings to the baker, just before closing, to buy a leftover loaf of bread at a reduced price. He would then carry it off as though he had stolen the bread and secretly eat it in his attic room. Sometimes he would stop by the butcher shop and buy a mutton cutlet for six or seven sous. This small piece of meat would last him three days, for the first day he would eat the meat, the second day he would eat the fat, and the third day he would gnaw the bone.

Over the next couple of years his Aunt Gillenormand made repeated attempts to send him sixty pistoles, as instructed by her father. Yet in spite of his miserable condition, Marius would return the money each time with a note stating that he needed nothing. The young man was still in mourning for his father as the stirrings of revolution within him were continuing to grow. Out of respect for his father and his father's politics, he wanted to wear only black garments, but his clothes were rapidly wearing out or disappearing. He had traded his coat away, and he knew his trousers would be worn out soon. Courfeyrac, concerned about his new friend, gave him an old coat. Marius was thankful for the gift, but was dismayed by the coat's green color. Therefore, he only wore it after nightfall, which caused the dark green to appear black. Since he always wanted to be seen in mourning, Marius began clothing himself with the darkness of the night.

In spite of the hardships, he continued his studies and finally was hired into a practice as a lawyer. Courfeyrac gave him access to his library of law books, which allowed Marius to meet the legal regulations for a practicing attorney. Almost immediately Marius sent a letter to his grandfather informing him that he had become a lawyer. The letter was not overly warm, but was respectful. Monsieur Gillenormand's hands trembled as he read the note, and then he tore it into four pieces and threw it into the wastebasket. A couple of days later, Marius's aunt could hear her father talking to himself while alone in his room. She knew he did this whenever he was especially agitated. The angry old man simply said, "If you were not such a fool, you would know that you could never be a baron and a lawyer at the same time."

Marius had now passed through the worst straits, and a narrow passage seemed to be opening before him. Through hard work, courage, determination, and perseverance he had managed to begin earning about seven hundred francs a year. In school he had become fluent in German and English, which he put to use by doing some work for a publisher who was a friend of Courfeyrac. Supplementing his law income by translating newspapers, editing books, and compiling biographies for the publishing house kept his income steady month after month.

With his prospects brighter, Marius moved from his attic room and rented one in the Gorbeau House. He paid thirty francs per year for rent and paid the housekeeper who lived downstairs an additional three francs per month to sweep his place and to bring him hot water, an egg, and a roll every morning. He had only the bare necessities of furniture, but what he had belonged to him. He ate only half portions of meat and vegetables, filling his stomach with bread instead. By doing this and other things, such as drinking water rather than wine, he was able to keep his expenses for food, lodging, and incidentals at no more than four hundred and fifty francs per year. With clothing costing him a hundred francs per year and his linens and laundry adding no more than another hundred francs, he was able to keep his total below six hundred and fifty francs. He owned an everyday suit and another for special occasions, and, of course, both were black. Owning two complete suits of clothes and keeping his expenses in line—he now felt rich!

Yet it had taken Marius three extremely difficult years to attain this somewhat flourishing condition. He had never given up, but had continued to forge ahead every single day. He had experienced everything the poor and destitute typically experience, except that he had never taken on any debt. To him debt was the beginning of slavery, if not worse. By his way of thinking a slave only had his person controlled by another, whereas a debtor lost his dignity as well. So rather than borrow, he went without food, and spent many a day fasting. Through all his trials he felt he possessed a secret, inner strength in his soul that always encouraged him and even lifted him up at times.

Besides his father's name, another name seemed to be engraved on Marius's heart—the name Thénardier. In his thoughts he had given the fearless sergeant who had saved his father's life, amid the flying bullets and cannonballs of Waterloo, a quite lofty—almost sacred—place of honor. Marius never separated the memory of this man from that of his father, and nearly worshiped each of them, with his father on the greater altar and Thénardier on the lesser one. And what led to even greater feelings of tenderness and gratitude toward Thénardier was what Marius had learned of the difficult circumstances of the former innkeeper in Montfermeil. Since learning of the innkeeper's ruin and bankruptcy, Marius had made untold efforts to find Thénardier, but it was as though the man had disappeared by falling into a dark abyss of misery.

Finding Thénardier and doing good to him was the only debt Marius's father had left him, and fulfilling it was a matter of honor to him. He thought that Thénardier had owed his father nothing, but had been willing to risk his own life to save the colonel. Marius felt he owed so much to Thénardier and could not ignore him now that he was in such darkness and perhaps suffering the pains of death himself.

Thinking aloud, Marius said, "Now is my turn to bring him from death to life. And I will find him!"

Three years had passed since Marius had left his grandfather, and the young man was now twenty years of age. The two of them were on no better terms than when Marius had walked out, and neither had even attempted to see or speak to the other. In spite of what Marius thought, he was mistaken in believing his grandfather did not love him. His grandfather was a harsh and crusty old man who had cursed, shouted, and stormed about with his cane, yet nevertheless he idolized Marius. Some fathers may not love their children, but no grandfather exists who does not adore his grandson.

Marius continued to work as a lawyer and did occasional work for the publishing house on the side. One of the publishers for whom he worked offered him a room in his house and a salary of fifteen hundred francs per year, which presented Marius with a difficult dilemma. His housing and pay would be considerably better, but he felt he would be giving up his liberty. He did not want to do what he considered to be menial work, although the pay would be certain—unlike the earnings of a lawyer. Marius believed if he accepted the job, he would be better off and worse off at the same time. He felt he would acquire comfort while losing his dignity. He saw it as similar to a blind man who had gotten used to his blindness, being offered partial sight in only one eye. He refused.

Toward the middle of this same year of 1831, the elderly housekeeper in Marius's rooming house told him of the plight of a family living in the building. It seems the Jondrette family was being evicted. Yet Marius, who spent the better part of every day at work, did not even know he had neighbors.

"Why are they being evicted?" he asked the woman.

"Because they are behind in their rent," the housekeeper responded.

"How much do they owe?"

"Twenty francs."

Marius, who had thirty francs hidden in a drawer, took twenty-five and gave it to the woman with these instructions, "Please use this for their rent, give the remaining five francs to the family, but do not tell them it was I who did this."

Actually, the Jondrette family had lived in the building for some time. During the period of Marius's most abject misery, he had noticed the family's two daughters as he would come and go. Yet each time he would quickly pass by, hoping not to be seen, for he believed they were making light of his old clothes and laughing at him. The fact is that they stared at him because of his good looks and the dignified way he carried himself, and they shared their dreams about him with each other.

Acting so shyly caused him to have no relationship with any young woman. Instead, he seemed to run from all of them, which led his friend Courfeyrac to give him a piece of advice. He told his shy friend, "Don't be stupid, Marius! Quit reading so many books and pay a little more attention to the ladies. Some of them do have some good points, but by blushing and running from them every time, you'll get such a reputation that no woman would ever have anything to do with you." At other times, to drive his point home, Courfeyrac would sarcastically say to Marius, "Good morning, Monsieur le Priest!"

After remarks of this nature, Marius would avoid women even more and would attempt to avoid Courfeyrac to boot. Nevertheless, in his entire world there were two women that did not cause him to flee. Yet if the truth were known he did not think of either as a woman. One was his elderly housekeeper, who had so much facial hair that Courfeyrac would joke, "That old woman wears Marius's beard so he doesn't have one of his own."

The other woman was really nothing more than a little girl. For more than a year he had seen her nearly every day, but had never made eye contact with her. Marius had first noticed her on one of his walks. Each day he would see her seated on the same bench near the end of a quiet alleyway next to Luxembourg Park, with a man seated next to her who appeared to Marius to be about sixty years of age. The man seemed somewhat serious and sad, and had an air of kindness. Yet the gentleman still seemed unapproachable to Marius, for he never looked up at anyone. The old man's hair was totally white, and from his sturdy build, Marius assumed he had once been a military man who was now retired from the service.

The first time Marius had seen the man and the young girl seated together on the bench they seemed to have adopted, the girl appeared to be about thirteen or fourteen years of age. She looked quite thin, homely, and awkward, but had the future promise of beautiful eyes. Her dress was very dated and childish and looked like the badly tailored woolen uniforms of a convent school. As Marius strolled by the old man and the girl, he made the assumption that they were father and daughter.

Marius got in the habit of walking back and forth by the pair at the end of the alleyway about five or six times each day. Yet, in spite of seeing them so often and because of his shyness, it had never occurred to him to exchange greetings with them. The fact that the old man and the girl seemed to shun all eyes glancing their way actually drew more attention on the part of some of Marius's friends. Courfeyrac, who thought of the girl as extremely homely, dubbed the pair with nicknames. To him, the distinctive feature for the old man was his hair, so he called him Monsieur Leblanc, meaning white; and because of her plain dress, the girl was dubbed Mademoiselle Lanoire, meaning black. The nicknames stuck, and even Marius found himself referring to the unknown man and girl as Monsieur Leblanc and Mademoiselle Lanoire.

For more than a year, Marius saw the two at the same time each day and he, too, thought of the young girl as homely. But sometime into the second year Marius's habit of walking through Luxembourg Park abruptly stopped, and even he wasn't sure why. Nevertheless, six months elapsed without the young man setting foot into the alleyway next to the park. Then one beautiful summer morning, being in a particularly happy mood, Marius returned.

Walking straight to "his alley," he saw two people sitting on the bench. The old man was certainly the same man as before, but it seemed that the girl next to him was not the same person. He now beheld a tall and beautiful creature who no longer had the figure of a girl, but that of a woman. Now fifteen years of age, she seemed to possess the charm and grace of a woman coupled with the innocence of a child. Her beautiful brown hair seemed to have threads of gold running through it, while her pale pink cheeks highlighted the soft white skin of her face. She had a radiant smile and an expression as beautiful as what Raphael would have given to the Virgin Mary, or what Jean Goujon would have sculpted for Venus.

As Marius walked past her, he could only see her long chestnut lashes, for she kept her eyes lowered out of a sense of modesty. However, this did not keep her from smiling as she listened to what the white-haired old man said to her, and her downcast eyes and smile only served to increase Marius's growing fascination.

Initially, he thought she must be another daughter of the man—no doubt the older sister of the little girl he had seen months ago. Yet upon walking by their bench a second time, he scrutinized her face more closely and realized she was the same girl. In six short months the little girl had become a young woman. As he passed by her, she raised her eyes toward him and he was finally able to see they were a deep, celestial blue. Yet this quick look was nothing more than the fleeting, innocent glance of a child. She looked at him indifferently as she would have watched any little boy run through the trees. For his part, Marius turned his thoughts to other things as well, and continued walking back and forth several more times without even turning his eyes in her direction.

As was his custom, Marius returned to Luxembourg Park on a regular basis and found what he assumed to be the father with his daughter, but paid no further attention to them. He thought no more about the young woman now that she was beautiful than when she appeared homely. Yet he continued to walk past her bench because it was his habit to do so.

CHAPTER TWENTY

———————— ❦ ————————

O ne day later, as springtime was in the air, the area where Marius walked seemed unusually bright, and the sky was such a pure blue it seemed as though the angels had washed it that very morning. As the young man listened to the chirping of the birds in the chestnut trees and was totally absorbed in the beauty of nature, he walked past the bench at the end of the alleyway next to Luxembourg Park once again.

The young girl seated with the white-haired old man raised her eyes toward Marius as he approached. Their eyes suddenly met, but today there was something different about her fleeting glance. "What is different about her today?" Marius wondered. There was nothing and yet there was everything. To the young man, something had flashed across the lovely young woman's eyes. Then as quickly as their eyes had met, she looked down, and he walked away.

What Marius had just seen was no longer the naïve innocence of a child. It appeared that a mysterious gulf had suddenly opened halfway and then had abruptly slammed shut just as quickly. It has been said that there comes a day when a young girl has the eyes of a woman, and woe to the man who happens to catch her glance on that day! For Marius everything had changed!

When he returned to his room that evening, he looked at his clothing with fresh eyes and was horrified to see how absurdly he had dressed. For the first time he realized his old clothes made him look so disheveled and unkempt he could hardly believe his eyes. How could he have gone for a walk each day in his everyday clothes; that is, wearing his battered hat, scuffed boots, black trousers worn out at the knees, and his black coat with its faded elbows!

So the following day Marius dressed himself in his finest suit, hat, boots, and even fancy gloves, and then left to take his walk. On his way he happened upon Courfeyrac but pretended not to see him. Yet when Courfeyrac saw their friends, he told them, "I just ran into Marius, who was wearing a completely new outfit. No doubt he was headed to an interview or something, but he looked utterly stupid!"

Before walking down the alleyway, Marius stopped at the fountain in Luxembourg Park. He stood there for some time, seemingly deep in thought, staring at the swans. Then he walked toward the alley, and upon reaching it he immediately saw "Monsieur Leblanc and Mademoiselle Lanoire" seated at the far end. Before continuing, Marius buttoned his coat to the very top, tugged on it to eliminate any wrinkles, and examined the lustrous material of his trousers. Finally he marched directly toward the bench, but as he drew closer his pace seemed to slow.

Suddenly he stopped, still some distance from the bench and the end of the alleyway. He could not even explain to himself why he had so abruptly stopped, or why he found himself now retracing his steps. Marius had stayed so far away from the young woman that it would have been difficult for her to even recognize him or to notice his fancy clothes. Nevertheless, he stood very erect just in case she was watching him from behind as he walked away.

Upon reaching the opposite end of the alley, Marius turned and headed back toward the bench, this time coming a little closer. Yet once again he felt it impossible to continue, and hesitated. Then, thinking he saw the young woman turn her face in his direction, he overcame his hesitancy with sheer determination and walked straight ahead. He passed by their bench standing straight and tall, but having turned so red that even his ears were crimson. He stuck his hand into his coat as though he were a statesman and did not dare to look to the right or to the left. His heart was beating wildly, and as he walked by her he could hear her voice, which sounded extremely pleasant and peaceful to him. She was quite lovely that day, and he had a feeling that must be true, although he made no attempt to look at her. Coming to the end of the alleyway again, he turned and walked past her once more—this time looking very pale. As he walked away from her, he hoped she was watching him, but the very thought caused him to stumble.

Then he did something he had not done before. He sat down on a nearby bench. After sitting there for about a quarter of an hour, he finally stood and nervously began tracing figures in the sand with a cane he had carried with him that day. And for the first time he was beginning to feel guilty for the way he and his friends had flippantly referred to this man and young woman with the somewhat irreverent nicknames: Monsieur Leblanc and Mademoiselle Lanoire—yet the names had stuck. Then he abruptly turned in the opposite direction of their bench and walked home.

Dressing the way he did, Marius began to raise the curiosity of his old housekeeper. Seeing him dressed in his best clothes three days in a row, she decided to follow him. Yet Marius walked so briskly and with such long strides that she lost sight of him within two minutes. Returning to her room, completely breathless because of her asthma, she was furious with him. She growled to herself, "How dare someone put on their best clothes every day, and then make people run like this!"

Two weeks passed with Marius heading for Luxembourg Park and that certain alleyway each day. He no longer went for the sake of taking a walk, but to stake out the bench that afforded him the best possible view of the man and his daughter. And once seated he did not stir.

Toward the end of that second week, Marius was seated on his bench as usual, holding an open book in his hands. Of course, he had not turned even one page in the book for the last two hours. To his surprise Leblanc and his daughter stood and walked in his direction. She held her father's arm as they walked slowly toward him. Now Marius forced himself to read and wished to appear handsome, but he could only imagine Monsieur Leblanc shooting darts at him with his eyes. He kept his eyes down, and just as they passed by him he glanced up to catch the young woman looking with a steady gaze at him. There was a certain sweetness in her eyes that thrilled Marius from head to toe, and reading between the lines, he imagined that she was saying, "If you will not walk as far as my bench, then I will come to you."

Marius was desperately in love.

A full month passed with Marius visiting the park every day. At the appropriate hour, nothing could have held him back. Courfeyrac would jokingly say of Marius, "He is on duty." Marius was living in a state of pure delight, for he was certain that the young woman was noticing him as well. Growing bolder all the time, but attempting to be prudent, he tried not to draw too much attention to himself from the girl's father. He would stand behind trees or by statues in the park where she could see him, but where her father could not.

Yet Monsieur Leblanc had apparently noticed something, for quite often, just as Marius would arrive, he would stand and walk around. The old gentleman had also chosen another bench at the far end of the alley, as though he were attempting to see whether Marius would follow them there. Doing that very thing, Marius believed he had made a grave error, for suddenly the old man and his daughter no longer came to the park every day, and occasionally the man would come alone. On those days Marius would not stay, which was another apparent blunder.

Marius, however, was oblivious to these mistakes, for he had moved right past the stage of timidity to that of blindness. His secret love for the young woman continued to grow, and he dreamed of her every night. Then one day something happened that was equal to throwing oil on the fire of his love, and which served to only thicken the scales covering his eyes. At dusk one evening, just as Monsieur Leblanc and his daughter left their bench, he noticed a handkerchief left on the seat. It was quite simple, without any embroidery on its edges, but it seemed to him to have an exquisite smell of perfume. He grabbed it with a sense of rapture in his heart, and upon doing so, noticed the letters *UF* sewn into it.

Marius knew nothing about this beautiful young woman—not her family name, her first name, nor her address. These two letters were the first items of hers that he possessed, and he immediately began to surmise what names the letters must stand for. "*U* must stand for Ursula," he thought, "and what a beautiful name it is!" This little handkerchief almost became an obsession for him. He kissed it, kept it between his shirt and his heart during the day, and laid it beneath his lips at night so he could fall asleep on it.

Marius exclaimed to himself, "I feel like her entire soul lies within it!" Yet little did he know, for the handkerchief belonged to the old gentleman, and it had simply fallen from his pocket.

Marius, having fallen in love, now saw his appetite for love only deepen. Knowing the young woman's name, which he assumed to be Ursula, meant everything to him. Yet very soon it was not nearly enough. Within three to four weeks he had totally consumed this blessing and wanted more. He wanted to know where she lived. So from that point on he began following the old gentleman and his daughter from the park to their home. He discovered that they lived in a relatively isolated area of Paris in a new, three-story house of modest appearance.

His hunger to know more continued to increase. He thought he knew her first name and now he knew where she lived, but he wanted to know who she really was. Then one evening, after following them home, he saw them enter through the carriage gate. Feeling quite bold, Marius approached the porter tending the gate, and asked, "Is the gentleman who just came in the one who lives on the first floor?"

"No," replied the porter, "he is the gentleman on the third floor."

With the success of learning something new, Marius forged ahead and asked, "And what profession is the gentleman engaged in, sir?"

"Oh, he's a gentleman of property. He's a very kind man who helps the poor, although he's not really rich himself."

"What is his name?" Marius continued.

At this, the porter raised his eyebrows and said, "Are you a spy for the police, sir?"

Not quite sure how to respond, and feeling somewhat embarrassed and confused, Marius simply turned and walked away. Nevertheless, he was delighted with the fact that he had learned a little more. He thought, "At least I now know her name is Ursula, that she is the daughter of a gentleman who has an income from his property, and that she lives on the third floor of that house."

The following day Monsieur Leblanc and his daughter made only a very brief appearance at the park, leaving long before dusk. As was his habit, Marius again followed them home, but when they got to the gate only the young woman went inside. The old gentleman paused for a moment, and then turned and stared intently at Marius. Finally, he entered the house as well.

The next day they did not go to the park at all, yet Marius waited all day for them. Finally realizing his wait was in vain, at nightfall he left and went to their house, only to see light shining through the windows of the third floor. He walked around the house beneath those windows until the light was extinguished.

Every day for a week that same scenario took place. The father and daughter did not reappear at their alley next to the park, and Marius would stay outside their windows until at least ten o'clock in the evening. Then, on the eighth day, there was no light shining through the windows. He paced back and forth and waited. Ten o'clock came and went, then midnight, and then one in the morning. Yet no light ever shone through the windows, and no one entered the house. Finally he left, albeit in a very depressed state of mind.

The next day the scene was repeated, with the third floor remaining totally dark. Unsure what to do next, Marius decided to knock on the door of the porter's station near the carriage gate. When the porter opened the door, Marius asked, "The gentleman on the third floor?"

"Has moved away," the porter replied.

Marius's mind reeled at the news, but he managed to feebly say, "How long ago?"

"Yesterday," was the answer.

"But where is he living now?" Marius demanded.

"I don't know anything else," the porter retorted, impatiently.

"So the gentleman did not leave a forwarding address?"

"No," the porter replied. Then suddenly recognizing Marius from their earlier meeting some weeks ago, he said, "So! It's you! You are a spy!"

CHAPTER TWENTY-ONE

~❦~

S ummer and autumn came and went. Now it was winter, and neither Monsieur Leblanc nor Mademoiselle Lanoire had set foot again in Luxembourg Park. Yet Marius had only one goal: to gaze once more on that sweet, adorable face. He searched constantly, looking everywhere for her, but found nothing.

The young man relentlessly heaped reproach upon reproach on himself. He would ask, "Why did I follow her? I was so happy with the mere sight of her. Why wasn't I satisfied with that? Her eyes seemed to offer me her love. Wasn't that enough? What more did I need? My actions have been absurd. This is my own fault." He was completely devastated, and spent more and more time alone. His inner anguish was overwhelming, and he felt like a wolf in a trap. He was dazed by his love, and searched for the object of that love every waking moment.

On one occasion he saw a man on the street dressed like a working man who was wearing a cap with a long visor. Protruding from beneath the cap, however, were locks of beautiful white hair. Seeing the man from behind, Marius noticed that the man's hair, build, and demeanor were nearly identical to that of Monsieur Leblanc. Yet for some unexplainable reason, perhaps the fact that Marius was so absorbed in his own painful thoughts, he walked very slowly behind the man. Finally, upon putting these clues together, he had a sudden impulse to follow the old man. But the thought came to him too late, and before he knew it the man was gone. He attempted to brush the encounter aside, saying to himself that the old gentleman he knew would never be dressed in such common working clothes anyway.

Having no other option, Marius was forced to move on with his life. His preoccupation with the young woman had taken its toll on his finances, so he now threw himself headlong into his work as an attorney. Then early one morning, around seven o'clock, as he was working on a pressing case in his room, he heard a soft knock on the door. Before he could respond, he heard a second gentle knock. Because he had so few possessions he typically kept his door unlocked, and upon hearing the second knock, he called out, "Come in!"

As the door swung open, he heard what he thought was the voice of an old man that had been hardened by too much liquor. The voice said, "Excuse me, sir," but when he turned to see who was speaking, he saw a young woman standing before him in the half-opened door. The faint light of early dawn fell across the frail figure that appeared emaciated and that was wearing nothing but a thin petticoat. She had the form of a young woman who had bypassed her youth, as she stood in the doorway shivering from the cold and looking more like a haggard old woman of fifty than her actual age of fifteen.

As Marius stared at her face, he thought he remembered having seen it somewhere. Then he asked the poor girl, "What do you want, Mademoiselle?"

She replied in her voice that sounded like that of a drunken convict, "I have a letter for you, Monsieur Marius."

The young woman had called Marius by his name, so he could not doubt that she had the right person, but he wondered who she could be and how she knew his name. As he pondered this, she stepped into the room and handed the letter to him. He broke its wax seal, and as he did so he noticed it was still moist, which told him the letter could not have traveled very far. Then he began reading the letter, which said:

My dear, gracious young man,

I am your next-door neighbor and have recently learned of your goodness to me—the fact that six months ago you paid the rent for my family and me. May God bless you for that, young man. My oldest daughter, who has delivered this letter to you, can confirm to you that we have not had even one morsel of bread for two days. There are four of us in our family without food, and now my wife is ill. Unless I am a terrible judge of character, I believe that your generous heart will be moved upon reading my words, and that you will overlook my forwardness in asking you for help. I close, wishing you the best for being such a worthy benefactor of those less fortunate.

Jondrette

P.S. My daughter will await your orders, dear Monsieur Marius.

Jondrette, in severe distress, was simply preying upon what he perceived to be a young man who could be easily persuaded to give and give again. As Marius read the letter, the young woman strutted back and forth across the room, seemingly unconcerned about her near nakedness. Then she walked to his table and grabbed a book that lay open on it. She said, "Ah, books! I know how to read!" To prove her point she read aloud, "General Bauduin received orders to take the chateau of Hougomont, which stands in the middle of the plain of Waterloo, with five battalions of his brigade." At this she stopped reading and proclaimed, "Waterloo! I know all about that. It was a battle fought long ago, and, in fact, my father served in the army there. We are all fine Bonapartist Democrats in our house—yes we are!"

She then grabbed a piece of paper and a pen, while saying, "I can write too! I'll show you. Here's what no Bonapartist ever wants to hear." As she said this, she dipped the pen in ink and wrote these words in capital letters: THE POLICE ARE HERE!

Suddenly the young woman seemed to scrutinize Marius, took on a totally different expression, and said to him, "Did you know, Monsieur Marius, that you are a very handsome man?" Then she smiled as he blushed. Placing her hand on his shoulder, she continued, "You have never paid any attention to me, but I know you, Monsieur Marius. You have passed right by me in the stairwell numerous times, and sometimes I have even followed you on your way to church. By the way, I really like your hair tossed over to the side this way."

These last few words she attempted to say very softly, but only succeeded in deepening her voice. In fact, a number of her words seemed to get lost somewhere between her larynx and her lips, like notes on a piano with a few missing keys. As she spoke, Marius slowly backed away, all the while thrusting both hands into his pockets as though he were searching for something. Finally he pulled five francs and sixteen sous from a pocket. At the moment this was all the money he had in the world, but he handed the five-francs coin to the girl, and only kept the sixteen sous for himself.

Grabbing the coin, she shouted with glee, "Great! The sun is shining again!" She then straightened the straps of her petticoat on her shoulders, bowed deeply toward Marius, and walked toward the door, while saying, "Good day, sir. I'll take this money to my old man." On the way out, however, she saw an old, dusty and moldy crust of bread sitting on a cabinet, which she quickly grabbed and bit into, before muttering with a smile, "This is good! But it breaks my teeth!" Then she departed.

At this point, Marius had lived five years in relative poverty—at least when compared to the years lived with his grandfather. He had lived through times of great distress, but had not known real misery and abject poverty such as he had just seen. Now perceiving the misery of his neighbors, he heaped reproach on himself for being so blind and uncaring, and for putting his own peace and passions above the needs of others. And to know that only a mere wall separated him from the misery of seemingly abandoned people only made him feel much worse. He had paid no heed to them, yet he was possibly their last link to the human race for help out of their agony.

Marius's thoughts had been elsewhere and had been totally devoted to his dreams. Yet all the while, people in his own building—people he saw as his brothers and sisters in Jesus Christ—were agonizing in vain right beside him! Yes, he saw them as corrupt, depraved, and vile, but gave them the benefit of the doubt, for he believed that it was rare for someone to fall to their level without becoming debased. He also believed there was something the unfortunate and the infamous had in common, and he summed it up by calling them Les Misérables—The Miserable.

As he reviewed his beliefs on this moral issue, Marius felt the further someone has fallen, the further someone else should go in extending charity. He saw destitution as something that was often not the fault of the destitute. Marius kept scolding himself, but often more harshly than he deserved. He would stare at the wall that separated his room from the Jondrette family, as though his gaze would bring warmth and hope to these wretchedly poor people.

Prior to this time, he had been so absorbed in his own problems that he had never noticed he could clearly distinguish the conversations taking place on the other side of the thin plaster wall. And as Marius stared at that wall, he noticed a small hole in the plaster near the top of it. He discovered by standing on his dresser that he could see straight through to the Jondrettes' room. His curiosity overwhelmed him at this point, and he began to rationalize that it was okay to gaze at misfortune if his goal was to relieve it.

He thought, "I'll just get some idea what these people are like and see just how bad their condition is." Marius climbed onto the dresser and began spying through the small hole. What he saw was miserable, filthy, and vile.

Marius was still poor, and his room was not elaborately furnished at all. Yet he maintained a sense of pride in his home, and at least his room was clean and neat. But what he was now seeing was total squalor. The poor family's room was a shrine to abject poverty, covered with dirt and obviously pest ridden. Their only furniture consisted of a broken-down wicker chair and a rickety old table with a few pieces of chipped dinnerware sitting on it. Their apparent beds were two filthy, makeshift pallets on the floor in opposing corners of the room. A single window, which was covered with spider webs and had a number of cracks in the panes, provided the only light. There was just enough light to make out the face of a man who had the hollow look of a ghost. Even the walls of the room were hideous. They seemed to have moisture exuding from them that was causing the plaster to peel, and they were covered with obscenities written in charcoal.

About an hour had passed since the desperate young woman had left his room, and while Marius continued to watch, he suddenly saw her burst into the room on the other side of his wall. Her cold, chapped ankles and the bulky pair of men's shoes she wore were splattered with mud, and she was now wrapped in a torn and ragged old coat. From this, Marius reasoned that she must have left the coat outside his door upon visiting him in order to elicit more pity. She entered her room completely breathless, as though she had been running, and then joyfully exclaimed with an air of triumph, "He is coming!"

Her ghostly looking father and her mother turned toward her, while her smaller sister did not stir. Then her father demanded, "Who is coming?"

"The gentleman!"

"You mean that charitable fellow?" he questioned.

"Yes, of course."

"The old man from Saint Jacques Church?" he persisted.

"Yes, one and the same," she answered.

"When is he coming?"

"He will be here soon. He is coming in his carriage."

"That's interesting," her father said, smiling, "He must be richer than I thought. A Rothschild!" Then questioning the young woman again, he asked, "If he is coming in a carriage, how did you get here before him? Did he read my letter?"

Attempting to explain fully, she said, "When I entered the church he was in his usual place, and I handed him the letter. After reading it he said, 'Where do you live, my child?' I told him I would show him, but he said, 'No, give me your address, for we have some purchases to make. Once we finish we will meet you at your house.' But when I told him we lived in the Gorbeau House he seemed surprised and hesitated for a moment. Then he said, 'Never mind. I'll be there soon.' When the mass was finished I saw him and his daughter leave in a carriage, and that same carriage has just turned down our street. I ran the last block or so, which is why I'm so out of breath."

Hearing this, the father suddenly seemed propelled to action, and yelled at his wife, "Put out the fire!" The woman, looking confused, just stared at him. Not waiting for her to act, he grabbed a jug of water and doused the fire in the stove, before explaining, "We can't have a wealthy man coming here without looking as poor as possible, and we certainly can't do that with a fire going in the stove!"

Then turning to his older daughter, he demanded, "You! Pull the straw out of that chair!" But the girl obviously did not understand, so he grabbed the wicker chair and with one kick knocked the seat out of it. As he pulled his leg out of the chair, he asked his daughter, "Is it cold outside?"

"Yes, it's very cold. In fact, it's snowing."

The father then turned to the younger daughter, who was sitting on one of the filthy pallets, and thundered at her, "Get off that bed, you lazy thing! You never do anything! Get up and break a pane of glass in the window." The smaller girl jumped off the bed with a shudder, but stood motionless before him in seeming bewilderment. So he screamed at her, "Can you hear me? Get over there and break some glass!" The poor child moved toward the window out of a sense of terrified obedience and struck one of the windowpanes with her fist. The glass broke and fell loudly to the floor.

"Good. Thank you," the father said, sarcastically. Turning once again toward his wife, he instructed, "Get into bed, my dear." She obeyed by falling heavily onto one of the pallets. Then he heard a quiet sob come from another corner, and seeing his younger daughter, he demanded, "What's wrong with you?" Not answering aloud, she simply held out her bleeding fist as she cowered in the corner.

At this, the mother began to shout as well. "Now see what you've done!" she yelled toward her husband. "She's cut herself on that windowpane!"

"Actually, I saw that coming. So much the better!" he said, slyly. Then tearing a strip of cloth from his own dirty shirt, he hastily wrapped the girl's bleeding hand and wrist. Finally, looking around the room and then examining his torn shirt with an air of satisfaction, he added, "This all looks great! We are now ready to receive our gentleman of charity."

Yet the father, with a worried expression on his face, abruptly said, "It's deathly cold in this demon's pit! What if our friend does not come? Right now he's probably saying to himself, 'Oh, they will wait. What else do they have to do!' Oh, how I hate the rich! I would love to strangle them all!" But just as he finished his ranting, a light knock could be heard on the door. The angry man rushed to the door, quickly opened it, smiled adoringly, and then while bowing said, "Enter, my dear sir, and your charming young daughter as well." Then using the assumed last name he had used to sign his letter to the man, Jondrette said, "We are the Fabantou family."

An old but rugged-looking man and a young girl entered the deceptive family's filthy room. At this point, Marius, who had continued to peer through the hole in the wall, was completely dumbstruck with what he saw. It was "She"!

His feelings at this moment completely surpassed the powers of the human tongue to describe. The beautiful vision that had been lost was found! Even more amazing was the fact that she had reappeared amidst such a horrific setting.

She was as pretty as ever. A soft velvet bonnet of pale lavender framed her delicate face, and her lovely figure was concealed beneath her floor-length dress of black satin. Her long dress partially revealed her petite feet that were wearing black silk boots. The young woman, who was accompanied by Monsieur Leblanc, took a few steps into the room and set a large package onto the table.

With a kind but sad look in his eyes, Monsieur Leblanc said to Monsieur Jondrette, "Sir, I was moved by the letter explaining your family's desperate situation, which your daughter gave me in church. So my daughter and I have brought you some new clothes, woolen socks, and blankets."

"You are an angel! Your kindness overwhelms me!" Jondrette exclaimed, bowing once again. Then hoping to take full advantage of his newfound resource, he continued, "See, dear sir, we have no bread and no fire for heat. My poor children and my wife, who is sick in bed, have no heat. My only chair is totally unusable without a seat. And this window! Look at it! Broken in this miserably cold weather!" Then Jondrette turned toward his younger daughter, who was continuing to sob in pain, and said, "My poor daughter is hurt. She badly cut her hand in an accident at a factory where she earned a meager six sous a day! Now she can't work, and it may even be necessary to remove her arm because of infection."

At this, the beautiful young woman, whom Marius referred to as "his Ursula," walked to the hurting girl and said, "You poor dear child!"

Then Jondrette continued with his long list of woes by saying, "All I have to wear is this torn shirt, so I am unable to go out because of my lack of a warm coat. And today is February third, which is the last day of grace my landlord has given me. If I am unable to pay my rent by tonight, all four of us will be turned out of here tomorrow with no shelter from the rain or the snow. My landlord has been very gracious, but we are a full year behind in our rent. I owe sixty francs, and you are the last hope for my poor family. If you do not help us, my sick wife, my hurt daughter—all four of us—will be thrown into the street!"

Still listening and watching from the other side of the wall, Marius knew Jondrette was lying. Marius himself had paid for two months rent for the family less than six months ago. Plus he knew that a year's rent for them was only forty francs.

Monsieur Leblanc took off his heavy brown outer coat and tossed it over the back of the broken chair. Then pulling five francs from his pocket, he set them on the table and said, "Monsieur Fabantou, this is all the money I have on me at the present time, but I will take my daughter home and return later this evening."

Jondrette's face lit up at the idea of the man returning later, and making a spirited reply, said, "Oh, thank you! I must be at my landlord's by eight o'clock."

"Then I will return promptly at six and will bring you sixty francs." Taking his daughter's arm, Monsieur Leblanc turned toward the door.

"Six o'clock will be fine," Jondrette replied.

As the man and his daughter were walking toward the door, the older of the Jondrette girls noticed the overcoat on the chair, and said, "Sir, you are forgetting your coat."

If looks could kill, Jondrette's angry glance at his daughter would have annihilated her. But Monsieur Leblanc turned around and said, with a smile, "I'm not forgetting it. I'm leaving it."

"You are too kind, sir!" Jondrette said, with all the sincerity he could muster, and added, "You nearly make me cry."

"I'll see you later tonight, sir," was Monsieur Leblanc's simple response.

During this entire encounter, Jondrette had been scrutinizing his benefactor as though he knew him from somewhere. As the charitable man spoke, there was something about him that reminded him of someone. Jondrette was frantically searching the dusty archives of his mind—yet he couldn't quite place him.

CHAPTER TWENTY-TWO

A fter a bit of respite from his perch, Marius resumed his post to peer through the wall just before six o'clock. The only light in his neighbors' nearly dark room was a coal fire that had been relit in the stove. Through the blue flame flickering above the coals he could see that an iron poker had been thrust into them. In one corner of the room he also saw what appeared to be a pile of rope that he had not noticed earlier, and in light of what he had already seen of Jondrette, he could not help but wonder if it were there for some sinister reason.

Jondrette had lit his pipe and was straddling his seatless chair. Obviously lost in thought, he finally looked up and said to his wife, "We're going to need two chairs in here."

"I'll go and get a couple of them from our next-door neighbor," she responded, as she quickly headed toward the door.

"Take a candle with you," Jondrette instructed.

"No, that will get me caught, and besides I have two chairs to carry. I'll be able to see by the moonlight," she said.

Realizing that his neighbor did not intend to ask to borrow his chairs, Marius jumped down from his dresser and hoped to hide himself beneath his bed. Yet he did not have enough time to do so, for he almost immediately heard the woman turning the door handle. He quickly blew out his candle, and simply concealed himself in the shadows of the night by leaning against the wall.

Marius was frozen in place out of shock and horror, and seemed to disappear into the darkness as the woman entered his room. In the moonlight she saw the only two chairs Marius owned, grabbed both of them, and quickly left, slamming the door behind her. Then reentering her own room, she set the two chairs on opposite sides of the table, jabbed the hot coals of the fire a few times with the poker, and walked over to the pile of rope in the corner. As she lifted it up to examine it, Marius realized that what he thought was simply a pile of rope was actually a sturdy-looking rope ladder with wooden rungs and two hooks with which to attach it to something such as a window ledge.

Jondrette, still straddling his chair, had allowed his pipe to go out—a sign that he was quite preoccupied with his plan for the evening. On the other side of the wall Marius had begun rummaging through his dresser drawer looking for something. Finally he pulled one of the two pistols he owned from underneath some clothes, pondered it for a moment, and cocked it.

As he did so, the pistol emitted a sharp, precise click. Jondrette, startled by the sound, partially rose from his chair, listened intently for a few seconds, but then began to laugh out loud and said, "I am such a fool! That was only the old plaster of this building cracking!"

Marius returned to his post as a spy, but kept the pistol in his hand.

Suddenly a distant sound lightly shook the windowpanes of the Jondrettes' room. Six o'clock was striking from the bell tower of Saint Médard's Church. Jondrette marked each stroke by nodding his head up and down. Then he began to pace back and forth across the room, but would stop occasionally to listen at the door. "I hope he shows," he muttered to himself, as he returned to his chair. Just as he sat, there was a knock at the door.

Jondrette's wife jumped toward the door, opened it, and said, "Please come in, sir."

"Yes, come in, kind sir!" Jondrette echoed, as he quickly stood.

Marius then saw Monsieur Leblanc enter the nearly dark room that was lit by only the glow of the fire. He set four louis on the table while saying, "Monsieur Fabantou, this is for your rent and your most pressing necessities. We will take care of your other needs later."

"Oh, you are too generous, sir!" Jondrette—or "Fabantou"—said, as he offered Monsieur Leblanc a chair.

Leblanc had hardly been seated before he noticed both pallets were now empty, and inquired, "How is your poor wounded little daughter?"

"Not well," Jondrette replied with a mournful look on his face. "Her older sister has taken her to a doctor to have her wound dressed, but they should be back soon."

"Madame Fabantou appears to be better," Leblanc said in a questioning tone.

The woman eyed their guest suspiciously and stood between him and the door, apparently guarding the exit. And her strange pose and body language seemed to say that she was ready for combat. Jondrette, continuing to play out his deception, stated, "Actually, she is dying. But just look at her! She has so much courage!"

While Jondrette was talking, Marius noticed a person quietly enter the dark room and move to the far end of it. He had entered so softly that no one had even heard the door swing open on its hinges. Yet suddenly Leblanc saw him, and as a startled look flashed across his face, he asked, "Who is that man?"

"Him?" Jondrette offered. "He's just a neighbor friend of mine. Don't worry about him."

"I'm sorry. What were you saying, Monsieur Fabantou?" Leblanc asked.

"I was about to tell you, sir," Jondrette answered, "that I have a painting to sell." Yet as he spoke, he eyed his guest with the deceptively fierce gaze of a boa constrictor that is stalking its prey.

Just then the door creaked ever so slightly as a second man entered the room and promptly sat on one of the pallets behind Jondrette. Endeavoring to head off his guest's suspicions, Jondrette said, "Don't mind them. They both live in this building, and . . . as I was saying, I have a valuable painting I would like you to see, sir."

Jondrette then lit a small candle and turned a wooden panel around that had been leaning with its face toward the wall. Because of the dim light, Leblanc leaned forward to examine the painting more closely, and when he leaned back and turned around again, he now saw four nameless men in the room—three seated on the pallet and one stationed near the door. All were quiet and still, and their bare arms and faces were smeared with something black.

Monsieur Leblanc was beginning to feel quite uneasy and kept his eyes fixed on the four men. Perceiving his uneasiness, Jondrette said, "These are friends of mine—my neighbors. Their faces are black because they are all chimney sweeps. Please don't trouble yourself about them, sir. Tell me . . . what do you think my painting is worth?"

"This is nothing but a sign from a tavern or something. It's probably only worth about three francs or so," he answered, reluctantly.

Jondrette responded, with a sly smile on his face, "You've brought your money pouch with you, I presume. I will be happy with no less than a thousand crowns!"

Hearing what sounded to him as nothing short of a threat, Leblanc sprang from his chair, put his back to the wall, and glanced quickly around the room. Jondrette was to his left, next to the window, and the man's wife and the four men were to his right, near the door. Jondrette, however, now knowing his ruse was becoming fully exposed, flashed a hideous smile. The little man stood as tall as he could, attempting to look Leblanc eye-to-eye, and yelled in a voice as loud as thunder, "Don't you recognize me?"

Just then the door of the room opened abruptly, revealing three more men standing in the hallway—each wearing masks of black cloth to hide their identity. It appeared that Jondrette had been awaiting their arrival, for he immediately said to them, "Is everything ready?"

"Yes," replied one of the men, who was quite thin, but carried an iron-tipped club in his hand.

With a sickening laugh, Jondrette turned to Leblanc and asked again, "Don't you recognize me?"

Leblanc scrutinized the man's face for a moment and said, "No."

Then Jondrette moved as close as possible to Leblanc's calm face without actually pushing him backward, and exclaimed with apparent glee, "My name is not Fabantou. My name is not Jondrette. My name is Thénardier—

the innkeeper in Montfermeil! Thénardier! Now do you remember me?"

An almost imperceptible tinge of red crossed Leblanc's face, yet he replied with an incredibly calm voice, "No more than before."

Marius did not hear Leblanc's answer, for he was in shock the moment he heard Jondrette say, "My name is Thénardier." His arms and legs began to tremble as he leaned against the wall, and he felt as though someone had just run a cold, steel blade through his heart. His right hand, which was still holding the pistol, fell to his side so abruptly that he nearly dropped the gun.

The news that Jondrette was really Thénardier had not seemed to faze Leblanc, but it had devastated Marius. His father's dying words had inscribed that name on his heart. To Marius, his father's instructions had become sacred—especially these: "A sergeant by the name of Thénardier saved my life. If my son ever meets him, I want him to do all the good that he can for Thénardier." And suddenly Jondrette's daughter's words came back to him as well: "Waterloo! My father served in the army there." Could there be any doubt that he was indeed the Thénardier who had saved his father's life?

Yet this man—the very man to whom Marius had sought to devote himself—was a monster! The man who had saved Colonel Pontmercy appeared to be on the verge of committing a crime so horrendous, Marius could not fully comprehend it. He now saw his father's liberator as capable of murder. For so long he had dreamed of throwing himself in gratitude at the man's feet, but now that he had actually found him, he was ready to hand him over to the executioner!

Marius shuddered as he considered his options. If he fired his pistol, Monsieur Leblanc would be saved, and Thénardier would be lost. Yet if he did not fire, Leblanc would be sacrificed, and a monster would escape!

In the meantime, Thénardier had been pacing back and forth, while raving like a mad conqueror in front of Leblanc. He exclaimed, "So, I've found you once again, Monsieur Philanthropist! Monsieur Threadbare Millionaire! You say you don't recognize me. So, it wasn't you who came to my inn in Montfermeil eight years ago, on Christmas Eve of 1823? Well, I recognize you!

Yes, I do! I recognized you the moment you poked your ugly snout in here. You scoundrel! You child stealer!"

Monsieur Leblanc responded in a quiet, calm voice, "You are mistaken, sir. I am a very poor man—anything but a millionaire. I don't know you. You are mistaking me for someone else."

"So," Thénardier roared, "you don't know who I am. That's a lie!"

"Excuse me, sir," Monsieur Leblanc said, with an extremely polite tone to his voice, "I see that you are a criminal!"

"Yes! A criminal! That's what rich gentlemen would call me! Yes, it's true that I became bankrupt, that I am in hiding, that I have no bread, that I don't have a single sou to my name, and that I am a criminal. So what!" the little man said defiantly. Then turning his bloodshot eyes toward Leblanc, he said impatiently, "Do you have anything else to say before we put handcuffs on you?" But Leblanc did not say one word, while Thénardier briefly turned his back to his captive.

Leblanc seized the moment before Thénardier could turn back around. He quickly kicked a chair over with his foot, threw the table over with his fists, and with what seemed to be a single bound, was at the window. He had climbed halfway through the window by the time six of the strong fists of "the chimney sweeps" had grabbed him and dragged him forcefully back into the filthy room. All the while, Madame Thénardier had grabbed him by his hair as well, and was pulling with the men toward the center of the room.

At this point, the other men who had been waiting in the hallway rushed into the room. One of them raised his club—ready to bludgeon poor Monsieur Leblanc's head. Marius could wait no longer. He thought to himself, "My dear father, forgive me!"

Yet just as Marius was about to pull the trigger of his pistol, he heard Thénardier shout, "Don't hurt him!" Instead of exasperating Thénardier, it seems that Leblanc's escape attempt had actually calmed the captor. He repeated, "Don't hurt him!"

With the urgency of his intervention having passed, Marius saw no reason not to wait a little longer, with his pistol still frozen to his hand. While he waited, however, a new struggle of Herculean proportions began to take place in the room across the wall. With one swift blow to the chest, Leblanc sent the small old man tumbling across the floor. Then sweeping the same hand back, he knocked down two more of his assailants, and pinned each one to the floor under each of his knees.

The wretched men were gasping for air under the tremendous pressure of what felt like a granite millstone sitting on their chests. Four more men finally grabbed Leblanc by his arms and his neck, yet he still managed to keep the two men pinned to the floor. In this strange position, he was in control of two, while being controlled by others. At this point Marius could hardly see Leblanc, for he had nearly disappeared beneath this horrible group of criminals. They looked to him like a pack of wild dogs fighting over their prey.

At last the men succeeded in throwing the poor man across the room and onto the pallet nearest the window, and then stood back staring at him with a kind of reverential awe because of his strength. All the while, Madame Thénardier had not released her grasp on his hair and had been tossed across the room as well. Seeing what appeared to him to be an amusing sight, Thénardier simply said to his wife, "You shouldn't get mixed up in this. You'll tear your shawl."

Then instructing his fellow criminals, he said, "Search him!" But to Thénardier's disappointment, they only found a leather pouch containing six francs, and a handkerchief that Thénardier immediately put in his own pocket. Next he walked to the corner of the room, threw some rope to the men, and said, "Tie him to that pallet." They tied him securely, so that he was sitting upright on the makeshift bed with his feet on the floor. As the last knot was being tied, Thénardier grabbed a chair and sat down directly in front of his prisoner.

Thénardier suddenly no longer looked like himself. In just a few moments his countenance had changed from a look of unbridled violence to one of tranquil yet cunning politeness. With a wave of his hand he dismissed his rough-looking mob of men who still held Leblanc in their grasp. He said, "Stand back a little. Let me have a chat with the gentleman." Then turning to his captive, he said, "Monsieur, you were wrong to try to escape out the window. You could have broken a leg. Now if you will allow me, I would like to have a civil conversation with you." Saying this, he stood, walked unpretentiously toward the fire and shoved the screen aside, so that his prisoner could then plainly see the white-hot poker still embedded in the glowing coals.

Finally returning to his seat, Thénardier continued, "I'm sure we can come to an amicable understanding. I was wrong to have lost my temper with you just now. I realize that in spite of your wealth, you have expenses of your own. Who doesn't? I'm not out to ruin you, for I'm really not a greedy person. I'm willing to make a personal sacrifice—so I'm only going to ask you for two hundred thousand francs."

Monsieur Leblanc did not utter a word as Thénardier went on to say, "This is a trifling amount of money to you. You will never miss it. And I promise you this will be the end of the matter—that I will make no further demands of you. I know you're going to tell me that you don't have that kind of money on you right now, but not to worry! There's only one thing I'm going to ask of you. I want you to write what I'm about to dictate to you."

At this point he paused, glanced at the hot poker sitting in the fire, and smiled as he said, "I warn you not to tell me that you don't know how to write—or else!" Then he pushed the table toward Leblanc and set a pen, ink, and paper before him, and demanded, "Write!"

The prisoner finally spoke, to say, "How do you expect me to write when my hands are bound?"

Turning to one of his cohorts, Thénardier instructed, "Untie the gentleman's right arm." Thénardier then dipped the pen in the ink, handed it to Leblanc, and said, "Write this, 'My dear daughter.'" Hearing this, the prisoner shuddered, hesitated, and then glared at his captor, who shouted, "Write it!"

Leblanc obeyed, as Thénardier continued his dictation by saying, "Come here immediately. It is imperative that I have your help. Come with the person who has delivered this note to you. I am waiting for you."

"Now," insisted Thénardier, "Sign your name. What is it?"

"Urbain Fabre," the prisoner said.

Thénardier, with the slyness of a cat, pulled the handkerchief from his pocket, which he had earlier taken from the man. Holding it near the candle, he saw the letters *UF.* Then he said, "So, your name is Urbain Fabre. Yet simply sign the letter *UF.*"

Once the prisoner signed the letter, Thénardier demanded, "Address it to your daughter at your address."

The prisoner thought for a moment, before writing, "Mademoiselle Fabre, 17 Rue Saint Dominique d'Enfer."

As soon as the man finished, Thénardier grabbed the letter and yelled to his wife, "Take this to his daughter. There is a carriage waiting at the door. And get back here quickly!"

The old woman left and was gone a short time before frantically reentering the room. She was nearly breathless and her eyes were obviously enraged as she declared, "He gave us a false address! There's no such street number, and no one in that area even knew his name."

Marius, still watching from across the wall, noticed one of Thénardier's men pick up an axe. Nevertheless, he breathed a sigh of relief knowing that his "Ursula" was safe for now.

Thénardier, now thoroughly exasperated with his prisoner, leaned against the table and remained silent for several minutes. Then staring at the hot poker, he roared at the man, "A false address! What did you hope to gain by that?"

"To gain time!" the prisoner thundered. At this, he jumped to his feet, and cast aside the rope that had once bound his left arm. While Madame Thénardier had been gone, he had secretly managed—with very little movement—to untie himself. Then before the mob could descend on him once again, he grabbed the white-hot poker from the fire and brandished it over his head, while defiantly saying, "If you think you can make me write what I don't choose to write—you are dead wrong!"

With the poker still in his hand, he then pulled up the sleeve of his left arm and added, "Watch this!" He proceeded to place the glowing tip of the poker against the flesh of his arm, which instantly began to sizzle from the extreme heat. This horrifying sight, and the resulting horrific odor, caused even the most hardened of the criminals who were watching to shudder. Marius reeled in horror as well, yet hardly a muscle of the prisoner's face even twitched at the pain as the hot iron sank deeply into the smoking wound.

Next he fixed his eyes on Thénardier. His look was stern, but not filled with any sign of hatred. Continuing to look his captor in the eyes, he said, "You should have no more fear of me than I have of you!" Finally pulling the poker away from his burned arm, he hurled it through the window, which had remained open from his previous escape attempt. It fell into the night, landed in the snow, and immediately sent up a plume of steam. Having done this, he added, "Do what you please with me."

"Grab him!" Thénardier yelled. Two men grabbed him once again, while the man with the axe faced him, threatening to crush his skull at the slightest movement.

As Marius watched, he suddenly heard Thénardier and his wife speaking quietly to one another, as they seemingly stood right below him on the other side of the wall. They agreed with one another that there was only one thing left to do, and that was, as they said, "Cut his throat." The evil old man then walked slowly toward the table, opened the drawer, and removed a sharp knife.

Marius, feeling time had run out for Monsieur Leblanc, glanced wildly around him out of a sense of instinct and desperation. Just as he did, his eyes fell upon a sheet of paper lying on the table, which was illuminated by a ray of light from the full moon. The words on the paper, which were written that very morning by the older of the Thénardier daughters, seemed to jump off the page at him. They read: THE POLICE ARE HERE!

Suddenly an idea flashed through Marius's mind—something that might possibly save Monsieur Leblanc's life. He grabbed the paper, hopped back onto his dresser, and quickly broke off a piece of plaster, making the hole in the wall somewhat larger. Then using the plaster as a weight, he wrapped the paper around it, and pushed it through the hole into the Thénardiers' room.

The note rolled noisily across the floor, just as Thénardier was heading for his prisoner with the knife. Madame Thénardier, seeing the note, yelled, "What is this?"

The old woman rushed to pick up the paper and handed it to her husband, as he demanded, "Where did this come from?"

"Thrown through the window. Where else?" the old woman reasoned.

Thénardier rapidly unfolded the paper and held it near the candle. "This is Éponine's handwriting!" he exclaimed. Not wanting to share the words with everyone, he simply handed the note to his wife, and quietly said, "Quickly! Grab the rope ladder! Let's get out of here! And leave the bacon in the mousetrap!"

"Without cutting his throat?" the woman asked.

"We don't have time!" Thénardier yelled, as he hooked the ladder to the window ledge and threw the other end down the side of the building. Then he added, "The bourgeoisie go first!" while he proceeded to climb through the window.

As he started to throw his leg over the ledge, however, one of his cohorts roughly grabbed him by the collar and pulled him back into the room. The brutally strong man then said with an air of anger, "Not so fast, you old dog! After us!"

"Quit acting like children!" Thénardier shouted. "The police are on our heels!"

One of the criminals then said, with a great deal of sarcasm in his voice, "Why don't we stand around, while we draw names from a hat to see who goes first?"

Yet just as he said these words, a deep voice came from the doorway, and said sternly, "Would you like to use my hat?" Every eye in the room was suddenly fixed on the man who had spoken. With a smile on his face, the man was holding his hat toward the motley group of criminals.

It was Javert.

Earlier that evening while making his usual rounds, Javert had noticed an unusual amount of activity at the Gorbeau House. Seeing men who had the seedy look of criminals, and noticing carriages coming and going, he had posted his men and himself among the trees across the street from the house. Growing increasingly impatient, and sure that these men were up to no good, he finally decided to enter the upstairs room of the Thénardiers.

Javert had arrived in the nick of time. He returned his hat to his head and walked into the room with his arms folded across his chest. His cane was stuck under one arm, and he had a sword that was still in its sheath at his side. As he walked toward the men, he spoke calmly, but very deliberately, and said, "You will not go out through the window, but down the stairway." Then he added with a sly smile, "The stairs are less dangerous." Immediately after warning the men, his entire squad of some fifteen men came tramping up the stairs and began handcuffing the criminals.

The large throng of men cast large shadows across the walls from the dim light of the only candle in the room, as Javert shouted, "Handcuff them all!"

As they grabbed Madame Thénardier, she stared at her shackled hands, began to weep, and asked through her sobs, "What about my poor daughters?"

"They are in good hands," Javert responded coldly. Then he glanced across the room and noticed the criminals' prisoner, who had not said a word and was sitting with his head bowed. "Untie that gentleman!" he instructed his men.

As they untied Leblanc, Javert sat down at the table by the candle and began to use the pen, ink, and paper that were there to begin preparing his police report. After he had written a few lines, he looked toward one of his officers, and said, "Have that gentleman who was tied up step forward." At this, the policemen looked behind them, as Javert added with surprise, "Well? Where is he?"

Marius apparently was the only one to notice that "the prisoner," Monsieur Leblanc, Monsieur Urbain Fabre, and the father of "his Ursula"—whoever he was—had disappeared. One of the policemen ran to the window, only to see the rope ladder slightly swinging. Yet no one was in sight.

Javert cursed under his breath, gritted his teeth, and said sadly, "He must have been the biggest catch of them all!"

CHAPTER TWENTY-THREE

No sooner had Javert left the Gorbeau House with his prisoners than Marius left as well. It was now around nine o'clock in the evening, and Marius ventured out to see Courfeyrac. His friend no longer lived in the Latin Quarter, but had moved to the Rue de la Verrerie for what he called "political reasons." And because of people such as Courfeyrac and his friends who populated the area, it was becoming known as a hotbed for insurrection.

Marius told Courfeyrac he needed a safe place to stay, so Courfeyrac immediately pulled a mattress from his bed onto the floor and offered, "You may sleep here." Early the next morning Marius returned to the Gorbeau House, loaded his books, bed, table, dressers, and two chairs onto a pushcart, and left without leaving a forwarding address. He wanted to avoid the possibility that Javert might return to question the inhabitants of the house about the events of the preceding evening. When Javert did arrive later that same day, he asked the old landlady about the resident of the adjoining room to that of the Thénardiers, but she answered by saying simply, "Moved away!"

Another visitor to the Gorbeau House had also questioned the landlady. He was a young lad who had the look of a street urchin. He told her he was looking for his parents and his sisters and that he had heard they lived upstairs. He said his last name was Thénardier, but the old woman answered coldly, by saying, "I don't know anyone by that name. Besides, the family that lived upstairs is in jail." The boy then walked down the street, happily whistling a tune. His name was Gavroche.

Marius's own hasty change of residence was prompted by two primary reasons. The first was that the previous nights' events had built a sense of horror in his mind when he thought of remaining there. And the second was that, despite Thénardier's evil behavior, he did not want to be forced to testify against him in a court of law. Out of respect for his father's memory, he could not bring himself to testify against the man who had risked his life to save his father in the heat of battle.

Yet Marius was once again heartbroken, as though everything in his life had suddenly plunged through a trapdoor. For a brief moment he had again beheld the lovely young woman he loved and the old man who appeared to be her father. Yet he still did not know the girl's identity or her address, which was the only information that he believed could ever bring him happiness. And just as she was nearly in his grasp, a gust of wind had swept his hopes away. Everything had vanished—except his love.

To make matters worse, the icy breath of poverty was once again breathing down Marius's neck. New law cases seemed to be few and far between, and in the midst of his mental torment, he found it difficult to concentrate on those he had. He began to avoid work altogether and felt he was on the verge of falling into a bottomless pit. One question occupied his mind: "Will I ever see the woman I love again?"

The young man's soul seemed paralyzed, and even during his waking hours he dreamed of her. He took long walks each day to think, and hoped against hope for the miracle of finding her again. Yet after several weeks, his thinking was becoming so clouded that he no longer even saw the sun.

One day as he walked in the shadows of the twin towers of Notre Dame, he suddenly heard a familiar voice saying, "Marius, is it you?" Stunned to hear his name, he raised his eyes. Standing before him was the poor young woman who had visited him weeks ago. It was Éponine, the older of the two Thénardier daughters. He now knew her name, having heard it during the notorious scene he had witnessed. She was barefoot and was wearing the same dirty rags she had worn the morning she had visited him—only now they were two months older and more tattered. She appeared poorer than before, yet in spite of it all, she was beautiful. She stood in front of Marius, totally speechless for a few moments, as a slight smile crossed her face.

"I have found you at last!" she said, excitedly. "I have searched these streets for weeks! If only you knew how hard I've looked! The police had me under lock and key for two weeks after that incident in our house, but realizing they had no evidence against me and that I was two months underage, they finally let me go. As soon as I was out I began looking for you. So you don't live at the Gorbeau House anymore?"

"No," Marius said.

"I guess I don't blame you for that, especially after such a disturbing incident," she said. "Where do you live now?"

Marius did not reply.

Éponine continued, "You don't seem glad to see me."

He remained silent, not really trusting the young woman because of the previous deception she had foisted upon him. He thought for a moment before offering, "There is a way you could make me glad to see you. The lovely young woman who visited your room that day with the old gentleman—have you discovered her address?"

Éponine had been able to discover the mysterious young woman's address—albeit quite by accident. It seems that one of Thénardier's cohorts in crime had sent her a message from prison. Éponine had been instructed to investigate a particular house on the Rue Plumet as a potential target for burglary, and had watched the house for several days. To her great surprise, the man who lived there with his daughter was the same man who had slipped through her father's grasp once before. Upon learning who lived there, however, Éponine had sent a message back to prison that this house would not make a good target after all. Yet her conclusion was to be ignored by her father.

Now upon hearing Marius's request for the young woman's address, a conflict welled up within Éponine. For years she had longed for Marius to notice her as he would come and go, and now he was asking her help in finding another woman. Her lower lip quivered slightly as she finally decided to give him what he asked. Simply desiring to please the man she had secretly come to love, she said, "You look so sad, poor Marius. I want to see you smile once again. Promise me you will smile. Yes, I know her address."

Marius's face turned pale, as all his blood seemed to flow back to his heart. He reached to take Éponine's hand, and pleaded, "Please take me to her."

After sighing deeply, she said, "I will show you where she lives. I know the house well. It is quite a distance from here, but I will take you there." Then she headed in the opposite direction from which she had come, but after a few steps she stopped, turned to him, and said, "Monsieur Marius, you are following me too closely. Let me go on ahead, and then follow me without appearing to do so. A nice young man like you should not be seen with a woman like me."

Éponine walked another dozen paces and stopped again. Marius walked up to her, as she said, "By the way, remember that you promised me something." Of course, she was referring to the smile she had hoped to see brighten his face. Yet Marius simply fumbled through his pockets and pulled out a five-francs piece and put it in her hand. She then opened her fingers and allowed the coin to fall to the ground, as she stared at him with sad eyes.

"It's not your money I want," she said.

A little more than two years before this, in October 1829, Jean Valjean had left the Convent of the Petit Picpus with Cosette. He had been completely happy with their lives there, but a matter of conscience began to overtake him. Living in the convent kept him safe from police capture and allowed him the opportunity to see his daughter every day. The convent had become his total universe, as well as hers, and he could easily envision growing quite old and dying there. Yet he began to ask himself that if by clutching this happiness for himself, was he in fact confiscating true happiness from Cosette. He knew that if they stayed at the convent, no one could ever take his daughter from him, but he also knew that if she were required to stay there much longer, she would probably become a nun. This probability became the root of his perplexing thoughts.

Many years ago he had resolved to never be a thief again, and yet he saw himself as perfectly willing to steal Cosette's future from her. If he did not allow her to know life before she renounced it as a nun, he was actually stealing her life from her—and he was depriving her without her consent.

Valjean began to see that he was depriving Cosette of many of the joys of life, under the pretext of saving her from the trials of life. Allowing her to grow in such continued isolation was to rob a human being from its true nature and to lie to God, he thought. If she stayed in the convent and later became a nun, would she someday come to hate him for his selfishness? Ironically, this last thought caused him to make a selfish decision—for he knew he could not live if she grew to hate him. He decided to leave the convent with Cosette.

With the decision made, Valjean waited for the perfect opportunity. It was not long before it presented itself, for Fauchelevent, his old gardener friend, died. Valjean asked to speak to the reverend mother, and told her that since he had received a small inheritance at the death of his "brother," he was now able to live without working, and desired to leave the convent with his "grand-daughter." Yet he wanted the sister to know that he did not take the last five years for granted, and since Cosette was not going to take the vows of a nun, he wished to make a donation for the education she had received. He gave the reverend mother five thousand francs.

After this Valjean continued to use the name he had taken at the convent: Ultimus Fauchelevent, and he and Cosette moved to the house on the Rue Plumet, where he endeavored to stay out of sight. Yet at the same time he rented two other rooms in Paris, which were quite pitiful in their appearance. By living in three different places and moving every couple of months, he felt he would draw much less attention to himself. And if he needed to escape the clutches of Javert, as in the past, he would have other hiding places as options.

Cosette was a little more than fourteen years old when they left the convent, and, except for her eyes, she was more homely than she was pretty. She was not quite a woman and was still somewhat awkward, thin, and timid, yet the woman within was beginning to appear. Her education was complete, which is to say, she had been taught of the importance of being devoted to God, along with the typical studies of history, geography, grammar, music, and art. Yet in all other respects she was totally naïve, which can be quite charming, but can also be quite dangerous.

Upon leaving the convent, Cosette could have found nothing more wonderful, yet more dangerous, than the house on the Rue Plumet. It became the continuation of solitude and the beginning of liberty for her, for its garden was enclosed, but had one gate that opened onto the street, allowing occasional glimpses of young men who would pass by. Valjean entrusted the garden to her, and said, "Do whatever you like with it." She loved the garden, which became for her a place to dream with the grass beneath her feet.

She also loved her father, Jean Valjean, with all her heart and soul and with such an innocent passion that the man had become a wonderful companion and friend for her. He had become more and more cultured over time, yet often his mind was still rough, while his heart had become tender. Valjean had never been happier. When they would go for walks she would take his arm, and he would feel his heart melt with delight.

Cosette had nothing but a confused recollection of her childhood. She prayed every morning and night for her mother, whom she did not remember, while the Thénardiers had become like two hideous creatures in a vague dream. She recalled going to fetch some water in a forest one evening, in a place that seemed very far away from Paris. The event was what she considered to be the turning point in her life, for she remembered her life then as one that was falling into a deep, dark pit, but one that was rescued by Jean Valjean.

The young woman did not even know her mother's name, and whenever she would ask her father, he would remain silent. If she persisted, however, and asked again, Valjean would simply smile. Once, when she insisted and repeated the question a second time, he was silent again, but she noticed tears welling up in his eyes.

One day Cosette said to him, "Father, I saw my mother in a dream last night. She had two large wings like an angel. My mother must have been a saint during her life."

"By way of her martyrdom, my child," Valjean replied.

CHAPTER TWENTY-FOUR

꧇

Jean Valjean and Cosette often spent their days taking bread to those who were hungry and clothes to those who were cold. Assisting many little children in distress, especially in light of her own distressing childhood, helped keep Cosette in a rather happy mood. It was during this very pleasant time in their lives, a time of helping others, that they had been deceptively lured to the Jondrettes'—or the Thénardiers'—room.

The evening of that terrible event, Valjean returned home emotionally calm, which was his nature, but with a large, inflamed wound on his left arm that looked very much like a burn. He gave Cosette some vague explanation in an effort to keep her from knowing that the family she had visited earlier that day was actually the very family who had mistreated her for so many years when she was just a child. Valjean wanted to protect her from the potential of reopening a wound of her own. Yet his wound became infected, causing him to be confined to bed with a fever for a full month. Cosette often urged him to summon a doctor, but he refused.

She dressed his wound each morning and evening with such an angelic sweetness that another kind of healing was engendered as well. After his recent encounter with Javert, and his horrific treatment at the hands of the Thénardiers, old fears and anxieties had returned. But as Cosette took care of him, those old emotions began to dissipate. He would gaze at her and think, "What a blessing this wound has become! What a wonderful misfortune!"

While Valjean was confined to bed, Cosette spent her days with him and read aloud any book he desired. He felt he was undergoing a new birth, for his happiness was being revived under rays of light that seemed indescribable. The troubling events of the recent past, not only the one with Javert and the Thénardiers, but also the one concerning the young spy who had been following him from Luxembourg Park, were clouds upon his soul. Now they were growing increasingly dim with each passing day. In fact, he came to the point where he thought, "I must have imagined all this. I am becoming such an old fool!"

His happiness was so complete that the unexpected discovery of the Thénardiers, as horrible as it was, had now glided past him. After all, he had made his escape and all trace of him had been lost by Javert, so what more did he care! Now he only thought of the wretched Thénardier family with a sense of pity because of their miserable poverty and the fact they were in prison, yet he was glad they would no longer be able to do harm to anyone.

Taking care of her father had gotten Cosette out of the habit of spending time in her garden. Yet spring was here, and now that Valjean was well he encouraged her to spend time in it again. So she resumed her walks in the garden, but primarily out of a sense of obedience. Usually she walked alone, for Valjean had a fear of being recognized through the gate and seldom went there.

In the garden there was a stone bench that was situated between the gate and a beautiful elm tree, which kept it shaded much of the day. The branches overhung the wall and kept the bench shielded from view from passers-by, but the bench was close enough to the gate for someone to reach it by extending an arm through the gate.

One evening during April, Cosette had gone out to stroll through her garden shortly after sundown. She sat on the bench for a while and then stood to walk around for a few moments. Yet when she returned, a large stone was sitting on the bench in the very place where she had been sitting. Realizing someone must have reached through the gate to place it there, she became alarmed and rushed inside. Locking the door behind her, she ran to her room, pulled her shutters closed, and bolted them as well.

When she awoke the next morning, she wondered if what she had experienced was simply a nightmare she had dreamed the previous night. She thought, "I'm being silly, and surely I was just dreaming." Yet, just to make sure, she dressed and hurried to the garden. She suddenly broke into a cold sweat, for the stone was indeed there, and in the light of day Cosette was able to see what appeared to be a white envelope sitting beneath the stone. Lifting the heavy stone, she grabbed the envelope and pulled several pages of paper from it. Each page was numbered and had several lines written on it with what she thought was rather pretty handwriting. The note was not signed by anyone, and was not addressed to anyone, although she assumed it was for her since it was left on her bench. The same beautiful handwriting comprised the entire note, but it was obvious to Cosette, because of the varying thickness of the black ink, that it had been written over some period of time—probably a period of days, if not weeks.

Cosette's hands began to tremble as she wondered who would have left this for her, and how this person, whoever it may be, would even have known she lived here. Yet she was intrigued with what the words might say, so she began to read. This is what she read:

> Love is the language of God and the angels who live amongst the stars of the universe.
>
> God created everything, yet His creation hides Him. Without love people appear dark, but love renders them transparent.
>
> Certain thoughts become prayers, and there are moments when, regardless of the position of the body, the soul is on its knees.
>
> People who love, though separate from one another, possess a reality of their own. Although they may not see or write the one they love, they discover a mysterious way to communicate. They send each other the song of the birds, the perfume of the flowers, the smiles of children, the light of the sun, the sighing of the breeze, the light of the stars—all of creation itself—and why not? All the works of God's creation are made to serve love. Love is sufficiently powerful to fill all of nature with its message. Oh, Spring! You are the letter I send to her!

The future belongs to our hearts more than it belongs to our minds. Love is the only thing that can fill eternity, for to fill that which is infinite requires that which is inexhaustible.

On the day a woman emits light as she passes you, you become lost in love. Only one thing remains for you—to think of her so intently that she is compelled to think of you.

What love commences can only be completed by God Himself, Who evidently made creation for the soul, and the soul for love!

If you are a stone, be strong; if you are a plant, be sensitive; but if you are a man, be love.

Nothing will satisfy but love. If we have happiness, we desire paradise; if we possess paradise, we demand heaven.

I saw in the street a very poor young man who was in love. His hat was old and his coat was threadbare. Water ran through the soles of his shoes—but through his soul passed the light of the stars.

True love ranges from despair to enchantment over a handkerchief lost and then found. Eternity is required to fulfill its devotion and its hopes, for they are comprised of both what is infinitely large and infinitely small.

God can add nothing to the happiness of those who love one another, but to grant them eternity together.

There is a being who has gone away and has carried the heavens with her.

Does she still go to Luxembourg Park? No. Does she still attend mass at Saint Jacques? No, she no longer goes there. Does she still live in the same house? No, she has moved away. Where has she gone? She did not say. What a miserable thing not to know the address of one's soul!

Yet those who suffer because of love—love all the more.

What a great thing to be loved! But what a far greater thing it is to love, for without someone who loves, the sun would become extinct.

As she pondered the words, the mind that had crafted them gradually unfolded before her, and the mysterious lines shone brightly in her eyes and filled her heart with a strange radiance. It was as if a fist had suddenly opened and flung a handful of rays of light toward her. In these few lines she felt a passionate, generous, and honest nature, yet one that had experienced an immense sorrow and despair. She felt a suffering heart—one that had one toe in the grave, but one finger in heaven—had composed the words. The lines to her were the drops of someone's soul, falling one by one onto paper.

Who could have penned them? Cosette did not hesitate even one moment—for it could only be one person. "He" had written them! And it was his arm that had reached through the gate to leave it! He had found her again! And although she had tried to force herself to forget him, she had always loved him—always adored him! Day had dawned once more in her spirit!

She clutched the letter to her heart, ran to the house, and locked herself in her room. She read the words over and over again, until she knew them by heart. And once she had thoroughly mastered them, she kissed the note, and dreamed of it at night. Cosette was deeply in love, and it seemed to her the gates of Eden had opened once again.

That first evening after she had found the note, Cosette dressed herself in one of her most beautiful dresses—one that by the slope of the neckline revealed the very top of her throat. As young girls would say, it was "a trifle indecent," but actually it was not indecent at all—it was simply prettier than usual. She combed her hair in a very becoming style and lightly touched her neck with just a hint of perfume.

She did all this without really knowing why, for she had not planned to go out, and she was not expecting a visitor. Nevertheless, at dusk she went down to the garden and began to stroll through the trees, occasionally pushing the branches aside, because some of them hung very low to the ground. Finally she sat down on her bench.

The stone was still there. Cosette gently laid her soft hand on the hard rock as though she wished to caress it and thank it. Then she suddenly had that indescribable feeling that people often experience when someone is nearby, even when they cannot see the person. She stood to her feet and turned around.

It was "He"! He was standing inside the open gate just behind the bench. Cosette did not make a sound, and felt ready to faint. She slowly backed away from him and would have fallen had she not bumped against the old elm and begun to lean upon it. He had not moved, but then suddenly she heard his voice—the voice she had never really heard. It was barely a whisper that rose above the rustle of the leaves, and said, "Excuse me. I didn't mean to startle you, but I had to come. Please don't be afraid. My heart is full, and I knew I could not go on living as I was. Have you read what I left for you on the bench? Do you recognize me at all? I know it's been a long time since you first saw me at Luxembourg Park—nearly a year has passed. You see, you are an angel to me! Please allow me to come here, or I believe I will die. If you only knew how I adore you! I hardly know myself what I am saying, so please forgive me if I seem to be too forward. Have I displeased you?"

All Cosette could manage to say was, "Oh, my dear!" as she sank down, feeling as though she were on the verge of death. He reached out as she fell and took her in his arms, and then pressed her to himself without knowing what he was doing. As he held her, he was beside himself with love.

After a few moments she took his hand and laid it near her heart. He felt the envelope she had placed there, and after a time he was finally able to stammer the question on his heart, "You love me?"

She replied in a voice that was nothing more than a breathless whisper, "Shhh! You know I do!" Then she hid her blushing face by pressing it against his chest.

As the stars were beginning to shine, they found themselves sitting by each other on the bench. Neither could have explained how it happened that their lips met, any more than they could have explained how it is that birds sing, that snow melts, that a rose bud unfolds, or that the dawn grows bright behind the dark trees on the shivering crest of the hills.

It was just a kiss. Yet it startled both of them, as they speechlessly gazed into the darkness with sparkling eyes. They did not feel the cool of the night, the cold bench, or the damp grass. They simply looked at each other, while their full hearts attempted to sort their thoughts. Without realizing it, they were holding hands.

Little by little they began to talk, until finally their words seemed to naturally overflow to one another. This pure man and woman told each other everything—their dreams, their fears, their weaknesses, how each had adored the other from afar, how they had longed for one another, and their despair when they had been unable to see each other again. She did not ask how he had found her, and she did not care, for it seemed so natural that he was there.

At last, when they had finished telling one another everything, she laid her head on his shoulder and asked, "What is your name?"

"My name is Marius," he said. "And yours?"

"My name is Cosette."

It was May 1832, and from the moment that sacred kiss engaged two souls, Marius came to the garden every evening. They both felt they were overflowing with the happiness of heaven, that they were living among angels more than mankind, and they had a pure and glowing radiance that shone for each other amid the shadows of the night. They touched each other, they gazed into each other's eyes, they held hands and pressed themselves close to one another, but there was a line they did not cross. In fact, their first kiss had also been their last. Marius would go no further than to touch Cosette's hand or a lock of her hair with his lips.

To Marius, his time with Cosette each evening was enough, and he did not picture a future life beyond just sitting elbow to elbow on their bench. He would be content to sit there night after night, gazing at Cosette through the scattered starlight shining through the trees. Yet certain shadows of complications were fast approaching that would soon cloud their skies.

One night at their normal rendezvous time, he arrived to find Cosette quite sad. She related to him, "My father told me this morning to get my things ready to move. He said he has business affairs to handle, and that we may go to England. Then he instructed me to be ready to travel a week from now."

Marius shuddered from head to toe, and stammered, "But this is outrageous!" Then in a weak voice, he asked, "When will you return?"

"He did not say," she answered. Marius was distraught, but when he looked at Cosette again, she smiled at him and added, "How silly we are being! I have an idea! If my father and I leave, why don't you just follow us?"

Yet reality had already set in for Marius, for he said, "Are you crazy? I would need money to go to England, and I have none. In fact, I owe my friend Courfeyrac more than ten louis, and all my clothes are worn out. My coat has buttons missing, my only shirt is ragged, and my boots let water in when it rains. You've only seen me at night and give me your love. But if you were to see me during the day, even you would think I was a beggar and would offer me some money yourself. Go to England? Impossible! I can't even afford a passport, much less the fare."

Marius then leaned against a tree and stared at the dark sky, looking like a statue of despair. After what seemed like hours, a faint noise behind him broke him from his dismal thoughts, and he realized Cosette was sobbing. He fell to his knees, took her hand, and while kissing it, said, "Cosette, I have never given my word to anyone. But I give you my most sacred word of honor, that if you go away, I will die."

Then, with a sudden sense of hopefulness in his voice, Marius added, "But now that I think of it, you should at least have my address, just in case something changes. Something might happen. You never know." He pulled a penknife from his pocket, as he said, "I live with the friend I mentioned— Courfeyrac—at this address." Then he scratched "16 Rue de la Verrerie" on the plaster of the garden wall with the blade of his knife.

Later that same week Jean Valjean was walking down the street and passed by a man he was certain was Thénardier. Yet, since Valjean was accustomed to wearing a disguise when he went out during the day, Thénardier did not recognize him. Several of the men who had conspired with Thénardier to hold Valjean captive were with him, and Valjean surmised that these criminals must have escaped from prison already and were on the prowl in the neighborhood.

To make matters worse for Valjean, political unrest was increasingly breaking the tranquillity of Paris. For the last few months, throughout the spring of 1832, the people had suffered through a cholera epidemic, which had cast a sense of gloom over the entire city, and the scene was set for insurrection. Then during the very month that Valjean was considering his journey to England—the month of June—the spark was lit. General Lamarque, who had been a stabilizing force somewhere between the left and the extreme left of the political spectrum, had suddenly died. He had served as a beloved leader of the people under Napoléon and was a calming force during the Restoration.

Now the city's primary symbol of stability was dead. For anyone wishing to conceal his identity, such as Valjean, this was a potential problem. The police were becoming more and more uneasy, and suspicious of nearly everyone. This had led Valjean to consider leaving Paris, and possibly France altogether, by going to England. He had told Cosette of his plans, and hoped to leave before the end of the week.

Adding to Valjean's concern was something that had happened the very next morning. He had awakened before Cosette and went for a stroll through the garden alone. There were a number of things rushing through his mind as he took a seat on her bench to ponder them. He was concerned about Thénardier, Javert and the police, his trip to England, and the difficulty of obtaining a legal passport as an ex-convict. As he sat on the bench, he saw something that greatly increased his alarm. He saw an address—16 Rue de la Verrerie—that appeared to have been scratched into the garden wall, probably with a nail. Examining the wall closely, he noticed that the thin grooves of the letters seemed freshly cut, and that the leaves below had a fine dusting of white plaster powder on them. From the looks of it, it had probably been carved into the wall the previous night.

What did this mean? Was it a signal for someone else? Or was it a warning to him in particular? Whatever the case, it was now quite evident that the security of the garden had been violated and that some stranger had made his way into it. His mind began racing, as he considered the various possibilities of what this could mean, and none of them were good. He made a determination not to share what he had found written on the wall with Cosette, for fear of alarming her.

Suddenly, while totally absorbed in these thoughts, Valjean saw a dark shadow fall across his feet. Immediately a folded piece of paper landed on his knees, as though someone had leaned over the wall and dropped it over his head. He quickly grabbed the paper, unfolded it, and read the following words written in capital letters: MOVE AWAY FROM YOUR HOUSE.

Valjean sprang to his feet, peered over the wall, and caught a quick glimpse of someone jumping over the retaining wall of the nearby bridge. The person seemed larger than a child, yet smaller than a man, and was dressed in a gray shirt, and what appeared to be dust-colored cotton velvet trousers. Valjean then went inside, wondering what all this meant, who would have sent him this message, and why.

In spite of not having answers to his questions, one thing was certain—his decision to leave this place had been confirmed.

CHAPTER TWENTY-FIVE

M arius began to wander the streets, which is often the only medicine for those who suffer. After learning the news that Cosette was going to England, he walked about for some time, returned to Courfeyrac's room at two o'clock in the morning, and then threw himself on his mattress without undressing. When he awoke he saw Courfeyrac and Enjolras standing in the room with their hats in hand, obviously ready to go somewhere.

Courfeyrac looked at him and said, "Are you coming with us to General Lamarque's funeral?" Marius told his friends to go on ahead of him, for his thoughts were only of Cosette. His plan was to visit her at their normal nine o'clock rendezvous time until the day she and her father left for England.

Marius soon left Courfeyrac's room, waiting for nine o'clock with feverish impatience. As he left, he tucked both his loaded pistols under his belt, and even he could not have explained what led him to take them with him. Yet the political unrest of Paris was becoming more and more violent, and as he roamed the deserted streets before seeing Cosette, he thought he heard the sounds of fighting.

Precisely at nine o'clock, just as the sun was setting, he went to the Rue Plumet as he had promised Cosette. Approaching her gate, his only thought was this momentary happiness that was soon to be taken from him. It had been forty-eight hours since he had seen Cosette, and he was filled with profound joy as he anticipated seeing her once more. He rushed into the garden, but she was not there, so he walked to the steps of the house, thinking she might be waiting for him in the recess of the doorway. Cosette was not there either. Then he walked through the entire garden, but it was deserted as well. Finally he returned to the house, noticing that all the shutters were closed. He repeatedly knocked at the door, risking being confronted by Cosette's father, yet there was no answer. He cried out repeatedly, "Cosette!" but again there was no reply. No one was in the garden or the house.

Everything was over for Marius! He was thankful that he had been blessed with such deep love for once in his life, but now that Cosette was gone, he thought all that was left for him was to die. As he sat on the front steps in a state of despair, he suddenly heard a voice calling to him from the street that said, "Monsieur Marius!" Startled, he jumped to his feet, as the voice added, "Your friends are waiting for you at the barricade being built on the Rue de la Chanvrerie."

The voice seemed somewhat familiar to him and sounded like the raspy, rough voice of Éponine. He rushed to the gate attempting to see whoever had spoken. Yet he simply caught a glimpse of someone who appeared to be a young man running into the darkness. This voice, which was summoning Marius through the shadows of the night to the barricade on the Rue de la Chanvrerie, seemed to him to be the voice of destiny. He wished to die, and now it appeared the opportunity was presenting itself.

Marius had decided to knock on the door of that tomb, and a hand in the darkness was offering him the key. These doors that open during times of despair can be quite tempting, and the young man made a decision to pass through its gate. Emerging from the garden, he said, "I will go!" He set out at a rapid pace, now understanding why he had earlier felt the need to arm himself with his pistols.

Not fifteen minutes had passed when riots broke out in more than twenty different places in the center of Paris. On both banks of the River Seine and throughout the Latin Quarter people read their proclamations and shouted, "To arms!" They broke street lanterns and began gathering anything they could find to build barricades. They uprooted trees on the boulevards, unhooked carriages, tore doors off houses, and used furniture and wooden planks to build their defenses.

In less than three hours, like a powder keg that had been torched, the center of Paris had been abruptly turned into a huge fortress of insurrection. In the Saint Jean Marketplace, the military guard had already been overwhelmed and disarmed by the revolutionaries, and the company of young men led by Enjolras and Courfeyrac was in control.

Their numbers were swelling quickly, and one of the lads to join this armed group was the son of the Thénardiers, Gavroche. He was merely eleven or twelve years of age, but was very accustomed to making his own way and surviving on the streets, living like a street urchin. He still appeared to have the happiness of a child on his face, yet his heart had grown sad and empty, like that of a hopeless old man. His ragged clothes were only what had been offered to him through charity. His parents nearly prided themselves on their cruelty to him, for his father said he never thought of his son, and his mother openly said she loved her daughters, but not him. Then, while he was still a child, they gave him a swift kick into the streets. As a result, Gavroche felt the pavement was less hard than his mother's heart, and came to love life on the streets. He was a child deserving of pity, and although his parents were still living, he was nevertheless an orphan.

Thus, this group of young revolutionaries had become Gavroche's family. They were ill prepared for fighting, yet even when the rain soaked their clothes, there was lightning in their eyes. The brigade continued to grow, with students, artists, and longshoremen joining their ranks. Most were armed with clubs and swords, while only a few had pistols.

One day, as Courfeyrac had led the group down the street, Gavroche had tagged along. And now that the rioting had broken out all across Paris, his "family" was growing by the minute.

One person finding his way to their barricade just as the rioting began was an older man of lofty stature whose hair was turning gray. He appeared to be a bold and daring man, and Courfeyrac and Enjolras remarked that they were glad to have him on board. Yet no one knew—or asked—his name.

As more and more recruits arrived, they brought with them gun powder, torches, and additional materials to construct their barricades. Courfeyrac and Enjolras divided the group into two smaller groups who worked simul-taneously on two barricades at one street corner. The two barricades sat at right angles to one another, effectively blocking two streets. Gavroche worked on the larger of the two, while the older man who had joined the group made himself useful on the smaller one. In total there were about fifty workers, with thirty having "borrowed" guns from the local armory on their way to the barricades. Gavroche was radiant and appeared to be completely taken with the work. He climbed up and down the barricade while generally whistling a tune. And although he was so young, his enthusiasm was contagious and seemed to be an encouragement to everyone.

Finally the two barricades were finished, so Courfeyrac raised their red flag to the top and then issued thirty bullets to each man who had a gun. It was now totally dark, and all was quiet in the surrounding area. The only fighting the men could hear was the sound of very distant and quite intermittent gunfire. These fifty men sat waiting for the sixty thousand they knew would ultimately arrive. While they waited, Enjolras went to find Gavroche, who had been instructed to make more bullets in the group's nearby headquarters in the Café Musain.

As soon as Enjolras found the young lad, he knew something was troubling Gavroche. The gray-haired man who had earlier been working on the barricade had also entered the café and had seated himself at the most poorly lit table. Initially Gavroche had simply admired the man's gun, but when Gavroche moved closer and got a good look at his face, he was startled. The boy pulled Enjolras aside and said in a quiet voice, "Do you see that big fellow over there?"

"What about him?" Enjolras demanded.

"He's a police spy," Gavroche whispered.

"How do you know?"

"Less than two weeks ago he grabbed me by my ear to question me. I was walking along, minding my own business, when he stopped me," the boy explained. At this, Enjolras walked across the room and whispered a few words to a longshoreman who was there. The man left the room and moments later returned with three other men. Then all four of these muscular men positioned themselves directly behind the older man, who was still seated at his dimly lit table. None of this activity had drawn any undo suspicion from the man. He simply remained seated, leaning over the table on his elbows.

With his men in place, Enjolras approached the man and demanded, "Who are you?"

Obviously not suspecting such a direct question, the man gazed up with a startled look. He fixed his eyes on Enjolras's, attempting to grasp the young man's meaning. Then he smiled an arrogant smile, and with a sense of haughtiness and disdain in his voice, he said, "Ah, I see what this is! Okay! I'll play your game."

"You are a police spy then?" Enjolras questioned.

"I am an agent of the authorities," was all the man answered.

"And your name?"

"Javert."

Enjolras signaled to the four men, who, in the blink of an eye—before Javert even had time to turn around—grabbed him, threw him to the floor, searched him, and then securely tied his hands and feet with rope. In his pocket they also found a small card that was engraved with the seal of France, and which said, "Javert—Police Inspector—age fifty-two." The card was signed by the Chief of Police: Monsieur Gisquet.

After they had finished searching Javert, they stood him to his feet, and with his hands still tied behind his back, they secured him with another rope to a pole in the middle of the café. Gavroche, who had watched this entire scene with a great deal of satisfaction, stepped forward, smiled slyly at Javert, and said; "I guess it's the mouse that has caught the cat this time."

Javert did not utter a word. Then Enjolras looked at the man with cold eyes of steel and said, "You will be shot ten minutes before these barricades are taken."

Marius was finally nearing the street where the voice had told him his friends were waiting for him on the barricades, and as he came within one block of them, everything was still quiet. Then, as ten o'clock sounded from a distant church bell, he could see Enjolras and Courfeyrac, who were seated on the larger of the two barricades with their guns in hand. They were not speaking, but were listening intently for even the faintest and most distant sound of marching. Suddenly, in the midst of the dismal calm, a clear, young voice could be heard singing. At the end of the short song, a sound like that of a rooster crowing rose through the night air.

Breaking his silence, Enjolras said, "It is Gavroche." They had sent the lad out as a sentinel, thinking he would not be suspected as a revolutionary by the authorities because of his young age.

"Yes, he is warning us," Courfeyrac agreed.

The calmness of the deserted street was abruptly broken, as they saw Gavroche hurriedly round the corner and run toward them. Two shots resounded, but apparently missed their mark, for the boy quickly bounded up the front of the barricade, and breathlessly said, "They're here! Give me a gun!" Then someone handed him the large gun he had previously admired. It was Javert's.

Several minutes passed until they distinctly heard the heavy, measured steps of numerous feet marching in their direction. At last they could also distinguish the sight of what appeared to be a multitude of metallic threads. It was the sight of bayonets and gun barrels glistening by the light of torches.

From the depths of the metallic threads came a sinister voice, which shouted toward the barricades, "Who goes there!" Then the fifty men heard the clicking of guns, as they were being cocked and lowered into position.

Enjolras answered the voice, with a proud and boisterous tone, "The French Revolution!"

"Fire!" was the answer to his cry. At the voice's command a flash emblazoned the once dark façades of the buildings lining the street. The red flag of the revolutionaries was immediately struck down, for the discharges had been so numerous and violent they had cut the pole in two. And although the men had hidden behind the barricades, bullets ricocheting from the cornices of the buildings had wounded a number of them.

After the first barrage, Courfeyrac shouted to his men, "Let's not waste our powder. Wait until they are in front of us in the street before firing."

Marius watched this eruption of gunfire while remaining concealed in the recess of a doorway one block behind one of the barricades. It had actually been his shots that had been heard as Gavroche had been bounding up the barricade moments earlier. Several sentries for the authorities had secretly made their way behind the revolutionaries, and Marius, seeing them from his hiding place, took careful aim. His first shot spared Gavroche just as he reached the top of the barricade, while his second round struck the other sentry who had leveled his aim at Courfeyrac.

Flinging his discharged pistols aside, Marius left the doorway and raced toward the barricade. Passing the Musain Café, he noticed a powder keg near the door and turned to pick it up. As he did so, another soldier took aim at him, but just as the man fired, a hand grabbed the muzzle of the gun and obstructed the musket ball. Through the resulting smoke, Marius could vaguely see that the person who had pushed the gun aside was a young workman, who appeared to be dressed in a gray shirt and velvet trousers. The young man fell to the ground after the shot, but it had missed Marius altogether. He then rushed into the café to take shelter.

Hearing the shots that had been fired from behind, Enjolras shouted,

"Wait! Don't fire at random!" Finally the soldiers were so close that the revolutionaries could have spoken to them without raising their voices. One of the officers yelled toward the barricade, as he extended his sword, "Lay down your arms!"

Enjolras replied by shouting, "Fire!" At this, both sides opened fire and everything seemed to disappear in smoke.

Once the smoke cleared, the combatants on both sides had been considerably thinned. Those remaining alive began reloading their guns in silence, when a voice suddenly thundered, "Get away or I'll blow up this barricade!" It was Marius who had grabbed the powder keg, and under the cover of the smoke, had rushed to the top of the barricade. As he held a torch near the keg, the soldiers simply stared at him in amazement. Then he demanded again, "Get back or I'll blow up this barricade and take you and me with it!"

Marius held the flame even closer to the keg, and finally the soldiers began to retreat. They ran for their lives, totally abandoning their dead and wounded, and at last disappeared into the darkness. For now the barricade was free, and the revolutionaries then retreated as well. There was a deafening calm as Marius, now alone on the barricade, began descending. Suddenly he heard his name being called from a voice in the darkness. The voice said feebly, "Monsieur Marius!"

To his surprise, it was the very same voice he had heard some two hours before at Cosette's garden gate. Yet now the voice was nothing more than a mere breath. He looked around, but saw no one. Marius thought, in light of the awful realities around him, that perhaps his mind was playing tricks on him. He took another step away from the barricade, just as the voice repeated, "Monsieur Marius!" This time he did not doubt that he had heard someone, but he looked around and still saw nothing.

Finally the voice said weakly, "I'm at your feet." He bent down and in nearly total darkness saw a small frame of a person dragging itself toward him along the pavement. As the person neared one of the lanterns left on the street by one of his comrades, he noticed the person was wearing a gray shirt and torn trousers made of coarse cotton velvet. The person also had bare feet and was lying in a pool of blood. At last the voice said, "Don't you recognize me? I'm Éponine."

Marius bent down more closely and saw that it was indeed that unfortunate girl—Éponine—but she was dressed in men's clothes. He spoke softly to her, "What are you doing here?"

Her simple response was, "I am dying."

Suddenly Marius noticed the pool of blood and exclaimed, "You are wounded! Hold on, Éponine! I'll carry you to the café and we'll take care of you there." Then as he reached under her arm to lift her, she cried out in pain. He asked, "Does that hurt? I only touched your hand." In response, she raised her hand toward him, and he could see a black hole in it. In horror, he asked, "What happened to your hand?"

"It stopped a bullet tonight," Éponine said, with a weak smile.

Hearing this, the scene of the small-framed person grabbing the gun of the soldier flashed across his consciousness. Marius realized it was Éponine who had saved his life, and he began to shudder. Finally he stammered, "My poor child! But no one dies of a bullet wound to the hand. I'll dress your wound, and you'll be fine."

Yet the young woman responded in a weak voice, "Yes, the bullet went through my hand. But it went through my chest and out my back as well. It is hopeless to remove me from here, but I will tell you how you can take better care of me than any surgeon. Please sit next to me."

Marius sat on one of the stones of the barricade, and Éponine feebly laid her head in his lap. With a sad smile on her face, and without looking into his eyes, she said, "Oh, how I've longed for this! Now I will suffer no longer!" Then with some effort, she turned to look at Marius, and added, "You know what, Monsieur Marius? I was so stupid for showing you the way to that garden and to her house." She paused for a moment, realizing she was overstepping the limits she had set in her own mind, and added, with a heart-rending smile,

"You thought I was ugly, didn't you?"

Not waiting for his answer, she continued, "Now you are lost as well, for no one will get out of here alive. And I'm to blame. It was I who told you to come here tonight. I wanted us to die together. Yet when I saw the man taking aim at you, I couldn't stop myself and grabbed the muzzle of his gun. How strange life is! I did it because I wanted to die before you."

Marius gazed at the unfortunate creature with deep compassion in his eyes. Suddenly her entire body stiffened and she gasped for air. At that moment, however, she heard the sound of the rooster crowing, and she recognized it as the sound made by little Gavroche. The boy could be heard from inside the café. He had climbed atop one of the tables and was singing as he reloaded his gun. Hearing the lad, Éponine said, "That's my brother. He must not see me here. I know he would scold me."

"Your brother?" asked Marius. Then his mind was suddenly taken to the words of his father that were etched on his heart regarding the Thénardiers.

"Yes, that little fellow who is singing is my brother," she explained. Marius started to move, but she pleaded, "Please don't go away. It won't be long now." Her voice was even softer now, and he could hear the occasional rattle of death in her breathing. Then she struggled to raise her face as closely as possible to his and whispered, "Listen carefully. I have a letter for you in my pocket. I was asked to mail it to you, but I kept it instead. Please don't be angry with me when we meet again soon. Take your letter."

Éponine jerked convulsively and grabbed his hand with her wounded one, but she no longer seemed to feel any pain. With her other hand she pulled the letter from her pocket and handed it to him. Marius took the letter and the young woman leaned back with a sense of contentment. Finally, she added, "Promise me something."

"Yes, of course," Marius said, with a look of true kindness in his eyes.

"Promise!" she demanded.

"Okay, I promise," he insisted.

"Promise to give me a kiss on my forehead once I am dead. I will feel it."

After whispering these final words, she laid her head on Marius's lap once again. Her eyelids closed and she breathed one final time.

Marius kept his promise. He placed a soft, sweet kiss on her forehead, where small beads of perspiration had already turned icy cold. Then with his letter in hand, he walked away. Something told him it would not be appropriate to read the letter in the presence of poor Éponine's body. He walked slowly into the café, broke the feminine-looking seal on the letter, and began reading. The letter was addressed: "Monsieur Marius Pontmercy, c/o Monsieur Courfeyrac, 16 Rue de la Verrerie," and said inside, "My dearest! Unfortunately my father insists on leaving immediately. This evening we are going to 7 Rue de l'Homme Armé. In one week, however, we will be in England. Cosette. June 4th."

Éponine had been the culprit of many of the changes in numerous lives. She had known of her father's plan to once again attack Valjean at his new residence and to steal his money. As a result, she had disguised herself, dressing like a man, and had been the one to throw the note over the wall warning Valjean to move away. Yet her note was written for another reason as well—to separate Marius and Cosette. Once Cosette knew they were moving, she had hastily penned a note to Marius, which she had entrusted to Éponine to deliver. But Éponine put the letter in her pocket, without any intention of ever delivering it. She knew Marius would come to see Cosette again, and upon finding her gone would be distraught—and she was not mistaken. She was also the one to call to him that his friends were waiting for him on the barricade. Therefore, Éponine died with the tragic joy of so many jealous hearts who attempt to drag their beloved into their own death, and who say, "If I can't have him, no one will!"

After having read Cosette's letter, Marius covered it with kisses. Now he knew she had not left without sending word, and that she truly loved him. For one brief moment a thought crossed his mind—perhaps he should now have the will to live. Yet, since he had already asked his grandfather for permission to marry her and had been refused, he realized nothing had really changed. Cosette was still leaving for England and he did not have permission to marry her. Their fates were sealed. However, there were still two duties needing to be fulfilled: to inform Cosette of his death with a final letter of farewell, and to attempt to save the poor Thénardier child, Gavroche, from the impending storm. He felt an obligation to Éponine and to his father to help Gavroche, who had been so mistreated by his own parents.

He pulled a notebook from his leather pouch, tore out a single sheet, and wrote a few lines to Cosette. His words read, "Dearest Cosette! Our marriage is impossible, for my grandfather has refused me permission. I have no money, and now I do not have you. Remember the promise I made to you? I'm going to keep it. For now that you are gone, I am going to die. By the time you read this, my soul will be with you, and you will smile. Marius." Then having nothing with which to seal the letter, he simply folded it and addressed it to: "Mademoiselle Cosette Fauchelevent, 7 Rue de l'Homme Armé."

Next he wrote on the first page of his notebook the following words: "My name is Marius Pontmercy. Please take my body to my grandfather, Monsieur Gillenormand, 6 Rue des Filles du Calvaire, in the Marais." Having finished, he put the notebook in his pocket, called Gavroche over to him, and said, "Will you do me a favor?"

"Anything," Gavroche said. And knowing Marius had saved his life by shooting the sentry, he continued, with a smile on his young face, "After all, if not for you, I would be dead."

"You would have done the same for me. Don't give it a second thought," Marius said humbly. Then he added, "See this letter? I want you to leave the barricade and this area immediately, and first thing tomorrow morning, I want you to deliver it to this address."

Gavroche scratched his ear nervously, but said, "All right." Then he left the café and ran down the street. An idea had occurred to the boy, but he had not mentioned it, for he knew that Marius would most likely object. It was around midnight, and instead of waiting until the morning, he decided to deliver the letter at once.

CHAPTER TWENTY-SIX

O n June fourth, when Jean Valjean and Cosette had left their home on the Rue Plumet, they had taken almost nothing with them. Full trunks would have required the help of porters, and, if questioned, porters would be witnesses. Around dusk they had summoned a carriage, and the only thing Cosette had taken with her was her writing paper and her blotting book. Valjean had told his daughter in the morning of his intention to leave later that day, which had allowed her time to write her note to Marius.

They arrived at their new address on the Rue de l'Homme Armé after nightfall, and had gone to bed shortly thereafter. Being in a new location greatly relieved Valjean's nervousness over being discovered, and he awoke the following morning feeling quite at ease. On this peaceful street where he had taken refuge, Valjean was gradually becoming free of all that had been troubling him for some time.

Yet something strange suddenly caught his attention. He happened to glance at the mirror hanging over the sideboard in the dining room. Upon arriving at their new house the night before, Cosette had been so absorbed in her grief over leaving Marius that she had left her blotting book open and in plain view on the sideboard. Valjean, upon seeing the reflection of the top page in the mirror, was able to make out a few lines of print. The page had obviously blotted her most recent note, and its text had been printed on the blotter as well, only in reverse. In the mirror, its reflection read as follows: "My dearest! Unfortunately my father insists on leaving immediately. This evening we are going to 7 Rue de l'Homme Armé. In one week, however, we will be in England. Cosette. June 4th."

Valjean was dumbfounded and stood before the mirror in disbelief. He read the lines again but still could not believe them. He reeled and then fell into the armchair beside the buffet in utter bewilderment. Finally he began putting times, dates, and events together in his mind regarding Cosette, and ultimately said to himself, "It is he!"

His arrow of despair had not missed its mark, for it was Marius he pictured in his mind, although he did not know the young man's name. He thought of him as "the prowler of Luxembourg Park" and as a coward, for he saw it as cowardly to make eyes at a young girl, especially when a father who loves her is seated beside her.

At nightfall he found himself outside, still thinking about the note and concerned that someone now knew their address. He sat on the wall surrounding the house near the deserted street and listened. In light of the nearby violence, a number of his uneasy bourgeois neighbors passed by but hardly noticed him. He sat there for more than an hour without stirring, when he suddenly heard two distant gunshots. Of course, he had no way of knowing that these were the shots Marius was firing in defense of the barricade on the Rue de la Chanvrerie.

The following sound of many weapons being fired startled him, and he finally rose to his feet. He turned toward the sound of the attack, walked a few steps, but then stopped again and leaned against the wall for some time. Then he heard the sound of footsteps, and upon turning, noticed a young lad coming toward him. It was Gavroche.

For some unknown reason, Valjean felt the urge to stop the boy, and speak somewhat sternly to him. He said, "What's the matter with you, little fellow?"

"What's the matter with me is that I'm hungry," Gavroche replied frankly.

At this, Valjean fumbled through his pocket and pulled out a five-franc piece, as he thought to himself, "Poor thing! He is hungry." He placed the coin in the boy's hand.

With a look of astonishment, the boy stared at the coin. He had only heard of a five-franc piece, but had never actually laid his eyes on one. He quickly thrust the coin into his pocket. Then, without a word of thanks, he said to Valjean, "Do you live on this street?"

"Yes, why?"

"I'm looking for house number 7."

"What do you want with number 7?" Valjean questioned. Fearing he might have said too much, Gavroche paused for a moment. A thought then flashed through Valjean's mind, and he quickly added, "Are you the one bringing the letter I'm expecting?"

With a puzzled look on his face, Gavroche answered, "But you are not a woman."

"The letter is for Mademoiselle Cosette, is it not?"

"Yes," muttered the lad, "I believe that's the name."

"Well, I'm the person to whom you are to deliver the letter. Give it to me," demanded Valjean.

"In that case, you probably ought to know that I was sent from the barricade," explained the child as he reached in his pocket and handed over the letter. Then he added, "Please hurry, for the mademoiselle is waiting for this."

As the boy turned to go, Valjean, seeking one last bit of information from the lad, asked, "Is it to Saint Merry that the answer should be sent?"

"No, the letter has come from the barricade on the Rue de la Chanvrerie, and I'm headed back there. Good evening, citizen!"

Valjean walked into the house clutching Marius's letter. He listened for a moment, wanting to be sure Cosette was asleep. His hand trembled as he struck a match to light a candle, for he knew that what he had just done smacked of theft. Nevertheless, he opened the letter and immediately these words jumped off the page at him: "I am going to die. By the time you read this, my soul will be with you."

He remained dazed for a moment, and was overwhelmed by the change of emotion taking place within himself. He uttered a frightening cry of inner joy, for he held in his hand the joyful news of the death of a hated individual. Now it was over, for the young man's demise had come sooner than he could have even dared to hope. Valjean felt delivered, and he was about to find himself once more alone with Cosette. All he had to do was to keep this letter from her, and she would never know what had become of the young man.

Valjean simply had to let things take their inevitable course. Apparently the young man could not escape his fate, and if he were not already dead, it seemed quite certain he was about to die. "What good fortune!" Valjean thought. Yet having said this to himself, he suddenly felt depressed and sad. Then he went downstairs, woke up the porter, and whispered some instructions to the man.

An hour later Jean Valjean left the house, wearing the complete uniform of the French National Guard and with a firearm at his side. At a brisk walk he headed in the direction of the Saint Jean Marketplace.

After the soldiers' retreat, the revolutionaries had put the barricade back in order and had begun using the kitchen of the café as their hospital. They had now finished tending to the wounded, had made more bullets, had cleaned up the gunpowder that had been scattered on the floor, and had removed the corpses of their dead. They had laid the bodies in a heap on one of the streets still in their control, and the pavement of that spot remained red for a very long time. Among the dead were four of the soldiers of the French National Guard, and Enjolras had their uniforms laid aside.

Enjolras addressed his band of men and said, "Gentlemen, this new republic is not rich enough to waste the lives of men. If it is to survive, some of us must escape. Vain glory is a waste, and if the duty of some is to leave here, that duty should be fulfilled like any other." Then pointing toward the uniforms taken from the dead soldiers, he continued, "With this uniform you can mingle with the troops and escape. There are enough for four."

Courfeyrac spoke up and said, "Any of you who are the sole support of your family do not have the right to sacrifice yourself, for that would be equal to desertion."

"That's true," said another young man to an older one, "You are a father and have a family to support."

The older man retorted, "Yes, but you yourself have two sisters who are depending on you."

With these words the group struggled with who should allow himself to be placed at the door of death's tomb, and who should go. "Whatever we do, we must do it quickly, for in another quarter of an hour it will be too late," Courfeyrac insisted.

"Citizens," added Enjolras, "this is a republic, and we should vote on who will stay and who will go." They obeyed, and after a few brief minutes five were unanimously selected to leave their ranks.

Marius exclaimed, "We have five names, but only four uniforms! One must stay behind." Just then, however, a fifth uniform seemed to miraculously fall from heaven onto the other four, and became the salvation for the fifth man. Marius looked across the dimly lit room, only to recognize the face of the man he knew as Monsieur Fauchelevent.

Under the cover of darkness Valjean had made his way to the barricade and had slipped undiscovered into the café. In utter shock and disbelief, one of the men demanded, "Who is this man?"

"He is a man who saves others," answered Marius soberly, and then added, "I know him."

Marius's apparent stamp of approval on the stranger seemed to pacify everyone. Then Enjolras turned to Valjean and offered, "Welcome, citizen." Finally, in a very somber tone, he added, "You know that we are going to die."

Jean Valjean did not reply. He simply helped the man he had saved to put on his uniform. Once the five chosen men were ready, no one could have known they were not members of the French National Guard. Before setting out the five embraced those who remained, and one of the five shed a tear as he walked away.

Day was beginning to break, and although the revolutionaries did not see their enemy, they could hear something happening some distance away. Finally they saw artillerymen pushing a cannon into place. And just before a cannonball smashed into the barricade, the men heard the happy voice of Gavroche announce, as he climbed toward them, "Present and accounted for, sir!" It had taken the boy a great deal of time to reach the barricade because the enemy had blocked what would have been his most direct route back to his comrades.

With a look of dismay, Marius pulled the boy aside and demanded, "What are you doing here?"

The child flippantly answered, "What are you doing here yourself?"

"Who told you to come back?" Marius asked. "Did you deliver my letter?"

Knowing he had not delivered the letter to Cosette, Gavroche lied to Marius by saying, "Citizen, I delivered the letter to the porter. The lady was asleep, but the porter said he would give it to her when she awakens." Yet because it had been a very dark night, Gavroche had not even seen the face of the man to whom he had handed the note. And since the boy had not completely followed Marius's instructions, Marius knew that at best only one of his two desires had been met. His objective had not only been to bid farewell to Cosette, but also to save Gavroche from nearly certain death at the barricades.

Shortly thereafter the fighting began again in earnest. Courfeyrac kept his eyes glued to the street just in front of the barricade when he suddenly caught sight of someone amid the gunfire. It was little Gavroche, who had taken a wine bottle basket from the café and was quietly moving among the bodies of the dead French soldiers, taking their unused ammunition. Courfeyrac angrily shouted to the boy, "What do you think you're doing?"

"I'm filling my basket with ammo, citizen!"

"Don't you know they're firing at us?" Courfeyrac asked in astonishment.

The boy answered smugly, "It's only rain!"

Courfeyrac demanded, "Get back here!" Yet the boy worked his way farther down the street. At least twenty bodies were scattered across the pavement, which to Gavroche meant plenty of bullets for the barricade. The boy was able to hide amid the smoke from the gunfire as it wafted its way down the street. Using the fog-like smoke as cover, he went quite a distance away without being seen by the enemy. But then the smoke began to dissipate, and one of the soldiers saw someone moving toward their troops. Just as Gavroche reached toward another dead soldier, a bullet struck the corpse.

"Great!" Gavroche yelled with a sly smile on his face. "They're killing the dead men for me—again!" A second bullet sparked as it hit the pavement beside him, and then a third overturned his basket of ammunition. The boy seemed to be enjoying himself and acted as though he were teasing the enemy. It was a strange yet terrifying sight, like a sparrow being shot at by hunters. With each shot the boy taunted his attackers. He would lie down as if shot, but would spring to his feet again and hide in a doorway. Then Gavroche would race across the street, scamper around, and thumb his nose at the soldiers. All the while the boy continued filling his basket with the dead men's bullets.

Gavroche's comrades trembled in fear for his safety, yet he seemed to be some invulnerable spirit. He was not a child, nor was he a man. The bullets flew past him, for he was more nimble, and he continued playing his terrifying game of hide-and-seek with death.

Finally, however, one bullet—better aimed and more deadly than the rest—struck its mark. Everyone on the barricade let out a scream as they watched the poor boy stagger and then fall to the street. Marius and Courfeyrac rushed to his aid, but it was too late. Gavroche was dead.

Courfeyrac picked up the basket of bullets and raced toward the barricade. Marius then bent down, picked up the lad, and carried Gavroche's small dead body back to his comrades. As he did so he thought, "This poor boy's father did this for my father, and now I'm doing this for his son. Yet Thénardier brought my father back alive. I'm bringing back the dead body of his child."

Javert remained tied to the pole inside the café. Enjolras pointed toward him, set a pistol on the table, and said, "I want the last man to leave here to blow this spy's brains out with this gun."

Someone asked, "You want him killed here?"

"No, I don't want his body left here. Take him to the barricade on the Rue Mondétour and do it there."

Just then Valjean stepped out of a dark corner of the café and asked Enjolras, "Are you in charge here?"

Recognizing Valjean as the man who had given his uniform to save another, Enjolras said, "Yes, I'm in charge. What do you need? Ask what you want, for there are now two saviors at this barricade—Marius Pontmercy and you."

"I only request one thing—that I be allowed to kill this man," Valjean said as he glanced toward Javert.

Javert then looked at Valjean, tensed almost imperceptibly, and said, "That's appropriate."

Enjolras responded, while reloading his rifle, "No objections here. Take the spy!"

Valjean moved toward the prisoner and untied the rope holding him to the pole. He then untied his feet, grabbed the end of the rope around his hands, and began pulling him toward the door of the café. The other men, preparing for the next attack, had their backs turned to the two men as they walked out of the building. Only Marius, who was at the extreme end of the barricade outside, noticed them as they walked away.

Once the two men were alone on the street, Valjean took the pistol he had gotten from Enjolras and tucked it into his belt. He fastened his eyes on Javert and said to his old nemesis, "Javert, it is I—Jean Valjean."

Javert replied, coldly, "Take your revenge."

Valjean pulled a pocketknife from his coat and began to open it. Seeing the knife, Javert exclaimed, "Ah, yes! A knife does suit the likes of you much better!"

Yet Valjean reached down and used the knife to cut the rope wrapped around Javert's hands. As the rope fell to the pavement, Valjean said, "You are free." Javert was not a man who was easily astonished, but at this, his jaw dropped and he stood before Valjean open-mouthed and totally motionless. Javert attempted to speak but was unable. Valjean then continued, "I doubt I will ever escape from these barricades with my life, but if by chance I do, I now live under the name of Fauchelevent at 7 Rue de l'Homme Armé."

Javert snarled at Valjean like a tiger, and then muttered through his now clenched teeth, "Take care."

"Go!" demanded Valjean. At this, Javert buttoned his coat, straightened his shoulders, turned around, and walked away. Valjean watched until Javert disappeared and then he fired his pistol into the air. Finally he returned to the barricade and said, "It is done."

The drums of the enemy suddenly sounded the signal to charge and a hurricane of an attack began. Enjolras was at one end of the barricade with Marius at the other. Marius stood unprotected with half his body exposed above the top of the barricade. Here this ragged and exhausted troop of revolutionaries, who had not slept or eaten in more than twenty-four hours, continued to fight. Soon nearly all of them were wounded, but they continued fumbling through their pockets for more bullets that would be quickly depleted.

Time after time—ten times in all—the barricade was attacked and successfully defended. Many of the defenders had died, and Courfeyrac was one of them. He had been run through with a sword, and as he died he only had time to cast a quick glance toward heaven. The few remaining men were covered with blood—but felt like Titans.

Marius fought on, but was so riddled with head wounds that his face seemed to disappear beneath the blood. From a distance one would have said that his face was covered with a red handkerchief. Only Enjolras had not yet been wounded, but was down to only the stumps of four broken swords to fight with.

Enjolras and Marius, the only leaders remaining alive, were still at opposite ends of the barricade when the center finally gave way and the enemy's assault succeeded. The few revolutionaries still alive were forced to retreat, yet in total confusion. Suddenly a bullet hit Marius's collarbone, knocking him from the barricade. As he fell, just before going into shock from the pain, he felt the grip of strong arms underneath him. His final thought was of Cosette, and just as he fainted he said to himself, "I have been taken prisoner. I will be shot!"

CHAPTER TWENTY-SEVEN

A ctually Marius was "the prisoner" of Jean Valjean. Through the thick smoke of combat, Valjean did not want to be seen watching Marius, but if the truth were known, he had hardly taken his eyes off him. Therefore, when the shot hit Marius, Valjean had moved toward the young man with the agility of a tiger, pounced on him as though he were his prey, and carried him away.

The street was in turmoil as Valjean quickly surveyed his situation. A house blocked one direction while the barricade blocked another. Bewildered, he stared at the ground as though he would have liked to pierce a hole in it with his eyes. Then, as if his wish were being miraculously fulfilled, something near his feet caught his attention. Amid the paving stones of the street he saw an iron grate, which was about two feet square. The stones meant to hold it in place had long since been broken and displaced, so that the grate was loose. Valjean quickly looked through it and saw a dark opening that looked like the flue of a chimney or the water pipe of a cistern.

Valjean moved quickly, as his old art of escape abruptly rose within him. Almost by instinct he pulled the grate aside and lifted Marius's dead weight to his shoulders. With the strength of a giant and the swiftness of an eagle, he descended the iron foot bars into the darkness of the hole, stopped to balance himself as he replaced the grate, and continued descending.

Some ten feet below the street, Valjean found himself with Marius, who was still unconscious, in some long subterranean corridor. Now safely away from the shooting, he was in a place of profound peace and absolute silence— yet in total darkness. Valjean's thoughts suddenly took him back to another

233

time—the night he had jumped from the wall into the convent. His feelings were much the same—only this time he carried Marius—not Cosette.

Valjean now found himself in the sewers of Paris. Marius did not stir, and Valjean did not know if the man he was carrying was a living being or a corpse. As he stood in that "grave" below Paris, his first sensation was one of blindness. Having gone from the daylight of the street to the darkness of the sewer, he could see nothing. However, after a few moments his eyes became adjusted, and he was soon able to see from the little bit of light shining through the manhole he had just descended. Yet a few paces ahead the light became so dim that he found himself plunging into a damp, massive gloominess, with Marius still across his shoulders.

He trudged forward, holding both of Marius's arms with one hand and groping along the slippery wall with the other. Valjean felt a warm stream of blood coming from Marius's head wounds that was trickling onto him and finding its way underneath his clothes. The mouth of the wounded man was near his ear, and Valjean knew the man was alive from the humid warmth of the faint respiration he could hear in the silence of the sewer.

He moved ahead with deliberate steps, but with a feeling of anxiety, for he could not see and did not know where he was going. All he knew was that his life, and that of Marius, was now fully engulfed in the hands of Providence Himself. Each time he encountered a branch splitting off from the main sewer he felt of the opening and then continued along the larger of the two. He correctly reasoned that the narrow opening would ultimately lead to a dead end and would only delay his progress toward finding a route to safety.

Valjean's trek became more and more strenuous. The height of the sewer was a mere five-and-a-half feet at best, so he walked stooped over in order to keep Marius from striking the top. Valjean was quite tall, which made walking in this way even more difficult, yet despite his age, he was still very strong. Nevertheless, carrying Marius like this quickly began to sap his strength. Finally, around three in the afternoon, he reached a major junction of the sewers. He was amazed by the sudden widening and was soon standing in a much larger passage. It was large enough for him to walk upright and was so wide that even with his arms outstretched he could not touch both walls.

Minutes later Valjean walked under the relatively bright light of a manhole. He stopped for a moment, and with a true gentleness that one brother would extend to another, he set Marius on a somewhat dry ledge. Marius's blood-stained face appeared ashen under the light, like the ashes scattered at the bottom of a tomb. His eyes were closed, and his hair was matted around the temples with clumps of dried blood that caused his face to look like it had been brushed with red paint. His arms and legs were limp and felt cold and dead. Blood oozed from the corners of his mouth, and puncture wounds to his body had thrust the fabric of his shirt into the wounds themselves. Through Marius's torn clothing, Valjean placed his hand over the young man's beating heart and realized he was still alive. He then tore his own shirt and bandaged Marius's wounds as best he could and stopped the flow of blood. However, after doing all he could to save the young man's life, he gazed at the unconscious soul before him with a feeling of inexpressible hatred.

Valjean quickly searched through Marius's pockets and found two things: a piece of bread the young man had stuffed into his pocket the previous day, but that he had forgotten, and a small notebook. He ate the bread and then opened to the first page of the notebook. On the page he saw the words: "My name is Marius Pontmercy. Please take my body to my grandfather, Monsieur Gillenormand, 6 Rue des Filles-du-Calvaire, in the Marais."

After this short break Valjean once again put Marius on his sturdy back, with the young man's head against his right shoulder, and resumed his laborious march along the sewer. He trudged through the darkness like this until his miserable situation abruptly became even worse. A downpour the previous day had filled this part of the sewer with a huge amount of water, and it seemed as though the pavement below his feet was washing away. He found himself standing amid a pit of slime in a cavern of absolute night. He moved ahead in what seemed to be water on the top and thick slime on the bottom. As he walked, he plunged deeper and deeper into the mire, until the water ultimately reached his shoulders.

Suddenly he felt he was sinking and only his head was above the water. He struggled with both arms to keep Marius's head above the muck and mire. With a nearly supernatural strength and sheer force of determination he forged ahead, yet with great difficulty. Nearing exhaustion, he made one last desperate effort to find secure footing just as his foot struck something solid. This one secure foothold became for him the first step on a staircase leading back to life. He stood there for a moment and braced himself against the flow of the filthy flood. After a brief rest he moved forward and came to realize that he was standing on what appeared to be a gradual incline leading him out of the water.

As Valjean emerged from the quagmire and was finally safe, he dropped to his knees on the stone floor of the sewer. With Marius still across his shoulders, he reflected on what had just taken place, and realized this humble position was quite appropriate. He remained there for some time with his soul totally absorbed in words of thanks addressed to God. Finally he rose to his feet. He was shivering with cold, foul smelling, dripping with slime, and bowed beneath a dying man. Yet his soul was somehow filled with a strange and glorious light.

Jean Valjean set out once more, now at a more deliberate pace. He walked briskly for about a hundred steps, almost without drawing a breath. Suddenly he saw what appeared to be daylight at the far end of the corridor in front of him. It was indeed a way out of the sewer, but across its archway was a heavy iron gate. The gate was clamped shut with a thick lock, which was red with rust and looked like an enormous brick to him. In the daylight beyond the gate he could see the Seine, and although its bank was quite narrow, it would be sufficient for his escape.

Hours had passed while he had trudged through the sewer. It was now eight-thirty in the evening, and the sun was beginning to set. Valjean carefully set Marius against the wall and then clenched his fists around the gate. He shook it vigorously, but it did not budge, and he began to realize he had only succeeded in escaping into a prison. With his back to the gate, he dropped to the pavement next to Marius, who was still unconscious. Valjean sat with his head between his knees and drank his last drop of anguish. In a state of deep depression, he had only one thought. He did not think of Marius or himself. He was thinking of Cosette.

In the midst of this despair, a hand was suddenly laid on his shoulder. Then a quiet voice said to him, "We'll split it." Beside him stood a man who was holding his shoes in his hand. He had evidently removed them in order to reach Valjean without his footsteps being heard.

Unexpected as this encounter was to Valjean, he did not hesitate for even an instant to recognize the man. It was Thénardier. Yet Valjean perceived that Thénardier had not recognized him. The two surveyed each other for a brief moment in the growing darkness, as though sizing up one another. Then Thénardier broke the silence by saying, "How do you plan to get out of here?" Valjean did not answer and Thénardier continued, "You know, it's impossible to pick that lock. But I tell you what—we'll split the spoils."

"What do you mean by that?" Valjean asked.

"It's quite obvious to me that you've killed that man, and probably emptied his pockets. I couldn't care less about that. But I have something you need—I have the key to this lock. I'll open the gate for you, if you give me half of what you found in his pockets," Thénardier said with a sneer on his face.

Valjean realized Thénardier mistakenly took him for a murderer. Thénardier reached under his tattered shirt and then held a large key temptingly before Valjean. Then he continued, "First let's settle our business. You've seen my key, now show me your money. For half I'll let you out of here."

It was typical for Valjean to have some money in his pockets, but on this occasion he had been caught unprepared. He fumbled through his blood-soaked pockets, turning them inside out, yet only produced one louis d'or, two five-franc pieces, and five or six sous. With a look of sadness on his face, and a curt tilt of his head, Thénardier stated, "Man! You've killed him for nearly nothing!" Not quite believing what he had seen, Thénardier, began searching Valjean's and Marius's pockets for himself. Valjean let him do so unhindered, for his primary concern at this point was keeping his back to the light, hoping to remain anonymous.

As Thénardier searched the pockets of Marius's coat, he removed a torn piece of fabric from it with the skill of a pickpocket. Valjean did not notice what he had done, so Thénardier was able to quickly conceal the strip of cloth underneath his own shirt. He thought the cloth might serve to be useful later in identifying the dead man and his killer. As he searched Marius he found another thirty francs. Then, commenting on the small amount of money on both men, he took it all, forgetting his words: "We'll split it."

Having finished his search, he took the key, turned it in the rusty lock, and opened the gate halfway. Then he said to Valjean, smugly, "Now, my friend, you must leave. This is just like the fair, where you pay as you leave. You've paid. Now clear out!"

Valjean put Marius on his back once again, and with just enough space to squeeze through the opening, he found himself in the open night air. Thénardier closed the gate, gave the key two turns in the lock, and plunged toward the darkness. He made less noise than a mere breath, and seemed to walk stealthily away on the velvet paws of a tiger.

Upon reaching the river, Valjean set Marius on its bank. As the darkness of night cast its shadows across him, Valjean could not refrain from basking underneath what appeared to him to be a vast sea of ecstasy and prayer in the majestic silence of the eternal heavens. His sense of his duty to his fellow man weighed upon him, and he bent down to dip some water with his hand, then sprinkled a few drops on Marius's face. The young man's eyes still remained closed, but he continued to breathe through his half-opened mouth. As Valjean dipped his hand once more into the river, he had the uneasy feeling that someone was standing just behind him.

Still crouching toward the ground, he spun around and was shocked to see Javert towering above him. When Valjean had allowed Javert to leave the barricade, Javert had caught sight of Thénardier and had pursued him as far as the river. Yet shortly thereafter Javert had lost sight of the escaped prisoner. Javert had waited by the river, only to see Valjean later emerge where he had last seen Thénardier. With Valjean's face cloaked by the darkness, Javert asked, "Who are you?"

"I am Jean Valjean." At this, Javert placed both hands on Valjean's shoulders, squeezed him with a viselike grip, and stood him to his feet, as Valjean continued, "Inspector Javert, you have me in your power. In fact, I have regarded myself as your prisoner since early this morning. I did not give you my address with any intention of escaping from you. You may take me into your custody. I only ask that you grant me one favor first."

Javert did not appear to hear Valjean, but simply kept his eyes riveted upon him. At last he released his grip, straightened himself, and murmured, "What are you doing here? And who is this man?"

"The favor I ask concerns him," Valjean began. "Dispose of me as you see fit, but first help me take him home. That is all I ask of you."

Javert wrinkled his brow, as someone who is incapable of ever making a concession. Nevertheless, he did not say no. He bent over, dipped his handkerchief in the water, began wiping Marius's bloodstained face, and finally said, as though speaking only to himself, "This young man was at the barricade. He is the one they call Marius." Then Javert grabbed Marius's hand and searched for a pulse.

"He is wounded," Valjean offered.

"He's a dead man," Javert answered.

"No, not yet," Valjean insisted.

"So, you've brought him here from the barricade?" questioned Javert.

Valjean simply nodded and said, "He lives in the Marais on the Rue des Filles-du-Calvaire with his grandfather. I don't remember his last name." Then Valjean pulled the notebook from Marius's pocket, opened it to the first page, and offered it to Javert.

After a moment Javert looked toward the street and shouted, "Carriage, please!" Then he thrust Marius's notebook into his own coat pocket. Seconds later Javert himself placed Marius on the back seat of a carriage and sat down on the front seat next to Valjean. Finally he slammed the door and the carriage drove rapidly away.

By the time the carriage reached its destination on the Rue des Filles-du-

Calvaire, it was completely dark outside and everyone in the house was asleep. Valjean grabbed Marius under the arms, while the carriage driver held him underneath his knees, and together they carried him toward the gate. Javert addressed the porter stationed there in a tone befitting a government official by saying, "Sir, we are looking for a gentleman by the name of Gillenormand. Is he here?"

"What do you want with him?" the porter questioned.

"We're bringing his grandson home," Javert answered with a hint of irritation in his voice. The porter, not wanting to wake the master of the house, woke one of his servants instead, a doorman by the name of Basque. Basque then woke Marius's Aunt Gillenormand, who made the decision to let the grandfather sleep, thinking he would hear of this matter soon enough in any case.

The men carried Marius to the main level of the house and set him on a sofa in Monsieur Gillenormand's waiting room. Immediately Basque set off in search of a physician, and just as he left, Valjean felt Javert touch him on the shoulder. Javert motioned to him, and Valjean, knowing what he meant, walked out of the house and toward the carriage once again, with Javert following directly behind him. As they climbed aboard the carriage, Valjean asked Javert, "Inspector Javert, may I ask yet another favor?"

"What is it?" Javert demanded, harshly.

"Let me go home for just one minute," Valjean pleaded. "Then you may do whatever you want with me."

Javert remained silent for several moments, but then lowered the window of the passenger compartment, and said, "Driver, 7 Rue de l'Homme Armé at once!"

As they approached the Rue de l'Homme Armé, Javert and Valjean stepped from the carriage, for the street was too narrow to accommodate one its size. When they reached the door of the house on the deserted street, Javert said to him, "Go on in." Then with a strange expression on his face, as though he were exerting great effort, he added, "I will wait for you here."

Valjean simply stared at Javert, because this was certainly not in accord with Javert's past habits. Yet he quickly dismissed any usual thoughts, supposing he should not be surprised by any amount of haughty confidence Javert might exhibit. He saw it as being the kind of confidence a cat has when granting a mouse the freedom to travel only to the length of its claws. Besides, he reasoned, Javert must now realize that he had made up his mind to surrender and to put an end to his running. With this thought firmly in his mind, Valjean opened the door and entered the house. He climbed the stairs, but before entering his room, he noticed the window on the landing was open. Without fully understanding why, he paused for a moment, and then leaned out the window to glance at the porch below. Valjean was overwhelmed with amazement by what he saw.

Javert had departed.

Police Inspector Javert walked slowly along the Rue de l'Homme Armé with his head down and his eyes downcast for the first time in his life. He took the shortest route to the Seine and walked halfway across a bridge near Notre Dame. With his elbows on the wall of the bridge and his head in his hands, he stared at the rapids below. It was a dangerous stretch of water, and was known by French sailors to be the most dreaded point on the Seine.

He considered his situation, which to him was intolerable. To owe his life to a criminal and to now be indebted to a fugitive from justice was more than he could bear. He had been set free by Valjean, and, for the first time in his life, had repaid one good deed with another. Yet he had betrayed the law and society by remaining true to his conscience, and had sacrificed his duty under that law to his personal motives. He was overwhelmed by the absurd thought that there could possibly be a law superior to the law he had known all his life—something he had never imagined before, and something which his mind could not reconcile with his heart.

One thing amazed Javert—that after all these years of being pursued, Jean

Valjean had set him free when he had the opportunity to kill him. And one thing terrified him—that he had returned the favor by setting the criminal free. He sought to comprehend his situation, but could no longer seem to find his bearings. He reeled as he examined his two possible options—neither of which was acceptable to him. To hand Valjean over to the authorities seemed unthinkable, and to give Valjean liberty seemed equally abhorrent.

Jean Valjean was an enigma to him. Here was a benevolent criminal—a merciful, gentle, and helpful convict, and one who repaid evil with good, hatred with pardon, and who preferred pity above vengeance. Valjean chose to ruin himself rather than to ruin his enemy, and to save the one who had wanted him dead. Here was a man who knelt on the heights of virtue itself, and responded more as an angel than a man. Javert was now forced to admit that someone like Valjean existed, and he saw Valjean as a hideous monster.

Some twenty times, as he had sat in the carriage face-to-face with Valjean, the legal tiger of the law had roared within Javert. He was forever a prisoner of the law, and the law could do with him as it wished. Yet in the depths of his being he had heard a voice crying out to him—a voice unknown to him, which said, "Very well! Have your savior killed. And while you are at it, why not ask for the basin of Pontius Pilate to be brought to you, so you can then wash the deed from your claws."

A whole new world was dawning within his soul. For the first time he had accepted a kindness, and he had repaid it with a kindness. Javert was seeing new things, such as mercy, forgiveness, and the possibility of a tear in the eye of the law. He stood in the shadow of an unknown moral sun that was rising in his soul, and it horrified and blinded him. He was forced to acknowledge that goodness existed—even within a convict. And now he had experienced something unprecedented in his life—he had done something good as well. But he saw it as becoming depraved.

His religion was law and order, and it had been enough for him. His faith was in the police, and he reported to his superior, yet to this point he had never dreamed of that other Superior—God. Tonight, however, he had unexpectedly become aware of Him, and he felt embarrassed and ashamed as he stood before Him.

In the light of this unforeseen Presence, Javert could not find his bearings. He did not know how to respond to this superior, yet he knew that a subordinate was always obligated to bow and to obey. He knew he should not argue, debate, or place blame in the presence of someone so amazing and much greater than he. He did not know what to do, but finally concluded that his only option was to hand in his resignation. But how was he to submit his resignation to God?

His thoughts swirled around him, yet one overriding issue kept rising to the top and dominated his thinking—he had committed a terrible infraction of the law! Two options waged war with each other in his mind. He could march resolutely to Jean Valjean, arrest him, and return the convict to his prison cell. And the other was to . . .

Immediately Javert straightened himself to his full stature, turned from the bridge, and began walking with a quick and determined pace. He headed to the closest police station, walked inside, took a sheet of paper and a pen, and began writing. At the top of the page he wrote, "My observations for the good of the Police Service." Then he listed ten abuses against prisoners he himself had witnessed many times, and suggested that these were "unworthy of the police who were to be servants of a great civilization." He signed the note, "Javert, Police Inspector of the 1st Class, 7 June 1832, one o'clock A.M.," left it on the table, and headed to the bridge once again.

With his head bowed, Javert gazed into the water. All he saw was darkness. He could hear the sound of the rushing water but could not see the river. He remained motionless for several minutes, gazing into the roaring blackness. He removed his hat and placed it on the wall of the bridge next to him. A moment later a tall black form, one that any distant passerby would have mistaken as a mere shadow or an apparition, stood erect on the wall of the bridge. The dark form bent over the Seine, stood erect once again, and then fell into the shadows.

A dull splash followed as the obscure form disappeared beneath the rapids.

———————— ⚜ ————————

CHAPTER TWENTY-EIGHT

Marius remained motionless on the sofa in his grandfather's waiting room. When the doctor arrived, he asked that a cot be set up so that he could better examine the young man. Miraculously, Marius had not suffered any major internal injuries. One bullet had apparently been slowed by impacting his leather pouch and had then been diverted toward his side. It had made a hideous laceration along his ribs, but was not terribly deep, and therefore was not life threatening. Yet the long underground trek through the sewer had put pressure on the fracture in his collarbone, which was now completely severed and quite serious. His arms had been slashed numerous times by swords and were covered with cuts. Although he had a number of wounds on his head, not a single cut was serious enough to disfigure his face.

As the doctor cleaned Marius's face, a door opened at the other end of the room and the tall, pale figure of the young man's grandfather walked toward the cot. The doctor had stripped Marius to the waist, and he lay motionless, with his eyes closed and his mouth open. His skin had a waxen whiteness, and his body was covered with slash marks, many of which were still bleeding. His grandfather began to tremble and then managed to mutter, "Marius!"

Basque, Monsieu r Gillenormand's doorman, began to explain, "Sir, your grandson has just been brought here. He was at the barricades, and . . ."

"He is dead!" the old man shrieked. "The rascal!" Then, attempting to regain his composure, he looked toward the doctor and said, "He is dead, is he not?" Before the doctor could answer, however, Marius slowly opened his eyes. As he fixed his still blurry gaze on his grandfather, Monsieur Gillenormand cried, "Marius! My beloved child! You're alive!"

Then the old man fainted and fell.

For many weeks it was as though Marius was neither dead nor alive. He ran a high fever and was delirious, simply repeating Cosette's name over and over—night after night. Each day, and sometimes twice a day, a well-dressed gentleman with white hair—as described by the porter—inquired about the wounded young man, and would leave a package of clean, linen bandages.

Finally, on September 7, 1832, exactly four months after Marius had been wounded, the doctor told Monsieur Gillenormand that his grandson was out of danger. However, his convalescence was not complete, for the young man would still be required to remain stretched out on a sofa for another two months, primarily because of his broken collarbone.

The news that Marius was out of danger nearly made his grandfather delirious himself—yet delirious with happiness. That same day he gave his porter a gift of three louis, which was out of character for him. And that evening, Basque, watching the old man through a half-open door, saw Monsieur Gillenormand kneeling beside a chair in prayer. He watched for some time to be sure he was praying, for up to that point the old man had never believed in God.

Once Marius's fever and delirium had subsided, he had no idea what had become of Cosette, and the entire episode at the barricade was nothing more than a cloud in his memory. Also, he did not know how his life had been saved, or by whom, and no one in his grandfather's household could fill in the details for him.

Day by day Marius's strength increased as his aunt and his grandfather took care of him. Monsieur Gillenormand seemed to treat his grandson more tenderly than ever, and one day said to him, "Listen, Marius. You need to start eating some meat for your strength. Fish is fine at the beginning of a convalescence, but a thick steak is what a sick man needs to put him back on his feet."

At this point Marius had almost entirely recovered, and taking advantage of his grandfather's cheerfulness, he said, "Grandfather, there is something I want to say to you." The young man had a determined look on his face, and was sitting straight up in his bed, with his fists clenched before him.

"What is it, my son?"

"I want to marry."

"Agreed!" exclaimed his grandfather as he burst into laughter.

"What do you mean, 'agreed'?"

"I mean," the old man said with a smile, "you shall have your little girl you asked me about some time ago." Marius was stunned, overwhelmed, and began to tremble. His grandfather then put his arm around his grandson's head and pulled Marius close to himself. Finally both of them began to weep from hearts overflowing with pure happiness.

"But, Grandfather, I no longer know where to find her!" Marius said, remembering the sad reality of his situation.

"Ah, but I do!" Monsieur Gillenormand exclaimed. "You see, she inquires of you every day—in the form of an old man. And it is she who makes the linen bandages that he brings each day. I have made inquiries myself, and I know their address. It is 7 Rue de l'Homme Armé. You shall see her tomorrow!"

"Why not today? I am quite well and up to it," Marius said, unable to wait another moment.

"Agreed! I will see to it," his grandfather assured him.

Cosette walked into the house with a white-haired man following close behind, whom Marius knew as Monsieur Fauchelevent. Marius and Cosette beheld each other once again, and then Marius noticed her father was smiling—albeit a heart-rending smile. Monsieur Fauchelevent had a package under his arm, which appeared to be a book wrapped in a moldy, greenish paper.

As Fauchelevent remained near the door, Mademoiselle Gillenormand, who did not like books, whispered under her breath, "I wonder if he always carries books like that with him?"

Overhearing his daughter's comment, Marius's grandfather responded, also in a whisper, "He's obviously a learned man. What of it?" Then, with a bow, he said aloud, "Welcome, Monsieur Fauchelevent. I have the honor of asking you, on behalf of my grandson, Le Baron Marius Pontmercy, for the hand of the mademoiselle."

Monsieur Fauchelevent simply bowed, and the grandfather quickly announced, "Then it's settled!" Next he turned toward Marius and Cosette, extended both arms over them as a blessing, and exclaimed, "Permission granted to adore each other!" Of course, they did not need his permission, for the adoring had already commenced. Finally he asked the two of them to sit before him, and he took their hands in his and resumed, "Love each other— and only each other. Be foolish about it! For love is the foolishness of men, but the wisdom of God. Cosette, you are a masterpiece and will be a very great lady." Suddenly his expression changed to one of dismay as he added, "Something just occurred to me! All my wealth is in the annuity I receive, but once I am gone it will end, and you will not have a sou! I am sorry, poor children."

At these words, Monsieur Fauchelevent stepped forward and said in a somber, but peaceful, tone, "Mademoiselle Cosette has nearly six hundred thousand francs."

"Six hundred thousand francs?" Monsieur Gillenormand asked in surprise.

"Less fifteen thousand or so," answered Fauchelevent, as he set the package he was carrying on the table. He unwrapped the package and revealed it was not a book, but was a bundle of money. In total, the bills added to five hundred and eighty-four thousand francs.

"That is some book!" Monsieur Gillenormand said, with a smile.

While the others were engrossed with the money, Marius and Cosette gazed into each other's eyes. The money was simply an unheeded detail to two young people in love.

The money had actually been hidden when Jean Valjean first found Cosette. He had buried it in a metal box in the forest in Montfermeil, in a place only he knew. Inside the box he had also placed his other treasure—the bishop's candlesticks. When he saw that Marius was recovering, Valjean resigned himself to the fact that Marius and Cosette would someday be married. He had then gone to retrieve his buried treasure, knowing the money would now prove useful to the young couple. As soon as he returned home, two candlesticks could be seen on the mantel of his fireplace.

Around this same time, Valjean learned he was finally and forever free of Javert. He had verified the rumors of his old nemesis's suicide by finding the newspaper report of his death. The report stated that the drowned body of "Police Inspector Javert has been found under a boat moored between two bridges, the Pont au Change and the Pont Neuf."

Life was indeed changing dramatically for Valjean, Cosette, and Marius—but especially Valjean. It was now December 1832, and as Marius continued to recover from his injuries, his doctor agreed to a February date for the wedding. Plans were in full swing for the happy event, and for his part, Valjean did everything he could to prepare Cosette for the big day. Yet there was one delicate problem still to be solved—Cosette's legal status and name.

He believed that simply announcing her origins bluntly might jeopardize the marriage and hurt Cosette's stature for some time to come—especially in the eyes of Marius's grandfather and aunt. So rather than revealing her past, Valjean concocted a story and fabricated a family of dead people for her, which he saw as a sure means of avoiding potential problems. He said that Cosette was the only living descendant of her entire family, and that she was not actually his daughter, but the daughter of the other Fauchelevent at the Convent of the Petit Picpus. He knew the nuns well enough to know that if anyone inquired about the Fauchelevent brothers, who had been gardeners there for many years, they would simply confirm whatever they were asked—

and would say it convincingly. They were never inclined to attach importance to questions of this kind at any rate, and, if the truth were known, they had never exactly understood whose daughter—or granddaughter—Cosette had been anyway.

As to the money, Valjean said it was an inheritance bequeathed to Cosette by someone who had desired to remain anonymous. Of course, a number of loose ends remained in his stories, but for the most part they were unnoticed or intentionally ignored by others. One of the interested parties had eyes that were blinded by love, and the others were blinded by nearly six hundred thousand francs. Any other time Cosette would have been broken-hearted to learn that the man she had called father for so long was not her real father. But her heart was filled with love for Marius, and the news that she was the daughter of another Fauchelevent, became only a passing cloud. Nevertheless, she thought of Valjean as hers, and would always refer to him as her father.

Marius and Cosette saw each other every day, but believing every young girl needed a chaperone, Valjean—or Monsieur Fauchelevent—would accompany her. There seemed to be some unspoken agreement between Marius and Fauchelevent, and as a result, the two men would see each other but would not speak. Cosette was not allowed to see Marius alone, and if Fauchelevent was the condition attached to her, Marius was willing to accept it.

In Marius's mind many questions still swirled around Monsieur Fauchelevent. He wondered many times if the Fauchelevent at the barricades was the same Fauchelevent who sat so solemnly beside Cosette each day. Often he would simply dismiss this possibility as something brought on by his many days of delirium. His questions lingered, but it seemed impossible for Marius to approach Fauchelevent with his concerns due to the rigid nature of both men.

As the wall of silence between the two men was gradually dissolved, Marius began to gain enough boldness to venture an attempt to discover the truth. In conversation he mentioned the Rue de la Chanvrerie, where the barricade had been, and turned casually to Fauchelevent and said, "I'm sure you're acquainted with that street."

"What street is that again?" Fauchelevent said, with a look of innocence.

"The Rue de la Chanvrerie."

"I'm sorry, but I don't know that street," replied Fauchelevent, in the most natural manner possible.

At this, Marius concluded that Fauchelevent was not at the barricades and that he must have him confused with someone who resembled him. Yet a few small doubts still lingered in the back of his mind.

Marius had two debts of gratitude still unpaid. One was to Thénardier on behalf of his father, and the other was to the unknown man who had returned him safely to his grandfather's house. Marius was a man of character and had no intention of becoming happily married, only to leave his debts unpaid. Doing that would forever leave a shadow over a life that looked to be promising and bright.

He endeavored to find these two men, searching for Thénardier first. But none of the various agents he hired succeeded in discovering any trace of the man. Next he turned to finding the man who had so recently saved his life. What had become of that mysterious man, whom the carriage driver had seen emerge from the Grand Sewer while carrying an unconscious Marius upon his back? The driver had also witnessed that very man being immediately arrested by the police, while in the process of rescuing the revolutionary he carried. Someone had carried him from the barricades to the Champs-Élysées. Who could have done this? And how? Marius surmised the man must have escaped with him through the sewer. "But what kind of devotion could lead to such personal sacrifice? And why has the man never come forward?" he wondered.

Marius had kept his bloodstained clothing in the hopes that it might prove useful in his search. He examined his coat and discovered that a strip of cloth had been torn from it in an unusual way. The tear seemed quite different from the tatters on various parts of the coat, but he had no recollection as to what had caused the piece to be missing.

One evening Marius was sharing with Cosette and her father the many inquiries he had been making, and of the fruitlessness of his efforts. As he shared he became somewhat frustrated by Monsieur Fauchelevent's blank stare and apparent lack of interest. This led Marius to exclaim, with a certain amount of anger in his voice, "That man who saved me must have been an angel! Do you know what he did, sir? He must have thrown himself headlong into the raging battle and rescued me after I was wounded. Apparently he opened the sewer himself and took me into it. Then he must have struggled in total darkness, weighed down with me, through mile after mile in that awful cesspool. Oh, if only Cosette's money were mine, I would . . ."

"But the money is yours," Fauchelevent interrupted.

"Well," Marius continued, "I would give it all away, if only I could find that man once more!"

Monsieur Fauchelevent—or Jean Valjean—remained silent.

CHAPTER TWENTY-NINE

T he wedding night of Marius and Cosette finally arrived. It was February 16, 1833, and was a blessed night, for it seemed the heavens shined down on the couple. The night before, Valjean had delivered the entire five hundred and eighty-four thousand francs to Marius in the presence of the young man's grandfather, and now it appeared that everything was in place for the joyous event.

Cosette could not believe this day was real and was finally here. She wore a beautiful long gown of white taffeta, a veil of English lace, a necklace of fine pearls, and a tiara of orange flowers—and her sense of amazement only added to her striking beauty and radiance. Marius wore a new black tuxedo and his long dark locks of hair were neatly groomed and nearly covered the last vestiges of the scrapes and cuts from the barricades.

As the wedding began, Marius's grandfather said to Valjean, "Monsieur Fauchelevent, this is a happy day, and I vote for the end of afflictions and sorrows! I decree joy!" Then the ceremony began as the happy couple exchanged their vows, then their rings, and knelt before God hand-in-hand. The young man and wife were duly pronounced before the mayor and the priest, and then almost as quickly as it had started, it was over.

Marius and Cosette stood at the arched doors of the church, and neither could believe it was real. They climbed into the carriage for the ride home, with Monsieur Gillenormand and Valjean sitting opposite them. "My children," Marius's grandfather said, "From now on you are Monsieur le Baron and Madame la Baronne!"

Cosette nestled close to Marius and whispered angelically into his ear, "I can't believe it's true! I now bear your name. I am Madame Marius Pontmercy!" Then as the beautiful folds of her wedding gown lay across Marius, she leaned toward him and added, "Soon we must visit our little garden on the Rue Plumet."

They returned home, and Marius, who seemed triumphant and radiant himself, strode side-by-side up the stairs with Cosette at his arm. How different was this trip up those stairs than that of months before, when the young man had been delivered to his house—wounded and unconscious!

Cosette had never treated Jean Valjean more tenderly than she did this day. After the wedding he seated himself in the drawing room of the house, behind the door in such a way as to nearly be hidden from view. Yet Cosette came to him, pushed the door closed, and then curtsied deeply, spreading out her bridal gown with both hands, and said, lovingly, "Father, are you satisfied?"

"Yes, I'm quite content," Valjean answered.

"Then be happy! Laugh!" she insisted.

Valjean smiled, and finally laughed, out of respect for Cosette's graceful command. Yet shortly thereafter, when no one was watching, he slipped out of the house and returned to his home. He lit a candle and climbed the stairs to his apartment. As he walked in, his footsteps seem to make more noise than usual. He entered Cosette's bedroom and stared at the bed, which no longer had sheets on it. The pillowcase had been removed from the pillow as well and was sitting at the foot of the bed with the blankets that had been removed and folded. All of Cosette's personal items had been carried away to her new home, and now nothing remained except the heavy furniture and four walls. Looking at the bed again, Valjean suddenly realized she would never sleep there again.

He walked from room to room, finally stopping in his own bedroom. He set the candle on the table and looked toward his bed. His eyes came to rest on a small trunk near the head of the bed. He had set the case on the candle stand on June 4, the day they had arrived at their new home, but had not opened it. Then he quickly took a key from his pocket and opened the small trunk. Inside were Cosette's clothes from ten years before, when they had walked hand-in-hand from the inn in Montfermeil.

Valjean took them from the case one-by-one and carefully placed them on his bed. There was a small coat, a dress, a soft scarf, and an apron with little pockets. Next he picked up a tiny pair of shoes and woolen socks that were no bigger than his hand. They were the garments he had bought for the child, and they were all in black, so that she could honor the death of a mother she could no longer remember. The items took him back to that very cold time one December, when Cosette was a shivering and half-dressed poor child, whose little feet were chapped and red in their hard wooden shoes. Perhaps her mother saw from above and was pleased to see her wearing mourning clothes in her honor, but above all, to see that she was finally properly clothed and warm.

He thought of that forest near Montfermeil where he had first seen Cosette as she had carried that heavy bucket of water. He thought of the cold weather, the leafless trees, and the darkened sky, but he remembered it all as wonderful. He arranged her tiny garments on the bed in an effort to remember just how small she had been. And he thought of how she laughed, how they walked hand-in-hand, and how she had no one in the world besides him. As his memories came flooding back, his head of solid white fell forward onto the bed, and his once stoic heart broke in two.

If anyone had happened to walk past that apartment that night, they would have heard the sorrowful sobs of an old man, muffled by a young child's clothes.

Jacob struggled with the angel only one night. Yet Valjean's long and difficult struggle of conscience, which had begun so many years ago, began once again in earnest, entering a new phase deep within his soul. For years his conscience would bodily seize him in the darkness, and he would struggle in desperation. That irrepressible spark of truth, lit so long ago by the bishop, shone brightly into his entire being to the point that often he would wish for blindness and beg for mercy. His conscience had worked within him to break and tear and dislocate him, and would ultimately stand over him with a sense of shining truth and tranquillity and say to him, "Now go in peace!" He would then rise, broken yet bold, vanquished yet victorious, seeking to do what was right and good—and in peace at last.

This particular night Valjean felt as though he were passing through his final conflict, as a heart-rending question presented itself to him. He saw his options as choosing either a stormy port or a friendly ambush—neither of which were pleasant. His struggle was this: How was he to relate to Cosette and Marius now that she was married? She was everything to him, and once he had been everything to her. But now she had Marius.

Valjean himself had willed her happiness and had actually brought it about by saving Marius and bringing the two young people back together. Yet now he was unsure of his place and how to behave in light of their marriage. He desired her happiness above all else, and he was happy to have provided for it, but his emotions were mixed. It was the sort of satisfaction a manufacturer of knives would experience upon recognizing his company's mark on a blade as it was pulled from his own chest in the heat of battle.

Should he simply hold on to whatever he could of Cosette? Or should he be a father that was seldom seen but respected, as he had been thus far? And what of his past? Should he now bring his past to their future? For Valjean, Cosette was the lifesaving raft of his shipwreck. What was he to do? Should he cling to the raft—or let go?

He remained on his bed, struggling with these thoughts until daylight. Stretched out, with his fists clenched, he looked like a crucified man who had been unnailed from his cross and had been flung facedown to the earth. For twelve long hours on that long winter night he did not lift his head even one time or utter a single word. All the while his thoughts ranged from the depths of the sea to the soaring heights of eagles' wings. He was as motionless as a corpse, and anyone who had seen him would have thought him dead. Then suddenly, after the long night had ended, he shuddered convulsively, and kissed the small garments that Cosette had once worn.

Then someone could have seen that he was indeed alive. But who could see, since Valjean was alone?

Only the One who sees all things—even through the shadows of night!

That morning, February 17, Basque heard a soft knock on the door. It was Jean Valjean, who was escorted into the drawing room that was still in disarray as a result of the wedding festivities the night before. His clothes were wrinkled, his skin appeared quite pale, and his eyes were so hollow and sunken that they nearly disappeared into their sockets, thanks to his night of sleeplessness.

He inquired of Basque, "Has Monsieur Marius risen this morning?"

"I will go and see," the servant answered. "I will tell him that Monsieur Fauchelevent is here to see him."

"No, please don't. Tell him that someone wishes to speak privately to him, but don't mention my name. I would like to surprise him," Valjean explained.

Soon Marius entered the room, his face lit with a radiant smile and his eyes bright—although he had not slept either. Seeing it was Valjean, he exclaimed, "Oh, it's you, Father! That silly Basque was so mysterious as to who was here! But you've come too early. Cosette is still asleep."

Hearing Marius refer to him as "Father" spoke volumes to Valjean regarding Marius's happiness, and showed that the icy wall between the two of them was finally beginning to melt. Valjean knew that someday it would either need to be melted or broken all at once, and apparently that point was beginning to come for Marius. He had already begun to see Monsieur Fauchelevent as Cosette did—as their father.

Marius continued, "Cosette and I have been talking about you. She loves you so dearly! And we would like you to know that you are welcome to live here. We would love to offer you the room that opens onto the garden. The room is ready. All you have to do is move in. Cosette and I are resolved to be happy, and you are a part of our happiness, Father."

"But, sir," Valjean began. "I have something I feel compelled to tell you. I am an ex-convict."

The term *ex-convict* entered Marius's ears, but seemed to overshoot its mark. It was as though something had been said to him, yet he had no idea what it was. He stood with his mouth gaping open, and finally managed to stammer, "What are you saying?"

"I'm saying," continued Valjean, "that I have been in prison. I was sentenced to nineteen years at hard labor for theft. I was a peasant in Faverolles and earned my living by pruning trees. And at this present time I am in violation of my parole. My name is not Fauchelevent, but is Jean Valjean. Yet you may reassure yourself with the fact that I am not related to Cosette."

"I can't believe this!" Marius interrupted, in obvious distress.

Then Valjean resumed, "I'm sure you must be asking, what am I to Cosette? I'm simply a passerby. Ten years ago I didn't even know that she existed. She was an orphan who needed my help, and as soon as I met her, I loved her. Immediately I became her protector and have fulfilled that duty to this day. But now she passes from my life. Our roads part, and from now on I can do nothing for her. She is Madame Pontmercy, and she is better off with that name." Pausing for a moment, he looked Marius in the eyes, and said, "You have not asked about the money, but I'm anticipating your thoughts. How did the six hundred thousand francs come into my hands? It doesn't really matter. It was a trust, and I've handed that trust over to you. Nothing more can be demanded of me. I have completed my restitution by telling you my real name. My name is actually only my concern, yet I have a reason for telling you who I am."

"But why have you told me all this?" Marius exclaimed. "You could have kept your secret to yourself."

"My motive may seem strange," replied Valjean in such a low tone that it seemed he was talking to himself rather than Marius. "It is out of honesty and honor. It is this thread that runs through my heart and holds my life together. Many times I have tried to break the thread, but the older I have become the stronger it has grown. And I have tried to pull it out, but it pulls out my heart as well. If only I could have broken that thread, I would have been safe, and could live here with you. But then I could no longer live with myself.

"We could never live as one family, for I belong to no family. I don't belong to yours, and, in fact, I don't belong to any family. It is not meant to be, and the day I gave Cosette in marriage it all came to an end for me. Now I see her happiness, married to a man she loves, and I have said to myself, 'Do not enter!' You ask what has forced me to speak—it is a very strange thing—my conscience. If I had continued to be Monsieur Fauchelevent, everything would be fine—except for my soul. You saw joy on the surface, but the bottom of my soul remained dark. It is not enough to be happy—a man must be content in his being.

"Monsieur Pontmercy, please understand. I did not do this out of common sense, but out of honesty. It is only through degrading myself in your eyes that I could elevate myself in my own. You saw me as an honest man, but I was not. And if you now despise me for my past, at least I am honest. Yes, now I am an honest man!" Then he drew a deep and painful breath, and added, with a sense of finality, "In days gone by I stole a loaf of bread in order to live. Today—in order to live—I will not steal a name."

Both men appeared to be plunged beneath a raging gulf of thoughts, but after a time of silence, Marius said, "My grandfather has prominent friends. We will get you a pardon."

"That would be useless," objected Valjean, "for I am thought to be dead. But that's all right, for the dead are not subjected to surveillance—they are supposed to rot in peace. Death is equal to a pardon."

Marius then made sure the door was closed, and said softly, "Poor Cosette. When she finds out . . ."

Hearing Cosette's name, Valjean began to tremble but kept his eyes fixed on Marius while saying, "Cosette! Yes, you would want to tell Cosette. I hadn't thought of that. I felt an obligation to tell you because she is now in your care, but I only had strength enough to think of that. But, sir, I plead with you—

give me your sacred word of honor that you will not tell her. Isn't it enough that you know? It would greatly trouble her." He dropped into an armchair and covered his face with his hands. His obvious grief was not audible, but from the shaking of his shoulders it was evident he was weeping. Finally, after a bit of hesitation, he stammered out the words, "One last thing. You are the master of this house. Now that you know the truth, do you think it would be better if I did not see Cosette any more?"

"I think it would be better," Marius replied coldly.

"Then I will not see her," Valjean muttered, as he walked toward the door. He opened the door, stood motionless for a moment, and closed the door once again. Then with a hint of desperation in his voice, as though he could not bear the thought, he said, "Sir, I ask that you reconsider. If you will allow it, I will come and visit her. I was like a father to her and she was my child. You may not be able to understand, Monsieur Pontmercy, but I could not bear to go away, never to see her again. I would have nothing. If you don't mind, I will visit from time to time, but I will not come often and I will not stay long. And you may give the order that I am to be received in the little room on the basement floor."

In a softened tone, and with a sense of understanding, Marius said, "You may come every evening, and Cosette will be waiting for you."

"You are very kind, sir," Valjean said.

Then a man of happiness escorted a man of despair to the door.

This surprising encounter with Valjean greatly upset Marius, and the feeling of uneasiness he had always felt around the old man with Cosette now began to make sense to him. Valjean had always been an enigma to Marius, and he now realized his own instincts had been attempting to warn him. Finally the puzzle had been solved—Monsieur Fauchelevent was the convict Jean Valjean—the most shocking kind of disgrace!

A secret such as this, especially when revealed amidst a time of such great happiness, was akin to suddenly discovering a scorpion in a nest of turtledoves.

It led Marius into the shadows of his memory to examine past events, troubling as they were. He thought of the events in the Jondrettes' room. He had always wondered why the man he then called Monsieur Leblanc had fled upon the arrival of the police, instead of registering a complaint. Finally he had his answer—the man was a fugitive from justice, having violated his parole.

Also, in light of these recent revelations, Marius realized that the Fauchelevent of the barricade must be Valjean, which was something he had previously dismissed because of his delirious condition after the battle. But now he knew that Fauchelevent had not "just happened" to come to the barricade, and as he thought of it again, a vision of someone suddenly sprang into his mind—Javert. The sight of Valjean dragging Javert from the barricade flashed through his mind, and he could still hear that lone, frightful gunshot ringing in his ears. Obviously Valjean had gone to the barricade to seek revenge.

The more Marius thought about what he had just heard, the more repulsive Valjean became to him. Marius saw him as a man of reproach, and the word *convict* resounded in his ears and stunned him as though he had heard the trumpet of Judgment Day. In his dismay, he made the decision to turn his mind from thoughts of Valjean. Yet how was he to do that? He was angry with himself for having allowed his swirling emotions to blind him to the point of allowing Valjean to visit Cosette, for he suspected those visits would ultimately become deeply repugnant to him.

The following evening around sunset Valjean knocked at the carriage gate of the Gillenormand house. Basque met him there and addressed him by saying, "Monsieur le Baron has instructed to inquire whether monsieur desires to go to the drawing room upstairs or to the basement below."

"The basement will be fine," replied Valjean. Basque then took him to a damp, poorly lit room. A fire was already burning in the small fireplace, which said to Valjean that his decision to choose that room had been anticipated. Two armchairs had been placed on each end of the hearth, and an old worn-out rug was lying between them. The rug had once been made of wool, but it was so worn that there was now more of the foundation of the rug showing than wool. And the only light in the room came from the fire itself.

Valjean looked haggard and tired, for he had now gone several days without food or sleep. He nearly fell into one of the chairs, and his head began to immediately nod in a somewhat agitated sleep. Therefore he did not notice that Basque lit a candle, set it on the mantel, and then walked from the room. Suddenly he was startled to look up and see Cosette standing beside him. He gazed at her and saw that she was incredibly lovely. Yet what he saw with his penetrating gaze was her soul, not her physical beauty.

"Father!" exclaimed Cosette, "I knew you were strange, but I would never have expected this. Marius said you wanted to see me here in the basement."

"Yes, that was my wish."

"I expected you to say that," Cosette said, as she reached to embrace Valjean, who was now standing before her. Yet it seemed that his feet were nailed to the floor and he did not return her embrace. At this, she leaned her face toward him, expecting a kiss, but he still did not move. Reacting to his apparent coldness, she endeavored to lighten his mood by saying, "Jesus said to turn the other cheek," and she then turned the other side of her face to him. Still there was no response. Finally, in exasperation she demanded, "What have I done to you? Your behavior is disturbing me! You will dine with us and we will discuss it."

"I have dined," Valjean responded.

"That's not true. It's too early for you to have eaten already," she said. Then, attempting to lift his spirits once again, she teased, "I will get Monsieur Gillenormand to scold you for that. Grandfathers were made to reprimand fathers. Come with me to the drawing room upstairs immediately."

"That's impossible," he said coldly.

At this point, Cosette became quite serious and asked, "But why? And why do you insist on seeing me here? This is the most unsightly room in the house. It's horrible here!"

"You know, madam, that I have my peculiarities," he answered, avoiding the issue.

Cosette slapped her hands together in frustration, and demanded, "'Madam'? Why are you suddenly addressing me as 'madam'? What do you mean by all of this?"

Valjean smiled a heart-rending smile, and said, "You wished to be married, so now you are madam."

"Yes, but not to you, Father," she insisted.

Then, only making matters worse, he said, "Do not call me Father."

"What!" Cosette said in total disbelief.

"Call me Monsieur Jean or simply Jean, if you like."

Now in desperation, Cosette sought for answers by asking, "So you are no longer my father? I'm no longer Cosette? And who is Monsieur Jean? And why won't you live with us? Look me in the eyes, and tell me what is going on here. Have I done something to you?"

"No, nothing," was his only answer.

"Then why have you changed your name?"

Valjean smiled sadly and said, "You've changed your name. If you can be Madame Pontmercy, why can't I be Monsieur Jean?"

Cosette exclaimed, "Don't be silly! This is idiotic! I don't understand any of this, and you're being no help whatsoever. All this seems so wicked—and from someone who is so good!" Valjean did not reply. Then taking his hands, she tenderly held them to her face and said softly, "Please be good!" Not waiting for a response, she added, "And this is what I call being good: moving from that hole of a room on the Rue de l'Homme Armé and living with us. Not giving me such riddles to figure out. Eating with us. And being my father!"

Pulling his hands away, he answered, "You no longer need a father. You have a husband."

Finally Cosette became angry and shouted, "I no longer need a father? How does someone respond to something so ridiculous? None of this makes any sense whatsoever!"

At the same time the following day Valjean arrived for another visit with Cosette. Yet this evening she attempted to make the best of a perplexing situation, and assured herself that the full truth would ultimately be revealed. She avoided questioning Valjean, but also avoided calling him either Father or Monsieur Jean. Her joy had been somewhat diminished, but it was impossible for her to be sad in light of the great happiness she enjoyed with Marius. And her curiosity did not outweigh her feelings of love.

Many weeks passed in this manner, and Valjean took Marius's words literally, coming to see Cosette each and every day. Yet at the hour Valjean was scheduled to arrive, Marius did his best to arrange his matters so that he was absent. And as the days went by other concerns and pleasures began to occupy Cosette's mind. She thought less and less about the questions that had once swirled around Valjean, and her greatest pleasure was simply spending time with Marius. The way that Valjean and Cosette addressed one another worked to somewhat detach them from each other. She became more and more happy and less and less tender with him, yet in spite of this, she still loved him greatly and he knew it.

However, one day she suddenly said to him, "You used to be my father, and now you're not. Then you were my uncle, and now you're not. You were Monsieur Fauchelevent, and now you're Jean. I'm tired of all this, and if I didn't know how good you are, I would be afraid of you. Who are you—really?" He did not reply.

Yet one day she slipped and called him Father. A distinct and radiant flash of joy brightened Jean Valjean's sad and wrinkled countenance. She laughed, as he lightly corrected her, by saying, "Call me Jean."

Then he turned aside so she would not see him wipe the tears from his eyes.

CHAPTER THIRTY

L ater that year, on a beautiful sunny day in early April, Marius said to
Cosette, "Let's visit our garden on the Rue Plumet, as we've discussed
since our wedding day." So they flitted away like two lovebirds in the
spring. They visited the garden and the house and lost themselves in their
happy thoughts of the past.

That evening, at the usual time, Valjean came for his visit with Cosette.
Basque told him, however, "Madam went out with Monsieur to visit the garden
on the Rue Plumet and has not yet returned." Valjean sat down in the basement
to wait, but after waiting a full hour, Cosette still had not returned. With a
sense of sadness, he decided to leave and returned to his home. Yet Cosette was
so thrilled with the stroll through "their garden" and so happy with having
lived an entire day in their past that she talked of nothing else, and totally
forgot that she had not seen Valjean.

The next day Valjean questioned her, thinking her trip to the garden
should not have taken so long. He asked, "How did you travel there?"

"On foot," she said.

"And how did you return?"

"We hired a carriage. Why do you ask?" Cosette responded.

For some time Valjean had noticed that the young couple was living a very
frugal life—far below what he knew they were able to afford. This troubled
him and prompted him to ask, "Why don't you have a carriage of your own?
With the money I have given you and Marius, you are rich."

Cosette replied as though she had never given it a thought, and said
casually, "I don't know."

Victor Hugo

Several weeks later, upon entering the basement room, Valjean noticed that the fire had not been lit before his arrival, as was the custom. When Cosette entered the room, she declared how cold it was, and summoned Basque, who lit the fire for her. Valjean did not give it a second thought, but the very next day the two armchairs were at the far end of the room near the door, instead of near the fireplace. He moved the chairs to their customary place near the fire, wondered briefly about the change, but then quickly got lost in conversation with Cosette. Yet just as he was preparing to leave, she said something that piqued his curiosity.

"Marius asked something strange yesterday," Cosette said, with a questioning look on her face.

"What was it?" Valjean asked.

"He asked me," Cosette said innocently, "if I would be willing for us to live on only the small income he receives from his grandfather. And, of course, I told Marius I would be willing to live on nothing at all, as long as it was with him. But then I asked him, 'Why do you ask me that?' and he replied, 'I was just wondering.'"

Valjean did not know how to respond, but it was obvious to him that Marius had his doubts as to the origin of the six hundred thousand francs. Perhaps he was thinking it was illegally gained. Then suddenly Valjean's thoughts went back to the incidents of the fire not being lit and the chairs being moved. He began to surmise that he was not so subtly being shown the door.

When he came for his visit the very next day, he was shocked to see that the chairs had been removed altogether. As Cosette walked into the room, she exclaimed, "Where are the chairs? This is ridiculous!"

Hoping to protect her from the truth, he stammered, "I told Basque that we wouldn't be needing the chairs and asked him to remove them. I can only stay for a few minutes tonight." That night he left utterly overwhelmed, having fully understood Marius's "message."

Valjean did not visit the next evening, and when Cosette mentioned that

266

"Monsieur Jean" had not visited, Marius diverted her thoughts with a kiss. Cosette felt only the slightest twinge in her heart from the absence of Valjean, for she and Marius were so happy.

⁓

Marius had done only what he considered to be necessary and just. He believed he had valid reasons for getting rid of Jean Valjean—yet without being harsh, and without showing weakness. He also believed that at some point he had a solemn duty that honesty would compel him to perform—returning the six hundred thousand francs to their rightful owner. Simply by coincidence he had gleaned some mysterious information that he believed cast additional doubt on Valjean regarding the money. Marius had once argued a case for a former cashier at the Bank of Laffitte, who had mentioned a manufacturer in the countryside who had gone out of business, putting hundreds of employees out of work. Marius's client explained that the manufacturer had been robbed of some six hundred thousand francs on deposit with the bank. The thief was suspected to be Jean Valjean. Therefore, in the meantime, and especially in light of this news, Marius refrained from using the money.

He kept his suspicions and concerns about Valjean from Cosette as much as possible. Nevertheless, she was conscious of Marius's feelings toward "Monsieur Jean," and she conformed to Marius's tacit yet clear intentions regarding him. There was a powerful magnetism between the young couple, which instinctively and almost mechanically caused her to do as her husband desired. She was still sincerely attached to the man whom she had called her father for so long, but it is fair to say that she was preoccupied with Marius and her new life and that she loved her husband more dearly than Valjean. Her soul had become completely one with her husband's and the fact that his mind was shrouded in gloom cast a shadow over her thinking as well. Gradually, Marius won Cosette away from Jean Valjean, but she allowed it to happen.

Valjean descended his staircase, took a few steps along the street, and then leaned against the stone wall around the house. It was the same place where he had met Gavroche on June 5 of the previous year. He remained there for only a few moments and then went upstairs again. This was to be the last swing of the pendulum, for on the following day he did not leave his apartment, and the day after that he did not leave his bed.

The housekeeper who prepared a small meal of cabbage or potatoes with bacon each day for Valjean brought him his next meal, only to discover he had not eaten yesterday's portion. She exclaimed, "My dear man, you didn't eat your meal!"

"I certainly did," Valjean responded.

"But the plate is still full!" she argued.

He pointed to the water jug, and said, "That's empty."

"Well, that proves you've drunk some water, but it doesn't prove you've eaten," she retorted. Then she added, "Sir, you must have a fever."

Yet Valjean dismissed her concerns and simply responded, "I'll eat tomorrow."

Later he left his apartment and with a few sous bought a copper crucifix that he hung on the wall across from his bed. "It's always good to look toward the Cross," he thought.

Shortly thereafter Valjean found it difficult to even lift himself on his elbow from his bed, and when he felt of his wrist, his heartbeat was so faint that he could not find a pulse. His breath was short and halting at times, and he finally admitted to himself that he was weaker than he had ever been in his life. Then out of a sense of sheer determination, he dressed himself in his old working-man's clothes. Since he never went out anymore, he preferred these old clothes because they were more comfortable. Yet just putting his arms through the sleeves caused perspiration to trickle down his forehead.

Next he took Cosette's small outfit from his trunk and spread it out on his bed once again. Then he took the bishop's candlesticks, placed two wax candles in them, and set them on the mantel. And although it was summer and still broad daylight, he lit them—something that was done at that time only in a room where a body was lying in state. Exhausted, he fell into a chair he had placed in front of his mirror. It was the mirror that had proved so fatal to him, yet so providential for Marius, when he had read Cosette's reversed writing in her blotting book.

Glancing in the mirror, he was shocked at what he saw and did not recognize himself. He was now in his mid-sixties, but he looked like he was eighty years old. Before Cosette's marriage, however, few people would have taken him to be even fifty years of age. The past year had counted for thirty, and what he saw on his brow was no longer the wrinkles brought on by aging, but was the mysterious mark of death.

Valjean sat there for hours, but then finally managed to drag a table and old chair to the fireplace. He collapsed into the chair again, slept in a cold faint for a few minutes, and then took a pen, some ink, and a piece of paper from the drawer of the table. His hand trembled as he began to write the following words:

Monsieur Pontmercy,
   Love my darling child well.

Cosette,
   I bless you. There is something that I wish to explain to you. Your husband was right in making me understand that I should go away, although there was a little error in what he believed. Still, he is a wonderful man. Love him well even after I am dead. I know this letter will be found after I am gone. But this is what I wish to say to you— you will see the numbers, if I have the strength to recall them. Please believe me—the money is really yours. Here is the whole matter . . .

Valjean paused and exclaimed to himself with sorrowful sobs heard by God alone, "My life is over. I will never see her again. Cosette is a beautiful smile that passed across my life, but now I am about to plunge into the night without ever seeing her again. If only I could have one minute, one instant to hear her voice, or one glimpse of her. She is such an angel! It is nothing to die. What is so frightful is to die without seeing her again!"

At that very moment there was a knock at the door.

CHAPTER THIRTY-ONE

J ust after dinner that same evening, while Cosette and Marius's
grandfather were strolling in the garden, Basque presented Marius with
a letter. As he did so, Basque said, "The man who wrote this is waiting
in the foyer and wishes to speak with you." Marius took the letter, which
smelled of tobacco. Immediately a vivid memory sprang into his mind, for he
knew that particular smell. It was the smell of the Jondrette's apartment! And
recognizing the tobacco scent caused him to recognize the handwriting as well.

Marius eagerly broke the seal, and began to read the following:

Monsieur le Baron,

*I know a secret concerning a particular individual that may be
of interest to you. I am offering you the means to drive someone from
your family that has no business being a part of it. I'm putting this
information at your disposal, for my desire is to have the honor to be
useful to you.*

With respect,

Thénardier

After his initial feeling of surprise, Marius was overwhelmed with feelings
of happiness. He had found Thénardier! Or actually, Thénardier had found
him. Now only one great desire remained for Marius—to find the man who
had saved his life.

Marius opened the drawer of his secretary and counted out some money,
which he folded and put in his pocket. He then rang the bell for Basque, who

stuck his head through the half-opened door, and Marius instructed, "Show the man in, please."

Moments later Basque announced, "Monsieur Thénardier."

Thénardier walked into the room with both hands in his pockets and stood as straight and as tall as possible. He looked quite unkempt, and as he approached Marius he immediately began to scrutinize him through his filthy glasses before saying, "Monsieur le Baron, I will not waste your time. I have a secret to sell to you."

"If it concerns me, then get to the point and tell me what it is," Marius demanded.

"Monsieur le Baron, you have a thief and a murderer in your family."

Marius replied simply, "In my family?"

Thénardier repeated, "A murderer and a thief." Then he added, "And, Monsieur le Baron, I will tell you more for . . . say . . . ten thousand francs."

"There is nothing you can tell me," Marius responded. "I already know what you have to say." Having said this, he paused for a moment to consider the situation. Before him stood the man he had so greatly desired to find, and at last he was in a position to honor his father's final request. Yet he was disturbed that Colonel Pontmercy should have had the misfortune to owe anything to this villain, Thénardier. Nevertheless, he realized the opportunity was presenting itself to repay his dead father's debt, and that his father's memory would no longer have to live in the shadow of such an unworthy creditor. The memory of his father would finally have been rescued from debtor's prison.

Marius also thought that perhaps there was another matter for which Thénardier could offer some information—the source of Cosette's fortune. Therefore, he decided it would be useful to play out the situation before him, and said, "Thénardier, I already know your 'secret.' I know about Jean Valjean—that he is a murderer and a thief. He's a thief because he brought about the ruin of a wealthy manufacturer after illegally depleting the man's bank account, and he's a murderer because he killed the police agent Javert."

"But, sir, I don't understand!" exclaimed Thénardier.

"I know the full truth, Thénardier. Allow me to share the details. I have learned that in 1823 in the town of Montreuil there was a man who had once been in trouble with the law, but had rehabilitated himself. His name was Monsieur Madeleine, and he became a just and good man, and, as a manufacturer and employer, he increased the fortunes of the entire town. However, a paroled convict knew of a secret crime the man had committed years before, and ultimately denounced him to the police, who arrested him. The convict, profiting from the man's arrest, then went to the Bank of Laffitte in Paris, and by using a note with a false signature, absconded with more than a half million francs of Monsieur Madeleine's money. I learned this information from the cashier himself, and, as you know, the convict who robbed Madeleine was Valjean.

"And as for the second matter—that he is a murderer—you have nothing to tell me about that either. Valjean killed the police agent Javert by shooting him with a pistol. I was there just before he shot him."

Initially Thénardier thought he had been conquered, but now he cast his eyes on Marius with a look of one about to snatch a victory from the very jaws of defeat. In an instant he felt he had regained all the ground he had lost, and a smile returned to his face, as he smugly believed the inferior had triumphed over the superior. He responded to Marius's accounting of the facts by saying, "Monsieur le Baron, you are on the wrong track."

"But," argued Marius, "these are the facts. How can you dispute them?"

"Your stories are pure fantasy! I appreciate the confidence you have placed in me by sharing what you believe to be true, but it is wrong, and I feel it is my duty to tell you so. After all, I always put truth and justice above everything else, and would never want to see someone unjustly accused. So, Monsieur le Baron, I must tell you that Jean Valjean did not rob Monsieur Madeleine and he certainly did not kill Police Inspector Javert.

Marius retorted, "How can this be? Tell me!"

"For two reasons," Thénardier began. "The first is, he did not rob Monsieur

Madeleine, because Valjean is Madeleine. Secondly, he did not murder Javert, because the person who killed Javert was Javert himself."

"What do you mean?" Marius said in disbelief.

"Javert committed suicide," Thénardier explained.

Marius, by now greatly angered and agitated, shouted, "Prove it . . . if you can!"

At this challenge, Thénardier pulled a large gray envelope from his pocket that was stuffed with various sheets of folded paper. He took two newspaper articles from the envelope and unfolded them. The paper of each was brittle, faded, and was saturated with the smell of tobacco. One of the articles was obviously much older than the other, for it broke along one of the folds as he opened it.

He handed the articles to Marius and offered smugly, "Two proofs for two facts!"

The older of the two reports was from 1823 and told of Mayor Madeleine admitting his true identity as Jean Valjean. It explained how another man had been accused of being Valjean, but that the mayor had proven that he himself was Valjean in a court of law. The second article was from June 15, 1832, and reported the suicide of Javert. It also reported that before he had taken his life he had made a verbal report to an officer at the police station. Javert reportedly told the officer he had been taken prisoner at the barricade on the Rue de la Chanvrerie, but owed his life to the noble generosity of one of the revolutionaries. His captor had fired the pistol into the air and then released him, instead of "blowing out his brains," as Javert had put it.

As Marius read he could barely contain his joy. Suddenly Jean Valjean was emerging from beneath a cloud. He blurted out, "So this man I've thought to be a miserable wretch is in fact an admirable man, and the entire fortune actually belongs to him. Madeleine is known to be the benefactor of that entire town. And he is Valjean! He's a hero, a saint, and a savior—not a murderer!"

"Not so fast!" demanded Thénardier. "He's not a saint, nor a hero. He is a murderer and a thief." Then he added, with an air of authority, "Let's remain calm."

The words *thief* and *murderer*, words that Marius had hoped no longer described Valjean, fell on him like an ice-cold shower. Yet Thénardier continued by saying, "Valjean did not rob Madeleine, but he is a thief, and he did not kill Javert, but he is a murderer."

Marius retorted, "If you're referring to that miserable theft of a loaf of bread committed some forty years ago, even your newspapers show that crime was atoned for by years in prison followed by an entire life of repentance, self-denial, and virtuous living."

"I said, Monsieur le Baron, not only a thief, but also a murderer. And may I repeat that I am speaking of actual facts," insisted Thénardier. Waiting for an explanation, Marius sat down and motioned for his visitor to do the same. Then Thénardier continued, "On the sixth of June about a year ago, on the day of the insurrection, a man was in the Grand Sewer of Paris near where it enters the Seine." This fact piqued Marius's interest, and he pulled his chair more closely to Thénardier, something that did not go unnoticed by the man. Knowing he had Marius's rapt attention, Thénardier continued like an orator who believes his audience is hanging on every word, "This man, who was forced to hide, had adopted the sewer as his home and had obtained a key to it. Around eight o'clock in the evening the man heard a noise in the sewer. Surprised, the man hid himself to lie in wait, as he heard footsteps approaching from the darkness. The iron gate of the sewer was not far away, and as the stranger came near, the light shining through the gate permitted the man to recognize the one walking through the sewer. The man recognized him as a convict, and was able to see that the convict was carrying something on his back. He walked bent over, for he was carrying a corpse. If ever someone was caught in the act of murder, it was he!

"As to the theft—that is obvious—for no one kills a person for nothing. The convict was on his way to dump the body into the river." Hearing this, Marius pulled his chair even closer. Thénardier took advantage of the young man's obvious interest by taking a dramatic breath, and then went on to say, "It was impossible for the man who was living in the sewer to actually hide because of the sewer's narrow width, so the two men finally came face-to-face, much to the dismay of both of them. The man carrying the corpse said to the other man, 'You see what I'm carrying. Surely you have a key to get out of here. Give it to me. I've killed once, and I'll kill again.' The convict was incredibly strong, and there was no way for the other man to refuse. Nevertheless, the man used the key to stall for time and to attempt to identify the dead man. All he could see, however, was that he was young, well dressed, and covered with blood. And without the convict noticing, the man was able to pull a piece of cloth from the back of the murdered man's torn coat—a damning piece of evidence, which he put in his pocket. The poor man who lived in the sewer then let the man out through the gate and ran away. He did not want to be mixed up in the murder, and certainly did not want to hang around while the murdered man was thrown into the river."

Having finally finished his tale, Thénardier asked, "Now do you understand? The man carrying the corpse was Jean Valjean. And the one with the key—and the piece of the coat—was I!" At that moment he pulled a piece of cloth from his pocket and dangled it temptingly before Marius's eyes. It was a torn strip of black cloth covered with dark spots of blood.

Marius had turned pale but sprang to his feet. Then, keeping his eyes riveted on that fragment of black cloth and without uttering a word, he walked backward to a cupboard near the fireplace. Still facing Thénardier, he ran his hand along the front of the cupboard and found the key still in the lock. He quickly turned the key, opened the door, and reached in, still without looking at anything except that strip of cloth.

While Marius did this, Thénardier continued by saying, "Monsieur le Baron, I have every reason to believe that the murdered young man was a wealthy stranger lured into a trap by Valjean, and he was probably robbed of a vast sum of money."

"Sir!" shouted Marius, "I was the young man! And here is the coat!" Then he tossed the bloodstained coat across the room at Thénardier's feet, and snatched the cloth fragment from his hand. Next he crouched over the coat and laid the torn strip onto it. The small piece was a perfect fit.

Thénardier's smugness disappeared in an instant and he appeared terrified. Marius was trembling as well, yet with anger, while his face became radiant. He fumbled through his pocket and nearly thrust a fist of money amounting to fifteen hundred francs at Thénardier's face, while declaring, "You are a despicable and wicked wretch! You are the criminal! You came to accuse Jean Valjean, yet you have only served to vindicate him. You endeavored to ruin him, but you have only succeeded in glorifying him. It is you who is a thief! It is you who is a murderer! I saw your plan to murder Valjean for his money, Monsieur Jondrette! I know enough about you to send you to prison and even to death if I choose. Here! This is fifteen hundred francs. Take it, you miserable man!" Then he threw the money in Thénardier's face, but continued by saying, "Let this serve as a lesson to you—you dealer in second-hand secrets and merchant of mysteries. Take this money and get out of here! Only Waterloo protects you!"

"Waterloo?" growled Thénardier, while pocketing the money.

"Yes, murderer! It was there you saved the life of a colonel . . ."

"He was a general!" Thénardier interrupted, with obvious conceit.

"A colonel!" Marius raged. "Get out of here! You are a monster. Here. Take three thousand more francs. But you will leave tomorrow for America and you will not come back. I know your wife is dead, as well as Éponine and Gavroche, but take your remaining daughter and go. I will wait for your departure, and at the moment you leave I will give you twenty thousand francs. Go get yourself hanged somewhere else! And get out of my sight once and for all!"

Finally, with nothing left to sell, Thénardier bowed to Marius and said, "Monsieur le Baron, I am eternally grateful." He left the house, having really understood nothing at all, and was more than thrilled with his newfound wealth. He felt as though a cloud had burst over his head and had rained money down on him. Two days later he bought two tickets for steamship passage to America and left with his daughter, Azelma. He traveled under an assumed name, and upon his arrival in his new country he used the remainder of Marius's money to become a slave trader.

As soon as Thénardier had left the house, Marius rushed to the garden, where Cosette was still walking. He shouted excitedly, "Cosette, come quickly! We need to go! It was he who saved my life! Hurry! Put on your shawl and let's go!" Then he called for Basque and asked him to summon a carriage for them. Cosette, totally unsure what was happening, nevertheless, hurried with Marius toward the carriage gate. Initially she thought Marius was going mad, and, in fact, Marius was completely stunned and bewildered.

Marius's encounter with Thénardier was transforming Jean Valjean into an indescribably wonderful yet miserably sad person right before his eyes. A totally new man was appearing before him—one with unparalleled virtue, the ultimate in sweetness and grace, and yet with immense humility and selfless-ness. In Marius's mind Jean Valjean had been transfigured into a savior, with qualities not unlike Jesus Christ Himself. Valjean, risking his own life, had saved Marius, and the young man now saw that as nothing short of miraculous. He was amazed, overpowered with a new light shining brightly into his soul, yet he was not totally sure what he beheld—he just knew it was wonderful and majestic.

By the time Marius and Cosette reached the gate, a carriage was waiting for them. Marius helped Cosette into her seat, and while climbing in he shouted to the driver, "Rue de l'Homme Armé, number 7!"

As the carriage drove off, Cosette said with obvious joy, "This is wonderful! I didn't dare to speak to you about my desire to see him. We're going to see Monsieur Jean!"

"Your father!" Marius said, as though correcting Cosette. "He's your father more than ever," beginning to explain to a still bewildered Cosette. "You told me you never received the letter I asked Gavroche to deliver to you. Now I realize Gavroche must have given it to your father. As a result, Cosette, he went to the barricade to save me! His nature is to be a guardian angel, for he not only saved me, but also saved the life of the police agent Javert.

"He rescued me from certain death in that terrible battle to give me to you. He carried me on his back for miles through that horrible sewer. And I've been nothing but a monster of ingratitude! Cosette, for so many years he has given you such godly care and protection, and then he chose to do the same for me. I can only imagine what he went through for me in that sewer. He could have drowned in that filthy quagmire, yet he took me safely through it. I was unconscious. I saw nothing and heard nothing. I was totally unaware of my dire situation. But now I know! And now that I know we are going to bring him back, and he will never be apart from us again.

"I hope he still lives at this address. I want to spend the rest of my life honoring him. That's how it should be. Don't you see, Cosette? Gavroche must have delivered my letter to him. This explains everything! Do you understand?"

While the carriage hurried on, Cosette said softly, "You are right, my dear." However, Cosette did not understand much of what Marius had shared so excitedly.

Yet all she cared to understand was this: she was going to see her father!

CHAPTER THIRTY-TWO

esponding to the knock on his door, Jean Valjean turned and feebly called, "Come in!" Marius pushed the door open and then leaned against it. But Cosette rushed into the room and Valjean immediately said, "Cosette!" As he sat up in his chair and held out his trembling arms, his sad, weary, and haggard eyes were suddenly filled with immense and overwhelming joy.

Cosette, sobbing with emotion, fell to her knees, embraced him, and said the one word she had longed to say: "Father!"

Valjean, now completely overcome with emotion himself, stammered, "Cosette! It is really you! Thank God!" Then, as he held Cosette tightly in his arms, he looked toward Marius and said, "You are here as well. Does this mean you forgive me?"

Marius blinked several times in an attempt to stem the flow of tears, took a step forward, and between sobs said, simply, "Father!"

"Thank you," was Valjean's happy response.

Cosette stood to take off her shawl and her hat and tossed them onto the bed. Then she sat on Valjean's knee, tenderly pushed his long white hair away from his face, and kissed him softly on the forehead. Valjean easily yielded to her display of affection, which only led to Cosette doubling her show of devotion, as though she were single-handedly attempting to repay Marius's debt.

Valjean then feebly managed to say, "How stupid I have been! I thought I would never see her again. Marius, you can't imagine what I was saying to myself just as you entered! I was looking at Cosette's little dress and saying, 'Everything is over for me. I am a miserable man, for I will never see my Cosette again.' How idiotic I have been! I was forgetting about our gracious God, Who said, 'You believe you are about to be abandoned? Don't be silly! No, things will not go as you think.' Then He said to one of His angels, 'There is a man over there who needs your help.' And the angel came, and the 'man over there' sees his Cosette again! Oh, I was so unhappy. But now you are here!"

Then looking Marius in the eyes, he asked again, as though it were too good to be true, "Marius, you forgive me?"

Hearing these words uttered once more was more than Marius could bear. His heart overflowed with emotions as he declared, "Cosette, did you hear that? He asks my forgiveness! Just think of what he has done for me! I owe my entire life to him. The battle at the barricade and the cesspool of the sewer—he walked through it all for me. For you, Cosette! He carried me through death itself and pushed it aside for me, yet was willing to accept death for himself on my account. He possesses all the courage, virtue, heroism, and godliness of an angel!"

"Hush! Hush!" said Valjean in a quiet voice. "Why tell all that?"

"Because you did not tell it!" Marius shouted angrily, but with an anger that included untold respect and honor. "It's your own fault. You save people's lives and conceal it from them! And then under the pretense of unmasking yourself, you actually scandalize yourself. It's terrible!"

"I told the truth," Valjean offered.

"No!" retorted Marius, "The truth is the whole truth—and that, you did not tell. You were Monsieur Madeleine. Why didn't you say so? You saved Javert? Why haven't you said that? I owe my life to you, but you never told me. Why not?"

"Because I was thinking as you do," Valjean answered. "I thought you were right, and that it would be better if I went away. And if you had known about the sewer, you would have kept me with you."

"But you are Cosette's father—and mine!" Marius argued. "And you will not spend another day in this dreadful apartment. Don't even think of staying here until tomorrow."

"Tomorrow?" Valjean questioned, with a faraway look in his eyes. "No, tomorrow I will not be here. But I will not be with you."

"What do you mean?" Marius demanded. "Come now, we're not going to allow any more journeys and good-byes. You belong to us and we will not lose you again."

"This time it's for good," added Cosette. "We have a carriage waiting, and we won't take no for an answer." Then with a smile, she said, "We'll steal you away, and use force, if necessary."

Valjean listened to Cosette but without really hearing her. He only heard the music of her voice, instead of catching the meaning of her words. Then large tears slowly welled up in his eyes—the type that seems to be the foreshadowing, dark pearls of the soul. As the tears ran down his face, he whispered, "The proof that God is gracious and good is that she is here."

Cosette took both of the old man's hands in hers, and cried, "Father! Your hands are so cold. Are you ill?"

"I am fine," Valjean replied. "Only . . ."

"Only what?" Cosette demanded.

"In a few minutes I will be dead," he said, in a matter-of-fact way.

"Father! You will live!" Cosette insisted. "I want you to live! Do you hear me?"

"Yes, forbid me to die," Valjean said, with a smile. "Who knows? Perhaps I will obey. I was dying just as you got here, but your presence stopped me. It was like being born again." Then in a very serious tone, he added, "It is nothing to die. And you see, Marius, God thought as you and I did, and He does not change His mind. He thinks it best that I go away. Death is a proper answer, and God knows better than we do what we need." Then he turned to Cosette and gazed at her as though he wished to remember her features throughout eternity. Although his life was already fading into the shadow, he was filled with pure rapture as he looked at her, and the radiance of her sweet face was reflected onto his pale countenance. He looked into her eyes and said, "How good your husband is, Cosette! You are much better off with him than with me."

Speaking barely above a whisper, he continued, "It is nothing to die. What is to be feared is not living beyond. . . ." Then pausing, he rose to his feet, which was a sudden display of strength not uncommon as one struggles with death. He summoned his last vestige of power, walked with a steady step to the wall, and lightly pushed Marius aside as he attempted to help him. He took his copper crucifix from the wall, and returned to his chair as someone who appeared to be in perfect health. Setting the crucifix on the table, he said in a loud voice, "Behold the great Martyr!"

Then his chest heaved abruptly as though the grave had placed its deadly grip upon him. His head also jerked convulsively, and his hands, which were resting on his knees, suddenly were clenched. Cosette held him by his shoulders and attempted to speak to him, but could not, for she was sobbing uncontrollably.

At that moment the housekeeper, who had come upstairs to check on him, since he had not been eating, stuck her head partially around the half-opened door. Seeing him in obvious distress, she asked, "Sir, would you like a priest?"

Pointing above his head as though he saw someone, Valjean replied, "I have had one." Of course, only Valjean saw the kind old bishop, who was now a witness to his final agony and battle with death.

The agony of death is said to meander toward the grave and then return to life, as there appears to be some grasping for life in the act of dying. For a moment he moved toward life again, and resumed, "Marius, I implore you not to worry about the money. The six hundred thousand francs really belongs to Cosette, and my life would be wasted if you do not enjoy them! We did very well with those glass trinkets and made some beautiful jewelry."

Jean Valjean's life turned once again toward the grave, and as the horizon of death approached, he seemed to become weaker by the moment. His breathing was now intermittent, and the rattle of death could be heard as he struggled. He had difficulty moving his hands, and he had lost all feeling in his feet and legs. Yet as his body became more and more feeble, the more the majesty of his soul was displayed across his countenance. And the light of the next world was already visible in his eyes.

He motioned for Cosette and Marius to lean more closely to him, and it was obvious to both of them that the last minute of the last hour had arrived.

Valjean spoke in a voice that seemed to be coming from some distant place, as though some unseen wall was now rising between them and him. He whispered, "I love you dearly. How wonderful it is to die like this, and to know that you love me, too, my dear Cosette! Deep within my soul I knew that you still loved your poor, old father. You will weep for me a little, won't you? But promise me—not too much. I don't want you to suffer.

"My children, don't forget that I am a poor man. Just have me buried in the first plot of earth you can find—under a stone to mark the spot. This is my wish. And put no name on the stone. Cosette, if you wish to visit the place from time to time, it will give me pleasure. And, Marius, you may come as well. By the way, monsieur, I must admit that I have not always loved you, and I ask your forgiveness for that. Now, however, Cosette and you are as one to me. I am very grateful to you, and I know that you make Cosette very happy."

Then pointing toward his dresser, Valjean said, "In there I have left some money for the poor. Please see that they receive it. And to you, Cosette, I leave the two candlesticks on the mantel. They are silver. Yet to me they are more than that. They are gold—even diamonds—for they change common wax candles that are placed in them into something sacred. I don't know if the man who gave them to me is satisfied with me from heaven, but I have done what I could.

"Cosette, see your little dress lying on the bed? Do you remember it? That was ten years ago. How time flies! We have been very happy, but now my life is over. Do not weep, my children, for I am not going very far. And I will see you from there. Just look up at night and you will see me smile. Cosette, do you remember that night in Montfermeil? You were in the forest and so terrified! Remember how I took hold of the handle of your water pail? That was the first time I touched your poor little hand. It was so cold! Oh, how cold, red, and chapped your little hands were then, mademoiselle, but now they are so soft and white!

"Oh, the forests through which one has walked with his child, the trees under which one has strolled, the convent where one hid himself and his child, and the games and the laughter of childhood—they are all but shadows now. They are things of the past—things that I thought I could hold on to forever, but that was my mistake. Oh, Cosette, I almost forgot—the Thénardiers! They were wicked people but you must forgive them.

"And now, Cosette, the moment has come for me to tell you of your mother. Never forget her name. It was Fantine. Kneel whenever you speak that name, for she suffered so much, but she loved you so dearly. She suffered as much unhappiness as you have enjoyed happiness. Yet that is the way God apportions things. He sits on His throne on high, He sees us all, and He knows what He is doing in the midst of each and every star in His heavens.

"My children, I am on the verge of my departure. Love each other dearly and forever. Nothing but love really matters in this world—love for one another. And when you think of love, sometimes think of the poor old man who died here who loves you.

"I am no longer seeing things very clearly. I had more things to tell you, but it makes no difference now. I die a happy man. Just one more thing—please move closer so that I may lay my hands upon your heads." Cosette and Marius knelt beside his chair, as he placed one hand upon each of them and said, "May you be blessed." The young couple sobbed through their tears of sadness and despair beneath his hands.

Valjean fell backward in his chair, and the light of the bishop's candlesticks shone across his face. He lifted his eyes toward heaven, and with a faraway look, said, "I don't know what's the matter with me. I see a light."

Cosette and Marius kissed his once strong, but still majestic hands—and then those hands moved no more. Jean Valjean was dead.

It was night—starless and extremely dark. Yet in that darkness, there can be no doubt that somewhere an angel stood with wings outstretched, awaiting the soul of Jean Valjean.

Far from the elegant quarter of the city there is a potter's field. Hidden from view in a deserted corner of the cemetery—next to the wall, and beneath a large tree—lies a stone. It lies amid the dandelions and is partially covered with moss, and has suffered the ravages of time and weather. Nothing has been carved on the stone—not even a name—except that many years ago, a hand scratched a few words, which over time have probably become illegible beneath the rain and the dust. Yet they once read:

He sleeps. Although his circumstance was very strange, he lived.
He died when he lost his little angel. The passing happened simply,
by itself, as the night comes when the day has gone.

ALSO AVAILABLE ON CD. A BEAUTIFULLY
ORCHESTRATED READING WITH FIVE SONGS
FROM THE ORIGINAL BROADWAY MUSICAL.

―――――0―――――

When *Les Misérables* was published in 1862, it generated more
excitement than any book in the history of publishing. Since then,
the excitement has continued as the novel has been transformed
into Broadway's longest running musical with over 8 million
viewers, producing a soundtrack that has won awards worldwide.
Discover the real message of this profound classic with the
companion CD that includes a beautifully orchestrated reading of
the book and five songs from the original Broadway musical.

―――――0―――――